Praise for Caroline Hulse

'I loved *The Adults*! Funny, dry and beautifully observed. Highly recommended for anyone whose Perfect Christmases never quite go according to plan!'
Gill Simms, author of *Why Mummy Swears*

'Genuinely unputdownable books are rare in my experience. This one … a brilliant, original comedy of contemporary manners'
Daily Mail

'I took this book on holiday and couldn't put it down! I found myself feeling tense as I became more and more invested in the unfolding drama of the weekend away. I've never read anything quite like it and Posey was a highlight'
The Unmumsy Mum

'Such a breath of fresh air! Witty, intensely human and (dare I say it) relatable … This novel is the perfect comedy of errors'
Katie Khan, author of *Hold Back The Stars*

'Packed with sharp wit, engaging characters and off-beat humour, this is a fresh and feisty thrill-ride of a novel'
Heat

'I have a feeling Caroline Hulse might be a genius, this book is so brilliant. It's funny, clever and original. I loved every minute of reading it'
Lucy Vine, author of *Hot Mess*

'Brilliantly funny'
Good Housekeeping

'*The Adults* gripped me from the start. With a razor-sharp eye, she dissects the nightmare of family politics ... Reminiscent of Liane Moriarty's *Big Little Lies*, this book is a sure-fire winner'
Cass Hunter, author of *The After Wife*

'Clever, perceptive and wickedly funny, this is a holiday-from-hell extravaganza not to be missed!'
Lancashire Evening Post

'Funny, poignant, real – *The Adults* is a truly original book that made me laugh, cry and cringe in equal measure. I loved it'
Charlotte Duckworth, author of *The Rival*

'Razor-sharp comedy'
Sunday Mirror

'I loved it. I couldn't believe it was a debut. It was so funny, and intriguing and I was desperate to know where it was all heading – a great read'
Mike Gayle, author of *The Man I Think I Know*

Caroline Hulse lives in Manchester with her husband and a small, controlling dog.

She is the author of *The Adults*, which has been published in fourteen languages and optioned for TV. *Like a House On Fire* is her second novel.

You can find out more at carolinehulseauthor.com

By Caroline Hulse

The Adults
Like A House On Fire

Like A House On Fire

Caroline Hulse

ORION

First published in Great Britain in 2020 by Orion Fiction,
an imprint of The Orion Publishing Group Ltd.,
Carmelite House, 50 Victoria Embankment
London EC4Y 0DZ

An Hachette UK Company

1 3 5 7 9 10 8 6 4 2

A CIP catalogue record for this book is
available from the British Library.

ISBN (Hardback) 978 1 4091 7834 7
ISBN (Export Trade Paperback) 978 1 4091 7835 4
ISBN (eBook) 978 1 4091 7837 8

Typeset by Input Data Services Ltd, Somerset

Printed and bound in Great Britain by Clays Ltd, Elcograf S.p.A.

www.orionbooks.co.uk

Like
A
House
On
Fire

Murder at Brockenhurst Manor:
an original murder mystery party
by Margaret Foy

DRAMATIS PERSONAE

CHARACTER	PLAYED BY
The Late Lord Alfred Brockenhurst, 80	No one – he's dead
Lord Brockenhurst, 50	Tommy Foy
Lady Brockenhurst, 43	Margaret Foy
Mr Shaker, Solicitor, 30	Pete Foy
The Honourable Mr Ashley Brockenhurst, 45	Scott Prentice
Ellie Brockenhurst, 25	Helen Wheatley
Mr Hapsworth, Private Secretary, 28	Nathan Wheatley
Mr Owlish, Butler, 50	George Mandani
Miss Cartwright, Housekeeper, 33	Adele Prentice
Agnes Fairbottom, Parlourmaid, 39	Stella Foy
Miss Evangeline, Vicar, 50	Cheryl Aspinal
Other below-stairs staff	Other party guests

DESCRIPTION

Cantankerous, selfish, tyrannical. Recently killed in a hunting accident, leaving two sons. His heir is:

The new owner of the manor. Charismatic, authoritative, kind yet firm. He is benevolent to his servants and conducts himself with impeccable control. Married to:

Sweet of nature. Retains an allure, a semblance of the society beauty she once was. Bravely bears the tragedy of her life, that she has been unable to produce an heir.

Handsome young solicitor. Inherited his business from his father, a dear friend of the Brockenhursts. Reliable and scrupulously honest.

Lord Brockenhurst's charming and wayward younger brother. Born with an eye for the ladies, it has always been hoped he will one day settle down and marry well.

Glamorous socialite and actress, niece of Lord and Lady Brockenhurst. Adopted by them after the untimely death of her mother, she is a credit to the Brockenhurst family.

Professional and discreet. Mr Hapsworth never stops – though his new-fangled ways of doing things occasionally need to be curbed.

Servile, proper, understated. Devoted to Lord Brockenhurst after they served in the army together in India. Mr Owlish is patient, and manages difficult staff with aplomb.

A recent addition to the manor. Efficient at running the household, despite rumours she has a rum past and previously trained as an exotic dancer. Sadly, she remains unmarried.

Rescued from poverty, aged fifteen, by the Brockenhursts. Rumours abound that she steals, but her master and mistress believe her unfairly maligned and pure of heart. She is always humble and grateful.

Trusted family confidant and moral authority. Whilst she generally keeps herself to herself, she has a nose for scandal and secrets. (Host's note: I know there were no lady vicars in the olden days, but I've updated it.)

(Host's note: Please play the game even though you don't have a named role. Remember, you don't need a character to be a detective!)

PROLOGUE

Eleven years before the party

Stella opened the door to the waiting room. 'Nimble Williams?'

She looked past the glum-looking terrier in an oversized cone, to a man sitting staring at the wall, a carry case on the floor next to him.

Stella went up to him. 'Nimble Williams?'

The man sat upright. 'That's me.' He followed her into her consulting room. 'Though I don't normally think to answer to that name.'

Stella lifted the tortoise out of the case and placed him on her metal table.

Nothing happened.

Stella looked up. The man looked a similar age to her, mid-twenties. 'What exactly's the trouble?'

'He's not himself.' The man pushed the sleeves of his hoodie up. 'He's my neighbour's tortoise and she says he's listless.'

Stella sighed. 'Are you able to tell me about his history? Eating patterns, toileting, change in movements?'

'All I know is, apparently, he's lost his spark.'

'I need to get the owner's consent to examine. Can I call her?'

'She's not good on the phone.'

Well, Stella thought. She'd tried. 'Then I'm sorry, I can't do anything. We have to get the history and owner's consent to do a clinical exam. And there's a reptile vet up the road, you know. Just saying.'

'I didn't know a tortoise was a reptile.'

'It is.'

The man leaned against the wall. 'I thought vets had to do everything. Mouse to elephant and back.'

Stella wondered why this man didn't look like he was leaving. 'Reptiles have quite specific anatomy and physiology. I *could* look at him, but you'd be much better at the specialists.'

'My neighbour can't get about.' Finally, the man picked the tortoise up off the table. 'I must have told her I'm teacher, which is always a mistake. People know when my holidays are.' He placed the tortoise slowly back in the case. 'She seemed worried. She's had this tortoise since she was seven. He's seen out her husband and her two brothers.'

Stella left a respectful pause.

The man looked around. He focused on the posters on the wall.

Stella followed his gaze. *Ask us about vaccinations. Are you antibiotic aware? Hydrotherapy for dogs.*

He looked back at Stella. 'This must be an interesting job.'

'Sometimes.'

'I saw a guinea pig on a lead in the waiting room.'

'That's not normal.'

The man clipped the carry case shut. He still didn't leave.

'I teach at the high school round the corner,' he said eventually. 'We have a career day coming up, they like to see young people talking about jobs. It's easier for them to relate.'

He met Stella's gaze. 'Would you like to come and talk to them?'

'What do you teach?'

He glanced away and back. 'History.'

Stella looked at the man for a second longer. She pulled a pad and pen towards her.

The man watched her write. 'Prescribing amphetamines? To give Nimble his spark back?'

'No.' Stella ripped the piece of paper from the pad and held it out to him. 'It's my number.'

Two weeks later, Stella stood on a school hall stage.

The teacher – who she now knew as George Mandani – stood against the wall at the side. He wore a crisp blue shirt and looked significantly less playful than he had in her surgery.

Stella looked at her audience of year nines. 'People think you should be a vet if you love animals, but most of the ones I see are in pain. You have to euthanise animals all the time. That means putting them out of their misery.'

She looked around the room, reading expressions. *Bored. Bored. Smirking. Bored. Disconcertingly keen. Super-bored. Actually asleep?*

'Any questions so far?' Stella asked.

A surprising number of hands went up. Stella looked at a girl with hair piled high.

'Don't ask her.' George Mandani pointed to a boy at the front. 'Jay?'

The boy put his hand down. 'Is it better to be a vet if you hate animals, so you can happily kill them?'

Stella smiled. 'Probably not.' She turned to another boy and nodded.

'Careful, Dylan.' George's voice was low.

Too late, Stella saw the pull of a smile at the side of this boy's mouth.

'How do you know Mandani?'

George's voice went dangerously quiet. '*Mr* Mandani.'

'And why've you ironed your shirt today, sir?' Another boy stood up. 'You normally look scruffy.'

'Not appropriate.'

'*And* you've done your hair. Do you like the vet, sir?'

'*Outside,* Samuel.'

'Samuel' left the room with a swagger.

'One more quip from *anyone,*' George turned to address the crowd, 'and you'll be sorry.'

'Let me make this clear.' Stella surveyed the room. 'Mr Mandani's asked me here to help *you.* He's a professional.'

Several eyebrows tweaked upwards.

'And he knows I'm gay,' Stella said.

There was silence.

A small voice said, 'Unlucky, sir.'

'Piper Briggs. Outside, *now.*'

A girl slumped out of the room, grinning as she went.

George turned to Stella. 'I'm sorry about the lack of respect,' he said loudly. 'When you're so generously giving your time.'

Stella waved a hand. She answered more questions.

What does it feel like to have your hand up a cow?

Do dogs mind having their testicles removed?

Which is better, a bird or a hamster?

Stella glanced at George occasionally. She took one long, focused glance.

The thing was, that shirt *was* well-ironed.

*

The bell went and the kids rushed out of the hall. George hurried over to Stella. 'I'm so sorry. The children deliberately misread things.'

'Deliberately misread things,' Stella repeated.

'It's because I'm one of the younger teachers.' George ran a hand through his hair. 'Apparently I'm having affairs with Ann Rothwell in drama, Jason Marks in P.E., and at least two of the dinner ladies.'

'OK.' Stella made eye contact. 'But I'm not gay, by the way.'

George put his hands in his pockets. 'Right.'

'Just in case the kids *weren't* misreading things.' Stella left a pause. 'And please never bring that tortoise back into my surgery, because I really don't know what to do with it.'

'That changes things, then.' George held her gaze. 'Can I call you tomorrow? After I've let the dinner ladies down gently?'

'OK.' Stella smiled at him. 'Yes, I'd like that.'

Eleven years later

'This is *ridiculous!*' George shouted in Grace's direction, his anger directed firmly at Stella. 'We can't end eleven years and a marriage because of a *Coke can!*'

'It's not about the can itself,' Stella said. 'It's about what the can *represents.*'

George slammed his hands onto his knees. 'It's bad enough having arguments about *real* Coke cans. I'm not having arguments where they're infused with meanings I don't even understand. That's not fair, Stella!'

The therapy room was silent.

Grace looked from George to Stella and back.

Eventually, Grace settled on Stella. 'Do you think George has a point? That you draw patterns from arguments and, as a result, make small points into large issues? Do you recognise that as something that happens?'

'He's *deliberately* being obtuse.' Stella shook her head. 'I thought having time apart was meant to help with all this. Help him get some perspective and realise how annoying he was.'

'Oh really?' George lifted himself up in his seat; he shifted himself till he was facing Stella. '*Really?* That's what this separation was for?'

Stella crossed her legs. A second later, she folded her arms.

The three armchairs felt very far apart.

'What are you thinking, George?' Grace said softly.

George said nothing.

'I'll go.' Stella sat forward. 'I know these sessions are meant to be about us finding a way to get back together. But I think – sometimes – that he's the single worst man in the world. I think I might *actually hate him*.'

Stella sat back and stared at Grace. *Go on. Fix that.*

George jumped up. 'You nasty—'

He stopped himself. He glanced at Grace and back.

'Piece of work,' he finished.

'This isn't working.' Stella addressed Grace rather than George. 'Why are we even doing this? We could have had *a hundred* Nando's for what we've spent in here.'

'We can't break up because of a Coke can,' George sat back down. 'I'm not telling people that.'

'Oh, that's what matters to you? You never used to care what people think.'

'You *know* I don't mean that.' George did his agitated tapping thing with his hands. 'Sometimes, you act like you've never even met me! Anyway, it wasn't the Coke can. It was *Jurassic Park*. The Coke can was just the last straw.'

'Stella?' Grace's voice was soft. 'I know you've always been reluctant to discuss the *Jurassic Park* conversation. But do you want to discuss it now?'

Stella couldn't trust herself to speak.

'Can't you see, Grace?' George said. 'We're sick of each other.'

'Maybe—' Grace looked from one to the other – 'maybe we should take a break on the joint sessions. Have some individual sessions.'

Stella looked at George.

'Forever?' George said eventually.

'We don't need to decide that now,' Grace said.

George looked at Stella. 'That sounds like a *yes*.'

Stella looked down into her folded arms.

George stood up and shoved his chair back. 'Fuck this. There's no point. It's been over for a long time. We just need to face it.'

He strode out of the room, briefly stopping to pick up his rucksack, before slamming the door behind him.

I

Two months later

George stood outside the block of flats. He looked down at the keys in his hand.

He put the keys in his pocket and rang the buzzer.

Stella's voice crackled through the intercom. 'Don't tell me you've lost your keys already.'

'I thought it was polite to buzz.' George focused on his trainers. '*Was* it polite?' He asked. 'Or should I have let myself in?'

The buzzer went; George hurried forward to catch the door. Stella got annoyed when people didn't stop the door in time – a lot of things annoyed Stella lately – and he wasn't going to add *catching the door* to the long list of *things George is shit at*.

Stella was already in the doorway of the flat when he got there. She studied him. 'You've got a new T-shirt.'

'I do buy new things occasionally.'

Stella eyed the T-shirt. 'It's quite . . . vibrant.'

George lifted his chin. 'I like it.'

'Not a criticism.'

'Sorry.'

George headed into the lounge. He looked around.

Where they had always had a sofa between the standard lamp and the side table, there was now an incongruous yoga ball. Disturbed by the weight of his footsteps, the ball now drifted lightly across the wooden floor. It came to a jellylike rest against the standard lamp.

George indicated the yoga ball. 'Is that the sofa now?'

'Yep.'

George watched the ball flutter against the lamp. 'Finally getting some use out of it, then. So that's something.'

'Every cloud,' Stella said.

George gave a faint smile.

'See, we can do polite,' Stella said.

George shut off his smile.

Stella turned and started walking. 'Your stuff's in the kitchen.'

George followed her. He looked past the bin bags on the table to the rest of the room. The kitchen surfaces looked cleaner than they had for the ten years he'd lived in that flat. He was about to say as much, but stopped himself. Stupid to gift Stella an open goal like that.

He opened the first bin bag to see CDs, a decade-plus redundant.

He glanced at Stella and looked into the second bag. Jeans and jumpers – clothes with a 32 waistband to fit a man who didn't exist anymore. George smelled his own smell coming back from the bag.

He looked up. 'You wanted me to come over for this junk?'

Stella indicated the spiraliser on the side. 'And this.'

George looked at all the sharp edges, the bulky plastic. 'I bought *you* that.'

'But I don't want it.'

'You used it more than me.'

'I only used it because you said, "Stella, why haven't you used that spiraliser I got you?"'

14

George didn't recognise this impression of his voice, still less the 'obedient wife' trope he was being fed. He picked up the spiraliser and thrust it in the clothes bag. 'You really brought me over for this on a school night?'

There was a long pause. 'Come through to the lounge.'

'Why?'

'Because I want to ask you something.'

George followed her through to the room and sank onto the yoga ball. He strained his thigh muscles. The yoga ball didn't work as a sofa.

It was down to him that Stella was now using gym equipment as furniture. He hadn't even needed to take the old sofa when he left, he reflected, it was way too big for his bedroom in his shared house. But he'd had a point to make and so he'd made it, however awkward that sofa was in his new bedroom. However many cups of tea he spilled getting past it.

'What do you want?'

Stella sank onto his sofa's estranged twin. 'What I'm about to say is such a stupid idea, I don't even know where to start.'

George brushed fluff off his trousers. 'Interesting.'

'Mum and Dad are having a party next month. A murder mystery anniversary party.'

George stopped brushing. 'Go on.'

Stella took a breath. 'I want you to come with me.'

She held his gaze defiantly.

A car beeped outside. A male voice shouted in anger.

George restarted his trouser brushing. 'That's insane.'

'I know. But still.'

'It's a terrible, *terrible* idea.'

'I agree completely, but here we are.'

George tried to sit back on the yoga ball. His thighs

screamed; he hunched forward again. 'Why on earth do you want me to come to the party?'

'Mum wants to have a do before her treatment starts. She wants one last party.'

George softened his voice. 'Right.'

'The cancer's aggressive.' Stella used her *say it briskly then it won't hurt as much* voice. 'If I try to ask Mum about it, she looks affronted, like I'm intruding into her personal business. Which I suppose I am. But I also think it's a *tiny* bit my business.'

'That's your mum's way of dealing with things,' George said. 'Don't talk about it and then it doesn't exist.'

'So we don't mention it, and pretend everything is normal. Except Dad keeps silently hugging Mum from behind when she's trying to refill the kettle.'

'Are you sure you're not reading too much into this? You sure your mum thinks it's the last time she'll get everyone together?'

'She's spending *four hundred pounds* on caterers.'

George tried to sit back on the ball again. 'Four hundred pounds? *Margaret?*'

'*And* she's arranged fireworks. She either thinks she's on the way out, or it's dementia.'

George shook his head. 'Wow.'

Margaret was as tight as a clam. She never passed a skip without a rootle inside, bringing out a lamp or a rug or a discarded toy. Blowing dust off the item, bright-faced with success. *A bit of a clean-up and this'll get a fiver on eBay.*

George focused on Stella. 'She wants a party, I get it. But why does that mean I have to go?'

Stella looked at her feet.

'Why so quiet?'

She didn't respond.

It hit him. 'Really?'

She still didn't say anything.

'For fuck's sake, Stella! You *still* haven't told them we're divorcing?'

Stella crossed her arms. 'They'll be devastated. I can't tell them now.'

George shook his head in wonder.

'It's fine,' Stella said. 'I'll tell them when I'm ready.'

George thought of the conversation they'd just had about Margaret. *Don't talk about it and then it doesn't exist.*

He couldn't supress a sniff of laughter. *The irony.*

Stella looked up. 'What?'

'Nothing.'

'What?' she said again.

'You're not going to like it.'

'Obviously you have to tell me now.'

'I was just thinking . . .' Was he really going to go there? He scratched his cheek. 'Like mother like daughter.'

Stella took a beat.

Yes, George thought, he went there. But that was a legitimate thing to say, because it was true.

'That's helpful.' Her voice was tight. 'You're really spoiling for a fight today, are you?'

'I don't want to fight, it's just how can I not notice?' He held his palms up. 'All you need is to do that hair-fluffing thing, or tell me how those vile squirrels have been at your bird feeder again, and you'll have turned full-on Margaret.'

Stella shook her head. 'You're trying to hurt me. I'm nothing like my mother.'

George raised his eyebrows.

'I don't give a shit about squirrels and I haven't even *got* a garden, let alone a bird feeder.'

George smiled. 'I must be mistaken then.'

'So, back to the point.' Stella looked away briskly. 'This is the last party, and it's going to be perfect for them.'

'Oh, *come on!*' George raised his palms. 'That's Margaret, again! And no good things ever start with *and it's going to be perfect*. I'm just saying.'

'You don't need to keep raining on my parade and managing my expectations down.' Stella's voice was even tighter now. 'It's not your job any longer.'

And with that, it wasn't funny anymore.

Stella must have seen his face. 'Sorry.'

George took a second. He nodded.

'I'm just a bit tense. I'll level with you, asking you this doesn't feel great.'

George felt his phone buzz in his pocket. He tensed.

'Do you need to get that?' Stella said.

'No.' He knew who it would be. And it really couldn't help the situation if he let Stella see a text from Nancy.

He had to get out of here. He might complain his new bedroom wasn't homely, but at least it didn't have Stella and all this *head fuck* in it.

Finally, he looked up. 'Aren't you worried we'll have a row when we're at the party and ruin everything?'

She crossed her arms more tightly. 'We won't though, will we?'

'So far tonight, we've argued over' – George raised one finger – 'whether I should have pressed the buzzer on my way in.' He raised another finger. 'You complimenting me on my shirt and me thinking it was a dig. Me buying shit birthday presents.'

Stella looked like she was about to say something.

'Raining on parades.' George was determined to finish his list. 'You being like your mother, which – by the way – I'd watch if I were you. And I've been here ten minutes.'

Stella's mouth twisted that way it did when she was biting her cheek from the inside.

'But we laughed about the yoga ball,' she said eventually. 'Which you look really uncomfortable on.'

George stayed grimly where he was, despite the pulsing ache in his thighs.

'And I didn't say the spiraliser was a shit birthday present, just that it was more your kind of thing than mine.'

He raised an eyebrow.

'Fine. It was a shit birthday present. Do you even know me *at all*?'

George got up and walked into the hallway. 'Apparently not.'

'Look.' Stella grabbed his arm. Her Stella-smell wafted towards him, grape-sweet. 'I'm not asking you to do it for me. I'm asking you to do it for them. It's just one day, then you can get on with your . . . life.'

George noted the lack of sarcasm in the word *life*.

She must really want him to come to this party.

'Please, George. For *them*. You're a good guy, really' – that must have hurt, George thought – 'and it *is* just a day. Can I tell them you're coming?'

'I'll think about it.' George opened the front door. 'Don't rush me.'

George hurried out the flat.

He was back home by the time he realised he'd left his bags of junk on Stella's kitchen table.

2

Grace looked up from her notes. 'Last week you mentioned you have a family party coming up.'

Stella nodded.

'I want to talk about that some more.' Grace kept her gaze on Stella. 'How do you feel about going to this party on your own?'

Stella shrugged. She wondered whether Grace used that neutral tone in real life. *Can you pass me a fork? Shall we do another episode?*

Grace tried again. 'Is it the first family event since you and George split up? That must be hard.'

'I'm fine with it. Fine, just dandy. Peachy, even.'

'Do your family know you and George are divorcing?'

Stella pressed her lips together. 'Yes.'

'And what are you looking forward to about this party?'

'Making Mum happy. It's what Mum wants.'

Grace left one of her special Grace-pauses.

'And I get to see the dog. It's always nice to see Goldie, assuming they don't put her in kennels for the party. But they can't, can they? That wouldn't be fair, all her favourite people there.'

'It must be a daunting prospect. Have you thought how you're going to handle it?'

Stella scrunched up her toes. 'I'm going to ring Mum and insist Goldie gets to come. I'll offer to man-mark her for the night so she doesn't send glasses flying everywhere. You know what Labrador tails are like. Solid.'

'It's – what – your first family party alone in eleven years?'

Stella straightened the tissue box in front of her, in line with the edge of the table.

It was still a little wonky, so she adjusted it again. *There. Better.*

'Tell me about your relationship with your family.'

'It's normal. Like everyone else's.'

'Do you get on?' Grace asked.

'Do any families get on?'

'I'm asking about yours.'

Stella shrugged.

'Stella? Have you got nothing to say about your family?'

'Is this really relevant? I'm *thirty-seven*.'

'Humour me.'

'I don't see the point.'

Minutely, Grace licked her lips. 'Do you remember how, last time, we talked about you shutting down our conversations? And you said you'd try to be more open?'

Stella flicked some lint off her jeans. She faintly remembered saying that. But why on earth would she?

'Tell me about your parents,' Grace said. 'What do you have in common?'

Stella tensed. *Like mother like daughter.* That was a low blow from George.

Grace was still waiting for a response.

'We all believe in the importance of recycling.' Stella thought some more. 'And that there's no such thing as bad clothes, just bad weather.'

'That's it?'

Stella sighed. 'My parents are getting older. That's hard.'

Grace gave an encouraging nod.

'My mum has cancer and is due to start treatment right after the party.'

'Shall we talk about your feelings regarding that?'

'Definitely not.' Stella held up a hand. 'And that's not me shutting this conversation down, that's not what I do. It's out of respect to Mum. She's in denial, and that's what this party is about. She wants to show us off, I think. Put a stake in the ground, get the photos taken. *This was my family, before it all went wrong.*'

'That's a lot of pressure for everyone to enjoy themselves.'

'I don't think it was ever the intention that anyone enjoys themselves. And I swear Dad doesn't want a party, he just gets pulled along with things.'

'Many of us think we understand the dynamics of our parents' relationship. We find it hard to see them as anything other than our parents, yet they have an inner life we know nothing about.'

'You think?'

Grace didn't reply.

Stella looked directly at her and waited. Stella had always been good at staring contests. Like Mum.

Eventually, Grace broke. 'What's your father like?'

Stella thought for a moment. 'He's in a period of change. He's given up his grocery shop – which was his business for over forty years, and his father's before him – and he's started working in a supermarket.'

'Yes?'

'"Yes" what?'

'Is there anything else you want to say about your father?'

Stella shrugged.

'What was your childhood like?'

'Same as everyone else's.'

Grace tapped her pen against her pad.

'We had a shit car, and you had to get up to change the TV channel. Everyone was skint, but in a different way from now, and I never did get that SodaStream. Then, of course, I'm a middle child. Do you want me to talk about being the middle child?'

'Do you want to talk about being the middle child?'

'If you like.'

'Do you think it has any relevance?'

'Not really.'

Grace looked at her pad again. 'And what roles did everyone take in your family?'

Stella glanced at the clock. Ten minutes to go. 'Helen's the eldest, she was always the good one, doing what was expected of her, making my parents happy. Pete was the youngest and he kept his distance, and my parents ignore his dodgy life choices. He does "a bit of this, a bit of that", all dodgy "get-rich-quick schemes" that don't work, even though Mum thinks he's Richard Branson. And me?' Stella paused. 'I was the pain in the arse.'

Stella lifted her chin. She decided Grace didn't look surprised enough at this revelation.

'And what about now? What are your roles in the family now?'

'Pretty much the same.' *Identical, in fact,* Stella thought. *But I'm not telling you that.*

'You'd be surprised how common it is that roles in the family are defined in early life.'

'I was meant to be the difficult one. That time I came home in a police car – just for messing about at the precinct, nothing major, and I wasn't even using spray paint, it was washable poster paint. I even used *a brush*!' Stella took a breath. 'But Mum said, "we knew it would be you, if any of our kids brought the police to our door." Then she completely ignored that Pete got a caution for possession at college later because, as she told everyone who'd listen, "he was just carrying that ketamine for a friend."'

'Were you jealous of Pete?'

'Absolutely not.'

'What about your sister? The one who did everything right?'

Stella gave a sniff of laughter. 'Helen did all the stuff Mum and Dad wanted and, when you think about it, that was all the rubbish stuff. We wouldn't speak if we weren't related. We have nothing in common.'

Stella glanced at the clock. Not long to go.

'Let's try a different angle. What were you afraid of as a child?'

'Ooh, I like that question!'

'Really?'

'So, I'm thinking – pylons.' Stella sat back in the chair. 'Quicksand, that was a big one back then.'

Grace stared at her. 'Right.'

'And swans. Everyone was always banging on about how swans could break your arm.'

The two sat in silence.

'We haven't talked about George today,' Grace said. 'Have you noticed?'

'I hadn't.'

'How does that make you feel?'

'Wonderful. It means that things couldn't be better. I'm growing and changing.' Stella looked at her watch and stood up. 'I think our time's up. See you next week.'

3

The next evening, after work, George sat on his bed, looking at a news site on his phone.

He was reading about Yemen. It had recently come to his attention he didn't know enough about Yemen.

Nancy had seemed surprised by his lack of knowledge on his last date, so he was doing research. *Yes,* he'd agreed, and meant it, *everyone should know about Yemen.*

Yet he was struggling to read. It was hard to ignore the sound of the podcast from the room above.

'And the countdown is on! Three, two, one – Splashdown! Hahahahahaha!'

George did not know what the podcast was, or what was going on. He just knew that no *real* people could find anything that funny.

George looked back at his phone, trying to ignore the podcast. And also, now, trying to ignore the bitter smell of what he assumed must be garlic bread, wafting up from the kitchen.

When he'd first checked out the room, George reflected, he should have asked, *'And this room isn't above the kitchen, is it?'*

Stella would have asked, if she'd been choosing the room. That kind of thing – practicality – had been her area.

Ah, well. Too late now. And at least this room could fit his sofa.

Kind of.

He sniffed. The smell of garlic bread seemed to have faded a little. You didn't notice these things after a few minutes, he decided. So that was fine.

And it could have been much worse. One of his house-mates – he deliberately hadn't asked which one, it wasn't that kind of house – liked to cook and eat fish after a night out. George hadn't known a smell could wake you up till he'd moved here. But it could.

There was another burst of laughter from the room above. Those podcasters were *really* enjoying themselves.

George tried to look at the news again.

He'd be out of here soon. It was only a six-month lease and he was halfway through. Once he'd properly saved a deposit, he'd get a flat of his own. Hopefully.

He looked at the clock.

Yes, right now, the room was OK. And, right now, he wanted to stay here all evening.

But probably, he admitted to himself as he reached for his coat on the sofa, because he knew where he was going instead.

George and Grace sat across from each other in the therapy room.

'How's this week been?' Grace asked.

'It's been a good week, ego-wise.' George stretched out his legs. 'I've got the moral high ground locked down after what Stella asked me on Tuesday.'

'Before we go into the detail of what you want to tell me, I want you to reflect on what you've just said.'

George blinked at her.

'"Moral high ground". How does that make you feel, that you're viewing your relationship with Stella as having a winner and a loser?'

'It feels great!' George sat forward. He'd cheered up on the bus on the way here, as he played out this conversation in his head. At least, this time, he had something satisfactory to share. 'Her parents are having an anniversary party and I've done the big thing and agreed I'll go with her, which makes me a good guy. Official, proven.'

Something on Grace's face twitched.

'What?'

'Nothing.' Grace gripped her chair arm slightly. 'Stella asked you to the party when?'

'Tuesday. Why?'

Grace looked at her diary. 'It's not relevant.'

The clock on the wall ticked.

Grace coughed. 'So, how do you feel about going to this party?'

'Stella hasn't told you she's asked me, has she?' George sat forward on his chair. 'Oh, this is *interesting*.'

This session was getting better and better.

Grace looked down at her pad. 'What I discuss with an individual in their sessions is completely confidential.'

Grace's expression was one he was familiar with from his place of work: *Sorry, sir? Who drew* what *cock on the whiteboard?*

'Interesting,' George repeated. '*Really* interesting. That's not a great use of her sessions, is it? Not very *mature?*'

Grace took a moment. 'Do you think you might get more out of this process if you focused on your own feelings, rather than what Stella might be saying?'

George thought about this for a minute.

'No,' he said. 'This has been my favourite session so far.'

'You're not meant to have favourite sessions.'

'But aren't you meant to be making me feel better?'

'Let's get back on track. Do you think it's a good thing to go to the family party when you've separated?'

'Is this for my session or Stella's?'

Grace put her pad down. 'This could be becoming an issue. Now you and Stella will no longer be coming back together for joint sessions, we may need to consider whether it's appropriate you both still come here to see me. It's something to think about in our next session. In the meantime, why are you going to this party? Really?'

George sat back in his chair. 'It's for her mum and dad. They were my family once. This is their last party and it's important their children reflect well on them and are seen to be successful.'

'And you equate divorcing with failure.'

'*They'd* equate divorcing with failure. I'm fine with it.'

'Fine with it,' Grace said. 'Yet, notice, you're attending a family party with your soon-to-be ex-wife. That's an unusual decision.'

'I'm just a good guy then, aren't I?' George stopped smiling. 'This matters to them. Her family are nice people, even though they're insane. You know?'

Grace shook her head.

'This is one last party. Margaret, that's Stella's mum, is about to start treatment for late-stage cancer, though they're deliberately all skirting round that topic as if nobody's looked up the recovery rates. This party is a big deal for her and Stella's dad, Tommy.'

'Have you thought about how you are going to manage at this party when people ask questions about you and Stella?'

'No one will ask questions.'

'People often ask questions when making small talk.'

'But they won't care about the answers, so it's fine.'

Grace gave a smile of acknowledgement. 'But people often underestimate the impact of dishonesty on their comfort levels. It can create a surprising level of anxiety. You don't think that will be the case for you?'

'I'll just remind myself I'm doing one final good thing for Margaret and Tommy. They got us a year's Sky subscription for Stella's thirtieth. And Tommy did replumb our new dishwasher that time. Only thing is, when I said yes to Stella about the party, I hadn't thought about Na—'

Damn it.

'What?'

George took a deep, stilted breath. 'Nothing.'

'Is there something you're not telling me?'

George rubbed the front of his trousers briskly. 'Absolutely not.'

'You look like you're experiencing a strong emotion right now.'

'I have nothing to feel guilty about. *Nothing.*'

The clock ticked.

'So what is it that you're thinking about?'

George pawed his neck in a restless swipe. 'The breakdown of my relationship with Stella.'

'And what exactly is making you feel guilty?'

'That's the point. There's nothing to feel bad about. This is all Stella's fault.' He held up his hand. 'OK, I know, it wasn't *all* Stella's fault.' He itched his neck again. 'Though it was at least seventy–thirty, and definitely ninety–ten by the end.'

Grace put her pen down. 'This isn't a test. It's not for me to decide what went wrong in your relationship. This is a safe space for you to talk about your feelings so you can assess them and move on.'

'Of course,' George said. 'I know that.'

'So let's talk about the feelings of guilt. What are you thinking about?'

Grace left one of her pauses.

George raised his gaze. He couldn't quite meet her eyes. 'I feel like you'll judge me.'

'That is the opposite of how you're meant to feel in this room.'

'I feel like you'll take Stella's side.'

'Do you? Really?'

'No.' George paused. 'I just don't want to tell you what I've done.'

Grace waited.

George sighed. 'I've started seeing someone else.'

Grace held his gaze. 'That sounds like quite an important thing to have shared.'

'I feel like I'm cheating on Stella.'

'But you're not cheating on Stella. You broke up several months ago.'

'And that's why it's *so* annoying to feel like this.' George looked at the carpet. He waited.

'Tell me about this person you're seeing. How do you feel about them?'

'She's called Nancy. I met her on a dating site and she's nice. Lovely, in fact. But it was an accident, and I know it's too soon.'

'It wasn't an accident.'

'You believe there's no such thing as an accident?' George shook his head tolerantly. 'Is this a Freudian therapist thing?'

'You don't *accidentally* put up an online dating profile.'

George stopped shaking his head.

'Unless you already had a profile when you were in a relationship with Stella?'

'No!' George sat up in outrage. '*Grace!*'

'We should talk openly here.'

'I put up a profile *several weeks* after we split up, because my mates are busy with kids and jobs and I had an empty half-term week. I was just kicking around on my own, feeling sorry for myself. And it wasn't like I was doing anything else, and I didn't have a telly. Of course, I could have bought a telly . . .' George tapped his tooth thoughtfully.

'You started online dating because you didn't have a TV.'

'My laptop has a faulty bit at the bottom of the screen, and it's too annoying to watch more than two episodes of anything in one go. And there's hardly any space in the bedroom as it is, what with the stupid sofa I took with me. I couldn't fit a telly in there as well.'

Grace held his gaze. 'But you weren't looking for a relationship?'

'It wasn't about meeting someone else. It was about practice for when I did. Last time I was dating, we had to leave the house. We met in bars and nightclubs where the music was too loud to talk. Everything was different.'

'Everything?'

'Everything.' George didn't want to talk specifically about body hair. 'I hadn't slept with anyone that wasn't Stella since I was *twenty-five*. But I didn't want to mess anyone about. On my online profile I made sure I ticked all the *looking for something fun* boxes. I deliberately made myself sound like a right shallow twat.'

Grace nodded. 'You were honest about your intentions. And what happened?'

George sat back in his chair. 'Nancy messaged a couple of times. We met for a drink, and I said straight away I'd just split up from my wife. I said I wanted something casual and she said it was fine, all the stuff I needed to hear. And I thought – *why wouldn't I see her again?* Nancy's pretty and funny, and it's not like I've got much else to do on a Wednesday night except sit in my shitty room with no telly.'

'So what's the problem?'

'I feel guilty.'

'Why?'

'I want things to feel simpler.' George scratched his cheek in thought. 'Maybe I should have bought that telly?'

'Things probably won't feel simple for some time. But Nancy definitely knows you only want things to be casual?'

'Are you saying I should be selfish?'

'I'm asking why you feel guilty about dating her, when you've been clear what the situation is.'

George shifted in his seat, irritated. 'She's nearly forty. You can't mess people about, especially if they're *so* understanding and fine not to rush things but, at the same time, they hold their mates' babies a little too long.' He shifted in his seat. 'I thought you were meant to be telling me not to leap into anything new? That I need time to heal?'

'I'm trying to reframe the situation so you can see the problem from a different angle.'

'Aha, so you *do* think it's a problem!'

Grace said nothing.

'Sorry. I just want to be a good guy. That's all I have left, being the good guy.'

'What if there's no such thing as the good guy?'

'There has to be. Otherwise—' George heard his voice creep up in pitch – 'otherwise, what do I do?'

4

It had been a great idea taking this retirement job, Tommy reflected, as he weaved down the seasonal goods aisle with a box of citronella candles in his arms.

He'd wanted less stress but hadn't been ready to retire. He'd known it would be hard to let go of the family shop but also knew none of his kids – Helen, Pete or Stella – would want to take over. But letting the shop go completely would have felt so *final*.

And then – the perfect compromise. Helen's husband Nathan had been made redundant and needed a new job. Tommy had inherited the shop from his father, keeping it in the family, and now he had passed it on to Nathan. Tommy hoped Nathan would hand the keys over to the next generation too, one day. It felt essential that the shop outlived him. That this was Tommy's legacy.

So here Tommy was, a supermarket assistant, still using his knowledge of produce to help customers, roaming the aisles with no stress, dressed in his smart pouch-pocketed uniform and peppy badge.

A man pushed his trolley up to Tommy. 'Baked beans?'

'Aisle five.' Tommy waved a hand. 'Midway down on the left, between the Green Giant and the tinned tomatoes.'

Tommy kneeled on the floor and opened the box of

candles. He started arranging them carefully on the shelf, labels facing forward.

A lady rushed up in a flurry of quick steps. 'Yoghurts?'

'You'll be wanting aisle thirteen. Make sure you look on the end, love, that's where the three-for-twos are.'

The woman smiled. 'Thanks.'

Tommy nodded. He continued unboxing and stacking the candles.

'Tommy?' Vanessa, the supermarket's assistant manager, stood over him. 'Have you got a minute?'

Tommy tried not to sigh. He looked down at his box of candles and back. 'Now?'

'Yes,' Vanessa said. 'Right now.'

Tommy followed Vanessa to the staffroom and the two sat on low spongy chairs. Across the room, the staff vending machine hummed gently.

'How do you think it's all going?' Vanessa crossed her legs. 'How do you think you're settling in?'

Tommy beamed. 'Fine.'

'And what about dealings with the customers? How are you finding that?'

'They seem satisfied.'

'Well, I'm afraid to tell you' – she didn't sound afraid at all, Tommy thought – 'we've had some complaints from customers.'

Tommy was still reflecting how unafraid Vanessa sounded, so it took a minute for the actual words to land. When they did, he stopped smiling. He sat up straight, despite the lack of back support in the chair.

'Tommy? Does what I'm saying surprise you?'

He straightened his apron. 'I just find that hard to believe.'

Vanessa looked at her notepad. 'One woman said when she asked where to find barbecues, you said "haven't you got a strong man to pick that up for you?"'

'I was being friendly.'

'She didn't like it.'

'I was sympathising! I wasn't implying she couldn't get a man! She was quite attractive actually. A little plump, maybe, but she had a nice friendly face.'

Vanessa's lip twitched. 'Another woman said you told her to smile and said "cheer up, it might never happen". Do you remember saying that?'

'No,' Tommy said. 'Not specifically.'

Vanessa waited.

'But I do say that quite a lot.' He shrugged. 'And if it was the blonde lass looking for the gluten-free bread last week, she was looking really harassed, and her little daughter was being a right madam. I was trying to perk her up a bit.'

Vanessa frowned. 'You say that a lot? Who do you say it to?'

'Whoever looks like they need cheering up! Some of those girls hurry around like they have the weight of the world of their shoulders.'

'Always women?'

Tommy felt his brow furrow. 'It would be a bit odd if I went round saying it to chaps, wouldn't it?'

'Please stop saying it.'

'Don't be friendly with the customers?'

'Don't be friendly with the customers *in a way that might offend them.*'

'But who could possibly be offended?'

Vanessa indicated with her hands. 'These people. Me, actually.'

Tommy just stared at her. He was so shocked, he couldn't even reply.

'She's completely overreacting,' Tommy said later that evening. He looked at Margaret over their steaming plates of chicken korma. 'If you can't tell a girl she'd look pretty if she smiled, what can you do?'

Margaret shook her head. 'Some people these days – it's like they *want* to find fault and get angry.'

'I never mean anything by it,' Tommy added.

'Of course you don't,' Margaret said. 'But that's the Internet for you. This is how it's made people now.'

'I tell you what.' Tommy held out a forkful of korma. 'I feel like never helping a woman take her shopping to her car again. However many kids are hanging off her. However many barbecues and baguettes she's juggling.'

Margaret shook her head again. 'I don't blame you.'

He ripped a piece of naan. 'Do you have conversations like that in the shop? Does Nathan tell you what to say to people, now he's running it?'

Margaret didn't answer.

'How was the shop today?' Tommy asked eventually. 'Is that hinge on the door still stiff?'

She put her knife and fork down.

He frowned. 'What?'

'Tommy.' She gave him that meaningful look. 'I don't think you should keep asking me what it's like working in the shop.'

'I'm just asking.'

'I don't think it's helpful. Onwards and upwards, remember?'

He looked down at his food. 'Onwards and upwards.'

But Margaret must have known he was upset, because when he fed a piece of naan to Goldie under the table, she pretended not to notice.

With Margaret on his side, Tommy rallied. Over the next few days, he directed people towards their eggs and anchovies solemnly, without comment. If he saw Vanessa approaching in her sleeveless business dresses, he hurried to the freezer aisle until the danger had passed.

But on Wednesday morning, Tommy was unboxing bananas after the staff 'energy huddle' when a blond man in cargo shorts strode up to him.

'I'm looking for soy sauce? I'm in a bit of a rush.'

Tommy stood up. 'No problem. Follow me.'

The two started walking side by side.

'I've looked with the vinegar and the tomato puree already,' the blond man said. 'I'm getting nowhere.'

'It'll be in the ethnic section.'

The man frowned. 'The ethnic section?'

Tommy smiled. 'Yes.'

The man stopped walking. 'You mean *world foods*.'

'Exactly, aisle eight.' Tommy slowed. 'So, do you think you'll be all right from here?'

The man stared at him.

'That way.' Tommy gestured with his hand. He waited. 'I thought you were in a hurry.'

The man raised his voice. 'Did anyone hear that?' He turned, as though the other customers were his audience. 'This guy just told me to go to "the ethnic section"!'

Some passers-by glanced over. All kept moving.

'For soy sauce!' Tommy looked round for someone appropriate to adjudicate. He waved at a passing dark-skinned man with dreadlocks. 'It's OK to say "the ethnic section", isn't it? For where you get soy sauce?'

The dreadlocked man shook his head. 'Mate, I'm just here for the spaghetti hoops.'

The blond man blinked at Tommy. 'You ignorant twat.'

The man walked straight over to the nearest member of staff. Who, unfortunately, happened to be Vanessa.

Damn it. Tommy knew he should have stayed in the freezer aisle.

Tommy watched helplessly while the man spoke to Vanessa, glaring and indicating in Tommy's direction.

Tommy adjusted his apron.

He adjusted his apron again.

The man left the aisle, shaking his head.

Tommy walked straight up to Vanessa. 'Before you say anything, he was completely off-track. My son-in-law George is Iranian. Half-Iranian,' Tommy corrected. 'Well, he's from Hertfordshire and speaks like he's from *EastEnders*, but definitely ethnic, it's complicated. Anyway, we're fine with it. Delighted.'

Vanessa held Tommy's gaze. 'It's not the first time this has happened.'

'I was being friendly.'

'And how did that work out for you?' Vanessa kept her voice level.

Was that sarcasm? Tommy shoved his hands in his apron pouch.

'I'm going to have to carefully consider the next steps.' Vanessa kept her face management-blank. 'We can't have staff making customers feel uncomfortable.'

'I've done nothing wrong! And I know all about the produce!'

'We are not doubting your knowledge.'

'Who's "we"?'

'I have repeatedly asked you not to say inappropriate things to customers, yet here we are. Discussing it again.'

'*We're* not discussing it.' Tommy gestured with his hands in his pouch. '*You're* discussing it.'

'I'm going to have to take advice. About disciplinary proceedings.'

Tommy gripped his hands together in his pouch. 'Disciplinary proceedings? For my retirement job?' He gestured his frustration, moving the pouch fabric up and down.

Vanessa said nothing.

'Ridiculous.' Tommy took a breath. 'If you don't want my skills, I'll resign.'

He waited, so Vanessa could make the appropriate noises of regret and despair.

She didn't. 'If that's how you feel in the morning, please put that in writing.'

Tommy blinked at her.

'We value our older colleagues and all their years of experience.' Vanessa spoke softly. Deceptively softly, Tommy thought. 'But you have to adhere to our company values.'

Tommy made a noise between a sniff and a cough.

'Regardless of what I may think personally,' she continued, 'can't you see it's bad business to have customers offended?'

'But I make other people very happy. Lots of people love my chat!'

'But when it's about sex and race, can't you see that's problematic? Have you seen what they've been saying online lately?'

Tommy pressed his lips together and walked away.

He wasn't going to dignify that question with a response.

*

Tommy had been determined not to tell Margaret about his day. It was his job to protect her from all that was wrong in the world.

Unfortunately, she hadn't even laid the table for tea that evening before he found it was all coming out, in a succession of jumbled breaths.

'I just don't understand.' Tommy put his head in his hands. 'I really don't understand what I've done wrong.'

'It's the nanny state.' Margaret got the knives and forks out of the drawer. 'No one will be as good at that job as you. *No one.*'

'I feel pointless.'

'You're not pointless.'

'They want to put me out to pasture.'

'Don't get emotional, love.'

He looked up at Margaret. 'But how am I supposed to not care?'

She laid the table hard, banging cutlery left and right. 'There are new rules now, whether we like it or not.'

'This never happened in the shop,' Tommy said. 'I knew what I was dealing with in there. I set the rules, and no one complained.'

Margaret patted his hand. 'Just try not to let it get to you. It doesn't matter what they think. You're a good man, and that's all that matters.'

Three days later, Tommy got the email.

Dear Tommy,

It has been recommended that you would immediately benefit from attending a *Be a Diversity Champion* workshop. Please get in touch with trainingadmin@groceryfresh.com to book your place on an upcoming session.

To help with your ongoing development, you will also be given a book to take away: *Embracing Difference* by A.S. Cranbourne.

After participating in the session, you will be asked to attend a meeting with your manager. Your manager will decide whether any further education in this area is still required.

Your attendance at this workshop is compulsory. Please be aware that non-attendance within a month of today's date, or any subsequent breach of the company's Code of Conduct, will result in disciplinary action.

Kind regards,
The Diversity Team

5

Margaret was chopping carrots in the kitchen. Tommy charged into the room and thrust a piece of paper into Margaret's eyeline.

Margaret put her knife down. She turned to reach for her downstairs reading glasses. She put them on and slowly, with a bad feeling, she unfolded the paper.

242 Cole Street
Manchester
M16 7XX

Dear Sirs/Madams,
Re: Invitation to Be a Diversity Champion Session
I want to say thank you for inviting me to the above workshop.
I want to say it, but I can't.

I do NOT appreciate the invitation, and I will NOT be attending the workshop.

Courses like this are a waste of precious supermarket resources. I am quite open enough to the changes in the world already and I do not have to justify myself to Vanessa or anyone.

I have a homosexual son. I have daughters. I have a half-Iranian son-in-law. Your suggestion that I need training in dealing with different types of people is an insult to me and my family.

Please do not send me a copy of Embracing Difference *by A.S. Cranbourne. If you try to, I will send it right back.*

This is my final statement on the matter.

If you wish to take this as my resignation, so be it. I will take my skills to a rival supermarket, where, with my forty years of delicatessen and customer service experience, I will be welcomed with open arms.

Yours faithfully,
Tommy Foy

Margaret let the letter droop. She removed her reading glasses.

Tommy was breathing deeply, like he'd been carrying boxes upstairs. 'What do you think?'

'Is there any way you could just see it as a game?' Margaret glanced at the letter and back at Tommy. 'Set your mind to just go to the session and sit through it regardless? Just rise above it.'

'That's impossible.'

'But they've made it clear they're not going to let you work there if you don't. And you love that job.'

'They've made my position untenable.' Tommy was still breathing heavily. 'But what do you think of my letter?'

'Have you already sent it?'

'Yes.'

'Physically placed it in the postbox?'

'Of course.'

Margaret put the letter and her glasses down. 'Then I think it's fine.'

Unexpectedly, Tommy grabbed her from behind. It was an

intense kind of hug – a hug that felt like heightened emotion and distress and inevitability and everything that Margaret *really* didn't want in a hug right now.

Tommy released her. She heard him bustle back upstairs.

Margaret pushed her chopping board away. She walked into the lounge to look out of the front window.

Across the road, men in overalls put the finishing touches to the new shop sign. Margaret had known this day would come, but why *today*? A week before her party?

It would have been bad enough, even if Tommy hadn't been still reeling from what had happened at the supermarket.

Nathan should have known better. Her son-in-law had no tact. Helen should have stopped him, she knew how sensitive her father could be. What *were* they thinking?

Any minute, Tommy was going to see the newly painted sign and realise Nathan was changing the name of the shop, and—

There was the thundering of agitated feet down the stairs. 'He's changing the name of *our* shop! How dare he!'

'Calm down, Tommy.'

Tommy was now in the doorway, followed, as always, by the slowly trotting Goldie.

'It's bad enough he's put in that fancy coffee machine and those café tables and started selling buckwheat. And you can't even get toilet roll there anymore, let alone a packet of custard. But it's been *Cole Street Groceries* since Father set it up! Nathan can't just change the name after seventy years.'

Margaret put a hand on Tommy's arm.

'That god-awful fake-French sign. What was wrong with *Cole Street Groceries*? He can't just say it's *The Jardin* from now on. He *can't*.'

'But it's *his* now, Tommy. We gave Nathan the business

to manage, and if he wants to be French now, he can. And I think it's *Le* Jardin.'

'Who does he think he is? Charles Aznavour? *Gainsbourg*?'

Margaret pursed her lips. When she and Tommy had first moved across from the shop, she hadn't thought about what that meant for their retirement. Stupid, really, to think you could live opposite a place in which you'd invested so much energy, that you could switch off from its life force somehow, even when, if there was no traffic, you could still hear the faint jangle of the door when watching *Cash in The Attic* in your own lounge.

'Don't you think it's a terrible name? And have you seen those crisps he's selling now! Four pound fifty a bag!'

'Have you been studying the contents of the shop again, Tommy? We've discussed this. It's not good for you.'

'Goldie wanted to go in, she was straining at the lead. It's hard for her, she doesn't understand why she doesn't get to go in the shop anymore.' Tommy leaned down and stroked Goldie's ears. 'It's been her favourite place all her life. She's all out of sorts.'

Margaret said nothing.

'Besides, I didn't have to go in to study anything. The crisps are arranged in an all-singing, all-dancing display in the window, it's lit up like Deansgate at Christmas. Four pound fifty,' Tommy repeated. 'For *crisps*.'

'Nathan says they're for special occasions.'

'What kind of fool pays four pound fifty for crisps?'

'Our customers do.' Margaret pressed her hand gently on Tommy's arm. 'And it's natural Nathan wants to put his own stamp on things. Don't you remember moving the counter when you first took over?'

But Tommy wasn't listening. 'I was doing Nathan a favour

when I said he could run the business. I didn't say he could *change* it.'

Margaret rubbed Tommy's back.

This was her fault, in a way – as much as anything was ever Margaret's fault. Helen had told her about Nathan being made redundant from the estate agency last winter, and Tommy was talking about taking it easier and getting a 'little' job for his last few working years, so Margaret had said, 'Well, how about we kill two birds with one stone?'

And everyone had thought it was a great idea. Nathan took himself onto a shopkeeping workshop and came back talking about *gentrification* and *proximity to ABC1s* and *bigger profit margins in the wealthier demographic* and sounding, Margaret thought, more like an estate agent than ever before.

But Margaret hadn't anticipated the supermarket fiasco. Or the name change.

Le Jardin, indeed.

'Tommy, this is why you had to step back. A business like that can only have one leader. You're two alpha males, knocking heads.'

Tommy reached for Margaret's hand. He smoothed her skin with his thumb. 'I'm still an alpha? Even now?'

'Of course. You were born an alpha. You'll die an alpha.'

The next day Tommy mooched about the house, being pointless in a surprisingly loud way. From the occasional scratching of chair sound across carpet upstairs, Margaret assumed he must be continuing his recent project, logging into TripAdvisor and systematically reviewing every restaurant he'd ever eaten in, every hotel he'd ever stayed at.

She hoped, at least, he wasn't writing to their MP again. That never ended well.

He appeared in the hallway at teatime. 'I'm going to ask Nathan if I can come back to work for him. I'll ask him at the party.'

'Don't ask him,' Margaret said automatically. 'Alphas, remember?'

He nodded. 'Maybe I'll take Goldie for another walk.'

'Are you sure?' Margaret looked behind Tommy to their slumped, arthritic dog. 'She looks like her back legs are giving her some gip.'

But Tommy grabbed his coat and took Goldie for another walk anyway.

The grandmother clock chimed.

Now Tommy was out of the study, Margaret went up there and sat down. She put her upstairs reading glasses on and turned to *Murder Mystery Parties – A Definitive Host's Guide*. It would have been helpful if it had had a chapter saying what to do about people and their awful mobile phones, but Margaret would just have to improvise.

She'd done everything on the list. She'd written the plot and the detailed character sheets and found she'd got quite a flair for detail. She'd even decided what specific item of clothing each guest should wear as a party talking point. Yes, she could have bought a murder mystery off the shelf, but why would she when she could write one herself?

After all. This was going to be a very special party.

Margaret unlocked the cabinet and got out her laptop from the bottom drawer. She checked her RSVP list, though she knew what she was going to find. Her youngest daughter was flaky and they were still missing George and Stella's RSVP.

Margaret shook her head and opened her address book. She could never remember mobile phone numbers. It was something about these new numbers starting with 07 that made them so much less distinctive than the old landline numbers, and—

Margaret caught herself. She deliberately stopped herself finishing what she considered an elderly person's thought and, instead, dialled Stella's (perfectly acceptable) 07 number.

A few rings, and Stella's phone was about to go to voicemail. Margaret coughed, getting her phone message voice ready.

'Hi, Mum, you OK?'

Margaret covered her confusion with brusqueness. 'I'm just going through my list of attendees and I can't find your RSVP email?'

'You can't seem to find it, or you know I haven't sent one?'

Margaret sighed.

'Whatever your list says, I've told you we're definitely coming. Wouldn't miss it.'

'And George?'

A pause. 'He's really looking forward to it.'

'And have you two studied the envelopes I gave you? You *have* done your preparation for the mystery?'

'Of course. We both know all good parties come with pre-work.'

Margaret narrowed her eyes. Was that sarcasm?

'Did you really write it yourself?'

'Of course.'

There was a long pause.

'Have you got a good crowd coming?' Stella asked.

'It'll be mainly neighbours and old friends. There's not enough characters for everyone, a lot of the guests are just going to have to be detectives. And the kids will have to entertain themselves in the garden or help their parents.

But that's fine. Kids know how to play without help, don't they?'

'I think so,' Stella said.

'Oh – you'll be pleased to know Adele is coming, and she's bringing Scott with her.'

'Scott?'

'You know Scott! Adele's son, the one with the property portfolio. He has a five-bedroom house in Didsbury now. He's having a cellar conversion, though the neighbours are up in arms. I feel so sorry for those neighbours. And surely no one needs more than five bedrooms. Do you remember him? You used to play in his sandpit when you were little. His wife runs that kids' boutique on Burton Road.'

Stella didn't answer.

'You used to ride around on your bikes with my laundry tubs on your backs, pretending to be Ninja turtles.'

'Why on earth would Scott come to your party? No offence.'

'Because his mother's coming and it's a nice thing to do! *Honestly,* Stella. And you know he owns our shop now. He bought the whole of Cole Street Precinct from the previous landlord.'

Stella didn't say anything.

Margaret paused. 'And your sister's doing some of her salmon parcels, you know, with the latticework on top.'

'Of course she is. Good old Helen.'

Margaret narrowed her eyes. 'Obviously we've got caterers bringing nibbly bits—'

'Still surprised about that.'

'—but if you had a signature dish you want me to factor in, let me know.'

'Thanks, Mum. I don't have a signature dish.'

'I was just giving you the opportunity to show off your skills.'

'Are you giving Pete the opportunity too? Or just me and Helen?'

This was Stella making some kind of point, Margaret knew. 'Do you think Pete will want to do some cooking?'

'No. I'm just asking.'

Margaret thought about this some more. Maybe she *should* give Pete the opportunity to cook. Her son was gay, after all, and wasn't that lovely nowadays? But it did make the rules less clear. She was expecting to ask Pete to man the bar, to tong ice and lemon slices – maybe send him down to the cellar if they needed the emergency garden chairs. But should she be asking him to cook?

Margaret decided to ask Pete what job he wanted to do at the party. He could choose whether he wanted men's jobs or women's jobs.

'Do you want me to bring anything?' Stella asked. 'Anything from Tesco, I mean. Or even M&S. I'll push the boat out for your anniversary, Mum.'

'No thank you,' Margaret said primly. 'If we need to buy in food, we'll get it from the shop.'

'*Le Jardin*, you mean.' There was something in Stella's voice – a question? Amusement? Mocking, even?

'Yes,' Margaret said firmly. '*Le Jardin*.'

She said goodbye and put the phone down on her youngest daughter, wondering why they could never have a proper conversation without Stella spiking it out of shape.

Margaret called Pete next. He didn't answer his phone, but that was OK. Pete was so busy with his London investments job – that's how she thought of it, *London investments job*, even though she wasn't exactly sure of the details – so she hadn't expected him to RSVP. Besides, he'd already said 'wouldn't miss it, Ma'.

She put a tick in the *RSVP* column and paused next to the *plus-one* column. She put a question mark. She hoped, one day, she would be able to put a tick there. And then maybe . . . She'd heard that the mother at a gay wedding got treated like royalty. Not that she could imagine any wedding of Pete's being *very* gay. He was unflamboyant and unsmiley, which is why, Margaret worried, he was always single. If you looked at him, thickening round the middle, always wearing baggy jeans and tired sweatshirts, you'd actually think he was *straight*.

In his own way, Pete was as unfathomable as Stella. So thank God for Helen. The final third of her offspring: the third she actually understood. The one who'd stayed in Manchester.

Maybe it was a generational thing – Helen was the oldest, nearly forty now. Perhaps she'd grown up before the rules changed completely.

Margaret phoned Helen next.

'How are you doing, Mum?' Helen's voice was bright. 'Are you looking forward to the party?'

'Everything's on track. I'm just trying to pin down some final RSVPs, but you know what people are like.' Margaret deliberately didn't say Stella's name, to be kind. 'Are you still going to do your salmon parcels?'

'Of course, Mum, don't stress. Do you need me to do anything else?'

'No, that wouldn't be fair. The others aren't. Unless . . . do you think Pete would want to cook anything?'

Helen laughed. 'No! Why do you say that?'

'No reason. And, Helen?'

'Yes?'

'Don't talk to your father about *Le Jardin* at the party.'

'Right.' Helen paused. 'I'm sorry to hear you say that.'

Margaret scratched her neck. 'And definitely don't ask him about his new job at the supermarket.'

'OK.' Helen paused again. 'Should I ask you, or . . .?'

'Best not.'

Margaret rounded up the conversation overquickly. She put her laptop away and locked the chest of drawers.

She should have told Helen about Tommy's *thing*. Helen might understand that Tommy was a bit down.

But then, Helen was always so bright-eyed. So jolly and helpful and in control. There was no way Helen would understand how Tommy was feeling – not at all.

6

Helen looked at the pasta shell on her fork.

Nope.

She put her fork down and watched Isobel over the dining-room table.

Isobel stabbed at her own pasta with careful jabs. Helen found her daughter's self-control disquieting. Next to Isobel, Charlie had his head down and was shovelling pasta in greedily. Five years younger and so much sunnier a disposition.

Helen would never be getting a call like the one she'd got today about Isobel about Charlie. *Never.*

'A meeting'. That's all the school secretary had said. He 'wouldn't elaborate on the phone. Ms Crawford will explain when you get there'.

Helen turned to Isobel. 'Do you know why they've asked me into your school tomorrow?'

Isobel looked up.

Helen softened her voice. 'Because they're busy people. They wouldn't invite me in for nothing.'

Isobel shrugged.

'Haven't you got *anything* to say?'

Isobel put her fork down. 'I suppose we'll find out tomorrow.'

Helen narrowed her eyes. Ten years old and Isobel was this

self-composed. Helen was *thirty-nine* and she never felt as calm as her daughter looked. But then, she should remember what that article in the magazine said. You shouldn't compare your insides with other people's outsides. It didn't say *especially your ten-year-old daughter's*, but this was probably because it was so obvious it shouldn't need to be written down.

Helen forced herself to eat some pasta. It stuck in a ball in her throat; she swallowed it painfully. She hoped this school meeting wasn't because Isobel had got into trouble with bad friends again. Isobel was easily led, that was the problem. She just needed to be easily led by better friends.

Isobel pushed her chair away from the table and placed her plate in the dishwasher.

'I love you,' Helen said.

Isobel slowed her pace for a moment, then sped up again. She headed out of the kitchen and up the stairs.

When Nathan got home, Helen scooped up the remaining pasta and put it in front of him.

Nathan picked up his fork. 'Your dad's getting right on my tits.'

'Sorry,' Helen said automatically.

'He keeps walking past the shop with the dog.'

'I suppose it's good he's keeping active?'

'Fifteen times he walked past this morning. And I swear he was dragging that dog.'

'Surely not.'

'Its lead looked taut. Its legs dug in at a seventy-five-degree angle on the pavement.'

Helen sighed. 'It's hard for Dad. He had that shop since he was twenty.'

'He even leaned inside the shop at one point, testing whether the hinge on the door needed oiling. And I know he took the chance to look round and check the fridges were properly shut. It's like I've got my own stalker.'

'It's hard for him,' she repeated.

'It's hard for *me*.'

'I don't think he expected you to make so many changes so soon. And the shop makes so much more money these days. It's galling for him.'

'But you can't just give something to someone and then say, "no, you can't do that, I gave this to you on the basis that you wouldn't improve it."'

Helen sighed again. That was exactly what her dad would have done.

'I'll have a look at the accounts again this weekend,' she said. 'Then maybe you can have a gentle conversation with Dad about how much profit you're making. That might help.'

'I don't think that'll help at all,' Nathan said.

'No. But I'll do the accounts anyway.'

'You don't need to. I'd rather you didn't,' Nathan said.

Helen tried not to notice that she was offering free help, using her professional skills, and her husband kept declining the offer. *Her* offer.

How had this happened? That she had become the person that smoothed things over, while all the real stuff happened to other people? Hadn't it once been Helen who was meant to take over the world? Take a hammer to all those glass ceilings and stand tall and proud, surveying the shards of glass all around her?

It was her own fault, she decided. She was the one who'd lowered her status, letting herself get too swirled up in kid stuff to keep thrusting forward at work. And now she wanted to thrust again, but no one seemed to want her to thrust. They didn't respect her as a thruster, or even an ex-thruster. It was like no one could remember she'd ever thrusted at all.

And here she was, about to talk about parenting again. 'I've been asked to go into Isobel's school.'

Nathan glanced up. He looked back at his pasta, like it was fascinating. 'Kids are kids,' he said into the pasta. 'What's she done?'

'No one's told me. They're saving it as a treat for tomorrow. A surprise.'

'It'll be some kind of joke,' he said eventually. 'She'll be letting off steam.'

'Yes,' Helen said.

'Kids are kids,' he said again.

'I just think we need to be better,' Helen said. 'Do family better.'

'Actually, Hel. On that note.' Nathan glanced up from his meal. 'You know your mum and dad's party next week? Do you mind taking the kids on your own? I have no time in my diary to catch up on admin.'

'You want to avoid my dad.'

'Well, wouldn't you? That big judging face looming over me the whole time.'

'You know it's the big, *last* party? You know how much it means to Mum to have the whole family there?'

'I'll try to come along later. I just really need some time to focus on work stuff.'

'But you've got a role. Mum's given you the role of Private Secretary. Have you looked at your envelope yet? You have to get an outfit. There're clues to learn. You *have* to come.'

'I'll do it, OK? I'll be there. I just might not be on time.

Your mum will have to improvise. Honestly, Hel, I've got bigger things on my mind than your mum's party.'

And what could Helen say to that?

'I love you,' she said.

Nathan gave her a humouring smile.

After tea, Helen hurried upstairs and sat cross-legged on the floor of the bedroom. She set her phone alarm for three minutes' time and rested her hands on her knees, making circles with her thumbs and forefingers.

She closed her eyes and breathed in. *In two three* – then she breathed out – *out two three.*

Everything was good. There was nothing wrong. Clearly.

In two three, out two three.

So Helen got frustrated, with that anxious feeling bubbling up in her stomach. But everyone felt like that sometimes.

In two three, out two three.

It was fine to have these thoughts, you just needed to acknowledge them and let them float away.

In two three, out two three.

So here Helen was, just acknowledging her thoughts. They still didn't seem to be floating away, but if Helen just acknowledged them some more, they definitely would.

In two three. Out two three.

Everything was going to be fine. That's why Helen had put her *forty at forty* plan in place. *Forty at forty* was a plan she'd found in a weekend supplement, and it sounded as good a template as any. A forty-point plan for middle age, to check your life was going the right way.

In two three. Out two three.

And she was following the plan carefully. Meditation helped, apparently. That was number sixteen on the plan, after number thirteen – take a spirulina supplement, fourteen – eat more blueberries for antioxidants, and fifteen – tell the special people in your life you love them at every opportunity.

Which Helen was trying to. Yet whenever she said *I love you* to Nathan or Isobel – *Charlie*, even – they just paused and blinked at her, then carried on with what they were doing.

Helen had even texted Stella to tell her how much she appreciated her, but Stella hadn't bothered to reply. And you'd think, when Helen texted her sister so rarely, Stella would at least have said *something*.

Number eighteen on the list was *get some hobbies*, so Helen had joined a book group. Which meant she always had extra homework to do, a whole extra book to read every week, on top of everything else. But, of course – that was a good thing. Because that was *fun* homework.

Shit. Helen realised she had stopped counting.

She was breathing heavily – and not in a good, meditative way.

She sat up straighter and refreshed the circles of her thumbs and forefingers.

In two three. Out two three.

If anyone could see her, watching from outside the room, she'd be looking pretty Zen right now.

In two three. Out two three.

Helen tried not to think about the school meeting tomorrow. About how her boss would look at her when she said she had to leave at lunchtime again. But she couldn't fire Helen for that – could she?

No. Helen was a good parent, and you didn't get fired for being a good parent. But her boss would give an understanding smile, like that was all she expected of Helen. Which felt worse.

Anyway, it was just a school visit. She hoped – really hoped – Isobel hadn't done something truly awful this time.

In two three. Out two three.

This had to be more than three minutes. *Had* to.

Surely her alarm would go off soon?

The next day, Isobel's teacher leaned over the desk, fingers interlinked in earnestness. 'We're sorry to tell you this, Mrs Wheatley . . .'

'Helen.'

'. . . but we have concerns about Isobel's behaviour.'

Helen felt her smile waver. With an effort, she boosted it.

'There are a few worrying aspects.'

Helen slumped in her chair. 'OK, let's cut to the chase. What's the worst bit?'

'She put a note in the headmaster's cubbyhole. Saying she was going to blow up the school.'

Helen slumped further down the chair. Notes, again. Isobel and her notes. They said kids were all Internet-based these days, yet here was Isobel, proving everyone wrong. She understood the archaic system of teachers' cubbyholes and everything.

'And in this day and age, we can't afford to ignore things like that,' Ms Crawford said. 'Not in the current climate.'

'Of course not.'

'Imagine if we ignored it and she actually *did it*?'

'Completely agree. You have to come down hard.'

The teacher waited.

'She will be punished. Properly.' Helen crossed her arms. 'But surely kids say stuff like that all the time?'

'No. No, they don't.'

'Really?' Helen couldn't bring herself to look up. 'And was it definitely Isobel?'

'She signed the note. Surname and everything.'

Helen was going to ask more but then she thought – *why?* Helen knew it was Isobel too. Her daughter and her creepy little notes.

'Also, she's quite intense and focused,' Ms Crawford continued. 'She asked the gardener about the fertiliser you use to make bombs.'

'My daughter can't even make a cake. She can only make a sandwich if I lay all the ingredients out.'

'Mrs Wheatley—'

'And I have to unscrew the lids *and* reseal the bread packet afterwards.'

Ms Crawford frowned.

'I'm not trying to undermine her potential I'm just . . . saying. It must be the crowd she's in.'

'She doesn't have a crowd, Mrs Wheatley. She sits on her own in the playground at lunchtime. She sits *still.*'

Helen shivered.

'Things have been a bit tough. At home.' Helen despised herself. Isobel didn't know how lucky she was, to have a mother with no ego left. 'Her grandmother's very ill. Cancer.'

Helen *couldn't* move Isobel to a new school again. She'd done it before, to get Isobel away from what she'd assumed to be a previous bad crowd. And nothing had got better about Isobel's behaviour – and now they had an extra twenty minutes each way on the school commute.

Helen risked a peek at Ms Crawford.

'I'm sorry to hear that. But I'm sure you understand, we have to think about the best interests of all the children.'

'Of course.'

Helen risked looking up again. Ms Crawford's expression wasn't unkind. It was balanced. Fair. Sympathetic, even.

And that, Helen decided, was worse.

Helen got up. 'I'll do something. I'll fix it.'

Ms Crawford stood up. 'Thank you.'

They said their goodbyes and Helen left the office. She realised Ms Crawford hadn't actually asked *how* Helen was going to fix it.

Which was a good thing, Helen thought, as she hurried through the chlorine-scented corridor. Because she didn't have a clue.

Helen went to the supermarket on the way back from the school. She drove home and threw the shopping bags on the table. The evening loomed ahead of her in a fat cloud of *task*. Several hundred pages of homework to read before tomorrow.

No. Not *homework*.

But she had to read a book a week. She'd made a commitment.

And she mustn't be late to the book group this time. It was getting embarrassing.

It was just so hard to get away from work on time, when colleagues were happy to talk for hours and let meetings overrun, because they didn't have to face the wrath of the surprisingly assertive assistant at Charlie's after-school club and—

Oh no . . .

Helen picked up her car keys and ran back to the car.

Helen spun the car into the car park with a squeal of tyres. The after-school club assistant stood on the steps, holding Charlie's hand.

Helen hurried out of the car. 'I'm so sorry.'

'Mrs Wheatley,' the assistant said.

'Call me Helen.' She wondered why everyone who wanted to tell her off was so keen to use her surname to do it.

'It is six ten. This is unacceptable.'

'I completely agree,' Helen said, 'and I can't apologise enough.'

Despite her best efforts, it was ten p.m. when Helen finally got round to picking up *We Need to Talk About Kevin*.

She eventually put it down at two a.m., half-finished. A failure, of course, but she mustn't be well. She had the chills. She couldn't get warm, even under the duvet.

She switched off the light and lay there next to the slumbering Nathan, knowing she wouldn't be getting to sleep for a very long time.

The next evening, the book group sat round the stark metal island in the floaty-skirted group leader's kitchen.

'I almost couldn't read it when he finally started shooting his classmates,' a woman said. 'Awful.'

The group leader nodded wisely. 'And is his behaviour a result of nature or nurture?'

'Nature,' Helen said automatically.

The leader gave a small nod. 'It's a complex point. How do we weigh up whether he was born like that or whether he became like that due to parental neglect?'

'Born,' Helen said. 'One hundred per cent born.'

'But what did the mother do to influence him? What could she have done differently?'

Helen pulled at the thin gold chain at her throat. 'She did her best. He hated his mother from the start.'

'That's interesting, Helen.' The woman leaned forward.

'But *did* he hate her? What about the time when he was ill? And how do you explain the gift of the eyeball?'

Helen clutched at her necklace again. She'd given up the book before those parts.

Helen found herself standing up. 'So sorry. The babysitter's just texted.'

She walked quickly out of the house, picking her coat off the hook without slowing.

In the car, she checked her phone. Nothing. Stella still hadn't bothered to reply to Helen's text from the day before. Which was pretty selfish. It wasn't like Stella had all the demands on her time that Helen did. All Helen was doing was trying to *connect*.

Helen shook her head to herself. *Selfish.*

She indicated and pulled away from the curb, wondering what it could possibly be like to have a life as simple as Stella's.

It was the small things, Stella thought, sitting on the wall outside Grace's house. It was the smoke that got you, not the fire.

Stella looked at her phone again. At that text.

I just wanted to say, I really appreciate having you in my life.

Stella stared at Helen's text for a while longer.

Grace opened the front door and Stella put her phone back into her bag. She followed Grace up the stairs and the two settled into their usual seats in the therapy room.

'How's your week been?' Grace asked.

It was so predictable. 'OK.'

'How are you feeling about the family party?'

Grace looked more intense than usual, Stella thought. Watchful.

'It's just inevitable. Something to get through, like a smear test. Though' – Stella sat back in her chair – 'Mum told me her friend's son's coming, a man called Scott. That's a bit bizarre. We were in the same year at school and I slept with him a couple of times, back in the day. First guy I ever slept with. Didn't even fancy him, he was just *there*. Under the bandstand in the park with a bottle of Martini when I had a virginity to get rid of.'

'Is it a problem for you? That he's coming to the party?'

'It's just weird, isn't it?'

'Do you have feelings for him?'

'God no. It's just I hate seeing him. I feel embarrassed for my teenage self. What was she thinking of?' Stella wrinkled her nose. 'And ever since then, even though it was over twenty years ago, he's given off a weird air when I've bumped into him. He lords it about, like because he saw me naked at fifteen it means we have a special connection. He gives me the shivers.'

Grace didn't respond.

'Shouldn't I have grown out of feeling like that by now?'

'I'm just wondering,' Grace tapped her pen against the pad, 'whether this is the best use of our time today.'

She waited. Stella shrugged.

'Is there anything else you want to tell me about the party?'

'I don't think so.'

Grace stared at her.

The clock ticked.

'And how are your family?'

I really appreciate having you in my life.

Grace leaned forward. 'You seem to be thinking about something.'

Stella recrossed her legs. 'My sister texted me two days ago. She never texts me. It threw me a little.'

'What did she say?'

'She said, "I really appreciate having you in my life."'

Grace nodded.

'It's not good, is it?' Stella asked.

'In what way not good?'

'I mean, what would have to be going through your mind to send a text like that?'

'Maybe she was just thinking about you and appreciating you?'

Stella made clear eye contact. 'Absolutely not.'

'It sounds like she's trying to reach out. Have you texted back?'

'God, no. What am I meant to say to *that*?'

'Stella.' Grace put her pad down suddenly. 'How do you think these sessions are going?'

Stella blinked at this sudden change of topic. 'Fine.'

'Do you think you're getting much value from them?'

Uh-oh. Stella sat forward. 'Am I not getting value?'

'I'm asking what *you* think. Whether you feel this is helping. Whether you feel you are able to open up completely with me.'

Stella said nothing.

'And I'm wondering whether, now you and George are divorcing, that you would benefit from seeing different therapists.'

Stella jerked further forward in her chair. 'You're not about to *sack* me from counselling, are you?'

'That's not how it works.'

'You're going to sack me and keep George?'

'I didn't say that. I'm asking what *you* think.'

Stella tried to twist her chair side-to-side nonchalantly. But it wasn't a spinning chair. It undermined every attempt she made to demonstrate casualness.

'This is your money you're spending, Stella. So why are you still coming here?'

Stella stared at the uncapped fountain pen on Grace's table. She wanted to ram that pen into her own hand, just to feel something. Something other than *this*.

'I'm coming here because I'm sad.' Stella stared fiercely at the pen. 'And I want you to help me. I don't think you can, but I *want* you to make things better. Magically. By asking magic questions that fix everything.'

Grace nodded. 'Thank you.'

Stella shrugged again.

'You have at the same time both pessimistic and unrealistically optimistic expectations of this process,' Grace said.

'Yep.' Stella pulled the collars of her jacket forward. 'I do.'

'So why are you still coming here if you have no expectations I can help?'

Stella glanced up. 'Honestly?'

'Honestly.'

'I don't want George to know I caved on the grown-up counselling thing first.' Stella looked at her watch and stood up. 'See you next week.'

Grace also stood up. 'After the party.' Her voice contained a challenge.

'Yes.'

'The family party.'

The two stared at each other.

'The party you're going to,' Grace enunciated carefully, 'completely on your own.'

There was something in Grace's voice Stella couldn't decipher.

No matter. 'Yes.' Stella stared directly at her. 'I'll see you after the party.'

8

George strained to reach round the bikes propped up in the hallway, picking up the pile of post. He was just sorting through, extracting his own letters, when he recognised Stella's handwriting on one of his envelopes.

He stopped sorting.

He'd never got a letter from Stella in his life. It couldn't be the solicitor thing. Could it? Surely she wouldn't do that in writing. Especially after he was doing this favour. That would be *shitty*.

The door at the back of the house opened and George looked up. He made himself smile at the housemate who was leaving a bedroom. This housemate was the one who ate a surprising amount of meals based on potato waffles and, George had noticed, liked to quote Tarantino films.

The man nodded at him and turned to lock his bedroom door. 'All right?'

George looked at his letter and back up. 'Yeah, you?'

The man pocketed his keys and edged past George to the front door. 'Yeah, good.'

George nodded. 'Nice.'

The man left the house and George took the pile of post to his room. He edged round the sofa, sat on his bed and opened the envelope from Stella.

But it was nothing about a solicitor. Instead, he pulled out a smaller, shiny envelope with *George* on the front. This envelope was written in a different script.

He turned it over and saw the Post-it note in Stella's handwriting.

From Mum, for Saturday. Thanks again.

George took a breath and opened the inner envelope. He pulled out some sheets of leaflet-effect paper, all printed with floating deerstalker hats and magnifying glasses.

Something fluttered to the floor; he picked it up. An oval sticker on a piece of paper, showing the words *Mr Owlish. The Butler.*

With a bad feeling, George looked at the first piece of paper.

Invitation

You are invited to experience
Murder at Brockenhurst Manor!

The murder will take place at 242 Cole Street, Manchester, on Saturday 14 July from 5 p.m. till late.

Enclosed are introductory details about your character, including what to wear at the party, and his or her big secret and cues! It is essential you prepare in advance. But shhh – keep this information to yourself! At the party, the plot will thicken! DON'T TELL ANYONE!

George read the invitation again. He wondered whether Margaret thought the success of a party was proportional to how many exclamation marks had been used on the invitation.

He looked at the next page.

Introduction

Murder at Brockenhurst Manor
By Margaret Foy

He didn't have time for this rubbish. He flicked past to the next sheet.

YOUR CHARACTER SHEET
Mr Owlish, the Butler

....

You are Mr Owlish, the new Lord Brockenhurst's butler. You served under your lord in the army in India and have dedicated your life to him for a decade since. You are devoted to your employer. You expect, when he dies, to receive a significant legacy from his will.

You take your job seriously. You feel others take advantage of your master's good nature and think Agnes, the parlourmaid, in particular, takes liberties in how she addresses him.

Character age: *50*

How to play him: *Servile, proper, understated*

Character's key item of clothing (please bring with you): *A double-breasted black waistcoat*

Where was he meant to get a waistcoat by the weekend? Margaret could piss off if she thought he was buying one. Not for this ludicrous party.

George turned over the piece of paper. He didn't want to keep reading, but somehow found he was.

Character secret: You have harboured a secret love for Lady Brockenhurst for years. However, you would never act on this. It would be inappropriate, due to your respective social statuses, and also because you hold a great admiration for Lord Brockenhurst. Your burning love will stay unspoken, and unrequited.

First character cue: Between Act One and Act Two you should reveal to at least three sources that you're aware Agnes, the parlourmaid, has let the waist of her pinafore out substantially in recent weeks.

George put the paper back in the envelope and wondered what was going on in Margaret's head and why he – or anyone else – was meant to care about a parlourmaid's pinafore.

George flicked to the character list, to see the identity of the person who his character was in love with.

He found the name. He closed his eyes again.

He didn't know why he'd ever – *ever* – agreed to go to this party.

9

The morning of the party, Nathan took the kids to the park without being asked. Helen, taken aback by her free time, wasn't sure quite what to do with it. She decided to do the shop accounts for Nathan. She opened the laptop at the kitchen table and uploaded the files into her accounting software. She glanced at the screen.

Odd.

Helen did some manual calculations and blinked at the screen. She felt herself frown and pushed her chair back from the table.

She was an *accountant*. Admittedly, she was working part-time these days, and maybe she was a bit distracted by what was going on with Isobel – but she should *at least* be able to make sense of numbers? She had been helping her parents with these accounts for fifteen years. It was second nature to know what kind of figures she should be dealing with.

But not these figures. These figures were different.

A distraction might help. Helen pushed herself further back from the table and called Mum.

'Six oh five five—'

'It's Helen. How's the party planning?'

'Wonderful! Your father's up a ladder with bunting as we speak.'

'His idea?'

'Obviously not, but your father does what he's told. Goldie's waiting right beneath the ladder – staring up at him, bless her.'

Helen smiled. 'Do you need me to get there early? Anything you need me to do?'

'Everything's under control. Just get here by five, or a little earlier if you want to make the salmon parcels in advance, and make sure the kids look adorable.'

'OK, then. I'm looking forward to it.'

Helen put the phone down.

With reluctance, she pulled herself back towards the kitchen table. She re-entered her computer password and looked at the figures on the screen again.

Still too high.

She sat back in her chair.

True, Nathan had made dramatic changes to the shop. But that didn't fit with the balance sheet. Because surely it takes time for improvements to bed in? You can't just change your stock and your clientele overnight?

Yet, apparently, you could.

Now Dad had gone and it was just Mum and Nathan in the shop, it looked like the two had been buying less stock, yet the profits had rocketed.

Helen must have missed something here. Obviously.

She got up and made a cup of coffee, lingering by the kettle, stirring for longer than necessary. She sat back at the kitchen table and blew on the coffee. She looked at the screen again.

Nothing had changed.

She slumped even lower in her chair.

Of course, Helen should be delighted that Nathan's vision with the tahini and the four-pound-fifty crisps had been vindicated. The area had gentrified, Nathan had been right to spot that. And yes, Nathan had put in a coffee machine and a little seated area, so that was always going to change the sales figures a little. They were moving from a commodity-based to a service-based business. 'Going up the value chain', Nathan called it.

Yet Helen was expected to believe that, on top of the much larger profit margins on Nathan's expensive new stock, *Le Jardin* was now selling, on average – she pulled herself closer to the desk and tapped some quick numbers on her calculator – *two hundred cappuccinos* a day? When the only people she'd ever seen sitting there were the same elderly lady and her (well-behaved but definitely non-coffee-ordering) dachshund?

The front door slammed. The sound of wellies hitting the wooden floor of the hallway.

'We're back!' Nathan shouted.

Helen smiled when he entered the kitchen. 'Hi,' she said brightly.

'Charlie's lost his lion top.'

'Poor thing.'

'He's still wearing his tail though.' Nathan opened the fridge. 'What are you doing?'

Helen tapped the keyboard to minimise the screen. 'Just Internet shopping.'

Nathan took out a fruit salad and shut the fridge door. 'I'm going to visit that supplier soon. So I'll see you at your parents' party?'

'Don't forget your murder mystery costume. And please try to get there at a decent time.'

'I will.'

Helen watched him go.

She turned back to the screen and, reluctantly, maximised the window.

She looked at the figures again.

No. It can't be.

Helen tried to ignore the muscle in her cheek that was starting to twitch as, slowly, she closed her laptop.

10

Nancy pulled up in the layby and clicked the handbrake on.

George leaned over and kissed her. 'Thanks for the lift.' He was relieved she'd kept the engine running: he needed her to leave immediately. Twenty minutes before Stella was due to arrive was a dangerously surmountable buffer.

'Text me, OK?' Nancy said. 'During the party. It's a strange day for me.'

George unclipped his seat belt. It retracted with more force than he expected; the clip narrowly missed his nose on the way past. 'I know. I will.'

Nancy put her hand on his knee. 'Are you feeling OK about all this?'

George looked at the door handle and back. 'It's fine,' he said shortly.

Nancy switched off the ignition. 'I'm not sure *I'm* OK about this.'

'That's fair.' George glanced over her shoulder at the road behind. It *was* fair for Nancy to be feeling like this. But George could not be having this conversation, not right now. 'We're here now though. The show must go on.' George knew he sounded terse. He softened his voice. 'I'll call you, OK?'

He tried not to make his eyes pleading. He gave Nancy a firm *goodbye* kiss and got out of the car.

He was just about to slam the door shut.

'George?'

He tried not to wince visibly. 'Yes?'

'Don't forget your waistcoat,' Nancy said.

'Oh.' He gave a tense smile. 'Good call.'

George grabbed the waistcoat from the back seat and closed the car door. He banged his hand on the roof twice, like they did in the movies, in what he hoped was a casual gesture of dismissal.

He relaxed a little as he heard Nancy start the ignition. He relaxed a little more as she drove away. But he still didn't breathe properly until he saw the red tail lights flash up and she was around the corner and out of sight.

He moved his weight from one foot to another. He hadn't worked out a story for how he got here, if Stella asked. The idea had seemed so simple when Nancy suggested she drop him off, the night before, their bellies warm from wine.

But now – he hadn't thought through the logistics.

He heard Stella's voice in his head. *George doesn't think about logistics, now there's a surprise.* Stella had said that kind of thing for years. The actual words hadn't changed, just the level of humour and tolerance behind them.

And now here was Stella, berating him in his own head. *That* was an unwelcome change of boundaries.

It wasn't like that with Nancy. Not yet. It was so much easier, having a new partner you hadn't disappointed a thousand times before. One that didn't know what faults to specifically tick off on the mental bingo sheet.

George looked at the waistcoat in his hand. It was a moment of genius when he remembered one of his housemates had an occasional evening job as a restaurant pianist.

Only Margaret would design a party that came with both homework *and* a uniform.

There was a beep of a horn and Stella pulled up into the layby next to him.

George steeled himself. He opened the passenger door and plumped into the seat. 'Hi.' He leaned over and kissed her cheek before he could overthink it.

'Thanks for this,' Stella said. 'Again.'

Stella indicated and pulled back into traffic.

George put his seat belt on. 'Just the kind of guy I am.' The comment sounded smugger than it had in his head.

She glanced at him. 'Why didn't you want me to come to where you're living?'

George touched his pocket self-soothingly, checking his e-cig was there.

'Is where you're living *that* shit?' Stella added. 'You didn't want me feeling sorry for you?'

George coughed. 'I just thought it was for the best. To keep a healthy distance. What with today being a purely transactional arrangement.'

Stella nodded. 'Fine.' She changed gear. 'Thanks for doing this.'

'You've said that already.' George peeked at her, but she was staring straight ahead. 'You'd do it for me, right?'

'I hope so.' Stella's hands tensed on the wheel. 'You don't need me to do it for you, do you?'

'No.'

'Phew.' Stella relaxed her hands. 'Now, we need to work on a story. For what we've been doing the last few weeks.'

George turned his e-cig over in his hand. 'That's a terrible idea.'

'We'll say we went down to London to see Johnny and

Nadia, then we went to the theatre, we'll mention some wank obscure production that no one will have seen—'

'As if there's not anything more suspicious than that. Like we've *ever* been to a play.'

'Or let's say we've been for a few meals out, then. Keep it general.'

George felt himself frown. 'Do you really think that's necessary? Better to keep it simple. No story. Just be vague.'

'That's easy for you.' Stella glanced at him. 'People expect you to be vague. They expect *actual conversation* from me.'

'Just try it. No acting. No imaginary weekends with imaginary friends.'

'Have you told your mum about us yet?' Stella asked.

'I told her ages ago.' George sucked on his e-cig. 'So when are you going to tell yours?'

'At a better time.'

'How many family parties am I going to have to come to?'

'Just this one.' Stella didn't look at him. 'What did your mum say when you told her about us?'

George said nothing. He shifted in his seat.

She glanced over. 'What?'

'It wasn't what she said as much as the noises she was making.'

Stella glanced at him.

'Her voice sounded full of mucus.'

Stella tipped her head to one side. 'Huh.'

'Huh?'

'I didn't even think your mum was that bothered about me.'

'Apparently, she liked you.'

'Amazing.' Stella scratched her chin. 'I wish she'd made it clearer at the time. I might have got you to visit her more often.'

'Then I'm pleased she didn't tell you.'

Stella snorted. 'Did she bring the kids thing up? Say we wouldn't be divorcing if we'd had kids?'

'Give her some credit. My mum's not that insensitive.' It wasn't a complete lie. She didn't say it on the first call. It was only on the follow-up call that his mum said, 'You should have had children. I told you it's senseless the two of you rattling around without children. You and Stella had no focus.'

They drove in silence for a while.

'I got a text from Helen last week,' Stella said.

'What did she want?'

'She said, "I really appreciate having you in my life".'

George thought about that for a minute. 'Wow.'

Stella shifted in her seat so she could see him. 'I know, right?'

'Did you do anything to spark that off?'

'No. I have literally done *nothing* for Helen to appreciate. Ever.'

'Wow,' George said again.

'It's not good, is it?' Stella said.

'It really isn't.'

'*Thank you!*' Stella thumped the steering wheel. 'I mentioned it to Grace, and she acted like people send texts like that *all the time.*'

'How's it going with Grace?'

'Let's not . . . do that.'

George nodded. 'Are you going to ask Helen about the text? You could try to talk to her today.'

'What do I say? You know we only ever see each other at funerals now.'

'There's nothing wrong with her,' George said. 'She's just a different kind of person than you.'

'Exactly,' Stella said. 'So God knows why she's decided to start *appreciating* me all of a sudden.'

They sat in silence. Was it a comfortable silence? George wondered. How did you define a comfortable silence?

George thought about it some more and decided it wasn't *un*comfortable. Not *yet*.

It could easily change though. Best to stick to safe topics.

He twisted in his seat to face her. 'Who's coming today? Anyone I know?'

'Mum's friend Adele is bringing her son Scott, apparently.' Stella tapped her hand on the steering wheel. 'God knows why. I learned he has a five-bedroom house in Didsbury now, though the neighbours are up in arms about their planned cellar conversion, apparently.'

'Scott?' George tried to place the reference. 'Is that the one you hate?'

'Not *hate*. He's just irritating. And he owns property. That's his job.' Stella gave a deliberate shudder. 'When you ask what he does, he says *I own property*. Apparently he owns Dad's shop now. Nathan's shop, I mean. Scott's the landlord.'

'Isn't he the one you first slept with? The one with the *special twinkle*?'

Stella looked round, clearly surprised. 'I didn't think you'd remember that. Yep, the one with all the eye contact to show me he can remember me naked. Don't you think there's something a bit queasy about remembering a fifteen-year-old girl naked?'

'I'm not sure how the etiquette works,' George said. 'And I never saw any fifteen-year-old girls naked.' Which felt like a failure at the time, George thought, but which should surely be a badge of honour now?

Stella changed gear. 'So what character are you playing in this mystery thing?'

'The butler. I'm devoted to your father, apparently. And in love with your mother, so there's nothing weird there at all. You?'

'I'm Agnes, the ruddy-cheeked parlourmaid. I was rescued from poverty in my teens by the Brockenhursts.' Stella's voice was matter-of-fact. 'They found me in the gutter, trying to swap my baby for food or something.'

'Brilliant.' George thought of something. 'I know something about you. A clue. Something about your pinafore.'

'Really? What?'

'Can't remember.'

'Never mind pinafores, I have to wear an apron for this party. If Mum thinks I'm going to curtsey to her and Dad, she can fuck right off.'

They drove a little further up the motorway.

Stella glanced over at George. As she twisted her neck, he noticed one of her dark hairs was caught in her thin necklace. He wondered whether to tell her, then decided not to.

Stella turned the car into her parents' street, a long, straight road of thirties semis with a row of shops on the opposite side. She parked on the drive.

George turned to look at the shop over the road. The *Under New Management* banner was still there, even though it had been several months since the handover, and where it had once said *Cole Street Grocers* there was a new rustic teal sign with swirly vine-like letters in red.

Inside, the shop was dark.

George turned to Stella. '*Le Jardin*? Really?'

Stella switched off the engine. 'Nathan's being pretentious.'

George studied the oversized display of fancy crisps in the window. 'What does your dad think?'

'I haven't asked. But I can guess.'

'Me too.' George stared through the windscreen. 'How long can we sit out here for, do you think?'

'Not much longer,' Stella indicated. 'Mum is looking right at us through the window.'

II

George had never expected to visit this house again. Even in the good times, it wasn't always fun. Stella had grown up here, in this, her family home, which always made it weird. And the problem with family homes was – well – *family*.

But it hadn't all been bad.

A decade before, Stella had driven this journey in a rented van, and it felt like they hadn't stopped laughing the whole way.

*

Halfway up the M6, George had twisted in the van's passenger seat so he could look at Stella. 'I've got a bad feeling about this whole enterprise.'

Stella concentrated on the motorway. 'You have bad feelings about getting up in the morning. It's your *thing*.'

'Your parents' furniture is going to be shit, right?'

Stella smiled. 'I suspect so.'

George closed his eyes. 'I mean, *really* shit, if *they're* throwing it out.'

'But we need something to sit on for a relaxed vibe when watching TV. And I want to be able to have friends over. You can't have friends over with no chairs.'

'I'm not sure we'd *want* friends over. I'm still imagining

the quality of this furniture if your parents have rejected it.' George shook his head. 'Your mum makes her own soap. Out of little leftover pieces of soap.'

Stella rolled her shoulders back, still keeping her hands on the wheel.

George felt a pang of guilt. 'Is it harder driving a van than a car?'

'My ankles are tired. The pedals are heavier.' She glanced at him. 'It would be so nice to share the driving sometime.'

'Is that because you have *delicate lady ankles*?'

'No, it's because I don't know what the fuck I'm doing with this van. Are you going to get your licence soon?'

George shrugged. 'There'll be self-driving cars soon. And it's better for the environment this way.'

'George Mandani. A man who never gets around to putting cans in a recycling bin, but he cares about the environment.'

'I'm a complex man.'

'You're going to have to recycle when we move in. We'll have the right bins, there'll be no excuse.' Stella glanced at him again. 'And you know I said I want this flat to have a relaxed vibe?'

She waited for an acknowledgement before continuing.

This, George knew, was bad news. Still, wordlessly, he turned to face her.

'Cupboard doors,' Stella said firmly.

'Cupboard doors?'

'I want you to shut all drawers and cupboard doors after using them. Every time.'

'What an oddly specific thing to say.'

'I've seen you.' Stella waved an arm. 'Roaming around, opening cupboards, not shutting them.' She gave a firm nod. 'I deserve to live in a home with closed cupboard doors.

86

Don't smile and ignore me, *I can see you.*' She shifted position so she could look at him. 'George. Seriously. It'll get right on my tits and, I promise, you'll have an easier life if you just shut drawers. It's not even hard. You just . . . open the drawer. Get something out.' Stella went through the motions with imaginary drawers with one hand. 'Shut it again.'

She opened and closed imaginary drawers for a little longer before rounding up her demonstration with way too much eye contact.

George slumped further down in his seat. 'What if I want to put something *in* a cupboard? How would I do that? Can you show me?'

Stella shoved his arm. 'Annoying.' She turned back to the road. 'Woah, this van scares me. How much do you think it weighs?'

Enough to crush those teenagers on that upcoming zebra crossing, so please be careful. Of course, George couldn't say it. If you couldn't drive, apparently you couldn't criticise the driving of others. It had been made clear to him before, that was one of life's rules.

'So. What do I need to know about my living habits?' Stella turned off the motorway. 'What annoys you about me?'

George blinked at her. This felt like a particularly unwise question to respond to.

'We're a team, right?' Stella glanced at him. 'And I want you to be able to relax at home too.'

'How kind.'

'So tell me what you want me to do differently.'

George watched a low-slung car overtake them on the dual carriageway. 'You're *asking* me to criticise you?'

'Yes. Constructively.'

'If you insist.' George sat forward in eagerness. 'You never lock the windows when you go out.' He held his hand up. 'I know we *probably* won't get burgled, but that's not the point.'

'Surely that's *exactly* the point. And we're on the second floor.'

'But what if there was a particularly catlike burglar who came in for all of our stuff? And we lost everything because you just couldn't be arsed locking the windows?'

'Fair enough,' Stella said. 'I'll lock the windows, you shut the cupboard doors.'

'And unplug your hairdryer when you've finished.'

Stella turned down a little high street. 'It must be awful being you. Everything a potential disaster. And I wish you wouldn't switch off the kettle and toaster at the mains, it keeps catching me out.'

'I just find it odd you seem to care more about cupboard doors than you do about electrical fires.'

Stella slowed the car and indicated to turn into her parents' driveway.

'Look!' She pointed at the man in the brown apron, who had flung open the door of Cole Street Grocers and was now sprinting over the road. He indicated where he wanted them to park on his drive with the seriousness of a surgeon. 'How has he got there so quickly?'

'He appears like magic.' George stared at Tommy. 'A magic, helpy man.'

'Can you unwind the window and tell him to go away?' Stella frowned. 'I know what I'm doing.'

George looked back at Tommy. 'I'm surprised he doesn't have special yellow sticks. You know, the ones they have on airport runways.' George gestured in the air with both hands with imaginary sticks. 'He's going to say something about it being a shame you always have to drive. I know it.'

Stella switched the engine off. 'You confuse him.'

'It's mutual.' George opened the van door. 'Come on then. Let's check out our hideous new furniture.'

George and Stella stood in Tommy's garage, looking at the sofa and the two spongey armchairs, all in the same vibrant blue and yellow fabric that looked like it came with the electric shocks sewn in.

George eyed a chair. 'They're ... retro.'

'They were my mother's. She bought them in the nineties,' Tommy added, unnecessarily. 'They were very fashionable then, though the cushions have lost a bit of plumpness. They'll still do the job.'

'Where on earth have you been storing them all this time that you can just produce them like this?' George turned to Stella. 'You're quiet.'

Stella had her arms crossed. She massaged her elbows in a gesture of self-soothing. 'I'm just picturing these in our beautiful new home.'

'Do you want the lampshade to match?' Tommy said. 'They should really stay together, as a set.'

'Definitely not,' George said.

'You'll find a spare shade useful. You might be grateful to cover up a bare bulb sometime. It's somewhere back here, hang on.' Tommy bent over at the waist and started shifting boxes on the floor.

'Have you given them the ironing board, Tommy?' Margaret's voice travelled through from the kitchen. 'And Nana's old set of pans?'

Tommy turned back to face Stella and George. 'There's also an ironing board.'

'And Nana's old set of pans.' George added.

Tommy got an elderly ironing board out from behind the chairs and stood it vertically, at person-height. George looked at the board. It was covered in brown water stains.

Tommy must have seen the dubious look on his face. 'Nothing comes off on your clothes. It still works perfectly well.'

To George's surprise, Stella took the ironing board and placed it next to the door. 'Great. Shall we go and play with the puppy again now?'

They sat drinking tea in the lounge. The puppy jumped up and sat next to Stella on the sofa.

'Stella.' Margaret frowned. 'Can you move Goldie?'

Stella looked at the dog. She still had fluffy puppy fur but was nearly at full size, almost grown into her paws now. 'I thought she was allowed on the sofa?'

'Not that part. That's the wrong part.'

Stella raised her eyebrows.

'We've taught Goldie she has to sit,' Margaret indicated a section, 'on *this* part of the sofa.'

Stella looked down at the dog dubiously. She looked back up at Margaret.

Margaret clucked her teeth. 'Those are the rules. She's too close to Helen's wedding cushion and I don't want her tempted to ruin the cross-stitch.'

George looked at the cushion. *Nathan and Helen* had been sewn on it, inside a heart with a previous year's date.

Stella lifted Goldie up and placed her back down where Mum had indicated. Goldie bounced over Stella in one furry leap and settled back happily against the *Nathan and Helen* cushion.

Stella stroked Goldie. 'She loves it. What can I say? Maybe move the cushion to the other bit of the sofa?'

'Don't encourage her.'

'How am I encouraging her, exactly?'

Margaret shook her head.

All this time, George was looking at Stella, thinking *I can't believe we've agreed to take that ironing board.*

It was only later, in the van driving back to Birmingham, that George realised why Stella hadn't complained.

Stella turned off onto a side road. 'We've just got a little stop to do.'

George read the upcoming sign: *Tip – 100 metres.*

He looked back at Stella.

'For the lampshade and the ironing board.' Stella saw George's face and laughed. 'It's a win-win. Mum and Dad get to think they've gone to a good home. We get to never look at them again.'

'I thought you believed in recycling?'

'I do, but not *these*. Anyway, they still might be recycled. Someone in need might take them. A homeless person.'

'A homeless person who needs a lampshade and an ironing board.'

'Maybe they could sell them. Either way,' Stella parked in a (fortunately wide) space, 'there's no way I'd have those *things* in our new home.'

'Good. And it's official.' George nodded to himself. 'First thing we do when we've saved some cash, we're going to get some new sofas.'

Stella smiled. She strained to reach over the van's central armrest and gave him a soft, lingering kiss.

Eventually, she pulled away. 'We're going to be so happy in that flat.'

Murder at Brockenhurst Manor By Margaret Foy

One cold winter evening, the family gather at the manor to hear the solicitor read the will of the late, elderly Lord Alfred Brockenhurst, who has recently died in a hunting accident.

But – peril!

Before the solicitor can read the will, a freak storm knocks out all of the phone lines, and the family and staff are trapped in the manor for the night.

The rain is torrential, there's no way to communicate with the outside world, and no one is to leave.

And when the clock strikes eight, a killer will be on the loose . . .

12

They didn't even have a chance to ring the doorbell before the door flew open.

'Hello you two!' Mum kissed Stella, then George. 'Before you go in, get your murder mystery outfits on. I'll just go and find my bowl.'

Mum rushed away; something on her head flashed.

Stella turned to George. 'Bowl?'

'Never mind that, is your mum wearing a *tiara*?'

'It's Lady Brockenhurst's!' Mum's voice travelled from the kitchen. 'Look at the flipchart.'

Stella turned to look at the incongruous flipchart that stood next to the staircase. The frame had *Happy Anniversary* balloons attached, the balloons bobbing slightly in the wake of Mum's exit.

The flipchart itself showed a table of information in Mum's handwriting, headed *Dramatis Personae*.

Stella looked at the top two lines of the table.

CHARACTER	PLAYED BY	DESCRIPTION
Lady Brockenhurst, 43	Margaret Foy	Sweet of nature. Retains an allure, a semblance of the society beauty she once was. Bravely bears the tragedy of her life, that she has been unable to produce an heir.

Stella turned back to look at George, who was buttoning his butler's waistcoat with obvious reluctance. Feeling a similar emotion, she tied her scratchy white apron over her favourite velvet trousers and pressed her name sticker on the chest pocket of her shirt.

Stella and George glanced at each other's stickers. Wordlessly, they looked back at the flipchart.

Mr Owlish, Butler, 50	George Mandani	Servile, proper, understated. Devoted to Lord Brockenhurst after they served in the army together in India. Mr Owlish is patient, and manages difficult staff with aplomb.
Agnes Fairbottom, Parlourmaid, 39	Stella Foy	Rescued from poverty, aged fifteen, by the Brockenhursts. Rumours abound that she steals, but her master and mistress believe her unfairly maligned and pure of heart. She is always humble and grateful.

'Fantastic.' Stella said. 'So I steal, as well.'

'It says you're *suspected* of stealing.' George said. 'You might be innocent.'

'Mud sticks though. Poor Agnes.'

'WHAT?' George frowned at the flipchart. 'Most of the guests don't even characters! They're just generic below-stairs detectives.'

'The lucky bastards.'

'I bet they aren't expected to bang on about the size of

parlourmaids' pinafores, or whatever the hell it is I'm meant to care about.'

'I'm starting to feel quite sorry for poor maligned Agnes.' Stella tapped a front tooth. 'And do you think Mum's sending a message with the "humble and grateful" dig?'

Mum returned with the washing-up bowl. She held it out in wordless anticipation.

The bowl's jaunty, handwritten sign said *Phone amnesty.* Inside, mobile phones rested amidst swirls of bubble wrap, labelled with handwritten Post-it notes. *Audrey from number 9. Mark P. Annabelle Ferguson (Ms).*

'You'll get the phones back at the end of the night.' Mum sounded proud of herself.

'That's a little passive-aggressive, don't you think?' Stella realised her tone was far from 'humble and grateful'. She wondered how much – and on how many different levels – today was going to mess with her head.

Mum waved a hand. 'I really just want a nice party without all you young people staring at your phones.'

'I'm thirty-six, Margaret.' George took the pen and Post-it notes and scribbled his name. 'Just saying.' He ripped off the Post-it and handed the pen and pad to Stella.

'And screens scratch, Mum.' But Stella wrote her name on the pad anyway. 'As I'm pretty sure someone will be pointing out to you at the end of the night.'

'I put some bubble wrap in there as a precaution.'

George put his phone in the bowl and took a step back. He whistled dramatically at Mum.

She stopped straightening the bubble wrap. She looked up. 'What?'

'You look really hot today, Margaret,' George said. 'And that's a lovely tiara.'

Mum narrowed her eyes.

'Mr Owlish wants to get it on with Lady Brockenhurst, remember?'

'George! Shhh!' Mum glanced towards the lounge door and back. 'Not in front of Stella. Besides, you haven't read your instructions properly, it's a secret, respectful love. Feudal. Nothing seedy.'

'Sounds seedy to me,' Stella said. 'Besides, George told me in the car.'

'Stop it, you two! Play properly.' Mum folded her arms. 'Now. After you've said hello to people, you'll have to coax your father down.'

'Down?' Stella repeated.

'He's . . . sitting upstairs.'

Stella frowned.

'With Goldie.' Mum smiled her brightest smile. 'Have you noticed she doesn't bark when people arrive at the house anymore? She just lifts her head and listens, then lays her head down again at your father's feet. Sad, really.'

'Mum? Why's Dad upstairs?'

'He's fine. He's absolutely fine.' Mum lowered her voice. 'But look after your father today.'

Stella shook her head. 'What does that even mean? Is he OK?'

Mum refreshed her smile. 'He's just – a tiny bit – not himself.'

'Mum?' That was alarming. *Not himself* meant *more himself, and not in a good way*. Stella stood up straighter. 'What's wrong with Dad?'

'Absolutely nothing. What a silly thing to say.' Mum looked past Stella. 'I need to go and check on the cold canapés.' She whisked out of the hallway on her kitten heels.

'Check on the cold canapés?' George said.

'Leave her alone,' Stella said forcefully, because she was also thinking, *Cold canapés?*

Mum returned from the kitchen. 'The canapés are fine.'

'That's a relief,' George said.

Stella touched him on the arm. 'I'm going to the toilet. Mingle.'

Two minutes later, Stella entered the lounge to join the hub of the party.

The room managed to look both emptier and fuller than usual. Around twenty people stood in groups, sipping Prosecco. Anniversary cards and flowers decorated the mantelpiece, and the furniture had been pushed back against the walls, leaving imprints in the carpet. Emergency chairs, Stella suspected borrowed from the neighbours, had been arranged round the room in a circle. Through the patio doors, Stella could see children sitting on the grass at the back.

Stella took a breath. She walked over to where Mum was standing with Adele, mother of Scott of the Five Bedrooms. George stood on the edge of their conversation, scraping one foot against the floor in an equine manner.

Stella glanced at a second flipchart frame in the corner of the lounge, identical to the one in the hallway.

Miss Cartwright, Housekeeper, 33	Adele Prentice	A recent addition to the manor. Efficient at running the household, despite rumours she has a rum past and previously trained as an exotic dancer. Sadly, she remains unmarried.

97

Stella wondered how long it had taken her mother to prepare for this party.

'It feels like only last week we paid for *last* term's Zumba.' Adele put a hand on the hip of her floor-length, housekeeper's black dress. She looked up. 'Hi, Stella! I've just met your lovely husband.'

Stella and Adele kissed hello and Adele turned back to Mum.

'They think we're *made* of money. And it's not like the church hall is even *nice*. There's draughts everywhere, and it's filthy with dust.' She looked around. 'Is Pete not here yet? I'd like to see that new fancy haircut you were telling us about.'

'He's on his way,' Mum said. 'It's a long way from London for Pete, and he's so busy. He does a lot of work with charities these days, there are so many demands on his time.'

Stella deliberately didn't let her expression change.

Adele nodded. 'But, of course, he'll be here soon. Men like Pete are so devoted to their mothers.'

Mum gave a weak smile.

George made eye contact with Stella. The two stepped slightly away.

'Your mum's paid for Zumba membership for next month, despite the chemo starting on Monday,' George said quietly.

Stella looked up to see if Mum could hear, but she and Adele were still safely talking about Pete's (definitely mythical) charity work.

'What's happened to her?' George muttered. 'Four hundred pounds on caterers and now paying for a Zumba class she won't be going to?'

'Stella?'

Stella stepped back towards Mum.

Mum was frowning. 'Helen's not here yet either. She was meant to get here early to do her salmon parcels.'

'And I'm sure she'll be here any moment.' Stella waved to a neighbour across the room. 'If not, the world will cope without her salmon parcels.'

'But I've told everyone about Helen's parcels.' Mum twisted her wedding ring round her finger. 'The salmon's thawing on the counter as we speak. There's no room to store it in the fridge.'

'It's not the end of the world if you have to throw away a bit of salmon.'

Mum looked aghast.

'She'll turn up,' Stella softened her voice. 'A good thing about Helen' – she stopped herself saying *the* good thing – 'is she's reliable.'

13

Helen stared at the wall, horizontal and motionless. She had her duvet tightly tucked round her neck.

This was . . . new.

Helen should have left for the party by now. Of course she should. She should have got her dress out of the wardrobe and laid it on the bed. She should have shaved her legs and moisturised carefully, letting her skin air before putting her tights on. She should have washed her hair and blow-dried it, should have pinned it up in her special clip, with soft pieces falling casually round her face in special tendrils.

She should *definitely* have checked the kids were Instagram-respectable. She should have fed them slow-release carbs. She should have packed a bag of raisins and rice cakes and ushered the kids into the car.

Of course she should. She should have done all those things.

Yet here she was, still on the bed, lying down.

Charlie came up to the bedroom holding his tablet in a trailing hand. 'I'm bored.'

Helen wanted to say something. But she found she couldn't move.

'Are you asleep?'

Charlie stood in the doorway a while longer. When she didn't respond, Helen heard the scampering of footsteps back down the stairs.

Helen remained there, unmoving.

But was *Helen* definitely here? she wondered. Or was *Helen* somewhere else, some*one* else, floating in the ether? A real Helen just imagining this fake Helen, here on this bed?

No. No, Helen was definitely here.

But was she?

Yes. Yes, she was. She could touch the edge of the duvet. She could feel the warmth from the sunshine, the heat through the window, on her cheek.

Sadly, she was still Helen.

Till this morning, she'd been holding everything together. The heart fluttering, the lack of sleep, the inability to meditate. She'd taken it all in her stride.

Now, something had clicked over. And she wanted to just stay under the duvet.

No. *Wanted* implied a level of activity that was false here. Helen didn't *want* anything. She was just – opting out.

Was this giving up?

It *felt like* giving up.

Helen continued to stare at the wall.

Maybe she was finally accepting that, no matter how much you did, you never got to win at life. If you got to the end of one level, there was always another, more challenging level ahead.

Helen let her head stay where it was. She closed her eyes.

It was interesting that she was just lying here. And not lying here in a good, meditative way. Lying here in the other, bad kind of way.

Helen was late. She was ruining everything. She knew that.

Yet, here she was. Still not moving.

Interesting.

14

'Scuse me.' Margaret left Adele with Stella and George in the lounge and hurried to the hallway. 'Tommy!' she shouted up the stairs. 'Stella's here!'

Margaret noticed her flipchart balloons weren't facing forward. She turned the balloons until the *Happy Anniversary* writing was visible from the front door.

She looked back up the stairs. 'Tommy? Don't make me keep shouting up there like a fishwife!'

Still no response.

Margaret let go of the balloons and watched them revolve back to their original position. But that didn't matter, she decided.

She glanced back up the stairs. No sound, or indication of movement.

This wasn't playing the game at all. He'd *promised*. And where on earth was Helen?

Margaret put her phone bowl down and reached for the landline on the table. She looked down at the chicken-shaped handset. Stella had bought her this handset for a birthday a decade before. Margaret never threw the children's presents away, no matter how ridiculous – but every time she used the phone, she wished Stella had bought something *a little* more sophisticated, especially as it was going to have to sit on Margaret's hallway table for evermore.

Margaret put the receiver to her ear, beak-first. She dialled; Helen's phone went to voicemail.

George came into the hallway, glass of Prosecco in hand. 'Interesting that you're allowed to use your phone?'

'Landline. For essential arrangements only.' Margaret looked George up and down. 'Do you want to get your stuff in from the car?'

'Stuff?'

'Your pyjamas and washbag and such.'

George wrinkled his forehead. 'Why would I want to do that?'

'Because you're staying tonight. Of course.'

'We're not staying!' George rushed his words. His eyes widened and the wrinkles on his forehead smoothed. 'We're heading back to Birmingham when the party winds down. I have to get back for . . . a thing.'

'I've made up your bedroom though. And blown up the lilo. So . . .'

'But we can't,' George said.

'I'll speak to Stella.'

There was a shuffling sound from above.

Margaret clapped her hands together with relief. 'Tommy!'

Tommy appeared on the landing. He lumbered downstairs, Goldie at his heel.

Rumpled, Margaret thought. These days, no matter how carefully she pressed his clothes, Tommy himself looked creased.

Lord Brockenhurst, 50	Tommy Foy	The new owner of Brockenhurst manor. Charismatic, authoritative, kind yet firm. He is benevolent to his servants and conducts himself with impeccable control.

Margaret gave a bright smile. 'Where's your Lord Brockenhurst cane?'

'I've left it upstairs.'

Margaret made a shooing gesture. 'You can't be charismatic without your cane. How will you swashbuckle?'

Tommy blinked. He turned and walked back upstairs, Goldie following in a sombre and, Margaret found, strangely vexing procession.

Margaret tried not to sigh. After all, a sigh was not a party noise.

She walked back into the lounge and headed for Stella and George by the fireplace.

'It's official, Stella.' Margaret covered her disappointment with terseness. 'Your sister's not here – you're going to have to make those salmon parcels.'

'No way!' Stella raised her palms, as though fending off an attack. 'I've never made a salmon parcel in my life!'

'You have to make them.'

'I certainly do not.'

Margaret just wanted Stella to do *one little thing* to help. 'Don't be difficult. If you don't make them, I will have to.'

'Can't it just be that no one makes them?'

'I promised people salmon parcels.'

'They can't hold you to it. It's not contractual. And I promise you, Mum, no one cares.'

'Everyone said how much they were looking forward to

them. *Everyone.* Do you really want me covered in flour at my own party?'

'No.' Stella pressed her lips together. 'But it isn't a problem because no one has to make them at all.'

'Which means I will have to be in the kitchen for an hour at my own party, and how's that right? Why do you have to make everything such a fight?'

The two stared at each other.

George looked like he was going to say something, then suddenly became fascinated by the lampshade overhead.

Margaret clucked her teeth. 'Well. I'm sorry to have to ruin the surprise, but I can't leave this room. Whereas *you're* dispensable.'

Stella inched her eyebrows upwards. 'I am?'

'Agnes the parlourmaid gets killed off in Act One. I'm going to make the announcement as soon as your brother and sister get here.'

Stella just stared.

Margaret reached up to straighten her tiara. 'So please just make the parcels. For your mother. On the day of her big party.'

Stella took a breath – preparing to argue again, Margaret knew.

Then Stella just said, 'OK.'

'Thank you,' Margaret said. '*Finally.*'

'Don't blame me if the parcels are a car crash.'

'Please *try* to make them nicely. That's all I ask.'

Margaret watched Stella walk to the kitchen. That *humble and grateful* hint hadn't worked as well as intended.

But Stella was doing the parcels, that's what mattered. Everything was fine.

Margaret steeled herself, turned her smile on and walked back into the lounge.

15

George sipped his drink and glanced at Scott. 'So how's life?'

'You know, working hard. Keeping out of mischief.' Scott snorted and indicated the flipchart. 'Though maybe not, if I'm the dashing Ashley Brockenhurst! He sounds like quite the Casanova.'

The Honourable Mr Ashley Brockenhurst, 45	Scott Prentice	Lord Brockenhurst's charming and wayward younger brother. Born with an eye for the ladies, it has always been hoped he will one day settle down and marry well.

George took another sip of his drink. He tried to imagine Stella having ever desired this five-bedroom man, even when overwhelmed with teenage hormones, twenty years ago.

He just couldn't comprehend it. The man was so *un-Stella*.

'Just thinking.' Scott laughed. 'If I'm going to be a ladies' man, it's a good thing I didn't bring my wife!' He indicated his glass. 'More Prosecco, I think. Back in a min.'

George smiled politely and watched Scott walked away. He tried to work out what it was that made this man the anti-Stella. Was it the spiky-fronted, over-gelled hair? The property ownership? The fact he had *even attended* this party in the first place, and was now apparently *enjoying* it?

But then – maybe George was being harsh. He knew his own small talk wasn't up to much. For example, he knew, if the discussion came up, that he was definitely against fracking. He just wasn't sure he'd be able to say why.

'George!' The slap on his back was hard from a new stranger. 'You're the teacher, right?'

'I'm the teacher.' George tried to place this back-slapper.

'History, is it? And a little bit of geography?'

'That's right.'

'Wonderful. You're a credit to Margaret and Tommy.' The man didn't stop, and went to join another group.

George watched the man chat to someone else. He was a little unnerved by how much Stella's parents' friends told him about himself. *You grew up in Tring, didn't you? It's your mother who's Greek and your father's Iranian – that's the right way round, isn't it? I'd offer you a canapé, but you don't like asparagus, of course.*

George looked around at the smiling strangers. He wondered where Stella had gone. Was he meant to stand next to her at all times?

He tried to remember how he and Stella used to behave at parties when they'd actually liked each other.

'George!' He was approached by a tiny round woman in a long, shapeless black gown, decorated with a vicar's dog collar. 'How's school? I hear you have some very bright sixth-formers this year, so that's lovely.'

'Things are good.' The *time* these people had on their hands. 'Thank you for asking.'

He looked at the flipchart surreptitiously.

Miss Evangeline, Vicar, 50	Cheryl Aspinal	Trusted family confidant and moral authority. Whilst she generally keeps herself to herself, she has a nose for scandal and secrets. (Host's note: I know there were no lady vicars in the olden days, but I've updated it.)

Cheryl. That was the woman who ran the newsagent a few doors down from the family shop. Margaret always referred to her specifically as 'my neighbour, Cheryl' rather than 'my friend' despite the fact they'd known each other for decades.

'Cheryl,' George added, a little too late to be truly polite.

'And you and Stella – you're still just the two of you in the house.'

'Yep.'

Cheryl tipped her head forward. 'But Margaret and Tommy have already got grandchildren, so that's lovely.' She paused. 'Though your kids would be . . . can I say this? I think it's OK to say this nowadays.'

George knew, whatever was coming, it definitely wasn't going to be OK to say nowadays.

'They'd be such a gorgeous tone. They could do the catalogues.'

George took a long sip of his drink.

'It's fine to say that, isn't it? Because it's a compliment. I've been reading that it's wrong, what the PC police have been telling us all these years, saying we should pretend we don't see different colours when we clearly do. That's what's caused the rise of this awful far right, and nobody wanted that, did they? Isn't that the case, Margaret?'

Margaret walked over, her glare fixed. 'Enough, Cheryl. I will *not* have the far right at my party.'

Cheryl watched Margaret head out of the doorway. She turned back to George. 'She's so clever.' Cheryl indicated the flipchart with her hand. 'I've told her, "I'm going to solve this one, Margaret!" I'm determined. Nothing gets past me! I've read every single Poirot and I know all the tricks. I've started sleuthing already.' She tapped the photo on the wall next to her. 'I love nosing round people's houses. He looks quite majestic here, don't you think?'

George looked at the photo she was indicating. Pete was leaning against a fence, smiling. It was the same picture Pete used on Facebook and George knew that, if you zoomed out, you'd be able to see the bookies' cabin and the greyhounds racing behind.

Margaret had edited out the bookies' and greyhounds for her wall, of course. Pete's life and Pete's life in Margaret's narrative were two very different things.

'Cheryl! You make a wonderful vicar.' A woman in an era-defying peppermint twinset swooped in. 'And George! How's the flat? Did the birthday rug Tommy and Margaret gave you fit in your hallway in the end?'

'It did.' George kissed the stranger; her face tasted of perfume. 'Lovely to see you!' George shook her hand excessively and let go. 'I'm just going to find my wife.'

He found Stella at the kitchen table, covered in flour. A section of fringe stuck to her forehead with sweat. The dog sat next to the table, staring at Stella.

George glanced at it. 'I thought Goldie didn't leave your dad's side?'

'She does if there's food to be had.' Stella looked down at her baking tray. 'Do you think these are all right?'

George followed her gaze. Squidgy, irregular shapes filled the tray. *Edible* was not a word that came to mind. 'You said your mum wanted a home-made party,' George said. 'So they're fine.'

'But do they look *too* home-made?'

George paused. 'Is there such a thing?'

'Of course there is, and you know it.' Stella wiped her forehead with the back of her hand. 'Mum's going to go off on one when she sees these. Where's Helen? She'd better *really appreciate having me in her life* after this one.'

George pulled a chair away from the table and sat down. 'Are you finished?'

'Can you believe this? That it's apparently fine for me to make the parcels because Agnes the Unlucky gets killed off in Act One. As if her life wasn't rubbish enough.'

Stella rolled more pastry. George looked at the baking tray in front of her. He watched a parcel unfurl slowly into a sweaty mess. Margaret was going to *shit* when she saw these.

'How many of those are you meant to make?'

Stella gave a wave of her hand. 'I keep wrapping till I run out of ingredients.'

There was the noise of movement from the floor. George watched the dog shuffle up straighter in an attempt to get Stella's attention.

Poor bastard, George thought. *Spending all day following Tommy around and then thinking these hideous parcels looked like a treat. What a life.*

Stella grabbed another pastry packet. 'So, is this hiding, I'm seeing? Are you hiding in here with me?'

'Well. Let me start by saying I've been told out there by a woman dressed as a vicar that it's good to talk about race these days.'

'Oh, God. One of them's been on Twitter again.'

'In fact, talking about race is to be encouraged. According to Cheryl who runs the newsagents.' George scratched his cheek. 'She explained to me about the Pantone range of baby colours and which ones can "do the catalogues".'

Goldie shuffled another inch higher. The dog's stretching didn't look comfortable, George decided.

'Do you want to try to make a parcel while you're skulking in here?' Stella said.

'Do *you* want me to?'

'Yes. *I* want you to.'

He watched Stella work, then grabbed some pastry. It felt slippery, yet floury. He pushed the pastry round the salmon, squeezing and wrapping.

There was something about the two of them sitting next to each other, working, that made George feel like he was doing something elicit. Because – *Nancy.*

He looked away. He couldn't risk Stella reading his expression. He didn't know why he felt guilty, but he did, and he *definitely* mustn't give her any reason to ask why. Today wasn't the day for Stella to learn about Nancy.

In fact – did Stella ever need to learn about Nancy at all?

Nancy, of course, knew about Stella. He'd fielded many questions. *Did Stella bring you a cup of tea in bed in the morning or did you do it for her? When did you and Stella stop having sex? Was Stella casual around the house, or did she put make-up on when it was just the two of you?*

The oven felt too hot, too close.

'Air,' he said. 'I need some air.'

'Lightweight. No stamina.' Stella moved some hair out of her face with a floury hand. 'Now. Where – *the fuck* – is Helen?'

16

In two three, out two three.

Could it count as meditation if you were lying down?

In two three, out two three.

'Mum!' Charlie shouted up the stairs. 'Can I have some crisps?'

Helen moved to speak. Her lips parted with a peeling sensation.

'There's an apple in the bowl!'

There, she'd spoken. That was progress.

She heard the rustling of a crisp packet downstairs.

In two three, out two three.

The kids had been playing downstairs on the tablets for hours. They were defying the half-an-hour-a-day rule that Helen had set but didn't enforce because – as Isobel had pointed out – Helen used her phone *way* more than that. Helen held the view, from her own childhood, that parenting should respond to rational challenges. But was she doing it right?

No. No, of course she wasn't.

Helen's phone vibrated. She listened. Buzz then pause, buzz then pause.

The buzzing stopped. One final vibration indicated she'd been left a voicemail.

Shit!

Helen forced herself up to a sitting position. She swung her feet from the bed to the floor. She pushed her hair out of her eyes.

She didn't need to look at the phone to know it was Mum calling.

What was Helen *playing at?* She was meant to be at the party *right this minute.*

She shouted downstairs. 'Kids! Get your shoes on!'

Helen looked in the mirror. There was no time to wash her hair, let alone dry or straighten it.

How had she let this happen?

She was ruining her parents' last party, just because she selfishly couldn't find the energy to move.

Helen sprayed her hair with dry shampoo and jiggled her hands through it roughly, trying to get rid of the chalky sheen.

She pinned her hair up severely. There was no other option at this late stage.

'Isobel!' Helen shouted.

Isobel appeared in the doorway.

'This is an important party for Grandma and Grandpa. You need to set an example to Charlie and behave there.'

'Of course, Mum.'

'That means – behave properly.'

'I know what *behave* means.'

Helen looked from Isobel to her own face in the mirror. She'd looked too quickly from one to another, and she'd inadvertently done a comparison. Her own face looked old. Tired.

She would have to do her make-up at traffic lights, and

ignore Isobel's expression in the rear-view mirror. She'd have to do *something*.

She was late. Super-late.

How *could* she have been so irresponsible?

17

George headed back into the lounge. He needed to end it with Nancy, right now, to make the guilt go away. To do that, he needed his phone.

And that meant – *Margaret*.

He watched her top up a glass across the room. He walked over and deliberately made himself a little taller, like Goldie had in the kitchen. 'Have you got a min, Margaret?'

'One sec. George, mingle while I fill up Cheryl.'

Cheryl adjusted her dog collar and took an olive from Margaret's tray. 'I'm sure Helen will be here soon. And Pete.'

'They wouldn't miss it. Another?' Margaret offered Cheryl the tray. 'Nathan gets the olives flown in from Italy now.'

Cheryl took another olive. 'Are we still on for jazz dance rehearsal next week?'

'I'll pick you up at the usual time,' Margaret said. 'Don't be late again.'

'Next week?' George frowned. 'Margaret, surely you can't do jazz . . .' He tailed off.

Margaret turned to him, her gaze dark.

'Don't you have' – he coughed – 'something on?' *Chemotherapy starting on Monday?*

Margaret held his gaze. 'Another olive, George?'

'No olives, but I do need my phone for just a minute.' George smiled. 'Thanks.'

'Sadly, I can't give you the phone.'

'"Can't" is a strange word to use in this situation, Margaret.'

'The whole point of the bowl is that the phones stay there.'

'OK. The thing is, I need to make a work call.'

Margaret looked sceptical. '*You* do?'

'Yes. *I* do.' That was the problem with being a teacher. People felt that they knew what you did and when you did it. 'Some children are on an outward-bound course. I need to check the coach driver has picked them up on time.' George found irritation a good imagination stimulant. 'Be responsible, Margaret.'

Wordlessly, Margaret left the room and came back with his phone.

'Thanks.'

George headed outside. He paced across the lawn, phone in hand. He reached some small children chattering in a circle; he took a drag of his e-cig and paced the other way.

An e-cig was golden today. A 'get out of conversation free' card. Yet, now, he'd be using his 'get out of conversation free' card to end things with Nancy.

He knew he had to, for his own self-respect. He couldn't be at this party lying to everyone, knowing he had a girlfriend. He'd have to avoid mirrors all day.

But it had been a long time since George had ended a relationship with a woman. And back then, it would have been at university, and the *woman* would have actually been a *girl*. And the *relationship* would have been *a few hours back at his shared house after a student club night*.

George paced under the tree in the opposite direction.

He looked down and spotted one of his shoelaces was undone; he pounced on it gratefully.

The vicar – Cheryl – came outside and closed the patio doors behind her.

George waved her over with excessive enthusiasm.

Cheryl walked over with bouncy steps. 'Who were you about to phone? Someone secret? A lover?'

George froze.

'A thief? A murdering accomplice?' Cheryl indicated the sticker on George's chest. 'Because you know what they say – the butler did it!'

George made himself relax. 'I don't think they had mobile phones in the olden days, Cheryl.'

'Good point.' Cheryl took an e-cig out of her handbag. 'Still, I'll be *watching you* very closely today, Mr Butler!'

George felt prickles up his neck.

He forced himself to smile. 'If I did it, no one's told me. And no one's been murdered yet.'

'Ah, but are you so sure about that?' She took a drag of her e-cig; the air she exhaled smelled like pear drops. 'Margaret will have a few tricks up her sleeve. And what about the old Lord – Alfred Brockenhurst? He died in a *hunting accident?* That's *convenient.*'

George eyed Cheryl's gown and dog collar. 'That's some impressive kit. Did you buy it just for the party?'

Cheryl looked down at her outfit and back. 'I hired it. My instruction card said just to wear a dog collar, but I thought, might as well make an effort!'

The two stood and smoked.

'Aren't the roses beautiful?' Cheryl gestured with an arm. 'Margaret's done great work with the grass too. But then, she's always been a dab hand with a lawn.'

George nodded.

'I hope Helen and Pete are here now. I'm itching to get the first clue.' Cheryl put her e-cig back in her bag. 'Magnificent roses.'

'Yes.'

George watched her go.

He turned to stare at the roses. They had stalks, petals. Maybe thorns. Everything as it should be.

He looked at his phone again. And decided maybe the roses would look better close up.

He headed over to the flower bed.

Yep. He poked a rose to check. *Thorns.*

Margaret stuck her head out of the kitchen window. She made a phone gesture with her hand.

George shook his head. 'Still waiting for a call back.'

She made a disappointed purse of the mouth and reversed back through the window.

George took another drag from his e-cig. He looked at the lawn. It was small, with a surface area the size of the lounge. But it had back-and-forth tracks and this, George knew, was the sign of a good lawn.

He slammed his hands down on top of the bench. *Come on, George!*

What was it they said about those people who had twenty-year affairs? That they managed to convince themselves they had two separate lives and compartmentalised things till they felt no kind of dissonance at all? Why couldn't *George* be more like one of those people?

The stupid thing was, he wasn't even having an affair. He was having a *legitimate* relationship with a *legitimate* woman after *legitimately* separating from his wife.

Just because it was too soon didn't mean he was in the

wrong. Just because it *felt* wrong didn't mean it *was* wrong. Just because he was tied up in this stupid day of lies, it didn't mean he was an *actual* liar.

The injustice of this situation was heinous.

Buoyed with outrage, George made himself dial the number.

The voicemail message started up. *Hi, you're through to Nancy Turner, I'm not around, so leave a message.*

He switched his phone off.

Nancy would call him back. Of course she would. Because Nancy was thoughtful. Reliable. Keen.

George put his phone in his pocket and headed back into the party, wondering how much more self-loathing he could take.

18

George, Margaret decided as she watched him walk back in through the patio doors, was being incredibly obtuse.

First, she'd given a casual wave of her arm. 'Can I have the phone back?'

George had just smiled and skaken his head.

Five minutes later: 'Shall I go and get my bowl? Then we can all relax.'

He raised his finger. *One minute.*

And now, with narrowed eyes – 'You really must have finished with your phone by now, George.'

'Just waiting for a call back, Margaret.' He'd slipped the phone in his trouser pocket, like that wasn't ignoring the party rules.

Inconveniently, Margaret had a flashback to her own mother's eightieth, where she had said, 'I know it's an inside party, but there's no way I'm not sitting in the garden on a sunny day like this!'

Margaret sighed. That party was right before her father died. Mother spent most of the time fussing about the food. Margaret remembered saying to Tommy at the time, there was *little joy in this room.* Margaret and her brother, they'd gone out of duty, not because they'd wanted to, but because they didn't want to let their mother down, and—

Margaret looked around the room. At her excessive number of canapés. At all the neighbours, moving politely around her lounge.

She felt suddenly cold. In a room full of people, yet completely alone.

She started trembling. She put one hand on top of the other to steady them.

Quickly, she picked up her cold canapé tray. 'More snacks, anyone?'

She smiled and smiled, and gave herself a firm nod. She kept hold of the tray and the trembling lessened.

Margaret concentrated hard on smiling at Cheryl, who was reaching for another handful of crisps.

'They're Manchego flavour,' Margaret said. 'Made by the Gourmet Snack Company, with no colours or preservatives.'

Margaret heard a familiar sniff of disapproval behind her.

'Tommy!' She looked at his empty hands. 'Where's your cane?'

'Those are *the* crisps?' Tommy eyed the bowl. 'The shop-window crisps? The ones Nathan says are the saviour of the business?' Tommy reached for a crisp and sniffed it. 'If they're *that* good, why don't we sell them at the supermarket?'

'They're not for supermarket people,' Margaret said.

'Do they come in cellophane or paper?'

'Paper.'

'Paper!' Tommy placed the crisp in his mouth. 'And how much do these cost?'

Cheryl wandered over to take another handful. Her vicar's gown rustled as she walked.

'They're four pound fifty a packet,' Margaret said pointedly in Cheryl's direction.

Tommy shook his head with what looked like sorrow.

'All this you know about food, and yet you've never cooked in your life!'

Yes, she should have stopped herself. But sometimes, at the moment, she found Tommy quite trying.

He widened his eyes at her. He strode out of the room and through the patio doors. He crossed the lawn to the shed with determination. Even without his cane he looked more like the decisive Lord Brockenhurst than he had all day.

'But *have* you, Margaret?'

Margaret blinked herself back into the room. 'Sorry, Cheryl?'

'I said, have you paid up for that retreat yet?' Cheryl took another handful of crisps. 'I wanted to check you were definitely going before I sign up.'

'I'm definitely going,' Margaret said. 'I paid last week.'

'Retreat?' George asked.

'We're going away with the choir next month to the Lake District,' Cheryl said. 'We're going to concentrate on our close harmonies.'

George turned to face Margaret. There was an unusual alertness in his eyes. Like he was *actually listening* to the logistics of their choir trip.

'Another olive, George?' Margaret glanced at Cheryl. 'Looks like we're running out of crisps.'

George shook his head.

'Ooh, I'll test another olive.' Cheryl took a handful. 'Are you having a good time?'

Margaret looked around the room. 'Of course.' The tray shook in her hand; she rested a corner of it on the edge of the sideboard.

Yes, she was *definitely* having a good time – despite everything being off track.

She'd wanted to take the family photo at the beginning of the party, but you couldn't take a photo with half the family missing. And, yes, they were running late for revelations of Act One of the murder mystery, but she couldn't start that without Helen and Pete.

She made accidental eye contact with George. She nodded at him and he nodded back. He looked at her for longer than necessary. Also checking she was having a good time, Margaret supposed. Thoughtful. She gave him a firm smile and picked up her tray.

19

George took a sip of his drink. He nodded at the neighbours he was standing with, but he didn't listen to their conversation. As long as these people had an audience and he made the right noises, George decided, it didn't matter whether he actually listened.

He looked again at Margaret. Her jolly demeanour had faded. She was now staring across the room, looking deep in thought.

But what was she thinking about?

George had never thought he'd care that much about what was going on inside Margaret's head. But he was fascinated now – *absolutely* fascinated. He'd started adding up in his head the activities she'd committed to that were coming up over the next few weeks and months.

Zumba classes.

Jazz dance.

Choir retreat.

All paid up by the cheapest woman in the world, a woman for whom plans were granite and unyielding, for times when she was meant to be recovering from chemotherapy. A woman who was clearly still cheap, because she was right now trying to embarrass Cheryl-the-vicar – someone who was *a guest at Margaret's own party* – out of eating too many posh crisps.

Cheryl walked over to him, empty Prosecco glass in hand. 'Have you made your mysterious phone call yet? All your cunning plans in place?'

'I promise you,' George made himself smile, 'I'm not mysterious at all. Nothing to see here.'

'That's what the killer would say.'

'Yes. Well. There's not much I can do about that.'

'Vicars learn all the secrets. I have God on my side tonight.'

Cheryl made a V-shape with her fingers and pointed to her eyes. She then turned her fingers to point the V-shape at George. She laughed, and turned to chat to someone else.

His neck prickled again. He could feel his own heartbeat in his chest.

She's joking, George. She knows nothing. She's talking about the butler, not you.

He looked back at Margaret, who was tipping Prosecco into a neighbour's glass with cautious precision.

'Margaret.' He put his glass down on the mantelpiece. 'Can I borrow you a sec?'

She turned. 'Are you *finally* giving me your phone back?'

George indicated the corner of the room with a jerk of his head. Margaret put the bottle down on the ottoman and picked up her glass. They both stepped away from the others.

'Because rules are rules,' Margaret said, 'and I don't know why *some* people find them so hard to follow.'

'Why do you keep making plans with your friends?' George kept his voice low. 'Don't they know about the chemo?'

Margaret raised her glass to someone across the room. She didn't look at George. 'And you feel this is *your* business?'

'I'm just wondering why you haven't told them?'

'Why *would* I have told them? It's miserable news.'

'You're paying for things you're not going to be able to do? You're happy with that?'

'No.' She raised her voice: 'Now, do we need some more canapés on that tray?'

Margaret whisked away.

George leaned back on the arm of the sofa. He was missing something here. Maybe Margaret was exaggerating. Maybe she had pre-cancerous cells, or something, and Stella and he had misunderstood completely.

But – no. That wouldn't explain everything. There were too many inconsistencies.

But how could Margaret, the queen of the tip dive, the woman who ironed wrapping paper for reuse, bring herself to shell out for activities she'd never be able to go on?

It couldn't be that ... Margaret was only *pretending* to have cancer?

20

In the kitchen, Stella kept rolling and folding, rolling and folding. She had got a third of the way through the pile of pastry packets, so that must be a good thing.

But when she looked at her output, it didn't *feel* like a good thing.

Stella got up and moved the trays of parcels from the table to the worktop that was furthest away. All those fleshy, sweaty lumps could start messing with your head if you looked at them too long.

Stella sat down and reached for more pastry. She listened to the conversation drifting through from the lounge.

'It's not just family you've got to watch. Which of the servants are going to benefit from the will? Remember, for some of them, it will be their one shot to set themselves up with financial independence.'

'Hold your horses, ladies.' Stella was familiar with that impatient tone. *'You're not meant to be able to solve it now. There are updates to come at various points in the evening. There are three acts to go.'*

'But I've solved it already, Margaret. I know who did it.'

'Did what?' Stella smiled at the steel in Mum's voice.

'Murdered Lord Alfred Brockenhurst in the hunting accident.'

'No one murdered him. Just forget the hunting accident, for

the love of God, Cheryl! The murder hasn't happened yet!'

Another voice, closer now. 'Hello, stranger.'

Stella flinched. Scott stood over her, still wearing his leather jacket.

'Is it cold out?' she said finally.

Scott laughed. He leaned down to kiss her cheek.

'You smell of leather.' Stella took in his jacket, his jeans, his surprisingly bright shoes. 'Really heavily of leather. Are you wearing that jacket for your character?'

Scott smiled. 'No.'

Stella shifted in her chair, so his hand dropped from her arm. 'What about your shiny shoes?'

'They're my favourites. *This* is what I'm wearing for my character.' Scott reached in his pocket and pulled out a monocle. He put it to his eye, trying to wedge it there with his cheek. 'Ashley Brockenhurst is quite the ladies' man.' He wrinkled his nose up in an attempt to keep the monocle in place. Still, it fell out. 'It's hard to wear when I'm speaking.' With what looked like regret, he put the monocle back in his pocket.

'Is your wife here?'

'Ashley Brockenhurst hasn't got a wife.'

'I mean *your* actual wife, Scott. I believe she's called Anneka.'

'My wife and I aren't joined at the hip. She's at home with the kids.'

'Wow. If I was going to a party like this,' Stella picked up more pastry, 'I'd want reinforcements.'

Stella glanced at Goldie. She weakened and threw a morsel of pastry in the dog's direction.

Goldie wolfed it without chewing. She sat up even straighter, her twitching nose inching closer to the parcels. She waited.

'Sorry, Goldie,' Stella got up and opened the back door, 'I love you, but you're not helping. And I shouldn't be feeding you uncooked pastry, it's not good.'

Goldie trotted outside and Stella shut the door after her.

Stella sat back down. She deliberately didn't look at what she knew would be wide, hurt eyes looking at her through the glass of the back door.

She looked back at Scott. 'Why *are* you here, anyway?'

'Our families work together now. In a way. I bought a portfolio of property and it included your dad's shop. Sorry, Nathan's shop. I still think of it as your dad's.'

'We all think of it like that. Even Dad.' Stella scratched her chin. '*Especially* Dad.'

Stella felt Scott looking at her intently. She turned away.

What was he looking for? A long-held flame? A spark of physical attraction?

His disappearing youth, Stella decided.

Scott leaned on the unit opposite. 'Did you mind me mentioning my wife before?' He tilted his head. 'Sorry if that's tactless.'

'No need to be sorry.' How was it this man managed to wind her up so well, and so quickly?

'I didn't know whether you knew I was married.'

Stella opened her arms in a *why the fuck would I care?* gesture.

'But then I thought – *Stella's tough.*'

'I'm not sure what you think the dynamic is here' – Stella stood up so she could eyeball him – 'but I assure you it's something different than you think.'

'I don't want to make you uncomfortable. Let's just keep things light.'

'Things *are* light.'

'You're a good sport, Stella.'

'My husband's here, you know.'

Stella looked away. She really didn't want to reflect that she'd just said that.

'That's great. Good for you.' Scott started to leave the room. He turned and smiled. 'Those parcels look delicious, by the way.'

'No, they don't,' Stella said.

'I can't wait to have one later.'

'You say the strangest things.'

'I was just being nice.'

'There's no need.'

Scott smiled again and left the room.

Stella slapped another piece of pastry on the table.

Mum had *better* be enjoying this party.

21

It turned out faking cancer was a *thing*.

George shook his head. Who knew?

He stood under the tree and opened another link on his phone, wondering when precisely he'd got so out of step with his fellow humans. Had it happened gradually, over a course of years? Or was there just a click-over point one day – a key moment in history when everything had changed, and he just hadn't noticed it?

Because there were *loads* of articles about people faking cancer.

He glanced up to see Goldie trotting across the lawn. She reached the closed shed door and slumped down in a movement that looked alarmingly like a collapse. She strained to rest her head awkwardly on an unturned flowerpot and closed her eyes.

George looked back at his phone.

Why do people do it?
In a lot of cases, it's to gain sympathy. Some people like being the centre of attention. In rare cases, it's a symptom of Munchausen's syndrome. Often, it's to scam. (One of the group we studied used the community monies raised to fund a breast enlargement.)

George accidentally thought about Margaret's chest. He quickly looked back to the article.

Most of the fakers in our study had a history as scam artists. Others clearly had a secondary motive – whether it was to avoid or delay consequences, or to gain something else. Often, people claimed they had cancer to avoid other problems, like money or relationship issues.

George let his phone rest against his leg. He glanced at the handful of primary-age children across the lawn, who were starting to look restless now, kicking heels and raising voices. He knew Margaret had tried to hand out a pile of stickers saying *Junior Detective*, but none of the kids were wearing them.

He looked at his phone again. He bounced it in his hand, thinking.

None of it made sense. *None of it.*

Margaret hadn't scammed them. Except maybe out of some lattes and the odd Bakewell tart when Stella visited her at the coffee shop near the hospital, but George didn't think that counted. But what was this party about if it wasn't about getting attention?

But why, if she wanted attention, would she not be telling her friends about it?

He looked back at his phone.

To avoid other problems, like money or relationship issues.

This was another possibility. If George had to live with perma-raincloud Tommy – well, George might actually *welcome* cancer, just to get away from it all.

George took a deep breath. He looked around the garden, trying to take in the trees, the birds. He noticed two older kids were sitting on the side gate, while another girl in a Japanese cartoon T-shirt pushed it from side to side.

He frowned. Really, Margaret expected teenagers to just sit in her garden for the whole party, no phones, no entertainment? What *was* she thinking of?

George coughed to get their attention. 'I wouldn't swing on that if I were you.'

The girl who was pushing kept moving the gate. 'We won't hurt ourselves, don't worry.'

Was she mocking him?

'Maybe not, but the lady of the house will kill you.'

He turned away so he didn't have to see whether the kids had obeyed him or not. He wasn't going to get caught up in playground duty. It was his *weekend*.

He put his phone in his pocket and looked at Goldie, still slumped in front of the shed, still trying to sleep in the most uncomfortable position. Was it true dogs could detect cancer? He noticed a flash of movement through the shed window. Tommy was in there, and appeared to be looking at him.

George forced his face into a smile and lifted his hand into a wave.

After what seemed like an age, Tommy lifted his arm and waved back.

Could George just ignore the fact that he'd seen one of the party's special guests hiding in the shed? Could George go back into the party like he hadn't even seen Tommy?

No, he supposed, he probably couldn't.

22

Tommy sat in his shed, squeezing the jaws of the secateurs closed and letting them spring open.

Margaret had made it clear the study was off limits for the rest of the day, so now he was back in the shed. It was a default thing, like setting off in the car and then finding you'd arrived somewhere without knowing quite how.

Tommy squeezed his secateurs again. Through the small shed window, he watched George tapping on his phone under the oak tree.

Tommy put his secateurs down. He turned back to look at the air rifle, leaning up against the workbench.

Yes, it was a party. But Margaret was dying. Everyone was just carrying on like before, but Margaret was dying. Properly dying, not just *we're all decaying over time, aren't we?* and *I could go under a bus tomorrow,* and all the other comments his family said to reassure him that a terminal diagnosis was neither here nor there.

Even Margaret was pretending it wasn't happening. 'Cheer up, love,' Margaret had said that first evening. 'And let's not talk about it again from hereon in.' She'd given his hand a pat of *that's that.*

Tommy couldn't change what was happening to Margaret. But without Margaret, he'd have nothing. He didn't understand this world anymore, the supermarket had showed him that. He *had* to swallow his pride. He *had* to ask Nathan if he could come back to work in the shop. And if Nathan said no, then Tommy would wait for Margaret to die, then take himself off somewhere that wasn't inconvenient, an—

He looked at the air rifle again.

But he needed to think about logistics. Putting an air rifle to the head wouldn't be easy, so he'd have to set up some kind of pulley system. Even for a man of his hands-on skill, the margin for error was alarmingly wide.

And definitely worse than shooting yourself in the head would be *not quite* shooting yourself in the head.

Tommy made himself look away from the air rifle. He watched George put his phone in his pocket.

George looked up and the two made eye contact.

He waved at Tommy. Tommy waved back.

He looked again at the air rifle.

That was low of Margaret, to kick him when he was down. She *knew* he was vulnerable.

All this you know about food and yet you've never cooked in your life.

It wasn't that he *couldn't* cook, he just *didn't* cook – but only because that was her job. She did the washing up and he did the bins. She did the sewing and he refilled the car washer fluid. They both had their jobs, and those had been their jobs for *forty* years, so why was she complaining now?

And it was his job to keep Margaret happy. So he needed his phone to give Pete a kick up the backside, tell him to get here now. Tommy knew where Margaret would have put the bowl of phones – he knew all her secret places. He'd do his bit and text Pete. He knew his end of the deal, even if Margaret was trying to change the rules.

There was a knock at the shed door.

Tommy didn't move. This was *his* shed. There was only one chair in this shed – and that was a clear statement of intent.

The door opened. 'You all right in here, Tom?'

George was giving him an odd, appraising look.

Tommy grabbed his box of lenses. 'I'm just checking my camera equipment.'

Goldie trotted through the open door and sagged down flat next to Tommy's chair. Tommy reached down to ruffle her ears.

George shifted his weight from one foot to the other. 'Aren't you, erm ... meant to be at the party?'

Tommy stopped stroking Goldie. He turned back to the box and pulled out a lens. He studied it and replaced it. 'Margaret's asked me to get a photo of all the family later.'

George looked at the lenses. 'I thought phone cameras were good enough these days.'

Tommy sniffed.

George sank slowly into a cross-legged position on the floor. 'Are you having a good time?'

'Of course.'

'So I don't put my foot in it,' George said carefully, 'what do people at the party know about Margaret's cancer?'

Tommy raised his head. 'Why would you be talking about something like that at a party?'

'I'm not. I'm just wondering.'

'They won't know anything. Margaret wouldn't have said.'

'She hasn't told anyone?'

'Why would she? She won't want any fuss.'

George furrowed his brow.

'It's our business,' Tommy said. 'No one else's.'

'She's behaving oddly, Tommy.' George trailed a finger

along the shed floor. 'She's paying for things she'll be too ill to do. Retreats. Dance classes. Zumba.'

'She doesn't want to talk about it, and that's her business.'

The two sat in silence.

'And Goldie?' George rubbed the back of his neck. 'Does she react differently to Margaret since the diagnosis? Is the dog a, er, comfort to her?'

Tommy reached out to touch his tripod. He let his hand fall back. 'George, do you cook? Do you cook for Stella?'

George took a beat. 'That's random.'

'I'm just wondering.'

'I would say "yes"' – George scratched his cheek – 'but mainly pizza or baked potatoes. Cheese on toast. Nothing gourmet.'

'And do you make the pizza or buy it?'

George frowned. 'Buy it. Obviously.' He stood up and put his hands in his pockets. 'Do you want to come back to the party with me?'

'No,' Tommy replied.

'OK.'

'Shut the door behind you.'

Tommy turned back to his Nikon. His trusty F3 SLR (with 50mm Nikkor f1.8 lens). Despite what others said about the quality of phone cameras now, this was a *real* camera. His Nikon had been three years old when he bought it, and they still went for a song on the Internet over thirty years later. Not that he'd ever sell it, it was just good to know the camera held its value.

He turned the Nikon over in his hand. He'd put in a FP4+ film, in preparation for the party, but it was getting late, and they were losing light. Maybe time for the HP5+ instead?

But – no. The FP4+ was fine for general use. Later, if it got too dark, Tommy would change for the HP5+. He'd use his tripod if the exposure time got too long. He could use the fill-in flash if necessary.

Tommy nodded in satisfaction.

Nathan, of course, might know about tahini and buck-wheat, but he wouldn't know about different exposure settings. Nor would Margaret. They wouldn't understand when you needed to use a tripod.

But Tommy was going to take a perfect picture as soon as Pete and Helen and her family turned up. Margaret had said how much she wanted some nice photos from this party. And Tommy didn't mind. Margaret cooked; Tommy kept the equipment in good order and took the photos.

That was how it had always been. And that was how it should be.

23

The photo Tommy was most proud of had been taken eight years before, at Stella's wedding on that Greek Island.

He'd been feeling pretty pointless on that holiday till he took that photo. The trip hadn't gone as expected at all. He'd thought it was going to be an idyllic trip. All the family, away together, celebrating something. All that free time.

It wasn't like that. No, it wasn't.

*

Two days before the wedding, he sat with Margaret at their hotel's pool bar, his camera on the table in front of them. He took a swig from a beautifully cold – if small – glass of lager.

He put the glass down and looked at his peeling feet.

He wasn't the only one who'd caught the sun. Margaret was giving herself several extra chins as she strained to study the white strap-lines next to her reddening cleavage.

She strained further. 'Will you be able to see these lines in the dress I'm wearing on the day?'

Tommy looked away. 'No,' he lied.

Margaret nodded.

Tommy went back to staring at his feet.

He heard shrieks of laughter from the pool nearby. He

looked up. A teenager ran and bombed into the water, and Tommy felt a sprinkling of spray on his arm.

He inched his plastic chair further away, towards Margaret.

'Are you feeling any better after last night?' she asked.

Tommy shrugged.

'It was a real shock.' Margaret looked out to sea. 'But Stella doesn't mean anything by it.'

Tommy scratched one foot with the other to scrape some skin off.

'You know what she's like,' Margaret added.

'She's ashamed of me.'

'She's *not* ashamed of you. She just doesn't want you to walk her down the aisle or do a speech because she has to be different, to prove a point. Like she always has.' Margaret leaned forward. 'Look at that!'

She pointed at a tiny lizard with an electric blue tail stripe. It scampered out of a wall and across the paving stones, pausing halfway across, as if taking in the sunshine.

Tommy picked up his camera, but the lizard was too quick. It streaked across the stones to the other side of the bar and darted into a gap in another low wall.

Tommy lowered his camera.

'You'll get one,' Margaret said reassuringly. 'We just have to be patient.'

Tommy put his camera back down on the table.

'Those lizards are everywhere here. Beautiful. The Greeks are lucky to have such lovely things running around in the wild. Much less trouble than squirrels.' Margaret narrowed her eyes. 'I bet their lizards don't dig through flowerpots.' She glanced at Tommy; her eyes softened. 'Hey.' She put her hand on his leg. 'Stop thinking about it.'

He shook her off. 'Stop fussing.'

'She doesn't understand it's a snub. At least you got to be a proper Father of the Bride at Helen's wedding. And your speech there was wonderful, and you looked so elegant walking her down the aisle.' Margaret looked down at her white strap marks again. 'Besides, we've got two days to work on Stella and make her realise how selfish she's being.'

Tommy took a sip of cold beer. He looked out to sea.

'Now, on a more positive note.' Margaret blinked. 'Shall we meet Pete at the airport tomorrow in the hire car? Though' – she scratched the side of her mouth – 'before we see him, I need to tell you something.'

Tommy waited.

'Don't get angry.'

Tommy put his beer down.

'We've paid for Pete's air fare.'

Tommy sat forward. 'What?'

'He's in some financial difficulty.'

Tommy needed to do something with his hands, so he picked up his camera. He gestured with it. 'But we haven't paid for the other kids' air fares.'

'They haven't asked. And remember, Pete needs more support.' Margaret pressed her lips together. 'He's an entrepreneur like you. Helen and Stella are just fine, they're self-sufficient. But entrepreneurs need that bit more help.'

'He's only coming for a day and a half and going straight home,' Tommy waved his camera jerkily, 'and now I find out I'm paying for his fare!'

Margaret put her hand gently on his camera till Tommy lowered it to the table. 'Think on, love. He's had so many more challenges to face than the others. He's a gay man in a straight family.' She shook her head sadly. 'And it's not your fault, but however delighted we were when he came out, it must have been hard for him, growing up with such a heterosexual male role model. It was bound to have an impact on his confidence.'

Tommy scuffed one foot against the other more violently now. 'I can't have us just paying for Pete.' A few flakes of foot skin floated onto the paving stones. 'We'll have to pay for Helen at least. But then – what about Stella? We give Pete and Helen money for the wedding, and nothing for the actual bride?'

'I can see you're getting agitated.' Margaret rubbed his arm. 'But there's no point going over this again. Stella won't let us give her any money for the wedding. Even though they clearly need it, as they've still got your mum's old sofa in their lounge, and I know for a fact Stella hates it, so I don't know why she insists on being so difficult when it's a *tradition.*'

Tommy felt that deep jitteriness in his stomach. He was going to have to face all those guests in two days. 'I can barely look George's parents in the face, I'm so ashamed. What *must* they think?'

He picked up his camera again. He pretended to see something that was photo-worthy so he could look through the lens instead of at Margaret.

'Maybe we should talk to George,' she said carefully. 'Without Stella knowing. Give him money and ask him not to tell her.'

Tommy lowered the camera. 'And he could spend the money on driving lessons.'

'He *could*,' Margaret said.

'Except . . .' Tommy picked up his drink. 'What if he actually accepts?'

Margaret looked away. 'We'd find the money somehow.

Things turn up when you need them, you'll see. That's how life works.'

'George wouldn't take it though. Not without Stella knowing, those two are funny about things like that.'

Tommy finished his lager and put his glass down.

'So there's nothing for it.' Margaret shook her head sadly. 'We'll have to keep it secret from the others that we've paid for Pete's flight.'

Tommy noticed the use of *we've*, not *I've*.

'Stella can't exactly complain as she keeps refusing our money,' Margaret continued. 'And Helen's gone back to work after having Isobel, and she says Nathan's doing well at the estate agents. So she's taken care of.'

Tommy nodded.

'Everything's fine. Stella will change her mind about the Father of the Bride thing, and we'll have a great family holiday once Pete's here.'

Tommy nodded.

'Ooh look!' Margaret pointed. 'Another lizard, just there! Next to that sunlounger!'

Obediently, Tommy picked up his camera.

ACT ONE

Why Didn't They Ask Agnes?

Card to be read at 6.30 p.m. by the solicitor,
Mr Shaker (a.k.a. Pete Foy).

*A typed, unsigned love letter, dated last week, has been
found in the greenhouse. The letter-writer declares a
deep, unyielding love for Lord Brockenhurst.*

*And now I, Mr Shaker, have gathered all the
family and servants in the study to hear the contents
of the will.*

*But before I can read the will – scandal! (Open
document case to show guests it's empty.) The will has
gone missing!*

*Worse, Agnes the parlourmaid has been found
stabbed to death in the music room!*

*What did Agnes know? What secret did she hide?
Who wanted to see her dead?*

24

Margaret couldn't wait any longer, so she fetched her reading glasses from the hallway table.

'Everyone! Act One.' She clapped her hands. 'Adele – can you please go and fetch Tommy from the shed? And make sure he brings his Lord Brockenhurst cane with him.'

'Can we even do Act One without Pete?' Cheryl turned to the room. 'He was a wonderful narrator at school. He did a power of a job at the junior four Nativity.'

'The show must go on, Cheryl.' Margaret wheeled over the librarian's stool she used to clean the top of the kitchen units. 'I'll read Act One and Pete can take over for Act Two.'

Adele came back through the patio doors with George and Tommy following.

Stella entered through the kitchen door, dusting her hands off on her servant's apron. 'Works well, having an apron as a prop. Who knew?'

Margaret stepped onto the stool and held her card in front of her. 'Act One.' She used a loud version of her telephone voice. 'A typed, unsigned love letter, dated last week, has been found in the greenhouse. The letter-writer declares a deep, unyielding love for Lord Brockenhurst.' Margaret looked down at her card. 'Mr Shaker has gathered all the family and servants in the study to hear the contents of the will.'

'Such a shame Pete's not here,' Cheryl said.

'But – scandal!' Margaret lowered her voice and gestured at the crowd. 'Imagine I'm opening a document case here and showing you it's empty.' She increased her volume again. 'The will has gone missing!'

There were exclamations and inhalations of breath, sarcastic or otherwise.

Margaret decided to continue. 'Worse, Agnes, the parlourmaid, has been found stabbed to death in the music room!'

Everyone turned to look at Stella.

Margaret lifted her card higher. 'What did Agnes know? What secret did she hide? Who wanted to see her dead?'

Stella folded her arms.

Cheryl looked at Margaret expectantly.

Margaret shook her head. She stepped off her stool. 'That's it.'

'Alas, poor Agnes,' Stella said. 'Your suffering is at an end. Though your apron's still useful.' She turned to walk away. 'I'll be in the kitchen if anyone wants me.'

The familiar shudder of the front door indicated someone had entered the house. Margaret turned to look at the doorway.

Isobel and Charlie rushed into the lounge. Helen followed, shedding a bag from each shoulder.

'Finally! Come here, my lovelies!' Margaret scooped Charlie up in her arms. She glanced at Helen. 'I was getting worried you'd been in an accident!'

| Ellie Brockenhurst, 25 | Helen Wheatley | Glamorous socialite and actress, niece of Lord and Lady Brockenhurst. Adopted by them after the untimely death of her mother, she is a credit to the Brockenhurst family. |

Helen's eyes flickered round without meeting Margaret's. 'I got held up, Mum. I'm so sorry!'

'If it had been Stella I would have understood. But *you*?'

'Car trouble. I'll explain later, Mum.' Was Helen about to *cry*?

'But nothing's really wrong . . .?'

Margaret wondered why she was asking. She definitely didn't want to know.

Helen gave a performance smile to the room. 'Hi everyone. Looks like a fun party.'

'It is, but everyone's been waiting for your salmon parcels.'

Helen closed her eyes. 'I forgot about the parcels.'

'Stella's had to do them, and none of us wanted that. She's been in the kitchen for an hour and I can't smell anything cooking.'

George leaned into their conversation. 'I definitely wouldn't get your expectations too high, Margaret.'

Margaret raised her gaze to the ceiling.

'Where's Nathan?' George asked.

Helen gave George a quick hug. 'He had to visit suppliers. He'll probably be along later.'

Margaret felt a surge of disappointment. George pursed his lips.

This made her feel a little better. Margaret had never been sure whether her sons-in-law liked each other or just tolerated each other, but here was the evidence, written across George's disappointed face.

George strode out of the room.

Margaret looked at Helen more closely. Helen's skin had an oily sheen, like she hadn't washed yesterday's make-up off before applying today's. Her eyeliner was unevenly done, and she had a mascara smudge high over one eyelid. And that hair! It wasn't party-fresh! It looked chalky at the top, almost as though . . .

'Is that . . . dry shampoo?'

Helen waved at a neighbour across the room. 'I've had a difficult day.'

Margaret looked Helen up and down again. 'And where's your outfit?'

'Outfit?'

'Ellie Brockenhurst? You're meant to be wearing a fur stole?'

Helen closed her eyes. 'Oh, Mum. I forgot.'

'You'll have to fashion something out of one of the spare-room blankets.' Margaret turned to Isobel. 'Have you had a difficult day too?'

'No. I've had a good day.' Isobel looked at Helen, 'Can I have your phone.'

While clearly a question, Margaret noticed the words didn't come with a question mark. She beamed at Isobel. The child was so wonderfully assertive. *Good girl.*

'Not today.' Helen waved a hand at the patio doors. 'Go and play with those lovely kids in the garden.'

'You can make your own entertainment.' Margaret winked at Isobel. 'That's much more fun.'

Isobel turned slowly to face her mother. 'If you don't give me the phone, I'm going to make my *own entertainment.*'

Helen's laugh had a thin edge. 'I said no, darling.'

Margaret looked at her grandson, Charlie, who was racing into the garden. Those lion-tail bottoms clearly shouldn't be paired with that elephant top.

Not ideal. But Charlie and Isobel were here now, and that's what mattered.

Margaret smiled at the people around her. Her party was nearly complete now. Of her children, there was just Pete to come, but he wouldn't be long. She wouldn't phone him again – she didn't want to harass him, he must be so busy not to be here. But she'd send him a message, just to make sure.

She gave herself a firm nod. 'Helen, come with me while I get my bowl.'

25

Isobel hadn't been looking forward to this party. But it was always nice to see Grandma.

Grandma never shouted at Isobel. Grandma never told her she was spending too much time on her own or couldn't she invite some nice friends over sometime? Grandma let her have whatever treats and drinks she wanted, because, 'you're such a skinny little whippet thing. Your mother had white bread and oven chips for tea and she looks well enough on it, doesn't she? She drank Panda Pops every day, and *her* teeth haven't fallen out.'

'Exactly, Grandma,' Isobel replied, not knowing what Panda Pops were, but knowing they meant it was OK to reach for another chocolate digestive.

Isobel watched Mum and Grandma have a row about Mum's phone, which Grandma won. Obviously. Isobel couldn't help feeling a small fire of victory. *See how* you *like it when your mum tells you you're not allowed your phone.*

Isobel licked the ulcer at the side of her mouth. She tested it with her tongue.

She could just bite that ulcer off now, maybe?

It would hurt more that way, of course. But she'd probably end up doing it anyway.

There's no point fighting these things, Isobel thought. *You know how this will end.*

She prodded it again with her tongue.

Mum stepped away from them to say hello to someone, and Grandma scooped a piece of Isobel's hair off her forehead. 'Is your mother all right?'

Isobel shrugged, and Grandma didn't ask anymore.

Isobel looked at the handful of kids outside. They milled around at the bottom of the garden, sitting on the grass and leaning against the fence. One boy concentrated hard on breaking a long stick into pieces. Two small girls were on the grass making daisy chains. Another little boy was on his hands and knees, his face all screwed up, making animal noises.

Grandma stood by Isobel's side. 'Those girls must have brought those daisies with them. They definitely won't have found any on my lawn.'

'Can't you grow daisies?' Isobel asked.

'I *could* grow daisies,' Grandma said, 'but I don't. Are you going to play with the other little ones?'

Isobel took a breath. She didn't want to let Grandma down, so she walked away. She was nearly out of the patio doors when she heard Grandma say, she wasn't sure who to, 'Isobel's so confident in social situations.'

Isobel hurried up to the group of kids, trying to get there before the scared feeling in her tummy got too big.

She stared at the older boy in a zip-up jacket. He leaned against the fence with his elbow, like he was in a film. His eyes looked big – like a boy's and a girl's at the same time. Eyeliner, Isobel decided.

She walked up to him. 'What a stupid party.'

The boy turned to a girl with messed-up hair on the grass.

'Shall we go to the park? Leave the little kids here. Have some fun.'

Isobel scuffed her shoes together. She wasn't one of the little ones. She may be younger than him, but she was *way* older than these other kids.

The girl with the messed-up hair stood up. 'Let's go and sit on the swings. Even without our phones, the park's got to be better than this. I told Mum earlier, "I'm not playing babysitter today."'

A teenage girl in a T-shirt showing a big-eyed manga girl pushed herself up and dusted her hands off. 'Me neither.'

Isobel looked at the little kids. She stood taller. 'I'm not playing babysitter either.'

The manga girl snorted. She and the other two older ones walked off.

Isobel shrank again.

She could follow them, she supposed. But they might pretend not to hear her if she spoke. Or, worse, run away – and Isobel would have to decide whether to chase them.

Isobel turned to look at the other kids. The daisy girls had finished their chains and were wearing them as crowns – like Isobel had, when she was little.

Isobel looked past the daisy girls and Charlie to a boy she hadn't noticed before, who was hiding behind the bin. He was concentrating hard, trying to peel off all the stickers saying *Junior Detective* that were stuck all over his face, hair and clothes.

A small boy made a roaring noise and clawed the air. 'I'm a tiger.'

Isobel looked at him. 'No you're not.'

'I am.'

Isobel shook her head. 'Shall we play a proper game?'

She waited till the six kids were all looking at her and, quietly, got her cigarette lighter out of her pocket. She held it up and flicked it and the flame came on.

The daisy chain girls stopped chattering. The tiger boy stopped roaring. The *Junior Detective* boy stopped peeling off his stickers.

'We need to get drawing paper.' Isobel looked round the group. 'You've got half an hour to split up and get hold of as much as you can.'

'Are we drawing today?' a daisy girl asked. 'I'm going to do a llama. Or a penguin. I'm good at zoo animals.'

'No.' Isobel flicked her lighter on again. 'No zoo animals.'

The tiger boy looked at the flame.

'We're not going to be drawing.' Isobel looked round the group, one at a time. 'Today, little ones, we're going to be playing *fire*.'

26

At the sound of striding footsteps, Stella looked up from the kitchen table.

George banged the kitchen door shut behind him. 'Helen's arrived.' His voice was tight.

'Oh, good. Right on time.' Stella side-eyed the parcels she'd made. 'You'd think they'd get easier. But if anything, they're getting worse.'

'Helen's here, but Nathan's not. Apparently' – he leaned forward to make eye contact – 'it's OK for sons-in-law not to come.'

Stella took a deep breath. 'Oh.'

'Exactly. *Oh.*'

Stella looked down at her lap. 'Nathan's really not coming?'

'*Apparently*, work is a good enough excuse.'

Stella felt hot. Any conversation with George with multiple *apparently*s never ended well. 'No one would believe it of you. We'd have had to come up with a mystery illness.'

'I work at the weekends. I do marking.'

'Yeah, but it's a sign of disorganisation if you have to miss a party on a Saturday.'

'It feels so unfair.' George deflated a little. 'My job's a social good.'

Stella shook her head. 'I can't believe Nathan's not here.'

George kicked the bin. It made a metallic clang.

'Woah!' Stella said. 'Steady.'

'This is your fault. When I get a solicitor, I'm going to get it written into the settlement. No more fucking family parties. No more secrets.'

The kitchen door opened.

'No more secrets?' Cheryl entered the room, Goldie scurrying behind her.

Stella froze.

'I'm sure Margaret will have *several* more secrets up her sleeve. And we need a cloth,' Cheryl said. 'There's been an incident with some orange juice and the ottoman.'

George reached into the sink and threw the cloth towards Cheryl. She caught it with both hands.

Goldie took up her familiar high-seated position, her wet nose an inch from Stella's parcels.

Cheryl waved the cloth at George. 'I'm watching you. You and your little secrets.' She turned to look at Stella. 'I've got my eye on your husband.'

Stella blinked.

Cheryl smiled and left the room.

George leaned down so his mouth was close to Stella's ear. 'She knows nothing.' He kept his voice low. 'She's saying that because she thinks the butler did it.'

Stella stared at him. 'She can't have heard what you said about a settlement, can she?'

'No. No way.'

After a moment, Stella nodded.

'Something's up with Dad.' She picked up more pastry and fed a piece automatically to the waiting Goldie. 'I don't think he can deal with a party right now.'

'He's clearly devastated about your mum.' George casually

turned over one of the parcels. 'Was he actually there when the doctor gave the news?'

'He's so gutted.' Stella swatted the air near her face. 'I just wish he wouldn't deal with it by hiding. I don't think that's helpful, do you?'

'Agreed.' George coughed. 'And do you think your mum's behaving normally?'

Stella put the pastry down. 'What do you mean?'

George turned his mobile phone over in his hand. 'Nothing.'

On the floor, Goldie shuffled a millimetre forward.

Stella indicated George's phone. 'How did you get that back from the passive-aggressive washing-up bowl?'

'I told your mother I had kids up a mountain and she didn't want them freezing to death on her conscience.'

'That's not true, is it? Anyway, give me that.'

Stella gestured for him to hand the phone over.

George, instead, inched it closer to his chest.

'I need to message Pete,' Stella said. 'Tell him he has to get here now, before I kill him.'

George pressed his lips together. He looked like he was about to say something but, instead, handed the phone over.

'Thanks.' Stella typed out her message and pressed send. She was just about to hand the phone back to George when the screen lit up. In her palm the phone started to ring.

Instantly, George wrenched the phone from her.

'Ow!' Stella watched him press the button to mute the ringtone. 'You scratched me!' She narrowed her eyes.

Look how scared he is of my mum. I can't believe I stayed with him so long.

'Whose phone is that?' Mum's voice could travel through walls.

'It's just me, Margaret,' George shouted back. 'Saving the kiddies.'

'Is it Pete ringing back?' Stella leaned over to look at the screen. *Nancy Turner.* 'Who's Nancy Turner?'

George paused. 'A colleague, from school. A work colleague.'

'Don't you need to take that? If you have those kids up a mountain?'

George looked at the screen. 'I can call back later.'

'Don't mind me.' Stella wiped the side of her nose with her floury hand. 'I won't be listening to your tedious work call.'

George stared at Stella for a second.

He answered the phone. 'Hi. Have you located the children?'

Stella fed Goldie another piece of pastry. *This is so bad for her. Shit vet I am.*

George listened into the phone for a minute. 'That's right.' He glanced at Stella. 'And have they got enough warm clothes?'

Stella batted Goldie's inching-forward nose back from the parcels. '*No!*'

George nodded into the phone. 'That *is* a relief. I'll call you back with the details once I've got them in front of me. Thank you for being so understanding.'

George put his phone down. He smiled at Stella.

She smiled back, and wondered *what the fuck* was going on with those kids up a mountain, and why *anyone* who'd met George would put him in charge of logistics from afar.

Stella looked back at the parcels. 'That's it. I've made a decision. We can't serve these monsters, can we?'

George didn't reply. He seemed far away.

Stella picked up the tray on the table. She stood up and

slid the parcels into the compost bin on the counter top. 'How long do you reckon we have to stay at this party?'

He focused. 'I think we have to wait till it's dark. And we have to get through all the mystery acts. Though your mother thinks we're staying tonight.'

'Didn't you tell her we aren't?'

'I certainly did.'

Stella ignored Goldie, who was now sitting directly underneath the compost bin. 'Did she listen?'

'She said she's made the bed up and everything. She said she was going to speak to you.'

'Right.' Ignoring the remaining tray of parcels, Stella unfastened her apron and threw it on the table. 'It's on.'

27

Helen had been standing by the fireplace, making polite conversation with someone she hadn't seen for twenty years, when she heard George's voice spike through from the kitchen.

'Apparently it's OK for sons-in-law not to come.'

Helen winced. 'Excuse me.' She edged backwards and pulled the kitchen door closed. She didn't want to hear George and Stella row, and definitely not about *her* husband.

Their marriage was so different, Helen reflected, to hers and Nathan's. Hers was polite to the point of no contact sometimes. Was that what contentment in a relationship felt like?

Contentment. Or indifference. Or even deception. On the off-chance her husband was committing embezzlement in the family business.

Not today. No more embezzlement thoughts today.

Stella entered the lounge, flour frosting her clothes, her nose, her hair. Only a circular patch around the lap of her velvet trousers was flour-free. George followed, dusting his hands off.

Helen felt another stomach-twist of guilt. 'Stella!' She gave her a hug. 'I'm sorry you had to do the parcels. I really appreciate it.'

Stella itched her face. White speckles stuck to her nose where her pores had sweated. 'You wouldn't appreciate it if you'd seen them. They've gone in the compost.'

'I'm sorry.'

'It's good to know you appreciate them though. Like you "really appreciate having me in your life".'

'I didn't know you'd got that text.'

'Oh,' Stella looked her up and down, 'I got it.'

'Mum tells everyone she really appreciates them now.' Helen hadn't seen Isobel approach, but here she was, standing next to them. 'She said it to me three times on Monday.'

'Why aren't you playing with the other kids?' Helen asked.

Isobel slowly lifted her gaze. 'The good ones have gone to the park. It's only the little ones left.'

Helen put on her best encouraging tone. 'You might be surprised how much fun you have.'

Isobel's gaze didn't waver. 'You want me to teach the other kids how to play?'

'Yes.' Helen stared at her. 'Yes, of course.'

'Hi, Scamp.' Stella turned to Isobel. 'What do you say to your mum when she says she appreciates having you in her life?'

'I just ignore her and hope she'll stop saying it.'

'Charming.' Helen wondered why Stella said 'Scamp'. Stella *did* know Isobel's name, didn't she?

Helen looked at the gaggle of kids roaming the lounge, badgering their parents for drawing paper. All the kids were younger than Isobel, but Isobel would just have to get over it.

Isobel fixed her gaze on Helen. 'I'm looking for drawing paper.'

'You'll have to ask Grandma. I don't know where she keeps it.'

Isobel walked away.

Stella looked from Isobel to Helen and back.

'She's a determined little character,' Helen said, keeping her voice light.

'Anyway, I've put my parcels out of their misery.' Stella folded her arms. 'I just need to find a way to break it to Mum. After . . .' Stella turned one-eighty. 'Mum!'

Mum looked up from her tray of canapés.

'Just so you know, we're not staying tonight. We were never staying.'

Mum shook her head. 'You can't be driving back to Birmingham tonight. It's dangerous if you're tired. And I've made up your bedroom.'

'It's not far.'

'We're having fireworks when it goes dark. And then it's the bacon butties. You don't want to be driving back in the early hours when there're perfectly good beds here.'

'I'm just explaining,' Stella said, 'that the real plans are different to the ones in your head. So don't act surprised later when we leave.'

'*Please* Stella.' Mum gestured widely with her arm. 'I have all these people to see to. Don't be difficult.'

'We're not staying.'

Cheryl was standing nearby and Stella caught her eye. She appeared to be studying Stella.

She didn't hear anything. She doesn't know anything.

'Well.' Mum sighed. 'I'm sorry it's come to this, but you should have said before. I told Jane she could park in front of your car. She's gone home in a taxi after having a funny turn.'

Stella stared at Mum. 'No!'

She turned to look at George.

162

George ran the fingers of one hand roughly through his hair. 'Margaret, say you're joking.'

'I didn't think it mattered because I thought you were staying!'

Stella rushed to the window.

'She's the yellow Citroen,' Mum said. 'Right across the drive.'

Stella span round. 'No, Mum, please. You'll have to get her and the keys back.'

Mum clucked her mouth. 'She's ill, Stella. She lives in Bolton and she went home in a *taxi*. That will have cost her twenty pounds.'

George paced across the room. 'If you give me Jane's address, I could get a taxi and get her keys and—'

'You'll miss the party, George, and I can't have that. Mr Owlish the butler has a key role in Act Two. And that would be a ridiculous waste of twenty pounds for poor Jane, she'd mull on that for days. So I won't tell you her address.'

Stella and George stared at each other.

Stella turned to Mum. 'Did you do this deliberately?'

'Stella, don't fuss. *Please.*' Mum gave a wave of the hand. 'I honestly thought you were staying.'

'Your filter is fascinating,' George said.

Mum threw up her hands. 'Sometimes, it's like I can't do right for doing wrong.'

George and Stella looked at each other again.

With a jerk of his head, George indicated for Stella to follow him upstairs.

Helen was surprised when, wordlessly, she did.

28

George ran up the last few steps and charged into Stella's old bedroom, gripping his hands into fists. Stella slammed the door behind them.

George got momentarily distracted by the room. Margaret had already made up the low double bed she always put together for them on the floor, out of a mattress and a blow-up holiday lilo.

He shook his head, hard. 'Let me get this straight.' He tried to pace across a tiny room that had no room to pace in. 'I have to be here so your family look strong and together for this last party.' He tried to pace over the mattress; he turned and paced round the edge. 'You're the shit daughter, yet you can't disappoint them and prove it by admitting we're divorcing.'

'For *their* sake,' Stella emphasised. 'I don't care about being the shit one, it's water off a duck's back.'

'Yet Helen's late. Nathan's off the hook completely with work, just like that – even though the shop's shut for today. And now *we've* got to stay over.'

'I'm sorry. I think it might have been an accident.'

'How can you even say that?'

'I genuinely think she thinks it's an accident. How do you do that? I want to be able to do that, be able to bend facts – and the *actual past* – with your mind. It's a skill.'

'Don't *you* play the victim here. This is way worse for me than you. *And* Pete isn't even bothering to come, to his own parents' party! Which makes him, officially, an arse.'

Stella looked at her hands. 'I know.'

'Yet I'm having to stand here making polite conversation with your parents' friends, who, by the way, know every fucking thing about me, like they've had me tagged, GPS-tracked and DNA-tested. And their own son and their real son-in-law, the one who's staying around, *aren't even here!*' George realised he was shouting into a shelf of *Sweet Valley High* books. He turned around so he was shouting at Stella instead.

'I didn't realise Nathan and Pete would be such weasels.' Stella ran a hand through her hair. 'It makes it even more important to Mum and Dad that you're here.'

'Can you hear yourself? *You're* the shit one. You're *meant* to be the shit one. Since when did you try to be the good one? What's even the point of being the shit one if you don't get the benefit?'

'I didn't choose to be the shit one,' Stella said. 'It was foisted on me.'

'Well, you can choose whether to use it or not. And you're clearly wasting it right now.'

'What could I say?' Stella shook her head. 'Mum's never going to give us that address, she'll just keep banging on about how ill that Jane woman is. You want to go back to Birmingham and me drive back to Manchester tomorrow for the car? Or get separate rooms in a hotel? We need to be saving money right now.'

'I'm not sleeping *there*.' George picked up the edge of the duvet and looked beneath. The bed was, as suspected, constructed from the single mattress and the holiday lilo, with a fitted sheet stretched over the two. He dropped the edge of the duvet in disgust.

'Look, I'm sorry I didn't get further with her on the staying over thing – really, really sorry, actually—'

Was that an apology? George wondered. It didn't sound like an apology.

'—but don't be a child. How many times have we slept in the same room?'

George didn't say anything.

'It changes nothing.' Stella looked away. 'We're not exactly going to jump on each other.'

George looked at the 'bed'. He tried not to think about how long it had been since they had shared a bed. How natural it had seemed at the time. And, by contrast, how unnatural it felt now.

'How far do you have to go to make your parents happy?' he said eventually.

'I think' – Stella narrowed her eyes – 'this is as far as it goes.'

'Whatever your twisted relationship with your parents is, I'm not playing. I'm leaving.'

'You can't! You promised you'd play along.'

'I never agreed to stay over.'

'You can't leave now. It's worse than if you never came at all. You would – literally – be ruining the party.'

George sank down onto the mattress. He crossed his legs.

'I know that sounds melodramatic,' Stella said.

'It does.'

'But it's true.'

George looked at his feet. She was right. *Of course* you don't tell your in-laws you're divorcing in the middle of a party. He'd made his bed (well, Margaret had, out of a mattress and a lilo) and now he had to lie in it.

'My mum's dying.'

'Low, Stella.'

'Just saying. And I'm not going to jump on you tonight. I think I can keep my hands off your paunch, waistcoat or no waistcoat.'

George tugged his shirt down automatically.

'That was meant to be a joke. Sorry.'

'Why am I here? Is this part of my punishment? Did you conspire with your mum to mess with my head one last time?'

'Conspire with my mum!' Stella said. 'You really think I want to sleep in a bed with you?'

George shrugged. 'I can't sleep in the same bed as you.'

'Don't be uptight.'

George indicated the high-backed armchair in the corner of the room. 'I'll sleep on that.'

'As you wish. It won't be comfortable, but it's your choice.'

George shook his head. 'For fuck's sake, Stella.'

Stella held her palms up. 'I'm sorry,' she said again. 'Look, I really am. But it's one night, and it means a lot to my mum.'

George looked at the lilo bed and tried, really hard, not to remember.

*

Eight years before, George and Stella had been having sex on this same half-lilo, half-mattress bed on a Tuesday at half-term at ten in the morning.

So George lay on his back on the lilo bed. He looked up at Stella; the two smiled at each other. He closed his eyes and—

'Stella?'

Margaret opened the bedroom door.

Stella sprang off George and back under the duvet. She grabbed the edge of the duvet and held it up to her neck.

'You would not *believe* what those squirrels have been up to.' Margaret strode into the room holding a pile of towels. 'Burying their nuts in my tulip pots like they own the place, digging up my precious bulbs.' She stopped in front of the lilo bed. 'I forgot to give you towels last night.'

George held the cover over his naked body, trying not to pant.

Margaret crouched down and set the stack of towels down next to George. 'It makes me hope poor Goldie will catch a squirrel one of these days. She's so keen, and I'd like to see how *they* like it when the tables are turned.' She stood up and looked at George and Stella. 'Sorry, did I wake you? And do you need anything from Asda? I'm just nipping out.'

George blinked. *She must have seen something, surely?*

'I know you like a different cereal to the ones we get, George, but honestly I can't remember which one it is and there are so many in that supermarket now, it's ridiculous. I don't know how anyone's meant to choose.'

'We're fine, Mum.' Stella's voice was hoarse.

She must *see our shoulders are naked. And that we're panting. Right?* Right?

George pulled the edge of the duvet further up his neck.

'Cheryl's son James is minding the shop, and guess what your father's doing with his bit of free time?' Margaret walked to the window and pulled back the curtains. George squinted in the newly sunlit room. 'He's reading a licencing agreement on the computer.' She turned to face the two of them. 'I keep telling him they don't expect you to *actually read* seventy pages of small type and, besides, I'm sure no one really wants *his* data, but he thinks the tech companies are out to get him and he has to thwart them.' She shook her head fondly. 'Right, I'm off to Asda. Don't laze in bed all day.'

With that, she was gone.

She didn't even shut the bedroom door after her.

Stella slipped out from under the duvet and crouch-walked to the window. She pulled the curtains shut, stood up properly and quietly shut the door.

She got back in bed. She looked drunk, George thought.

They didn't say anything for a long time.

She stared straight ahead. 'Do you think she noticed?'

'How couldn't she have? But no.'

'You sure?'

'Unless – you know your mum. She might have brazened it out.' George's heart was still beating at an alarming pace. 'But – no. No way. She can't have seen that and then – squirrels and Asda and licencing agreements.'

They lay there in silence, the duvet still pulled up to their shoulders.

'*Surely* she couldn't have noticed?' Stella said.

'Your mum is an odd one. What if she saw my sex-face?'

'*Surely*,' Stella said again.

'Either way, I'm not going to be able to look Margaret in the eyes for a very long time.'

They lay there together, not moving.

Eventually, Stella sat up and pulled the duvet back. 'Let's not think about it. It's way too disturbing.' She indicated George's body, a question on her face. 'Shall I hop back on?'

'Nice thought.' George put his hand over hers. 'Really nice. But don't be offended when I say that the moment has definitely – *definitely* – passed.'

29

In the lounge, Helen couldn't help looking at the ceiling. George and Stella had taken their row up another – literal – level.

Helen couldn't hear their voices, but she'd recognised that dangerous exchange of glances, saw the angular shapes their bodies made when they ran up the stairs. Heard the familiar slamming sound of Stella's bedroom door.

Helen recognised that sound from her childhood and knew, with certainty, which particular bedroom door was slamming. But then – Stella's door had slammed more than most, twenty years ago.

Helen didn't remember slamming her own door at all. But Stella's husband had come to this party. So maybe Helen should have slammed more doors over the years.

'Helen.'

Helen turned to face her mother.

'Can you find out what Stella's done to those parcels? I still can't smell any cooking.'

Helen glanced at Isobel. She seemed to be organising the other kids, collecting newspapers and leaflets. One kid brought Isobel a book from the shelf – Simon Schama's *History of Britain*. Isobel shook her head at him and he put the book back.

Helen turned back to Mum. 'No problem.'

She glanced at Charlie, who was holding an Indian take-away leaflet out to his sister – *nice they were playing together* – and headed for the kitchen.

She found Dad there, staring out of the window to the garden. Goldie sat at his feet.

'Hey, Dad.' She kissed his cheek. 'Happy anniversary.'

Dad gave Helen a stiff hug. 'When did everyone start saying *Hey* not *Hi*?'

'I've never really thought about it.'

Helen noticed a tray of parcels that Stella had abandoned on the sideboard. Were those meant to be *her* parcels? Surely not.

'We don't say *hey*. We say *hi*. I just don't know when all this became normal.' Dad was still going. 'We're just letting our culture be Americanised.'

'I'll say *hi* next time.' Helen noticed the worktop was smeared with greasy patches. Potato peelings and tea bags were everywhere, some scattered on the floor. 'What's happened over there?'

'Looks like Goldie managed to get her paws on the work-top and tip over the compost bin. I was about to clean it up.'

They both looked at Goldie.

'It's not her fault, she hasn't done that for years,' Dad stroked the dog's head. 'She must be unsettled, all these people in her house without her say-so. It's not fair to her *at all.*' Dad stopped stroking Goldie and got up. 'Helen.' He reached into the sink for the kitchen cloth. 'Do you mind that I never cooked for you when you were growing up?'

'What?' Helen couldn't help looking back at Stella's sci-fi pastry. 'No. No, why?'

'It's just something your mother said.' Dad deposited some potato peelings back in the compost bin. 'Do you think I'm hypocritical for knowing all about produce but never actually cooking?'

'You OK, Dad?'

No reply.

Helen put her hand on his shoulder and rubbed it softly.

'Nathan doesn't cook either,' Helen said. 'Not everyone does.'

'He doesn't?' Dad wiped the surface, concentrating hard on it. 'Men don't all cook now?'

'Nathan doesn't. Toast and cereal ... microwave soup ... that's about his level.'

Dad stood up straighter. 'I'll help you with those parcels then.' He wiped the floor and looked at Stella's tray. 'They're not meant to look like that, are they?'

'No.' Helen smiled. 'They're meant to look different.'

'Will I be able to do them, Helen?'

'Of course.'

'I've done plastering, but never pastry.'

'You just have to get your eye in. And you'll be able to do it if I show you.' She glanced at Stella's tray. 'Better than Stella did, at least.'

Dad walked over to the table. He sat down and turned a pastry packet over. 'Cornish farm pastry?' He said it like *unicorn milk?*

Helen reached for the rolling pin.

'All butter – I thought so. Christ, Helen, are you *made* of money?' Dad puffed himself up, filling his skin more with every second. 'You're practically throwing pound notes on the fire.'

'I bought it for your party. Because you and Mum are worth it.'

Dad held the packet at arm's length, narrowing his eyes to read the small print.

Helen dusted the table with flour. She started rolling the pastry. 'So, you need to roll it to about five millimetres thick. Keep dusting the table with flour and turn the pastry regularly so it doesn't stick.'

Dad was still studying the packet. 'It's got endless E-numbers. Look, Helen.'

Helen shaped the pastry with a knife. 'I'll do this bit,' she said tactfully, 'and you can help me with the filling.'

Dad stood up, suddenly. 'I've made a mistake.'

Helen screwed up the offcuts. 'It's no problem, Dad. You don't have to help if you don't want to.'

'I made a mistake when I decided to give up the shop.' Dad looked over her shoulder. 'I want to come back.'

Helen put the ball of pastry down. 'What's brought this on?'

'I'm nothing without the shop. Will you tell Nathan to have me back?'

'But what about taking it easier for the next few years?'

'How do I take it easy, with what's happening to your mother? I need a focus.'

'What about the supermarket? I thought you liked it there.'

Dad waved a hand dismissively. 'It's not me. I like to set the tone for a place. There, I feel like a sheep in an apron.'

Helen picked up her knife. 'Right.'

'Your mum says I shouldn't go back to the shop. She says I shouldn't ask, that it will upset the ecosystem. That Nathan and I will lock horns like two alpha stags and there can only be one pack leader. But what else can I do?' Dad looked at his lap, making himself appear smaller. 'Let them put me out to pasture?'

Helen took care with her words. 'Has something happened at the supermarket?'

Dad waved a hand. 'My boss is a robot. She's impossible to work for.'

'It must be hard to have a boss after it being just you for so long. Do you want the rolling pin?'

'It's not just being an employee.' Dad didn't take the rolling pin. 'It's working for *her*. She deliberately misunderstands my intentions.'

'There are other supermarkets?'

'I want to be somewhere smaller. Somewhere I have influence.'

'But maybe you'd feel the same about working for Nathan? Maybe that's what Mum meant with the *alpha stags* thing. It's hard to go from being in charge to taking orders.'

'I'll have some influence. Nathan will listen to me.'

Helen wondered where her dad had got *that* idea from.

'I'm going to ask Nathan when he gets here.' Dad stood straighter. 'I'm going to go cap in hand and ask him to take me back.'

'Today?'

'Why not today?'

'Dad. You're meant to be chatting to guests.'

'It will only take a few minutes.'

'It's a celebratory day,' Helen said. 'Not one for serious talk.'

'You'll barely notice. I'll just slip it into conversation when Nathan and I are on our own.'

Helen had that bad feeling in her stomach. 'How do you feel about the new stock?'

Dad stiffened. 'It's Nathan's shop. It's Nathan's choice.'

'I can see how hard it is for you to say that. But are you going to be able to recommend the expensive crisps without rolling your eyes?'

'If he wants to sell overpriced food to idiots, that's his lookout.'

'You know those people in cartoons who are trying to hold something in? Who have steam coming out of their ears like kettles?'

'Maybe if we become co-partners I'll have more influence on the stock selection.'

'I don't think Nathan would want a co-partner. He's a lone wolf. I know that's a phrase you use for terrorists and serial killers, but you know what I mean.'

'Or I could just work *for* him, not *with* him. Like a member of staff. I could wear a name badge. I could doff my hat and call him *boss*. I could scurry to his every command.'

'You *could*,' Helen said carefully.

The doorbell rang.

Helen heard the shudder of the front door opening.

'Better late than never.' Mum managed to sound both welcoming and critical.

'I'm finished with the suppliers now' – Helen was surprised to hear her husband's voice – 'so you've got me for the rest of the evening.'

Helen looked at her watch. It wasn't even eight o'clock. He'd arrived earlier than she'd expected.

She should be grateful. She *really* should be grateful . . .

'Is that Nathan?' Dad said hopefully.

| Mr Hapsworth, Private Secretary, 28 | Nathan Wheatley | Professional and discreet. Mr Hapsworth never stops – though his new-fangled ways of doing things occasionally need to be curbed. |

The conversation continued in the hallway. 'I just don't understand what you want from me, Margaret.'

'Your phone, that's all.'

'You need to make a call? Hey! Where are you going with that?'

'Don't make a commotion, Nathan. Everyone else followed the rules without complaining.'

Nathan's and Mum's voices faded as they moved through the house.

Helen turned to Dad and gave him a bright smile. She picked up another piece of pastry.

Nathan was here. She probably should go and say hello. But she might just stay in the kitchen for a bit, do some cleaning up after finishing the parcels. Talk was too risky today. *Fancy a drink? Oh, and Dad wants to come back and work for you, won't that be fun? And, while we're chatting ... have you been committing a tiny bit of fraud in the business?*

Helen placed a finished parcel on the tray. She looked out of the window. The kids weren't in the garden anymore. She realised she hadn't seen Isobel and Charlie for a while. But someone would be supervising the kids at a party like this, surely?

Yes. Yes, they would. The kids would be fine. Doing their drawings, nice and quietly.

Mum walked into the kitchen. She waved Nathan's

phone at Helen. 'Just Pete to come now. Then we'll have a full set.'

'Of phones?' Helen asked.

'Of phones *and* people. So we're nearly there. And I know I can rely on Pete.'

30

| Mr Shaker, Solicitor, 30 | Pete Foy | Handsome young solicitor. Inherited his business from his father, a dear friend of the Brockenhursts. Reliable and scrupulously honest. |

Message notifications on Pete's phone:

You're on your way, I hope, Pete love? Struggling to get hold of you, I think you must have a bad reception. Please call me on landline – 0161 888 6055 but you know that. Your silly mother xx 😊😊😵

This is Stella on George's phone. Mine's been kidnapped. You'd BETTER be on your way here or I will Hunt – You – Down.

BetLucky July Jamboree continues! Remember – if you deposit into your BetLucky account in July, your money goes further with extra bonuses and free spins. Stay lucky!

PETER PHONE YOUR MOTHER SHES GETTING UPSET DAD NO MOBILES PARTY SWITCHING OFF NOW

31

Isobel found Grandma in the lounge, trying to get everyone to eat more food.

'Honestly, Margaret, I'm full.'

'No, I'm saving myself for Helen's parcels.'

'I couldn't possibly.'

Isobel strode up to her. 'Can I have a bucket, Grandma? Me and the little ones are playing lucky dip.'

Grandma beamed at her. 'What a lovely thing to do.'

Isobel waited while Grandma went into the cupboard under the stairs. Grandma hadn't noticed that Isobel was too old for lucky dip.

'Here,' Grandma handed Isobel the bucket. 'You kids have fun!'

Isobel looked at the other kids. She jerked her head for them to follow with their 'drawing paper' – mainly toilet roll, it turned out.

Isobel walked through the garden, past the hunched-over Goldie, who was making a strange pumping noise.

A daisy girl wrinkled her nose. 'Ew.'

Isobel realised Goldie was throwing up beige and pink chunks onto Grandma's best flower bed.

'Just don't look. Walk past it quickly.' Isobel didn't like dogs – especially not old dogs, *especially* not if they were being sick. 'Don't stop till we get in the ginnel.'

She unlatched the gate to the ginnel, then latched the gate after them.

'It smells here,' the daisy girl said. 'Of wee.'

'It doesn't.' It did a bit. The ginnel was no man's land between the gardens. And the only person she'd ever seen use it was a taxi driver, who needed to *find somewhere proper next time you're caught short or I'll report you to the council!* Grandma had shouted as he was doing up his flies.

But there was no one weeing here today. Today, the ginnel was hers.

Isobel set her bucket down. She looked around the group of kids.

'You have to undo the toilet roll.' Isobel unravelled it into the bucket till it piled like spaghetti. 'And screw the paper up so it's still got air in, see?'

Isobel watched the little kids copy her and stuff their paper in the bucket. She picked Charlie's piece out and gave it back to be refolded.

When she was satisfied, she took the bucket by the handle and moved it further away from the group.

Isobel waited for silence. 'Stand back.'

She stepped forward with her cigarette lighter. Carefully, she lit the edge of a piece of paper that peeked out of the bucket.

The paper burned for a moment, then went out.

Isobel's face went hot. 'Hang on.'

She pushed her hand down into the bucket. She lit the paper from the bottom this time, jerking her hand back quickly.

Isobel watched as the flames grew. They licked over the top of the bucket, nearly as high as Isobel's waist.

'Is it going to stop?' a girl with a French plait asked.

'Shhh,' Isobel said. 'Isn't it beautiful?'

Other kids *umm*-ed and *aah*-ed.

Eventually, the flames shrank back. The paper curled into blackness; the fire went out.

Some of the kids started coughing.

'Step back if it hurts,' Isobel said. 'I can't be thinking of everything here.'

Isobel glanced into the garden again. There was no sign of the big kids coming back yet.

She looked at the little ones. 'Was that fun?'

The kids nodded.

'Good.' Isobel looked back round at the crowd. 'But if we're going to make the fire bigger next time, we need to find some fuel.'

ACT TWO

What the Butler Knew

Card to be read at 8.00 p.m. by the solicitor,
Mr Shaker (a.k.a. Pete Foy)

*By now, you should all know that Agnes the
parlourmaid let her pinafore out in the weeks before
she died. And the rumours should have reached you of
that October night-time assignation between Agnes
and Lord Brockenhurst, in the folly at the rear of the
estate.*

*You should also be aware that Ellie Brockenhurst's
late mother's priceless necklace has been stolen from
Ellie's bedroom.*

But what's this?

*Tragedy strikes the manor for a second time! Miss
Evangeline, the Vicar, is found in the armoury,
strangled with a scarf!*

It was Mr Owlish, the butler, who found the body.

*Could it be there's something the butler isn't telling
us?*

32

Stella padded quietly down the stairs, leaving George in the bedroom, trying not to think about anything. Anything at all.

She'd thought she and George would at least be able to get through today – *one day* – without arguing.

She was wrong.

Stella reached the lounge. She watched Mum laugh as she circled a group of neighbours with a tray of snacks.

At the sound of the front door slamming, Stella glanced out of the window. George strode down the street, head down, hands in pockets. He'd taken his waistcoat off.

Mum swivelled her head to face Stella. 'Who just left?'

'George just went to get something from the shop.' Stella felt Cheryl studying her; she turned away.

'Now, Stella? You let him go *now*?'

Stella raised her palms to the ceiling. 'Why not now?'

'It's Act Two!'

'I didn't know that, did I?'

Mum shook her head. She tapped her wedding ring against her wine glass and raised her voice to the room. 'Act Two in five minutes! Just enough time to fill up your glasses.'

'Stella?' Helen steered her by the arm. 'Talk to me.'

Stella let herself be guided into the alcove by the mantel-piece. 'Why?'

'What do you mean, "why?"'

Stella paused. 'Sorry.'

'OK. Honestly?' Helen looked over her shoulder and back. 'I'm avoiding Nathan.'

Stella peered at Helen. 'Interesting.'

'Never mind about that. We don't talk, but we *should* talk. We're sisters.' Helen indicated the photo on the mantelpiece. 'I always think that's such a lovely picture of you two.'

Stella looked to the picture of Stella and George on the beach on their wedding day, sand and light in their eyes.

'Dad took it,' Stella said. 'He was so proud of that picture.'

'He was so proud *that whole day*. It was kind of you to let him walk you down the aisle. In the end.'

'That was a mistake. I bowed to wedding pressure. But he did love that picture.' Stella deliberately didn't look at it. 'He reckons it was the best one from our wedding. That the official photographer never got the lighting right.'

'I don't know about the lighting.' Helen stared at the picture. 'But you two look so happy.'

Stella looked at the carpet. She knew every inch of that picture. It had been everywhere in the last ten years. Screen-savers. Mouse mats. Phone lock screens.

And she and George *had* looked happy on that beach in Greece. But that day wasn't as picture-perfect as it looked. She and George had rowed that morning over whose fault it was that piece of buttered toast had ended up face-down on the thick cream carpet of the honeymoon suite. (George's, of course. Yes, it was her toast, but he was the one who'd moved the duvet so thoughtlessly.)

In retrospect, it was an ominous sign. They'd rowed on

their *wedding day.* They should have recognised it, right then. Just walked away. Saved themselves all this pain.

'Are you two OK?' Helen asked. 'Do you want to talk about it?'

Stella frowned. 'We're fine.' When did Helen get astute? And since when did she assume Stella wanted to talk to her about *feelings*? This was an unwelcome double-down on *I really appreciate having you in my life.*

There was a clap of hands behind her; Stella looked round.

Mum clapped her hands again. 'Gather round! Act Two!'

Stella shuffled forward with the crowd. She caught Nathan's eye across the room. He waved and she waved back. After a second, Helen did the same. She looked – vacant.

It hit Stella right then. She needed to be nicer to her sister.

Mum stepped onto her librarian's stool, card in hand. She surveyed the room and coughed.

'Agnes the parlourmaid is dead.'

Everyone turned to look at Stella.

'And, by now,' Mum continued, 'you should know that Agnes let her pinafore out in the weeks before she died—'

Everyone turned to look at Stella again.

Stella shrugged. 'Parlourmaids get hungry. It's an active job.'

'I didn't know about the pinafore, Margaret,' Adele said.

Mum narrowed her eyes. 'Mr Owlish should have told you. George.'

Adele looked at Stella. She shook her head.

Mum turned to Stella too. 'George *has* been following instructions?'

'I've been in the kitchen. You'll have to ask him.'

'But he's not here!'

Stella held her palms up. 'I don't know!'

Mum licked her lips. She looked down at her card and raised her face to the group again.

'And the rumours should have reached you of that October night-time assignation between Agnes and Lord Brockenhurst—'

Stella frowned. 'A *night-time assignation?*'

'—in the folly at the rear of the estate—'

'My character's been at it with *Dad?*'

Cheryl took in a deep breath. 'I've got it! Agnes the parlourmaid was *pregnant!* With Lord Brockenhurst's *baby!*'

Mum tapped her card against her leg. 'You were meant to get there *an hour ago*, Cheryl.'

'That's disgusting,' Stella said.

'Stella.' Mum pressed her lips together again. 'You're not helping. You *know* Lord Brockenhurst isn't Agnes' actual father.'

'*Do* I? Or is that lovely little snippet coming in Act Three?'

Mum stared at her. Something in her cheek twinged.

'I'm sorry.' Stella felt her face heat up. 'Where were we? Agnes was pregnant by Lord Brockenhurst? That's cool, I'm fine with that. Keep going.'

Mum gave Stella a single nod. She turned back to the crowd. 'You should also be aware that Ellie Brockenhurst's late mother's priceless necklace has been stolen from Ellie's bedroom.'

Everyone looked at Helen. Helen fingered her own (not priceless) necklace nervously.

'But what's this?' Mum moved her eyebrows up. 'Tragedy strikes the manor for a second time!' She left a pause. 'Miss Evangeline, the Vicar – that's Cheryl – is found in the armoury, strangled with a scarf!'

Everyone looked at Cheryl.

'Oh, shoot.' Cheryl pursed her lips. 'Was it definitely me?'

'Yes,' Mum said.

'It couldn't be someone who looks a bit like me? An imposter, or someone wearing a similar dress? Maybe a mix-up?'

Mum gave a sad smile. 'Sorry, Cheryl. Can't be helped.'

'An evil twin? Could I have had an evil twin?'

Mum stopped smiling. 'Absolutely not.'

Stella patted Cheryl on the shoulder. 'Unlucky.'

People started dispersing.

'Don't go yet.' Mum put her hand out in a stop sign. 'There're two more sentences. It was Mr Owlish, the butler, who found the body.'

Cheryl sniffed. '*Body*. Just a *body*, now.'

'Could it be there's something the butler isn't telling us?' Mum paused. 'If he was actually here, of course.'

Stella heard the shudder of the front door.

'George?' Mum froze. 'Is that you?'

No response.

'He mustn't have heard me.' Mum stepped off her librarian's stool. 'Anyway, that's Act Two.' She turned up the music on the speaker and walked out of the room. 'George!'

Stella watched Cheryl put her hands behind her neck and unclip her dog collar. She placed it on the mantelpiece unspeaking and, alone in the now noisy room, peeled the *Miss Evangeline, the vicar* badge slowly and sadly from her robe.

187

33

George had watched Stella leave her old bedroom with his hands bunched into fists. He unbuttoned the *stupid* waistcoat and threw it onto the bed. He walked down the stairs, out of the door and down the road, without knowing where he was going.

He hurried down Cole Street and turned left at the junction, heading for the off-licence now. If he was going to stay over, he might as well get some decent ales in. Margaret never had ales in because she thought them old-fashioned. She wanted her guests to drink continental lager instead.

He hadn't been drinking much, out of solidarity with Stella (and, OK, he didn't want to risk having the *I always have to drive* conversation again), but, yes, George might as well drink now they were staying.

George bought the box of beer and headed back to the house. The lounge curtains weren't shut; he could see Margaret standing above the crowd, waving her hands with importance.

He opened the front door.

'George?' Margaret's voice carried. 'Is that you?'

George walked through to the kitchen and put the box of beers on the side.

After a moment, Margaret followed him in. 'You *have*

been telling everyone your key reveals, haven't you? There was some confusion out there about Agnes' pinafore.'

'Maybe I didn't want to tell people.' George ripped open the cardboard packaging. 'Maybe I found it quite rude for the butler to be telling everyone about the parlourmaid's weight gain.'

'And where's your waistcoat?'

George got an ale from the box. He looked around for a bottle opener. 'I wasn't going to wear it to the shop.'

Margaret put her hand in her pocket and handed him an opener. 'Try to stay in character, George. While you were gone, Miss Evangeline, the vicar, got strangled. Don't mention it to Cheryl because she's a bit sensitive.' Margaret handed him a card. 'But now you need to make sure everyone hears your second character cue. *Please*, George.'

George took a swig of his ale. This woman had (knowingly or not) kidnapped him for the night. He really didn't feel like helping.

Still, he looked at the card.

Second character cue: Mr Owlish.
To be revealed to guests between Act Two and Act Three.
Despite the rumours, you know Agnes wasn't pregnant with Lord Brockenhurst's baby. You caught her sneaking to the kitchen and eating extra midnight meals on a nightly basis. You also had it on good authority from Miss Cartwright, the housekeeper, that Agnes had been through an early menopause.

Extra note: You may find it enlightening to ask Ellie Brockenhurst whether she ever found her late mother's necklace.

George tried to give the card back to Margaret, but she moved her hand away.

'Two people have just been murdered, and I'm the kind of guy who goes round talking about menopauses and necklaces.'

He offered the card again; Margaret still wouldn't take it. 'You keep it. In case it slips your mind. Again.'

George put the card in his pocket. 'Sounds like Mr Owlish is *way* too interested in other people's business. Why's he watching the parlourmaid? It's a bit stalky.'

'He's not *stalky*. He's responsible for her. He has an avuncular relationship with the women of the house.'

'Yeah,' George leaned forward. '*Avuncular*. Nice and *avuncular*.'

'You and Stella!' Margaret slammed her hands on the table. 'You have to snipe and twist everything. You're like peas in a pod.'

George had been about to take a drink; he stopped. He made himself continue.

Bottle in hand, he walked out to the garden. He pulled his e-cig out of the pocket and took a deep inhalation.

The patio door slid open. Scott headed outside and over to George.

Scott lit a cigarette and slid his lighter into his coat pocket. 'That Cheryl's really upset about being killed off. She keeps asking people to check her pulse. Margaret says you have something to tell me about Agnes?'

Silently, George handed Scott the cue card.

Scott read it and handed it back. 'Early menopause. Right.'

George pocketed it. 'Can you tell everyone about it so I don't have to keep getting harassed by Margaret's friends?'

Scott nodded. 'Then will you do me a humiliating favour in return? If my mum comes out, can I throw this cig on the ground and we can pretend it was yours?'

George looked at the silvery streaks round Scott's temples, the lines round his eyes.

'It's just easier this way.'

'No problem,' George said. 'None of my business.'

'Thanks.'

'Out of interest, how long have you been hiding that you smoke from your mum?'

'Must be twenty years.' Scott put his cigarette out. 'No, twenty-five.'

'Right,' George said.

They smoked in silence.

Scott put his cigarette out and offered George a breath mint. 'I can't tell her now, can I?'

George declined the mint; he watched Scott put two in his mouth and head back inside.

George took a drag of his e-cig. It was running out of liquid.

He was in no rush to get back inside. He took the little bottle of liquid from his pocket and injected it into the cigarette.

'What's that stuff?'

George looked round into the clear eyes of Isobel.

She gestured at his e-cig. 'Is it fuel for your cigarette?'

George looked down at the bottle. 'In a way.'

'Can I buy some off you?'

He blinked. 'Of course not.'

'Why?'

'Just no.'

'It's not a real cigarette,' Isobel said. 'So what's the problem?'

George scratched around his brain, trying to get the logic together. 'It's not for you.'

'Why not?'

'You're ten. Eleven?'

She narrowed her eyes.

'You've never smoked. You don't need a cigarette replacement. Smoking is stupid.'

'But you started smoking once.'

'*I* was stupid.'

'Everyone starts somewhere.'

'But not you, not with my liquid. Not today.'

'So that's double standards.'

'Isobel.' George took a drag on his e-cig. 'I have enough pointless debates with children in the week. Can't I have weekends off, at least?'

Isobel stared at him for a second. She wandered back towards the house.

George's mood improved momentarily. He took a celebratory puff of his e-cig.

He watched Isobel open the back door and his good mood faded. He thought of the time he and Stella had first had The Conversation about kids. Here, in this house. Three years before.

*

George and Stella had studiously avoided The Conversation until their mid-thirties. Friends thought it unusual that they hadn't discussed it, but the topic always felt so *weighted*. George was pretty sure neither he nor Stella knew what they thought – and even if they had known, they definitely weren't ready, so why discuss it?

Obviously they needed to think about kids at some point. *Obviously.* Except – no, no *except* about it. Lovely, *lovely* kids, bright shiny faces, with all that cute energy and those lovely loud voices and crusty, gloopy nostrils.

The two had discussed kids in passing. A friend of a friend had asked in the kitchen at a house party, 'Are you two going to have children?'

Stella was quick to reply. 'What am I going to give a kid?' She gave a snarky laugh. 'Freckles? A genetic predisposition to Alzheimer's? A world where they'll be fighting for water in thirty years? Who's going to thank me for that?'

George had smiled politely, and the conversation was hurried on.

So George and Stella had breezed through the first seven years of their relationship. They listened to audio tours of European cities on weekend mini-breaks, did the electric slide at weddings, shivered their way through surprisingly religious christenings and lay under parasols clutching damp-paged paperbacks in Majorca. They gave up drugs, took up exercising, started going into work without hangovers, joined and left social media and gave up (then restarted) reading the newspaper.

Still, no conversations about kids.

It was strange, George reflected, because they talked about everything else. Teenage masturbation habits. How she thought her toenails tasted. The nightmarish images on the screen of his own colonoscopy, the waves of throbbing internal flesh coming together in a wormish optical illusion.

After a particularly non-productive few weeks, when all they'd done was work and sit around, George had turned to Stella in bed. He'd stared sideways into her eyes and nearly asked. 'What do you think about kids?' But the question seemed so absurd. Once you'd said it, it was *out there*. You couldn't *unsay* it. And he really didn't know what he thought himself, and surely you should have some idea of your own

opinions before you asked someone else's? It was only sensible. If not sensible, polite.

Then there were days his mates' kids didn't have restaurant
meltdowns and were spectacularly cute with the mispronun-
ciations, and he'd thought – *maybe?* Then, there would be
the other types of days – the more frequent types – when his
bank account was down to zero before payday and he would
smell the teenage boy fug of the classroom and have to disci-
pline a twelve-year-old for smearing jism over another kid's
pencil case, *again.* And he'd think, *no. No, no, NO.*

But what he didn't expect was that when he and Stella
finally had the conversation, it would be with Stella's parents
there, and that he wouldn't even be an active participant.

*

Three years before the party, Margaret had answered the
door of 242 Cole Street.

Stella brandished the bouquet at her. 'Happy Birthday,
Mum! Sorry it's so unimaginative but I didn't know what to
get you.'

Margaret took the flowers with a smile. She peered into
the street and shut the door after them.

'What were you looking for out there?'

'A delivery driver. I haven't heard from Pete today.'

Stella took a beat. She smiled. 'Pete's very busy and he
didn't know what to get you, so he asked to go in on these
with me.'

Margaret stopped in the hallway. 'He did?'

Stella made eye contact with George. 'He specifically
asked me to get peonies because he knows how much you
like them.'

'He's so thoughtful.' Margaret took the flowers and took a

deep breath of their scent. She beamed. 'They're even lovelier now.'

Stella kept her smile in position. 'So what else have you got today?'

'Your father got me the new microwave we needed. And Cheryl from the newsagents – you know Cheryl?'

'Of course I do.'

'She brought round a nice ham.' Margaret reached up to the top of the sideboard in the hallway and pulled down a vase. 'Helen got me some bath things – it looked like an expensive make from the packaging, I think I was meant to know who they were. I'll look it up later. I really hope she didn't spend too much.'

'Lovely.'

Tommy entered the room through the back door. A minute later, Goldie followed. She jumped up at Stella and George, and they greeted her.

Tommy kissed Stella hello and shook George's hand with what felt like excessive formality. 'Have you started the driving lessons yet, George?'

George made himself give a polite smile. 'Nearly, Tommy.'

'Dad, stop it.' Stella put her hand on Tommy's arm. 'He'll do it in his own time. I know you think the man should drive, but you're just ridiculously old-fashioned. I can drive perfectly well.'

Tommy looked from Stella to George.

'He does his bit. We do the cleaning together. Even though he is a bit shit at it, he tries.'

George smiled at Tommy – a smile that said *It's true. What ya gonna do?*

The three sat at the kitchen table while Margaret busied about.

Mindlessly, George picked at a bunch of grapes in the fruit bowl and put one in his mouth.

Margaret rested the flowers on the side. 'Look what Isobel's made me at school!' she held up what might have been a picture of Margaret. It might have been a picture of someone very different. 'Isn't this lovely?'

'Charming,' George said.

Margaret ran a vase full of water. 'That's the thing about little ones. They make everything so much fun.'

Stella gave a loud sigh – a sigh designed for an audience.

George helped himself to another grape.

'I can't say how wonderful it is, seeing them grow and change. Admittedly, Charlie's still a baby but—'

'Mum. Stop it. You're completely transparent.'

Margaret unwrapped the flowers with her back to Stella. 'I'm not sure what you mean.'

'Shall we do this now?' Stella leaned forward and placed her hands palms down on the table. 'Have this conversation, once and for all, and then you can forever hold your peace?'

Margaret concentrated on cutting the peonies' stems. 'I don't know what you're talking about.'

Stella glanced at George and back. 'George and I have talked about having kids. And we've decided we're not doing it. It looks *way* too much like hard work.'

George stopped, a grape halfway to his mouth.

'We don't even have the energy for the car seats, so we can't even get past the first hurdle.' Stella waved a hand. 'It's all so much hassle. Putting the car seats *in* the car. Taking the car seats *out* of the car when you need to pick up other people. Working out if you *have the right number* of car seats when you pick up your kids' friends. *Talking* about car seats, even.'

George shoved his hands in his pockets. His left hand landed on a receipt. He fiddled with it.

Margaret and Tommy looked at each other.

'You don't have to say now,' Margaret said.

'It's none of our business,' Tommy said into the table.

'We've thought about it, Mum. We really have . . .'

George tried to keep his face still.

'. . . and we've watched everyone with their car seats and it looks like a right faff. We just don't think we have the headspace to deal with them.'

'There's a bit more to it than car seats,' Margaret said.

'I know, right?' Stella twisted in her chair impatiently. 'They're just the tip of the iceberg.'

George crunched the receipt between his fingers.

'I'm just saying.' Stella brushed a slice of hair out of her eyes. 'You know that "bag of flour" thing they do with teenage girls? They have to carry a bag of flour for a week without destroying it to show how challenging parenthood is? Which is laughably patronising to both parents and teenage girls, I feel, but that's by the by. I mean, *flour*. Jesus.'

She turned to Margaret, who said nothing. George had never seen Margaret look less sure of herself.

Stella turned back to face into the middle distance. 'If George and I ever started thinking about kids, we'd do the same with car seats. Carry a car seat around for a week. Keep putting it in and out of the car any time we went anywhere. Get a dose of cold, hard reality.'

Tommy and Margaret looked at each other again.

'And don't even get me started on the sun-cream thing,' Stella added. 'That's a full-time job in itself, it's not like when we were kids and you could just leave us playing all day on a beach with just a swipe of factor three.' Stella stood up. 'I've got something in my teeth from that sandwich at the service station. Back in five.'

She pushed her chair back and left the table, leaving George only to smile weakly at Margaret and Tommy.

'Well, that was a surprising conversation,' George said later, when Tommy and Margaret had left the room and he and Stella were on their own in the kitchen.

Stella took a grape from the bowl. 'It needed to be had.'

'But we haven't even talked about it.'

Stella threw the grape in her mouth. 'I know.'

'So why would you say we had?'

Stella took another grape. 'It's not what you think. I'm not making decisions for us.'

'It *sounds* like you're making decisions.'

'I'm just making it clear to them.' Stella chewed her grape. She wiped some juice from her mouth with the back of her hand. 'Whatever we decide – if we ever do decide to, or not – it's nothing to do with them.'

George thought about this. 'So you *don't* feel like that about car seats?'

'I just don't think it's a question for right now. And *definitely* not a question for my parents.' Stella reached for his hand. 'Besides, wouldn't you agree? Things are just fine as they are.'

'Yes.' George nodded thoughtfully. 'Yes, things are just fine as they are.'

34

Tommy held his cane tight throughout Margaret's Act Two speech. He kept glancing towards Nathan.

While Cheryl begged to be kept alive, Tommy edged closer to Nathan. He didn't see Goldie move, but she'd been at his feet at the start of the speech and was still here, across the room, at the end. She looked off colour, Tommy decided. She was sitting even closer to him than usual and, while there was a tray of fancy cheese-on-toast canapés on a dog-height side table, she hadn't helped herself to any of them.

After the speech, Tommy, turned to his son-in-law. 'Good evening.'

'Tommy.' Nathan shook his hand. 'What is Margaret playing at with that washing-up bowl? I thought it was a joke, but she's taken my phone, *seriously* taken it.'

Tommy patted him on the shoulder. 'It's *her* party, son.'

'I'm trying to explain it's actually rude, practically theft, but she just won't—'

'You got a second?'

'For you, Tom?' Nathan smiled. 'Always.'

Tommy narrowed his eyes. He guided Nathan round to the alcove so they could speak in private.

'I've made a big mistake,' Tommy said.

Nathan smiled. 'I'm sure it's not all that bad.'

'I want to come back to the shop.'

Nathan stopped smiling.

The silence stretched between them.

Nathan took a careful sip of his drink.

The silence stretched further.

Tommy looked up to see Helen walking into the room. She took one look at them, turned and hurried out again.

'Was that Helen?' Nathan asked. 'I need to—'

'I know it would have to be different. *I'd* work for *you*,' Tommy said quietly. 'Be your assistant. Your – shop boy.' His voice was barely audible now. 'I'd do the sweeping up and the cleaning and—'

'I don't need a shop boy.'

'You could still run the place, I'd just be there in the background. Margaret won't be able to keep working when she starts her treatment anyway. You'll need someone to cover the late shift.'

Nathan patted him on the shoulder. 'That's a big discussion. Let's talk about this another time.'

'It's not a big discussion. Not at all. You just say *that's great, Tommy, welcome back.* And then we all move on.'

Nathan took another sip of his drink.

'You just say, *welcome back to the fold,*' Tommy continued. '*It'll be great to have you on the team again, I value all of your experience.*' Tommy gave a wave of the hand. 'We don't have to do details now. Just agree in general it's a good idea.'

Nathan took *another* sip. Tommy wondered how thirsty this man could be.

Tommy puffed up his chest in a pre-emptive gesture of defiance. 'Helen thinks it's a good idea. And so does Margaret.'

Nathan had been raising his glass to his mouth again. He stopped. 'They do? *Really?*'

Tommy let the air out of his chest. 'No, but they got it when I explained it to them. They were very supportive.' *Were they?* Tommy wondered. 'They said nobody can twist down those overheads like I can. I leapt to shut those fridge doors a hundred times a day. I bet your electricity costs have tripled since I left.'

Tommy looked around for support; he spotted his wife by the patio doors.

'Margaret!' he shouted.

'What?'

'Can you come here?'

Margaret strode over. 'You wouldn't believe how many toilet rolls we've got through at this party, it beggars belief. Now, is Nathan still going on about the phone thing? Because I told him no one else has complained and—'

'I've just asked Nathan if I can go back to the shop.'

Margaret closed her eyes.

'And he hasn't answered me yet. But it's such an easy conversation to finish. What could be easier than saying *welcome back*?'

Margaret raised her gaze to look at Tommy.

He shifted his weight from foot to foot.

'Tommy.' Margaret glanced over his shoulder and back. 'There's so much other stuff to focus on today. I'm sure Helen would appreciate some help washing up.'

'I've been helping her lots today already.'

'And Nathan wants a day off today. He works so hard. He doesn't want to be thinking about work on a day like today.'

Nathan gave a quick nod.

Tommy looked from Margaret to Nathan. 'Why *not* talk about it now?'

Margaret took his hand in hers. 'Please don't ruin the party.'

It hit Tommy then. The kind voices. The lack of eye contact.

Tommy staggered backwards. He looked at Nathan. 'You don't want me back.'

Nathan looked at Margaret helplessly.

Tommy turned to Margaret. 'And *you* don't want me to come back either. *You.*'

'It's not that, Tommy. It's a big decision and we need to discuss it seriously.'

'Look, Tom,' Nathan said, 'I know you're upset about what happened at the supermarket—'

'What do you mean, "what happened at the supermarket"?' Tommy turned to Margaret. '*How* does he know?'

'Love,' Margaret touched his arm, 'Nathan and I talk in the shop. He could see I was distracted, so I told him. He's family. He's on your side.'

Tommy narrowed his eyes at Nathan. 'Is he?'

'Course I am, matey.'

Tommy looked up. 'Stella! George!'

The two were entering the room from different directions, Stella from the hallway, George through the patio doors.

Tommy gestured at them both. 'Come here, you two! Just wait till you hear this!'

The two glanced at each other. Slowly they walked over to join Tommy.

Tommy rocked on his heels. 'It appears Nathan doesn't want me to come back to work at the shop.'

Stella looked from Tommy to Nathan. George looked down at his bottle.

'And neither does your mother. How do you like that for gratitude?'

Nathan coughed. 'Tommy, please, let's not do this now.'

'You're just raw about what happened at the supermarket,' Margaret said. 'In time, you'll decide a little job is best. You don't need that responsibility.'

'What happened at the supermarket?' Stella asked.

'But you're going in for treatment, Margaret,' Tommy said. 'Nathan's going to need some more help.'

George jerked his head up. He studied Margaret's face carefully.

Margaret flapped a dismissive hand. 'How many times do I have to say "not now"?'

'But you won't be able to work there anymore, will you, Margaret?' George said quietly. 'Soon?'

'Stay out of this, George.'

'What happened at the supermarket?' Stella asked again.

Margaret spun round. 'Stella. Your father doesn't want to talk about it.'

Tommy took a deep breath. He mustn't let them see how much this hurt him. He had to protect his family from the truth.

'So,' Margaret turned and smiled at them all, like that conversation had never happened, 'George, I hope you've been telling everyone about Agnes' menopause.'

Tommy felt Margaret's hand slip into his. It felt like *she* thought she was protecting *him*.

He had to rally.

'It's been a great murder mystery, love. First Stella dies, then Cheryl.' Tommy made himself smile. 'Are we all going to be killed off tonight, one by one? Like that Agatha Christie set on the island, *Ten Little—*'

Stella shoved her hand out, palm first. 'No, Dad!'

Outrage swelled Tommy's chest. 'I wasn't going to say *that one*! I'm not completely out of touch, Stella. I was going to say "*Ten Little* Indians"!'

'But the book's been called *And Then There Were None* for decades! There was that TV adaptation a few years ago, don't you remember? Even that *Indian* title was junked by the eighties.'

Tommy let his cane drop. He heard it clatter to the floor.

Everyone was looking at him.

He put his hands to his face, trembling.

He rushed out of the room without picking up his cane, making sure he didn't look up till he was safely back in his shed, Goldie slumped silently next to him.

35

'What was that about?' George asked.

Margaret leaned down to pick up Tommy's cane. 'When he needs to go, he needs to go.' She rested the cane against the fire guard. 'It's a prostate thing, give it twenty years and you'll learn.'

Nathan turned to Stella and George. 'Thing is, Tommy's got himself into a bit of trouble at the supermarket.

Margaret frowned. 'Nathan. That's private.'

Nathan nodded. But Margaret knew as soon as she moved away, he'd tell the others. He wasn't even close to Stella and George – he just wanted to share this gossip with them. Have a good old laugh at poor Tommy.

After everything Margaret and Tommy had done for Nathan. *This* was how he rewarded them.

She was powerless. The supermarket story would be told somehow. It would either be told in the open now or in guarded whispers later.

Poor Tommy.

Margaret took a step away. She started collecting up glassware but she could still hear the conversation.

'The problem is,' Nathan said, 'he's used to working for himself. He's been in a bubble of his own rules for so long.'

'And now the bubble has burst?' George asked.

'Has it ever. He's made a series of *Carry On* comments to customers. He keeps telling women to "cheer up, it might never happen."'

Stella made a face. 'Ew.'

'He thinks he's being friendly,' Nathan added.

'I thought he only did that to me,' Stella said, 'and I always tell him to fuck off. I'm surprised he thinks it's friendly.'

'Another of his lines is "you'd look lovely if you smiled".'

'Dad?' Stella's eyes widened in horror. 'No.'

'And then he said something about the world foods aisle. Called it the "ethnic section".'

Stella closed her eyes.

'It caused quite a stir online,' Nathan said. 'He doesn't get it.'

Margaret shook her head angrily. She scrubbed furiously at a ring from a wet glass on the top of the TV cabinet. There was at least one selfish guest in this room who wasn't respecting the role of the coaster.

'He felt like king of his castle in the shop. He was making *jokes*. He thought women liked being told to "smile, it might never happen".' Nathan glanced around. 'Which is why he's *never* coming to work for me.'

'Have they sacked him at the supermarket?' Stella said.

'Worse, from his perspective. They asked him to go on a diversity course. He's resigned.'

'Why doesn't he just suck it up and do the course?' George asked.

Nathan shook his head. 'Margaret says he can't bring himself to.'

Margaret was about to say, 'It's too humiliating,' but she realised she wasn't meant to be listening. She collected more glassware together.

'How do you know all this?' Stella asked.

'Your mum,' Nathan said. 'She was upset when she came in for a shift one night. She wanted to tell me how unfairly Tommy had been treated. Of course, she doesn't understand either.'

Margaret lifted a vase and swept her cloth underneath it. She banged the vase down hard.

Behind her, the conversation stopped.

Margaret imagined there must be gesturing going on. *She can hear you.*

There were footsteps behind her. George moved next to her. He lifted the coasters up, so she could wipe underneath them. The coasters said *Three Cheers for White Wine.*

Were they still allowed *Three Cheers for White Wine?* Margaret wondered. Or did *that* offend somebody these days?

'Is Tommy OK?' George asked.

Margaret turned to face him. 'He's in the shed, I suspect. What do *you* think?'

George gave a nod.

'Can you imagine what it's like to be told you don't get the world anymore?' Margaret said. 'That the rules have changed and you're a laughing stock?'

'He's not a laughing stock.'

'You were all gossiping about him.'

'But no one was laughing. No one thinks it's funny. We know he loved that job. It's a shame he won't just suck it up and go on that diversity course.'

'He will never go within a hundred miles of that course.'

'But he'd be getting paid to sit down for an afternoon. They'd probably have coffee and biscuits. Maybe good biscuits, chocolate ones.'

'He can get biscuits at home.'

'He might learn something new. It's fun, learning something new.'

Margaret gave that statement a sniff.

George scratched his face. 'Margaret, can I borrow you for a second? I need to ask something.' He indicated the stairs.

Margaret put her cloth down and followed him.

As they walked, Margaret calmed a little. George must want her advice. He, at least, still respected her opinions.

'I hope I can help.' She slid her hand up the bannister. 'But if you want advice about how to deal with Stella when she's in one of her moods, I've no idea. She's always been like this, even when she was in the Brownies.'

'Shall we go in her old room?'

George closed the door behind them. Margaret looked around at the teenage books and the shelves of old jewellery. It seemed strange that George, a grown-up, was sleeping in a little girl's bedroom. She could automatically see George as a grown-up, in a way she struggled to see Stella. She had to force herself to remember how old Stella was. *Nearly forty. When you were her age, you had three teenagers.*

George indicated the chair in the corner and Margaret sat down.

George got down awkwardly onto the lilo. He steadied himself. 'It's something sensitive. You're not going to like it.'

Margaret sniffed. 'Everything's sensitive these days. It's like everyone's had a layer of skin peeled off.'

'Right.' George gave himself what appeared to be a nod of encouragement. He looked directly at her. 'You haven't told anyone here at the party about the cancer. Or the chemo.'

Margaret gave him a shake of the head. *Rude.* She shook her head again for no reason, trying to distract herself from the chill that had crept across her chest.

'And that's your prerogative.'

Margaret's chest tightened further. She straightened the duvet in a stiff gesture. '*Thank* you.'

'Why are you booking retreats and classes you're not going to be able to do?'

'That's my business.' Margaret took a deep breath. 'You shouldn't have been eavesdropping.'

George waited.

'Why are you doing this now?' She tried to control the tone of her voice. This was a time to be practical, not emotional. This was a day of *celebration*.

'Unless you've come into money,' George said, 'or had some kind of epiphany – you're acting ... unMargaretlike. Something doesn't fit together.'

Margaret looked at her hands. She knew she was going to have to have this conversation with someone, at some point – she just hadn't expected it to be George.

Margaret ignored the tightness in her chest. She gave George her fiercest glare.

He didn't seem to care. 'You are lying. To some of us, at least.'

She jerked her head up at that. 'Are you asking me whether I've been making up cancer?'

She stared at him. That was good. Outrage was much easier to process than fear.

'I'm confused. You've got to admit, the story's inconsistent.'

Margaret stretched her legs out in front of her, trying to release the tension. Her outrage was ebbing. She desperately tried to get hold of it again, but it was slipping away.

Margaret rubbed her eyes. 'I've got a year or two left, George. Maybe more, maybe less. And we all die eventually.'

George nodded.

'And I thought to myself, do I really want to spend that last year ill and weak and tired and in hospitals?'

George stared at her. 'You've paid for the retreats and dance classes because you're actually planning to *go* to them?'

Margaret held his gaze. 'Can this be the end of it now?'

'You're not having the treatment.'

Margaret jiggled her legs up and down, trying to make sure they didn't quiver.

'But why? You might get better with the treatment.'

'I *might*. Have you looked at the recovery rates?'

George didn't answer.

'Course you have.' She jiggled her legs again. 'I *might* get better with treatment. It's unlikely. So why would I do that to myself, when I could just plan to take the next year and do what I want with it? Stay out of hospitals?'

It was so obvious, when she said it out loud. So why she was having to stop her body trembling like this, she didn't know.

'Does Tommy know?'

Margaret looked at her skirt. 'He wouldn't understand. He gets emotional about this kind of thing. He's scared of death.'

'And you're not.'

'Absolutely not.' Margaret glanced away.

George gave Margaret a long look. 'Have you told your doctor? What did she say?'

Margaret sat up straighter. 'She said that they can't make me have the treatment, but that they strongly recommend it. She's covering her own backside, and good on her. She's all very nice and reassuring. They can't make me have the treatment unless I lack capacity to make decisions.' She glared at him. 'Would you say I lack capacity?'

George didn't say anything.

'So, well done, Miss Marple.' Margaret stood up abruptly. 'Don't mention it to Stella. She'll only ask intrusive questions. And, George—' she focused on him closely – 'I don't need this today. We're doing the piñata now, then we're doing the speeches in a few minutes. So you need to be downstairs and smiling by then, please. Promise me.'

'Margaret, wait—'

But Margaret made sure she was up and out of the room, hurrying down the stairs, before he had the chance to ask anything else.

36

George looked across Stella's bedroom to the armchair where Margaret had been. He twisted his hands together.

How many times did George have to learn the lesson that life was better if you knew as little about it as possible? Retaining plausible deniability was his main aim.

This was *bad*.

He couldn't face Stella. Margaret might be able to compartmentalise and self-justify, but George didn't have the skills of self-deceit, or the bullheadedness, or whatever it was that meant Margaret could happily lie to everyone, including herself, and still *actually* sleep at night.

'What are you doing up here on your own?'

George looked up to see Cheryl in the doorway. 'Just – thinking, really. Sometimes you can have too much of your extended family, you know?'

Cheryl nodded. 'Of course. Though I don't know that, really – my boy James married a lovely Swede and they moved to Gothenburg.' She smiled brightly. 'But I'm sure you're right.'

George shifted his position on the lilo.

'Margaret said I could come up here to look for a cardigan. She keeps her old ones in Stella's room. She's so petite these days since taking up Zumba.' Cheryl looked down at her black robe. 'And I feel silly in this outfit now I'm dead. I could go home to get changed, but I don't want to miss any clues.'

'I'm sorry to hear you died,' George said. 'Deepest sympathies.'

Cheryl accepted his sympathies with a nod. She indicated the wardrobe. 'Do you mind?'

'Please.' George waved a hand. 'Help yourself.'

He watched Cheryl pull out two cardigans on hangers. She held them both up to study them.

'I like the turquoise one,' George said.

'You do?' She dropped the rejected navy cardigan onto the bed and held the turquoise one up over her robe. 'Nice and jolly?'

'Very jolly.'

'Good.' She pushed her sleeves into the cardigan and fastened it across her chest. It sat awkwardly, scrunching up the front of the robe beneath.

'Cheryl.' George got out the card from his pocket. 'Don't read too much into being dead.' He unfolded the card. 'Margaret would still want you to investigate. In fact,' he held out the card, 'she asked me to tell you this.'

Cheryl took the card and started to read.

'Aha!' Cheryl's eyes looked instantly lighter. 'So Agnes *wasn't* pregnant. She was overeating!' She clucked her teeth. 'Oh, I've got the measure of you, Margaret. I *know* Ellie's necklace is a red herring.'

'How've you worked that out?'

'I just notice things.' She gave him a look for longer than necessary and put the card down.

George shivered. He mustn't have eaten enough today. It had suddenly got cold in here.

'You know, I caught Stella in the newsagent's once.

Stealing.' Cheryl held up the navy cardigan as though she was studying it. 'I could tell what she was going to do before she did it. The look on her face was furtive.'

Something about the way she was talking made a prickle cross George's neck. Under the breeziness, there was an intensity he hadn't seen before.

Cheryl straightened the cardigan back on the hanger. 'It was Stella's first year of high school. I caught her on the way out of the shop.'

George heard whooping and cheering from outside. The kids must have started that piñata. And there was that laugh, again and again – Margaret's laugh.

'I put my hand on her arm.' Cheryl placed the rejected cardigan back in the wardrobe. 'She tried to wrestle me off, but I knew. I fished that packet of cola bottles out of her pocket.' Cheryl closed the wardrobe door. 'She said she was sorry. I told her if I ever caught her again, I'd tell Margaret and Tommy. I asked her to help with the next stocktake and she did. Not another word was said.'

Cheryl turned round to look in the mirror. 'But I didn't tell her parents. In case you're wondering if I tell Margaret everything – I don't.' Cheryl straightened her cardigan. 'Especially things she doesn't want to know.'

She turned. The two made eye contact.

She turned back to look at her reflection. 'Now, I want to go and watch that piñata.' She smoothed down her robe. 'I've never seen one before and it sounds wonderful.'

With that, she left the room, leaving George to wonder if she could have possibly meant what he thought she meant.

He closed his eyes. *Not now.*

No, now he had to think about how to tell Stella about Margaret.

If Margaret didn't tell her, George was going to have to. But how?

He and Stella hadn't been able to talk for a long time. Often, they'd found themselves arguing about trivia – and often, later on, George had wondered whether he'd taken the right corner in the argument or whether he agreed, secretly, with Stella's side. And he *just knew* sometimes Stella argued points in absolute terms, when her actual view was fuzzier, and sometimes even *opposite* to what she was saying.

He and Stella couldn't talk anymore. Not about serious stuff. Not without it going weird.

Like the *Jurassic Park* conversation. The one that felt so seminal.

The one that, on reflection, had felt like the beginning of the end.

*

A year before, George had walked into the flat after school as usual. He threw his keys into the bowl on the hall table and frowned.

Stella's keys were already there.

He walked through to the kitchen. 'Stella?'

Stella sat at the table, still in her woolly hat and gloves.

'How come you're back so early?'

'I got my period,' she said dully.

George closed his eyes. She hadn't even given him time to take off his coat. 'Definitely? Are you sure?'

She just looked at him.

He shook his coat off his shoulders. He bent down and put his arms round her, reaching down into the chair, hugging her from above.

She was limp in his arms. 'I think this might be it for me.'

215

'We don't have to make any decisions today. And there's always IVF.'

'I can't do the hormones and the hoping. And shelling out thousands of pounds we haven't got.'

He said nothing.

'We weren't even sure we wanted kids.' Stella balled her hands into fists. 'We just said "if it happens it happens". And now it hasn't happened. I just want life to be simple and fun, back to how it was. No more thinking or wondering.'

'Today's not the day to make any decisions,' he said again.

'Oh, you're so fucking balanced about this, aren't you?'

George released her immediately, like he was dropping something toxic.

He turned away. 'It's hard for both of us.'

George stood in the kitchen, across the table from Stella in her gloves. He didn't sit down. He didn't know why, but he didn't.

He took a deep breath. 'We can adopt.'

'I'm not sure I want to.'

George frowned. 'They'd still be our kids.'

'It would still be out of our control, and we wouldn't be able to get on with our lives. And I'm not sure whether I ever really wanted this, or whether I'm trying to just fill some kind of "what happens next" hole. Maybe the fact it isn't working is a sign we shouldn't be doing this. You know, *life shows the way.*'

George slammed his hands on the table in frustration. 'That's *Jurassic Park.*'

'I know that.'

'That's *Jurassic Park* and you're quoting it wrong. It's life *finds* a way. And it's basically the opposite of what you're saying. It means that—'

'I know what it means. But what do you think? Should we keep trying?'

'You know me, I don't have strong views about anything.'

'*Fuck you!*'

At the fury in Stella's voice, George took a step back.

'You *should* have strong views on this one.' Stella lowered her voice. 'If you're going to have one opinion in your life – just *one* – it should be about this.'

'Are you asking me to make the decision for us? You'd be happy if I did?'

'I'm tired of this. I don't want to be upset and confused anymore. I want to know what's happening, a hundred per cent, either way.' Stella spoke downwards, into her folded arms. 'You just always get to be the calm one. The one who doesn't make decisions or push things forward. It all gets put on me. Like you saying you'll get round to booking driving lessons and then you don't. It isn't fair to put everything on me.'

George slammed his hands on the table again. 'If you say the words "mental load" again, I'm walking out of this flat.'

Stella kept looking downwards.

'I don't *care* about learning to drive. I've *said* I'll get round to it, I just haven't yet. Driving lessons are expensive and it's not like we could even afford two cars, and I can walk to school, so I don't see the point. And you *knew* what I was like,' George tried to control his voice, 'when you married me. You can't start minding a fundamental part of my personality. That's changing the rules.'

'I need someone to tell me what to do about the kid thing,' Stella said into her lap. 'I'm too confused to work it out.'

'That's not *us*, Stella. You want us to be *actually different people*.' George took a deep breath. 'Let's take some time. You need to relax. They say that with trying for a baby, getting anxious is the last thing—'

'Oh, keep going, that's lovely.' Stella's sarcasm was humourless. 'You're telling me your sperm senses my anxiety and says *fuck no to that, I'm not into high-maintenance women?*'

'That's not what I'm saying. Of course.'

'Maybe your sperm just don't like my eggs. Maybe we're not suited to have babies. Maybe we just repel each other because we're wrong together. Like angry magnets.'

'Angry magnets,' George repeated.

'Or maybe your sperm just can't be arsed. Maybe they're just not sure what they think because *you're* not sure, so they've got no direction.' Stella gave a violent shake of the head. 'I think some things are bigger than science. Maybe this was wrong from the start. You and me. And our bodies know.'

George took a step back. 'Are you really saying we should split up and go and have kids with other people? How can you say that?'

Stella stared straight ahead, like she couldn't even hear him.

'I thought you and me was it,' George said. 'Blankets on knees, osteoporosis together. Rocking chairs.'

'That was before,' Stella said. 'Before we tried all this and it all went wrong.'

'So what are you saying?'

'I don't know,' Stella said.

*

George didn't want to remember this anymore. He didn't want to remember this ever again.

He brushed hair from his eyes.

He looked down at the worn carpet of Stella's bedroom and took a breath. He tried to focus on the cheering from the garden.

Eventually, George pushed himself up from the lilo. He looked at himself in the mirror, observed the lines between his eyebrows and made himself smile.

He watched himself in the mirror as his smile faded to nothing. It was several minutes before he was finally able to head back to the party.

37

Helen was emptying the washing-up bowl into the sink when she heard her mother's distinctive footsteps hurrying down the stairs.

'Piñata time!' Mum's voice was sing-song.

Helen swilled the sink free of the last dregs from the washing-up. She wiped her hands on a tea towel and headed out into the garden.

'Hi.' Nathan grazed his cheek against hers. He'd been here for half an hour and this was the first time they'd greeted each other. And this felt wrong. Too polite. Of all the emotions Helen had expected to feel after being married for so long, politeness wasn't one of them.

'I'm pleased you're here,' Helen said.

'I'm not pleased I'm here,' Nathan said. 'I've just been accosted by your father.'

Helen noticed something liquid on the flower bed. A chunky puddle of beige and pink gunk. One of the kids must have been sick.

Helen glanced at her mother, then kicked some soil over the vomit before anyone else noticed.

Stella walked up to her and Nathan. 'Classy.'

'I'm guessing it was a child,' Helen said.

Stella sniffed. 'I suppose so.' To Helen's surprise, Stella

hooked her arm in hers. 'It's a long time since I've thrown up on Mum's flower bed.'

Helen watched Mum place the donkey on the 'hook' – the wire top of a coat hanger, tied to the washing line. How had her mum even heard about piñatas? They weren't around for Helen's childhood – or they were around, they just happened to kids in books or on TV, like trick or treating or chocolate advent calendars. Piñatas seemed way too foreign and materialistic and all-round twenty-first century for her mother. She must have seen them on *The One Show*.

Helen clutched Stella closer. She hadn't known it till right this moment, but she hated piñatas.

Stella gave her a surprised look, but didn't say anything.

Helen looked at the donkey again. Obviously, it wasn't a real one – it didn't even *look* like a donkey, being multi-coloured and made of the cheapest cuts of crepe paper – but, still, the activity implied a cruelty Helen didn't want to think about.

People were gathering in the garden around her, walking tentatively, kitten heels sinking into grass.

Helen saw a glint of movement in the shed and beckoned for her father to come out.

There was rustling and scraping from within. Eventually, he emerged.

'Your lawn is magnificent,' Adele said to Mum.

Mum nodded.

Helen tried to imagine herself ever accepting a compliment like that.

Goldie trotted out of the shed. She sniffed at the pool of soil-covered vomit.

Stella flapped her hands at Goldie. 'Shoo.' She looked up.

'Dad? Will you lock Goldie in the shed for the piñata? All those sweets are going to hit the ground.'

Dad didn't say anything, but he reached down to Goldie's collar and steered her into the shed.

Charlie slipped his hand into hers. 'What's a piñata?'

'It's a toy,' Helen said. 'A toy donkey. You hit it. With a stick.'

'Why do we hit a donkey?'

'So sweets come out.' Helen paused. 'But it's not a real donkey. Sweets definitely don't come out if you hit a real donkey.'

'How do you know?' Charlie asked.

'I just do,' Helen said.

'Have you ever hit a real donkey?'

'I just *promise* it doesn't happen,' Helen said.

She glanced at Isobel and glanced away. She rubbed her neck violently.

'Rosa,' Mum crouched in front of her neighbour's toddler. 'The youngest goes first. Do you want me to help you reach the donkey?'

Mum handed the child Rosa the rounders bat. Rosa gripped it with both hands, but, still, the bat drooped heavily. Mum lifted Rosa by the waist so she could reach the donkey on the washing line.

Rosa took a swipe with the heavy bat. It barely glanced it. The donkey twisted gently in the breeze.

'Woo!' Mum placed Rosa on the floor again. 'Nearly!' She smiled brightly and turned to the crowd. *Next*. 'Charlie!'

Helen watched her son step up to her mother. Rosa handed him the bat and he took a step towards the donkey, studying it. He swiped upwards with the bat.

Charlie made better contact than Rosa had. The donkey

swung jerkily on the line this time; a sliver of dislodged crepe paper wafted to the ground. Still, the donkey stayed clearly intact.

One by one, in reverse age order, the younger kids took turns to swipe at the donkey. The swipes were accompanied by screams and shouts of excitement, but the donkey clung resolutely on to the washing line.

Watching all these children hitting the donkey, knowing Isobel was waiting, a sense of panic filled Helen's throat. She span around to say something to Nathan.

What could she say? *Nathan. I'm drowning?*

She turned back to look at the donkey.

'Isobel, your turn,' her grandmother said brightly.

The garden hushed. The crowd of kids seemed to split down the middle.

Helen clutched Stella more tightly still.

Isobel took precise little steps through the crowd. She took the rounders bat and adjusted it in her hands carefully. She stood in a baseball stance. She pulled her arms back, preparing to swing.

Helen turned away.

At the sound of impact, the children roared.

The donkey hit the floor with a crispy thud.

Helen closed her eyes. She heard the rustling of wrappers as the children gathered round, clawing at the donkey's guts.

'Your girl's got a good arm,' Scott said.

Helen looked at Isobel. She looked to Charlie, who held the donkey carcase to his chest, prying the stomach further open. Other children crowded round it now, pulling and shoving to get to the innards, unwrapping the sweets.

'And a very calm way about her,' Scott added. 'Her face

wasn't screwed up in concentration like the other kids. She makes a natural batswoman.'

Helen made herself smile. She watched Isobel stand up from the crowd of children, leaving the others to the sweets on the lawn. Isobel picked the last few pieces of crepe paper off the coat hanger hook. She let them fall to the floor and breeze along the grass.

She didn't pick up a single sweet.

38

Isobel waited for the grown-ups to leave the garden, then headed back to the ginnel at the back of the house. The little kids mingled around her while she stood in the centre like the Pied Piper.

But even with all her little rats on the case, rooting through their parents' handbags and her Grandma's drawers, they hadn't managed to get much more paper. Grandma was guarding the toilet roll, and only one pizza delivery leaflet had come through the door in the meantime.

The tiger boy came running up, offering up a roll of kitchen foil with both hands.

'No good,' Isobel said firmly.

Tiger boy's foil drooped.

Isobel looked down at the fire bucket. It was black now on the inside, with bits stuck to it. It looked so empty.

One of the daisy girls' mouths was stained raspberry from sweets.

'You look sad.'

'No I don't,' Isobel replied. She watched the girl put another sweet in her mouth.

All those kids had loved the piñata. It was almost like they enjoyed the piñata more than the fire. Isobel needed to do something special now, to show the kids the magic of fire.

But they didn't have any paper, or fuel. One of the daisy girls had got hold of another lighter, but what was the point of a lighter if there was nothing to light?

Isobel had looked through Grandma's kitchen cupboards, considering options – *Pasta? Salad cream? Flour? Ketchup?* – but there was nothing she thought would work.

It turned out, without the Internet, Isobel didn't know enough about fire.

Grandma had said there would be fireworks later, but fireworks weren't the same. They were good, but they were only so much fun from a distance, and her parents had always been really clear: only grown-ups were allowed to set off fireworks.

Watching fireworks was like going to the zoo and not being allowed to touch the monkeys.

Isobel scraped a foot against the rotting leaves in the ginnel. She watched the little kids scoffing their piñata sweets.

At the sound of voices, she looked up.

The eyeliner boy and the two teenage girls let themselves in through the side gate of Grandma and Grandpa's house.

Isobel rushed through the gate from the ginnel into her grandparents' garden. She slowed as she walked across the lawn towards them. She heard noises behind her and knew the little children must have followed.

Isobel turned and scowled. 'Go away!'

The eyeliner boy turned to Charlie. 'Hi, kid. Give me some of those sweets.'

Charlie, surprisingly, gave him a handful.

Manga T-shirt girl took a sweet from Charlie and un-wrapped it. 'Where did you get all these?'

'We did a piñata.' Isobel puffed herself up. 'I was the one who hit it properly. I was the one who broke the donkey.'

The eyeliner boy turned to look at the girl with messed-up hair. He had laughter in his eyes.

Messed-up-hair girl and manga girl both snorted.

Eyeliner boy turned back to Isobel. 'You hit a *toy donkey* with a *little stick*.'

Isobel looked at her feet. 'Not a stick. A rounders bat.'

'A rounders bat.' The boy looked from Isobel to the teenage girls. 'And you're telling us this *why*?'

Manga T-shirt girl rolled her eyes at Isobel. 'How about, little one,' she leaned down towards her, 'you leave some sweets and take your troop to go and play fairies in the garden?'

Isobel blinked at her.

The older three looked at each other and laughed.

Some of the younger kids started laughing, even though they were too stupid to know what they were laughing at.

Isobel turned slowly. She walked back to the house on her own, like she'd been planning to do that all along.

As she walked, she bit the ulcer at the side of her mouth, hard. Pain rushed in. Isobel stopped herself shouting out. She tasted the piece of her skin that was floating loose in her mouth. She chewed it. She was eating meat made of herself, and she didn't even care.

Everyone was ignoring her. Everyone that mattered.

And, for that, they were going to pay.

39

After the piñata, there was a bottleneck at the patio doors, with people milling around and funnelling inside.

Tommy automatically headed back towards the shed.

Helen grabbed his arm and spun him off track. 'It's speeches next.'

'I don't want to do speeches.' Tommy smiled benignly at a neighbour. 'Not *now*.' Tommy turned to Helen. 'Your *husband* doesn't want me to come back to the shop.'

'Oh. I'm sorry to hear that.' She didn't look surprised.

'He thinks I'm past it.'

Helen shook her head firmly. 'No, he doesn't.'

'A liability.'

'I *know* he didn't say that. What a ridiculous suggestion.'

'And now your mother wants to do speeches and how can I do a speech at a time like this?'

Helen brushed flour from her sleeve. 'Mum is a force of nature, maybe it's best not to fight it. Besides, our parcels are ready to come out of the oven. Do you want to help me hand them out?'

Tommy sighed. He could hand out salmon parcels, he supposed. But what was the point?

The sound of clinking, a spoon against glass, came through from the lounge. Wordlessly, Tommy let Helen steer him inside. He let her hand him a glass of Prosecco.

Stella caught up with them. 'Dad, is it true?'

Helen gave her a *not now* look.

Stella kept her gaze focused on Tommy. 'Have you been going around telling women to "cheer up, it might never happen"?'

Stella linked arms with him. Tommy tried to work out if the gesture was supportive or to keep him captive.

'People say that all the time,' Tommy said gruffly to his daughter/captor. 'There's nothing wrong with it. I've said it to *you* before.'

'But do you remember, whenever you've said that to me, I said it made me want to punch you in the face?'

Tommy frowned. 'Really?' Admittedly, it did ring a bell. He'd always put it down to Stella's oversensitivity.

'If you want any help in understanding the context and the situation—'

'Oh, I understand the *situation*,' Tommy said. 'I understand the situation all right.'

'Dad. It's a patronising thing to say.'

Tommy whirled round to face her, shaking off her arm. '*I* don't understand what it's like to be patronised?'

'Stella, you're being a bit uptight about this.' Scott had appeared from apparently nowhere to join their conversation. He gave Stella a smile and turned to Tommy. 'Some women can overreact to this kind of thing, but most reasonable women think it's fine.'

'Thank you!' Tommy said gruffly.

'"Uptight"? "Most reasonable women"? I have no idea, whatsoever' – Stella got momentarily distracted by Scott's shiny shoes – 'why you'd say that.'

Scott smiled kindly. 'Think about it.'

Stella brought her palms up in what was clearly frustration. 'Your view is even worse! You definitely shouldn't have that opinion. It's bad enough in someone of Dad's generation.' Stella took a breath. 'And another thing' – she said hotly – 'while we're on the topic of being patronising—'

The sound of the spoon hitting glass again interrupted her.

Stella let her arms fall to her side. She muttered something, clearly finishing the conversation with herself. It was something she used to do as a child, Tommy reflected. If she couldn't win an argument, she'd win it to herself, on her own, afterwards.

The crowd in the lounge grew quiet. Margaret stepped atop the wheeled librarian's stool with a flute of Prosecco held aloft.

In front of Tommy, people moved to the side and smiled at him. Tommy realised they were making space so he could go and stand next to his wife.

He stepped into position.

Margaret gave a bright all-room smile. She'd reapplied her lipstick, Tommy noticed. The deep red colour brought out the yellow of her teeth. He wondered whether he should tell Margaret that she looked so much prettier with something softer, something pink. But he thought – *No. Women don't want me making helpful comments anymore.*

Margaret clinked her spoon against her glass again. 'I didn't really want to do speeches till Pete got here, but he's clearly delayed at work' – Tommy noticed Stella roll her eyes – 'so it's best we go ahead.'

Tommy stood up straighter.

'This isn't part of the mystery,' Margaret clarified. She looked down at him from her librarian's step. 'Tommy and I have been married for forty years.'

Tommy stood below her, in her shadow. Robin to her Batman. Smiling, and smiling and smiling.

'And it feels the right time to take stock.' Margaret glanced at Tommy again. 'Because most of the time, we don't celebrate things when they're actually right there in front of us, and it's imperative we enjoy what we have while it lasts. So I'm so pleased you're all here to celebrate with us on this special occasion.'

She glanced at George who was just entering the room.

She looked back at the crowd. 'My husband, Tommy Foy. What can I possibly say about Tommy?'

Tommy made himself beam.

Nathan held a glass up towards him, as though making eye contact. But Nathan held his gaze a clear inch to the side of Tommy's, operating it like a dodgy gun sight.

Tommy's hand gripped tighter on his own glass.

'I don't want to get all gushy in front of the kids—'

'Is that us?' Stella said.

'But if you'll allow me to gush, just a little, Tommy is the greatest man I've ever known.'

Tommy frowned.

There was an awkward silence.

Margaret smiled brightly.

'Why did you say that?' Tommy asked.

Margaret shrugged and kept smiling to the crowd.

'But – that's patently untrue,' Tommy said. 'I'm adequate, more than adequate, but the *greatest*? That's not me.'

Margaret gave a dismissive wave.

'It's nice to get a compliment,' Tommy said, 'don't think I don't appreciate it, but can't you use an honest compliment? *He fills up the watering can after he's used it. He knows his grana padano from his parmigiana and he always remembers to bleed the radiators.'*

There was nervous laughter in the crowd.

'He doesn't mind being the one who takes the dog out last thing before bed.'

Margaret smiled indulgently at him. 'The greatest man – *to me*. How about that?'

'That's even worse,' Tommy said.

'Everyone else here thinks you're great too,' Margaret said.

Tommy noticed Nathan smiling at him again. He glared back, to show Nathan he didn't have Tommy's permission to smile. Tommy wasn't a man for drama, but there was something about this situation – all these people watching him, the feeling of being patted on the head – that made him want to throw his glass in the air and walk out.

Because no one pats a man on the head who's just smashed a glass all over them. It doesn't happen.

A low buzzing sound came from somewhere. George jerked something out of his pocket under Margaret's unblinking glare. He made a *one minute* sign with a finger and hurried out of the room, putting his phone to his ear.

'So thank you everyone for coming,' Margaret said. 'We're lucky to have such good friends and family around to help us celebrate.'

Tommy gave a louder-than-intended sniff.

She narrowed her eyes at Tommy. 'Do you want to say anything?'

Tommy cleared his throat. 'Forty-two years ago, I met the most beautiful girl in the world – not the most beautiful girl *to me*, I mean *actually* the most beautiful in the world – in a chip shop in Stretford. She was ordering a cone of chips and carrying a handbag decorated with beads, and she had the loveliest laugh. The forty years I've been with her have been the happiest I could have imagined.'

He'd said all this before, he realised. He'd said this at their twenty-fifth wedding anniversary party, with all the same people here. He might even be wearing the same tie.

He looked down at his tie. It *was* an old favourite. But *how* old?

Tommy turned back to address the audience. 'My wife. My shop. My family. For forty years, I had everything I needed. I was a lucky man.'

'Hear, hear,' a deep voice said.

'I was *such* a lucky man.'

The crowd held an unnatural stillness.

Tommy lifted his glass. 'Enjoy the party.'

He left the room abruptly, not knowing where he was heading until he shut the shed door behind him and slumped back into his wicker chair, next to the subdued Goldie.

He watched George pace outside, between the oak tree and the shed, talking hurriedly into his phone. He was gesturing with his free hand, with what looked like desperation.

George paced closer to the shed and stopped. 'I think if I don't do it now, I'll keep things going when things aren't right.' George touched the tree lightly with the knuckles of his free hand. 'Because I'm lazy. So it feels like I have to do it now. I have to give myself some time alone, or I'll look back in five years and—' He paused for a moment. 'That's fine. I deserved that.'

Tommy wasn't actively listening, he just wasn't doing anything else. You can't sit in silence if someone is filling that silence with words.

'Nancy?' George's voice was filled with uncertainty. 'You sound really angry.'

Nancy?

'They won't.' George sounded exhausted. 'They'll say I'm a lazy good-for-nothing, but they don't care about the length of my legs.'

Tommy felt himself frown.

'I know,' George continued. 'I know. It's not an easy conversation for you.'

Tommy sat forward in his wicker chair.

And now, Tommy was properly listening.

40

Of course Nancy rang back during the speeches. There was no worse time to ring than during the speeches, and that was just how George's day was going, wasn't it?

But George couldn't ignore her again. He wouldn't put it past Margaret actually picking his pocket for the phone like an elderly Artful Dodger.

Despite the awful timing George rushed outside, buzzing phone held tightly in hand.

Margaret would get him for this.

He reached his pacing tree and answered the phone. 'Nancy. Hi.'

'How's it going?' The sound of Nancy's voice pulled something within him. 'Is it awful?'

George turned to look through the patio doors, at the speeches still going on in the lounge. Tommy looked *angry*. Angrier than a man soaking up goodwill from friends and family should look.

'Yep,' George said to Nancy. 'Awful.'

'Stella owes you for this.' The kindness in Nancy's voice was hard to take. 'In what way is it awful?'

'Stella's family keep saying what a good guy I am.' George paced under the oak tree and turned and paced in the opposite direction. 'I *swear* they never said that when we were together.'

'Enjoy it while it lasts. They'll say different when they know about the divorce.'

'I hope so,' George said. 'Or it's going to be a pretty shit time for Stella. Unless . . .'

'Unless?'

'Unless – maybe they *do* know we've split up, that's why they're saying I'm a good guy? Is this whole party just an elaborate exercise in making me feel bad?'

Nancy laughed. 'I don't think people use their parties to make others feel bad.'

'They don't?' George said hopefully.

'After they know about the divorce, you'll be Satan. They'll say there was always something a bit shifty about you. Shifty eyes, they'll say you had.'

George stopped pacing. 'Do I have shifty eyes?'

Nancy's laugh made his stomach twist.

'That's just an example,' she said. 'That's not really what they'll say.'

'No?' George knew he was getting distracted from his task. 'Then what *will* they say?'

'How would I know?' Nancy laughed again – *why wouldn't she stop?* 'Anyway, a few hours down, can't be more than a few to go, right?'

'Right.' She definitely didn't need to hear about the sleeping arrangements. Not while he was ending it.

Not that he was *exactly* ending it. Not right this second.

At this point in the conversation, Nancy could be forgiven for not realising he was ending it at all.

George's gaze settled on the hook on the washing line. It glinted and twisted in the breeze. Without the piñata attached, the hook looked sinister.

'Nancy, I had to call you.'

'I'm pleased you did. It's odd for me, you being there.'

George looked at his feet. 'I'm feeling more and more un-comfortable. About us.'

'What?'

'All this family stuff has reminded me how raw everything is. How I'm not in a position to start anything new. I need to end this now, before our lives get any more entwined.'

He waited.

She didn't say anything.

It's not you.

He didn't say that. He wanted to, but he didn't.

'I'm feeling guilty about letting you down in the future, when I really should be thinking about me. I need to work out what I want, and I don't want to be the bad guy, now or then. I've got swept along with things, but I think I need to stop sweeping. For both of us.'

George waited.

He took his phone away from his ear, to check he hadn't accidentally put it on mute.

Nope.

He put the phone back to his ear. 'It's not fair of me to be with you now. I'm not ready.'

'Don't I get to decide what's fair on me?' Nancy's voice no longer had laughter in it.

'Of course.'

'Don't tell me you don't want to *hurt* me or treat me like a fragile woman who's being taken advantage of, having sex with a *big bad man*, acting like you're doing me a favour, and—'

'It's nothing to do with that. It's to do with me being a fuckwit. You deserve better.'

'Deserve,' Nancy repeated tonelessly.

'Deserve,' George said firmly.

'You want to be a good guy by dumping me, and you think if you slag yourself off it makes you nicer?'

'Of course not.' Oh, Nancy had the measure of him all right.

'Even though dumping me doesn't make you a good guy. It makes you an *absolute shit*.'

This change of pace made George pause. 'A short-term shit though, if I end it now.'

'There's no such thing as a *short-term shit*.'

'I'm so sorry I've hurt you.'

'Are we talking about you being a good guy again? Is that what all this is about?'

There was a pause.

'You absolute knob.'

George blinked.

'And you still told me about your problems at the party – how selfish is that? Just squeezing out the last bit of girl-friend support while you could? How much of a *good guy* thing to do is that?'

George looked at the tree in desperation. He balled up his fist and lightly touched the tree in a practice punch, feeling the bark against his knuckles, imagining what it would be like to follow the punch through. To just hit this tree right now, see the blood explode outwards, feel that rush of lovely distracting pain.

Nancy's voice softened again. 'Look, let's not talk now. This must be a strange day for you.'

'I' – George was finding it hard to follow the jolting turns of this conversation – 'I think if I don't do it now, I'll keep things going when things aren't right.' He practice-punched the tree again. 'Because I'm lazy. So it feels like I have to do it now. I have to give myself some time alone, or I'll look back in five years and—'

'Fuck you then.'

'That's fine. I deserve that.'

'Don't you say *that's fine*. You don't get to approve. And don't you *dare* text me at midnight in two years' time, when you've had a drink and there's nothing on TV.' Her tone sharpened by the second. 'Do you want to know what your in-laws will say about you? When you're gone?'

'Nancy?' George said. 'You sound really angry.'

'They'll say that your forehead's too small, and your body is too long for your legs.'

George hit the shed lightly. 'They won't. They'll say I'm a lazy good-for-nothing, but they don't care about the length of my legs.'

George touched his forehead, felt the size of it, measuring it with his forefinger and thumb.

'I didn't mean that,' Nancy said.

'I know.'

'I'm just trying to be cruel.'

'I know.'

'You're bringing out the worst in me.'

'It's not an easy conversation for you,' George said.

'How understanding of you. Hope you feel like the *good guy* now.'

'Nanc—'

Nancy hung up.

George sank onto the wooden bench next to the bird feeder.

He was so engrossed in thinking how badly he'd handled

that conversation – really, he couldn't have managed it any worse – that he didn't take in the security light coming on or the sound of footsteps striding towards him.

'Who's Nancy, George?'

41

Stella watched the speeches, distracted. She couldn't pinpoint when the feeling had started.

Maybe when she and George had been joking about poor, downtrodden, murdered Agnes.

Maybe when the two had teased her mother about the mobile phones or when they were laughing together at Stella's dead-sci-fi-creature parcels. Or maybe, above all, it was reflecting on the fact that George had come here today for her family. That he was going to spend the night here, even though he hated her.

She'd been angry at this man for so long. Yet, inexplicably, the anger was dissipating.

And this was cause for alarm. She felt the need to gather her anger up, nurture it, fan it with oxygen.

And it was getting worse. Now, during the speeches, George had got a phone call and hurried out of the room under her mother's icy glare. He gave Mum that wave of both acknowledgement and dismissal, and Stella felt that confusing fondness bloom further in her chest.

Because that guy in the garden – the guy who was, right now, pissing her mum off by taking a call – felt more like family than anyone else in the house.

Was it just, Stella wondered, the proximity to her parents

and sister (and the kind-of proximity to her absent brother), to her kin, the people in her life she was *meant* to fit in with, that made her realise how much better she fitted with George?

Stella had a word with herself. *I just need to make more effort with my family. Especially Helen. That's all.*

Stella half-listened to the end of her parents' speeches. She tried to shake the unwelcome feeling off. Unwelcome, because her time with George, at the end, had been so exhausting. She *liked* being single. She *liked* having no one else in the house to have to think about, to argue with or resent. Life was simpler this way.

Stella saw her dad head to the shed. She smiled as she watched George pace outside on his phone. She even found herself thinking fondly about things that used to irritate her. His keenness for afternoon naps. His inability to pass a newsagent without coming out with fizzy snakes or some other over-bright, over-sweet semblance of food he was thirty years too old for. That day's observations that his butler character, Mr Owlish, was a seedy authority figure, who took way too much interest in the weight and hormonal statuses of his female staff.

No. Stella had to draw a line. *That's definitely not right. Those stops for fizzy snakes were really annoying. Stop romanticising it.*

Stella looked at Scott. Scott, of the retro gender opinions, the patronising comments. Scott, who owned the building that housed her family's business and thought that was a personal achievement. Scott, who George had told her earlier, hid the fact he smoked from his mother.

No, seeing Scott hadn't helped today. *This is what you could have won.*

At some point, Stella was going to have to start dating

again. And there were many, *many* men out there who were a hundred times worse than George. *Exhibit A* was currently standing next to a tray of canapés in her mother's lounge, explaining the logistics of a cellar conversion.

Stella watched George outside the window. What was he doing? Was he *punching the tree*?

Yes, it appeared he was. And that was because he was passionate, he cared about something.

Stella shook her head. She needed to drive these thoughts away.

Because they weren't real thoughts. They were just thoughts fuelled by this strange day.

Because she was being unrealistic. Sentimental. Unfounded.

It was ridiculous.

Somewhere along the way, Stella had made a massive mistake.

42

'Who's Nancy, George?'

George jerked his head up. He looked at Tommy, panic clear in his eyes.

Tommy glowered down at George on the bench. He still *looked* the same. Same eyes, same hapless expression. But now Tommy knew different. There was a shark's fin behind this dolphin's façade.

'I was in the shed.' Tommy was too angry to sit. 'I heard you on the phone.'

George twisted his hands together. 'What did you hear?'

'Don't try to shy away from it. You've got a bit on the side.'

'No. *No.*'

Was this one of those situations, Tommy wondered, where he was meant to actually *fight* someone? 'Does Stella know?'

George widened his eyes. 'It's not what you think! I can't explain today, but it's not that.'

'I thought you were a solid kind of man. Faithful.'

'You've got it wrong. And Stella doesn't need to know, you'll hurt her.'

Tommy set his jaw. 'It's like that, is it? I'm meant to ignore your affair, for her sake? That's meant to be OK, as long as she doesn't know. How very *French*. You and The *Jardin* deserve each other.'

'I—' George hunched his eyebrows. 'Sorry, *Le Jardin*? What's the shop got to do with—'

'How very old-fashioned.' Tommy folded his arms. 'Yet you all think *I'm* the dinosaur.'

'No one thinks you're a dinosaur, Tommy.'

'I didn't think you were that kind of man, George.'

'I'm not.'

'I think so much less of you. We always knew you and Stella weren't perfect, but I thought you respected her.'

'You don't understand.'

'I don't understand. Ha! But look at you, sitting there. And look at me, standing here.' Tommy gestured jerkily between them. 'I have *ears*, George. *Ears*.' He flicked one of his ears at George. It hurt.

George lowered his head. 'I can't talk about this today.'

Tommy wished George would stand up. Tommy considered putting his hands up in a fighting gesture. He raised them a little, but thought about all the people in the lounge through the glass patio doors. He thought of Margaret, and lowered his fists again.

'I understand why you'd be upset,' George said, 'You'd be right to be, if I was doing what you think I was doing. But you're wrong.'

Tommy bunched his fists at his sides. He was being *understood*, again. And he was just meant to *take it*? Smile as he was patted on the head, and told, *You don't get the world today, Tommy. Bless.*

George stood up slowly. He turned to walk back towards the house. 'You just look after Stella, Tommy. When the time comes. She's going to need support from you. She thinks the world of you.'

'Don't go!' Tommy said. 'You can't go! Stay and fight!'

But George just shoved his hands in his pockets and walked away.

43

At first, Margaret wasn't sure what she was watching. In theory, she was in the lounge, listening to Adele talk about the roadworks on the M60. In reality, she was watching the activity through the patio doors.

The darkness was setting in quickly now, but to Margaret it *looked like* a heated conversation between George and Tommy. Margaret was only able to watch intermittently, she had to wait for one of the men to gesture and trigger the security light.

But this last flick of the security light had confirmed it. She was watching an argument – admittedly, a one-way argument. Tommy was gesturing angrily and the tops of his ears were reddening. Now, he was flicking one of his red-topped ears at George in a way that looked painful and that suggested it might be time for Tommy to have a little sit down. Margaret could see the clear battleground of his body, as he tried to both express his emotions and keep them firmly hidden at the same time.

Not like Margaret. She had no problems with emotions; she was in charge of hers. She kept them firmly boxed and labelled, mothballed in places neither she or anyone else would ever find them.

Tommy waved another angry hand in George's direction.

Margaret thought about going outside but didn't want to draw attention to the scene. Right now, nobody was looking towards the garden except her.

'This salmon is wonderful,' Adele said. 'Worth waiting for.'

Margaret turned slightly so Adele had to move to face her, further from the window. 'Helen is great with pastry.'

'How's Pete's import business?' Adele asked. 'Can he still get those cheap mobile phones?'

'Unfortunately not. He was doing so well, until that enterprise got scuppered by the weak pound.'

Margaret glanced back into the garden. George couldn't ... George couldn't be telling Tommy Margaret's secret, could he?

No. *This* would not be how Tommy would react to the news of Margaret's secret. That reaction wouldn't trip the security light. There'd be no red-tipped ears, just shuffling feet and long, weighted silences.

'Well, well, Margaret Foy.' Cheryl had a bounce in her step as she walked up to Margaret and Adele. 'I know what you're doing with Ellie Brockenhurst's necklace. But you can't fool me!'

'Why? What's going on with the necklace?' Adele asked. 'Is it still missing?'

Cheryl just tapped her nose.

Margaret made herself smile and looked back towards the garden.

The patio doors opened with a hiss.

George strode up, his phone held out. 'You can have this now.'

Margaret picked up a tissue. She dabbed the corners of her mouth.

George waggled the phone impatiently. He looked a little out of breath.

Margaret dabbed again. 'Are those kiddies well?'

George didn't reply.

'George? George, are those kiddies safely down the mountain?'

He snapped back into the room. 'Yes, thanks for asking. They're back at base camp now, sipping hot chocolate. Eating Kendal mint cake. Singing "The Wheels on the Bus".'

'How old are these kids meant to be again?'

George held the phone out further. 'Don't you want it? I thought you'd snap my hand off.'

Margaret gave George a narrow look. She pushed a tiny piece of pastry from her finger to her mouth. She wiped her finger on her napkin, took the phone and headed upstairs to her bedroom.

She got her phone bowl out of the wardrobe, labelled George's phone and placed it cosily into some bubble wrap.

She looked at her bowl with satisfaction.

Finally. A complete set of phones.

44

'What are you doing in here, monkey?'

At the sound of her dad's voice, Isobel looked up from the kitchen table. Isobel's chest was full, like something was about to explode out of it.

Dad was smiling down at her. 'Why weren't you there for the speeches?'

'Speeches are boring.' Isobel kicked the table leg. 'Everything's boring.'

'I thought you were having a great time with your little pals?'

Isobel stared at the table leg. 'They're not my pals.'

Being teenagers was wasted on those kids. They might wear eyeliner and manga T-shirts, but they'd gone to play on the swings, and where was the fun in that? Swings weren't even fun. While the big kids had been on the swings, playing like children, Isobel had been setting things on fire, like a grown-up.

'Hi, you two.' Mum came through the doorway holding an empty plate. She moved in that weird puppety way she had all day. 'Hi, Nathan.'

'You said hello to Dad twice,' Isobel pointed out. 'Because you'd already said "Hi, you two".'

Mum put the plate down on the table.

'I'm bored,' Isobel said decisively.

Not *angry*. Not *left out*. Just *bored*. That was definitely what she was feeling.

Dad smiled at her. 'Why don't you go and get some more crisps from the shop?'

Isobel stared at Dad. She wanted someone to listen and make it better. Not to be given a job.

'I hate the shop.'

'Fair enough.' Dad raised his eyebrows. 'I can see you're in one of your little moods.'

Isobel picked up the salt cellar and turned it upside down. She poured a pile of salt onto the kitchen table. The salt heaped into the shape of a molehill.

When no one said anything, Isobel put the salt cellar down again.

Mum was too busy looking at Dad with Important Eyes. 'Nathan. Do you want to step outside for a second?'

'I thought you wanted me to mingle.'

'Now I want you to mingle *with me*.' She glanced at Isobel and back. 'Just grown-up stuff.'

Dad looked at Isobel. 'You mind being left alone for a sec, monkey?'

Isobel shrugged. *Grown-up stuff.*

She watched her parents head out of the back door. They stood slightly away from the door, but not far enough.

Isobel pushed herself up from the kitchen chair. She tip-toed to the doorway and peeked outside.

'Is there something going on?' Mum said. 'Something we need to discuss?'

Dad stood completely still. 'I don't know what you mean.'

'Nathan.'

'You're not yourself today. I know today must have been stressful.'

'Don't do that to me, Nathan. I'm your wife.' Mum's eyes were getting wet. 'Don't disrespect me.'

Isobel pulled back from the doorway. *She'd* managed to stop herself crying earlier. Isobel didn't like being tougher than her mum.

'We need to talk *at some point*.'

'There's nothing to talk about,' Dad said.

Isobel rushed back to her original spot on the kitchen chair. She felt her heart beat as she thumped back into the seat. She shook the salt shaker again, turning it over, making the salt form another little pile.

She stared at it. Could she burn salt?

No. Probably not.

Mum came back into the kitchen and didn't even look at Isobel. She stood with her arms folded, staring out of the window. Her eyes looked stupid, like a cow's.

'Helen.' Aunty Stella strode into the kitchen. She winked at Isobel and turned to Mum. 'Glad I've found you. Today's put me in a weird mood, I don't know if it's nostalgia or *way* too much family time, but I'm having crazy thoughts. And you're right – we *should* spend some actual time together. You *should* appreciate having me in your life, and I should appreciate having you in mine. So we're going to have a drink.'

Mum broke away from staring out of the window and turned to Stella.

'Come on, Hel.' Stella grabbed her arm. 'Let's get pissed together. Cocktails for two, no arguments.' She walked over to the far kitchen cupboard and started getting bottles out and putting them on the side. 'Now. Do you know how you make a vodka Martini?'

Mum looked at her and laughed. A proper laugh, Isobel thought. 'When do you think I go around making vodka Martinis?'

Aunty Stella looked at the bottles. 'I'll improvise, then.'

'Can I have a cocktail?' Isobel said.

Aunty Stella looked at Isobel. 'Sorry, mate, you'd hate it. But I'll make you one in a few years, and that's a promise.'

Aunty Stella clanked around with her bottles, pouring liquids into a metal rocket thing.

Too young for everything, Isobel thought. *That's what* they *think.*

She put her hand in her pocket and flicked the wheel of the lighter.

'Helen?' Aunty Stella shook the metal rocket thing, whooshing the liquid within. 'You're quiet. There are some glasses on the side and you're not even tidying them up. You OK?'

'I'm just thinking about work. Don't worry about it.'

Aunty Stella poured the liquid into two glasses shaped like ice cream cones on stilts.

'Then forget about whatever it is for now. This will help.' Aunty Stella handed Mum a glass. The two clinked their glasses together. 'To a good, drunk rest of the day.'

Isobel watched them both drink. It was like they'd forgotten she was there.

Isobel picked up the salt cellar again. She made another molehill.

When neither of them noticed, she put the salt cellar down.

She put her hand in her pocket and turned the wheel of the lighter again.

45

Margaret put the phone bowl in the wardrobe and turned around.

She started. George had followed her into her bedroom.

'What was all that about in the garden with Tommy?' She had long learned that acting surprised relinquished control of a situation.

'He's not himself today. He's a bit agitated.'

'He has nothing to be agitated about. He's king of his domain, he's *Lord Brockenhurst*. And why are you in my bedroom, Mr Owlish?'

George closed the bedroom door with a bang. 'I'm here in a non-butler capacity. Let's continue that conversation while I'm having a bad day.'

Margaret shut her eyes. *Give me strength*. 'You're not meant to tell the party host you're having a bad day. It's rude. So, if you don't mind, I'll just—'

'You have to tell Stella, or I will.'

And there was that lightness in Margaret's legs again. How could George *do* this to her? 'It's not your business to tell.'

'I can't know this and not tell her.'

'You *can*. Not doing anything is *always* the easiest thing of all. And remember – *you* did this yourself, George. I didn't want you to know, but you skulked about and forced the issue, with your investigations and your attention and all your *listening*.'

Margaret made her gaze icy. That was better. The more authority she showed, the more the other feelings receded.

George scratched his chin. 'Your family deserve to hear. It's your decision, but shouldn't they know, at least?'

'It's about me, not them.'

'You can't really think that.'

Margaret held her body rigid. 'There are levels of being affected. You're being too sentimental.' Margaret saw the blankness on George's face. 'Think of this situation as like an earthquake.'

George blinked. 'OK. Like it's shaking the family foundations, or . . .'

'*Try* to follow me, George. *Listen*.'

George twitched his mouth.

'Others feel the ripples, but I am at the epicentre of what's going on. Everyone else has secondary tremors.'

George put his hands in his pockets. 'You know I teach some geography as well as history, right?'

'It's an *analogy*.'

'OK. So do you want me to help you?'

'I am the epicentre. Stella and Tommy are in wave one – not in the centre but affected by the fall out.'

'So, *fall out* is an expression for nuclear—'

'You're in wave two.' Margaret looked him up and down. 'Or three, or four, I haven't given it much thought.'

'Right. How many waves are there?'

'Cheryl is about wave eight. She'll have to find someone else to give her a lift to Zumba, but it would be excessive if she were to cry when she heard the news.'

'You even think you get to decide what the *exact* appropriate reaction is from everyone when they hear your news? This is the world you live in?'

'The point is, every wave should recognise where they are in relation to the epicentre. You're thinking about Stella, rightly, because she's nearer to the centre, so you want to support her. And so on and so on. You're in an earlier wave than Cheryl, and Cheryl should be supporting *you*.'

'That would be kind of her, but I don't think it's strictly necessary.'

'But you're forgetting that I am the centre. No one else's feelings matter here. Stella – *all of you* – should be supporting *me*.'

Margaret stood as tall as she possibly could. This was not the time to show weakness.

George looked like he was about to speak, but stopped.

'What were you going to say?'

He raised his gaze. 'Just that the sacrifices of motherhood came naturally to you.'

'If it was Stella who was ill, she'd be the epicentre. But she's not. So this whole thing should be looked at from the perspective of *what does Margaret want? What would inconvenience her the least? How do we make sure she enjoys her anniversary party with the minimum fuss?*'

'I have to tell Stella.'

'Not today.'

'If I can't tell Stella, you have to. This weekend.'

'George, don't ruin my party.'

'Today, or tomorrow at the latest.'

'It will all come out in the wash. They know I'm not around for long, it's only a tiny change. Eventually, life will move on.' Margaret took a deep breath, determined to sound more certain than she felt. 'It'll be your job to support Stella and make sure Tommy opens the curtains once in a while. And to make him buy new jeans when the old ones go thin at the back.'

George didn't say anything. That meant Margaret had won.

'I was going to say this later, but what the hell. Don't let Tommy be taken in by some floozy afterwards. He can get married again, but not immediately, and it has to be to someone he likes and not just because he doesn't know anything about washing-machine spin cycles.' Margaret took another breath. 'Tommy is quite a catch for a single woman.' She kept her voice as light as she could. Seeing the expression on George's face, she added, 'He *is*. Physically able. Still wanting to work. No bad habits. No really strong opinions on anything.'

George leaned back against the bedroom wall.

Margaret picked a bath towel off the bed. She took it into the en suite and put it back on the rail. She held the towel rail until she was confident her hands weren't shaking.

She stepped back into the bedroom. 'So? Are you going to allow this to ruin my day?'

George held her gaze. 'Are you going to tell Stella tomorrow?'

'No.'

'Then I'm not going to say anything today. But I *am* going to tell Stella tomorrow.'

'Even though I've asked you not to?'

'Even though. I'm sorry.'

'If you were sorry, you wouldn't tell her.'

'OK. Then I'm not sorry. I'm just . . . sad.'

Margaret watched George leave. She looked around the bedroom carefully, making herself focus on individual items, one at a time.

She pulled loose hair out of her hairbrush and dropped it into the bin.

She put the cap back on her deodorant.

Through the doorway, in the en suite, she saw the mouthwash sitting on the edge of the basin.

She shook her head.

She reached for the mouthwash bottle and wiped it down. She placed it back, carefully, in the bathroom cabinet, tucking it away from view, where it belonged.

46

Tommy picked up a stray sweet wrapper from the lawn. He plucked pieces of battered piñata from the hedge and screwed the rubbish up in his hand. *Making himself useful,* he thought, lifting the lid of the recycling bin and depositing the paper inside.

He let the bin lid drop. It banged shut.

Poor Stella.

'Poor Stella' weren't words that naturally sat together in his mind – there was something about Stella that repelled any thought of sympathy, had done even when she'd been in pigtails, chalking hopscotch games on the pavement. But, today, those words felt right. *Poor Stella.*

'Dad?'

There she was. Opening the patio doors, walking outside with Helen, holding a cocktail glass.

Stella linked arms with him. 'We came to look for you. We were worried you were in the shed again.'

Tommy forced a smile. 'I'm just clearing up the garden.' He looked from Stella to Helen. It hit him how rarely he ever saw his two daughters together. There was no over-lap in their lives. Or Pete's, even. The three didn't even look alike. They had nothing in common – except, per-haps, that they heard about each other's progress through politely received tales from Tommy and Margaret.

Tommy wondered if, when he and Margaret died, these people would even see each other.

'Ambush!' Helen linked her arm through his other side. He had a daughter on each wing.

Tommy knew he should like this experience. Yet he'd shrunk at an alarming rate lately and now was shorter than both his daughters. He felt like a pet.

Tommy stepped out of their reach. 'Stella, we need to talk.'

'Is it the stickiness in the bottom of the fridge? Because that was there before I started making the cocktails.'

Tommy kept his gaze focused on Stella. 'Helen, could you leave us?'

Helen took a tactful step towards the rose bushes.

Tommy turned to Stella. 'I heard George on the phone before.'

She waited. 'OK?'

Tommy licked his lips. 'I'm sorry to do this to you, love, but' – he reached out to touch her arm – 'George is having an affair.'

Stella didn't respond.

'There's no doubt about it, I'm afraid,' he said. 'Though George said the woman sounded angry, so he might not actually be having an affair anymore. But still. He definitely had a girlfriend of sorts. I'm so sorry.'

Stella stood unmoving.

The security light flicked off, leaving them in darkness.

Tommy wrung his hands. 'I felt you should know.'

The patio doors hissed. The security light came on as George stepped outside.

Tommy and George looked at each other.

'I've told her, George,' Tommy pulled Stella towards him by the arm. 'And I'll pick up the pieces of what you've broken.'

George looked at Stella.

'You're confused, Dad.' She disentangled herself from Tommy's grasp. 'Again.'

'The girlfriend's called Nancy,' Tommy said.

Stella turned to face him. 'Will you go inside now, Dad? You've got confused, and it's not helpful.'

Tommy looked from Stella to George.

'You've got it wrong,' Stella said. '*Please*, Dad. Just go.'

Tommy pulled roughly at his shirt. *No. No, no, no!*

Were they really saying Tommy couldn't trust his own ears anymore?

'But – but, Stella—'

'What are you all doing out there?' Margaret's voice rang out; she stood outside the patio doors, rubbing her arms. 'We need you all inside for Act Three!'

'We'll be in in a sec.' Helen had been standing a tactful distance away this whole time.

'Helen, will you make Dad go in, please?' Stella wasn't looking at Tommy. 'And George too. Make them both go inside, so Mum can do her party update.'

George took a step towards her. 'Stella—'

Stella turned to face the shed. 'No.'

She folded her arms; Tommy could just make out the spikes of her shoulder blades through her silk shirt.

Tommy took one last glance at Stella. He let Helen usher him inside.

He heard George say, 'Please. Let me explain.'

'George. I can't deal with this. Leave me alone. *Please*.'

With reluctance, Tommy stepped though the patio doors into the lounge. George followed.

Tommy turned to look outside.

The security light in the garden stayed on and, through the glass, Tommy watched Helen pace slowly back towards Stella.

47

Helen had intended to follow George and Tommy into the house. Yet Stella looked so vulnerable, standing there with her arms folded, Helen found herself walking towards her sister. Her sister, who never wanted any sympathy from anyone, especially Helen.

'Hey,' Helen said softly.

Stella's voice was quiet. 'I've fucked everything up.'

Helen took another tentative step forward. She put a hand on Stella's arm.

'George and I have split up.'

Helen tried to process this.

'He's doing me a favour, being here.' Stella glanced up at Helen and back at the grass. 'Pretending we're still a couple so Mum and Dad don't get upset on their big day.'

Helen took a deep breath.

'So I can't be angry if he's seeing someone. Right? Right. Fair's fair. It's over, so he's allowed to move on, isn't he? And yet ...'

Helen pulled Stella towards her.

Stella kept her body limp. She let herself be hugged.

'And I can't even think what I feel about it,' Stella said into Helen's shoulder. 'And now George has let Dad hear he's got a girlfriend – and, as an aside, I can't believe he's got a new girlfriend so quickly, she must live in his house or be *his fucking cousin* or something.' Stella took a stilted breath. 'Dad'll tell Mum, of course. So I've ruined their day by letting this happen, and that was the *exact opposite* of the plan. And now I'm going to have to come up with some explanation for Dad to make it OK. But what?'

'Is it irretrievable?' Helen asked finally. 'I thought you two were tight.'

'I *think* it's irretrievable. Especially if he's seeing someone else. And I should *want it* to be irretrievable now, shouldn't I?' Stella stared at her. 'This is the bit where I say that I'm stronger than I ever was before, right? That I've grown and realised how much happier I am without him?'

'Can George really be seeing someone else?' Helen said. 'You know how Dad gets things wrong.'

'You saw George's face. It's true.'

'You should let him explain,' Helen said. 'It might not have been quite what you think. It's not always helpful to have delicate conversations funnelled through Dad.'

They both snorted.

Helen had forgotten she and Stella had the same snort.

'So what do you want?' Helen looked over the fence, into the darkness of the ginnel behind. 'Have you and George really run out of tries? All relationships can be rubbish sometimes.' She thought about Nathan. '*Most* of the time.'

'It feels final. *I* made it final. And I wasn't behaving well at the end. Neither of us were.' Stella gave a strained laugh. 'I fuck everything up.'

'Don't say that.'

'Well, I *really* fucked this one up.'

'Everyone fucks up.'

Stella studied her.

Helen put her hand to her face self-consciously. 'What?'

'You've never fucked up in your life.'

'Not true. Why do you say that?'

Stella shrugged.

'I've fucked up way worse than you. Seriously. Compared to me, you've got everything together.'

Stella shook her head. 'Thanks for trying, but you've got your shit together. Proof positive: you wear sun cream in the UK.'

Helen brushed a strand of hair out of her eyes. 'How would you know that?'

Stella gave a wave of her hand. 'Mum.'

'Right.'

'You wear it every day, even on cloudy ones. *Sun cream.* And you do *Pilates.* And not just six times in January and then never again. You do it *every week.* And you have a *salad spinner.*'

'Mum again?'

'On the phone, after she does Pete and your kids, she does you.'

Helen smiled. 'But always Pete first.'

'Of course. Apparently his new business is going well. I don't know what it is this time, maybe hoof warmers for unicorns, or he's single-handedly invented a cure for obesity, but apparently he's going to start paying Mum and Dad back any day now. He says he's even going to buy the shop building off that throbber Scott and give it to Dad.'

'I don't know that word,' Helen said. 'But Scott *is* a throbber.'

Stella glanced at her. 'You think that too?'

'Doesn't everyone?'

'You're going to laugh when I tell you this then. I had sex

with him once. Lost my virginity with him.' Stella scratched her lips. 'Technically. We were outdoors, it wasn't *sexy* sex. We were still in our coats and jeans.'

'Well.' Helen raised her eyebrows. '*That's* going to take a while to process.'

'So—'

Helen held up a hand. 'Hang on. I know it's not the time. I just – wow. *Scott.*'

Stella reached out and held Helen's hand. 'Back to you being fucked up, despite the clear evidence of the salad spinner.'

Helen stopped laughing instantly. 'Having a salad spinner means I've not fucked up?'

Stella raised her palms in a gesture, clearly intended to communicate *what other explanation is there?*

'Salad spinner evidence can be overridden by other factors.'

Stella raised a sceptical eyebrow.

Helen took a deep breath. 'I was late today because I couldn't get out of bed. Literally couldn't make myself move even a centimetre.' Helen made herself hold Stella's eye contact. 'I was screaming at myself to get up, but I still couldn't.' Helen was surprised she could sound so matter-of-fact. 'I was paralysed with self-hate, and I just lay there making things worse. I think I've been having a breakdown coming for a while and today – well, I found something out, something bad, and it brought everything crashing down. I've just finally accepted I can't cope. I went to bed and I couldn't physically move. That's why I was late.'

Stella blinked at her.

'I haven't had a shower today. I haven't cleaned my teeth. I haven't fed the kids anything with any nutritional value, hence Charlie has gone crazy with the Haribo and is running around with a shoebox on his head.'

Stella's eyebrows moved higher.

'I don't know where Isobel is,' Helen continued, 'and that fills me with fear. Because I've tried and tried to not see it, and I'll love her whatever, like the mum in the book, but there's only so long I can fool myself. She's a Kevin.'

'A Kevin?'

'A Kevin. And the real question is whether I've made her a Kevin, or whether someone else has made her a Kevin, or whether she was born a Kevin. And, really – that's a stupid question because we all know it's the mother's fault.'

'What's a Kevin?'

'And your relationship's gone to shit?' Helen waved a hand. 'Nathan and I have the politest of conversations these days. There's no way that man's ever going to fuck me against a kitchen counter again. Last Christmas we agreed to buy each other a new sideboard and just get each other thoughtful little gesture presents. And the gesture present he got me was a book called *Channelling Your Inner Calm.*'

'No!' Stella said.

Helen took a breath. 'And the worst thing? I can't meditate.'

Stella scrunched her eyebrows together. '*That's* the worst thing?'

'I've tried and tried, and I just can't. Every day, I read somewhere how meditation's the solution, but I'm failing at the solution. I'm failing at it all. I can't force myself to be calm at all.' Helen stopped. She dug her fingernails into her palms. 'I'm sorry to bore you with my stuff.'

'Oh, H. That sounds shit.'

Helen was momentarily triumphant. 'Thank you!'

Stella reached for Helen's hand. She gave it a squeeze. 'Oh, God, Helen. It's over. He's seeing someone else. It hurts.'

Helen squeezed back. 'I know.'

The two stared straight ahead, towards the house, as the security light went off again, leaving them in silent darkness.

48

Three months before the party, it was a Saturday afternoon and George was feeling proud of himself.

He'd cleaned the flat that morning, as they'd agreed that he would in their latest session with Grace. He'd cleaned the whole place, top to bottom, and Stella had hardly had to chase him at all.

Now he sat on the sofa on the lounge, marking exercise books containing some near-identical essays about the history of the Suez Canal. He was just wondering how much to ignore this 'coincidence' when Stella strode into the room holding a can stiffly ahead of her. It was a purposeful grip, George noticed, showing both that the can was empty and that it represented bad news.

George riffled through his recent head-history, trying to remember any incident in which his behaviour might be found wanting – particularly any incident associated with a can of soft drink.

'I found this.'

'Yes?'

'On the side of the bath.'

'So?'

'Not only does the bath still have rings round it, it now has a *fuck you Stella* Coke can on top!'

'That's not what the can says.'

'It's *exactly* what it says. You were *meant* to be *cleaning*. Not sprinkling more junk around.'

'I *have* cleaned! OK, so I clearly haven't done the bath brilliantly if there are still rings round it, but I did everything else.'

'You left the bath dirty, with a can on top of it. You left the top of the bleach on the window ledge *and* – wait for it – you left the bathroom cupboard open! And that's just one room. And, while I'm at it, I've begged you not to switch off the toaster at the mains, but you did it anyway. It made me late for work this morning.'

'What the fuck has the toaster got to do with anything? Is this just the day for telling me everything you hate about me? I'm working. Can't you see?'

Stella raised her gaze to the ceiling and made a revving noise in her throat.

George looked briefly at the ceiling and back. 'What?'

'Did you decide not to do the cobwebs in the flat after all?'

'No, I definitely did the cobwebs.' He looked away. 'I just forgot we had this room.'

To be fair, he thought he'd done this room. Was it better to have done the room and missed the cobweb or not to have done the room at all?

Stella put her face in her hands. 'You just *refuse* to get it right,' she said through the gap between her fingers. 'It's like you don't even *try*.'

'Of course I try. That was me trying my best.'

At that, Stella burrowed her face further into her hands.

'I just forgot we had a lounge. Anyone can forget they have a lounge.'

'Four rooms, this flat has, George. Four fucking rooms.'

'Five. Six, if you count the hallway.'

'Stop talking. Please.'

'I do my bit,' George said. 'I'm a good man.'

'A good man who I have to beg to clean the flat and, when he eventually does it, is shit at it? Do you agree?'

'I just think we don't need to row about it, that's all.'

'You say that, like you're Captain fucking Zen, but it takes two to row.'

'But only one of us has a raised voice. And only one of us has spittle at the edge of her mouth.'

Stella wiped the spit with her hand. 'But it's so unreasonable you get to be the calm one! It takes two to row because *you caused it.*'

'How did I cause the row?'

'By leaving the can on the bath.'

George walked out of the room. 'I'm not doing this.'

Two days later, after work, George had managed to convince his workmates to have a pint in the pub round the corner from school, even though it was a Monday.

He was just mid-anecdote about the intricacy of one of the desk carvings he'd found in his year nine form room when he felt his phone buzz on the table.

He looked at the screen.

Stella.

He took a beat and turned back to his mates. 'If you'd seen it, you'd understand. It was the attention to detail – he'd got the shading just right. I need to give him hell about not defacing school property with knob carvings – and also make sure he's put himself down for art at GCSE. Anyone fancy another?'

He got another round in.

When he came back from the bar, he saw he'd got a voicemail. He moved the phone slightly further away to make room for his new pint, and joined in the conversation about the odd teaching style of the new deputy head.

Twenty minutes later, Stella charged in to the pub.

George ignored the fact that her face was red. 'How did you know I was here?'

'Have you been here all the *fucking time?*' Stella looked at the phone on the table in front of him, the evidence of the missed call on the lock screen. 'Not even taking my calls anymore?'

George looked at his mates and back at Stella.

It hit him. *Shit.*

'I forgot. I just forgot. I'm sorry.'

Stella turned to his mates. 'Apologies for ruining your afternoon, but I need to speak to George because I'm fucking *fuming*. He was meant to meet me at the White Swan. We had a meeting with a driving instructor.' She turned back to George. 'And I just waited there like a dickhead. Ringing you.'

George stood up. 'Maybe we can stop playing this out in public and embarrassing everyone?'

'It was the last day we could do it. You *know* that meant the lessons voucher I got you will expire.'

'I said sorry. I accept it's my fault and I'll reimburse you from my personal account. I'm really not sure what the big deal is.'

'The big deal is we're skint, you've made us skinter, and you have *no respect* and I always have to do fucking everything!' Stella turned to look at his mates. 'Sorry, guys. I'm really so so sorry.'

She rushed out of the pub.

No one round the table said anything.

With a shaky hand, George drank from his pint glass.

After a moment, he downed the rest and got up without saying goodbye.

He saw Stella's tail lights flash up in the car park. She didn't stop, though he chased her, waving his arms.

He half-ran, half-walked home.

He threw his keys into the hallway bowl, on top of Stella's, and strode into the kitchen. 'OK. Let's do this.'

Stella stood in front of the open cutlery drawer. 'Why the fuck is this drawer open?'

George looked at the drawer and back. 'You're angry, but you haven't even shut it.' He gave a tight laugh. 'That's what I find hilarious. You just left it there, annoying yourself, so you could have a go at me. That's *healthy*, isn't it?'

'But I've asked you and asked you. I've begged you not to leave the drawers open. And you did it on Saturday with the Coke can too.'

'Listen to yourself. And look, you're nearly crying. Over a Coke can and a fucking drawer. You're *crazy*.'

'That's such an easy thing for you to say, isn't it, to win an argument? Crazy, crazy, *crazy* wife.'

'If the cap fits,' George muttered.

'I'm in charge of *fucking everything*.'

'Don't say it.'

'How can I not say it?'

'If you say mental load *one more time,* I'm walking straight out. We will have split up. Eleven years, and we will have split up. Over a Coke can and a *drawer*.'

'Oh, run away!' Stella was really crying now. 'Well, let me tell you, if you walk out now, you're leaving forever. I'm warning you. There's no way back from here.'

George stared at her. He couldn't do this again. He *couldn't*.

He turned and walked into the hallway. She could still see him from the kitchen, so he picked his keys up off the table with deliberate precision.

He walked out of the flat and slammed the door behind him.

ACT THREE

A (Double) Murder is Announced

Card to be read at 9.30 p.m. by the solicitor,
Mr Shaker (a.k.a. Pete Foy)

*By now you should know that Agnes and Lord
Brockenhurst were having an affair, but she was
definitely not pregnant with his baby.*

    *You will also be aware that Mr Hapsworth, the
Private Secretary, has found a telegram from Somerset
House, confirming that Lord Ashley Brockenhurst and
Ellie recently eloped in secret.*

    *You will also know that Ellie Brockenhurst's
mother's priceless necklace has been found in the
dressing-up box in the attic, and that the will has been
found in the pantry, leaving everything to Mr Owlish,
the butler.*

    But, now, I declare that will a forgery!

    And, finally – the last reveal.

    *I am sorry to have to tell you that Lord and Lady
Brockenhurst have died. Found by the chauffeur, gassed
to death in their second Bentley.*

    May they rest, together, in peace.

49

George followed Tommy and the trailing Goldie through the patio doors. He knew he was shaking. He wanted to run away and never come back, but he couldn't bring himself to ruin this party any more than he already had. And he had to be there for this stupid card reading, for Margaret's sake.

He watched Margaret step onto her librarian's step.

Tommy stopped walking suddenly; George walked into the now-stationary dog.

Tommy span round. 'How can you dare to *enter my house?*'

'I'm sorry to have upset you.' George took a sidestep round the dog and kept moving. 'But you've got it wrong. And we can't do this today.'

'You've got some nerve.'

'I'm not going to argue with you. Tommy. And I'm just going to stand over there now.' George walked across the room and stood behind the yucca on the sideboard so Tommy couldn't see his face.

He peeked round the plant.

Tommy held his arms stiffly to his side, his hands bunched into fists.

George pulled back behind the yucca again.

Margaret clapped her hands together. 'Act Three, everyone!'

The room quietened. Everyone turned to look at Margaret.

'To recap, everyone should know that Agnes wasn't pregnant with Lord Brockenhurst's baby, after all?' She looked at George meaningfully.

George held her gaze. 'I told Scott. And Cheryl.'

'Right.' Margaret looked down at her card. 'And by now you should know that Agnes and Lord Brockenhurst were having an affair, but that she wasn't pregnant with his baby.'

There were nods around the room.

'And that Mr Hapsworth, the Private Secretary, has found a telegram from Somerset House, confirming that Lord Ashley Brockenhurst and Ellie recently eloped in secret.' Margaret looked round the room. 'Cheryl? You were going to say something?'

'It doesn't matter really.' Cheryl straightened her cardigan. 'I was just still trying to work out the family tree and if that was legal. Or incest.'

Margaret glared at her. 'It definitely *wasn't* incest.' She turned to face the crowd. 'You will also know that Ellie Brockenhurst's mother's priceless necklace has been found in the dressing-up box in the attic, and that the will has been found in the pantry, leaving everything to Mr Owlish, the butler.'

'Course the necklace has been found.' Cheryl nodded in satisfaction. 'It was never really missing.'

'But, now, I declare that will a forgery!'

Everyone turned to look at George.

George held his hands up. 'I'm disappointed too.' George tried to hide the harsh speed of his breathing; the tightness in his chest. 'I thought I was loyal to my master.'

He leaned forward and peeked round the yucca. One look at Tommy's face, and he leaned straight back.

Margaret indicated for Tommy to stand next to her. Slowly, he walked up.

'I am sorry to tell you,' she pressed her lips together, 'that Lord and Lady Brockenhurst have died. Found by the chauffeur, gassed to death in their second Bentley.'

Tommy turned to stare at her.

'We're both dead.' Margaret stepped down from her stool and slipped her hand into his. 'Together, side by side. So that's nice, isn't it?'

Around Tommy, people expressed sympathy. George watched him pull his hand out of Margaret's and slip out of the room, Goldie following.

Cheryl turned to Adele and started chattering excitedly about the logistics of a double gassing.

Behind them all, Margaret, with a certain nobility, put her card on the sideboard and graciously accepted the condolences.

50

Tommy shut the door of Margaret's study behind him.

How *could* she? He *could she* joke about her death today? And talk about it like a nice thing they were going to do together, when she knew she was going to leave him alone?

Tommy couldn't take this anymore. He needed to *do something*. Anything.

He opened the desk drawer and got the shop keys. He looked at the scratched-up Pacha Ibiza key ring.

Tommy had never been to Ibiza. One of the kids must have bought it – he couldn't remember which one – and he'd had the shop keys on it for fifteen years.

He smoothed his thumb over the metal.

It was so tactless of Margaret to joke about her death today. Especially when it was all about to come to a head. Any moment now, probably tomorrow, Margaret was going to have to tell Tommy she wasn't having the treatment.

He jiggled the keys in his hand.

Of course, she wasn't definitely planning to tell him. She might even keep up the pretence. Get the bus to the hospital – even let Tommy drive her there – and sit in the coffee shop for hours.

But that would be a bridge too far. He respected her privacy, but driving her to the hospital for pretend appointments was above and beyond.

Tommy had known she wouldn't have the treatment all along. They hadn't discussed it and, of course, Margaret hadn't told him. But he'd known. He'd known from the look on her face when she was told the news.

They didn't need to discuss it. He'd been married to this woman for *forty years.*

And Margaret had stopped him from coming to the consultations with the oncologist. 'You'd find it too upsetting, Tommy. You're getting yourself all out of sorts. Why not spend the time fixing up that bird box?'

She was just pretending to get the treatment, while everyone was getting used to the idea. That was why she was saying she was going to keep working in the shop. It was true, of course. She had no plans to be recovering in bed. That's why there was no room for Tommy.

Tommy gripped the shop keys and stood up.

They were out of crisps downstairs. Those bowls were empty of all but the saddest of crumbs. It was his duty. He would leave a note with the cash on the counter. He wasn't going to just take the crisps, he'd check the price and count out the correct money. Tommy Foy paid his way.

And while he was there, he could fix that dripping tap in the storeroom that Nathan still hadn't got round to looking at. Even though Nathan kept telling Tommy not to help. Which was ridiculous, seeing as Nathan clearly wasn't doing it.

Whatever Nathan said – whether he wanted Tommy there or not – that tap still needed fixing.

Tommy might not be needed in the supermarket. He might not understand conversations between George and

Stella. He might be letting his wife lie to him about the most important topic of all. He might have just been gassed to death in a Bentley. But Tommy Foy could still make himself useful.

Tommy Foy could *definitely* still fix a tap.

51

Grandpa walked through the kitchen towards the back door.

From the kitchen table in the alcove, Isobel went to speak up. But something about the way Grandpa moved made her stop.

He was *sneaking*.

Isobel watched Grandpa head out of the back door. He let himself through the side gate, Goldie following, keys on a ring covered with red writing dangling from his hand.

Isobel got up from the kitchen table and scampered out of the back door. She followed him through the gate, leaving the little kids playing behind her in the garden.

Isobel trailed him across the street, ducking behind a car along the way. She stopped to watch him.

After all that, he was just going to the shop.

Isobel sighed. *Oh, Grandpa.*

Isobel checked no one was watching her from the house, then hurried the last few steps to the shop door. She peered in, watching Grandpa's shape as he moved around behind the glass. He disappeared into the storeroom.

Isobel kept watching through the window, even though there was nothing to see.

She leaned her forehead against the glass and scuffed her

shoes together. If it hadn't been for Grandpa's sneaky look, she wouldn't have bothered being here at all.

She jiggled her weight from one foot to another.

It was like he'd disappeared.

Isobel took a big breath. Maybe he *had* disappeared. Maybe there was a magic back room, and you had to do a special knock or pull a secret handle that turned some of the shelves round? And then a secret door led to a passage into a different world? Not Narnia, obviously, but *like* Narnia.

She knew places like that didn't exist.

But a proper spy would follow Grandpa anyway. Just in case.

Isobel pushed on the shop's front door. A loud jangling made her start; she pulled the door shut behind her and ran to crouch in front of the display of crisps in the window.

She felt her bum press against the cold glass at the front of the shop. She hoped no one was standing outside. She'd look very silly right now.

She heard the sound of footsteps.

Grandpa used a voice deeper and tougher than usual. 'Who's there?'

Isobel's heart beat in her ears. She pressed her hands to her heart, trying to squash the thumping down.

'Is someone there? Come out where I can see you.'

Isobel watched Grandpa's scuffed old shoes move under the display. His left shoe squeaked as he walked.

'I've got a gun right here. And a large dog. She's not barking because she's so well trained, but she's vicious. Don't test me, sunshine!'

'It's me! Isobel!' Hurriedly, Isobel put her hand up so he could see it over the crisp display. 'I'm down here. Don't shoot me.'

Grandpa leaned over the display and looked at her.

'Hi,' she said.

'I'd never have shot *you*.'

'Have you really got a gun? Can I see?'

'No. Not with me, at any road.'

'Oh,' Isobel said.

'I thought you were a burglar, lovey.'

'I'm not a burglar.'

'I can see that.' He looked down at her. 'What are you doing here?'

'I'm hiding.'

'From me?'

'From everyone.'

Grandpa sat down next to her. 'Then maybe I'll hide with you. If that's OK.'

The dog slumped between them. It smelt of bad breath and rotten vegetables.

Isobel inched away and looked back at Grandpa. 'You need some new shoes.'

'They've got years left in them.'

'The left one squeaks. I can't believe Grandma let you wear a squeaky shoe to your party.'

Grandpa looked at his shoes. 'Your Grandma is used to my little ways.'

Isobel stuck her legs out. 'My shoes are new.' She clicked her silver heels together. The light shone off the glitter and made her shoes sparkle.

'Wow!' Grandpa gave a loud whistle. 'You're the bee's knees in those! You look like a proper princess.'

He smiled at her. She smiled back.

Grandpa's smile faded. 'Do you mind me calling you a princess?'

Isobel frowned. 'Why would *anybody* mind being called a princess?'

Grandpa smiled more. He gave her shoes another whistle. 'Look at that! It's like you've got diamonds on your feet.'

'You have the best whistle, Grandpa.'

'You think so? I can do better than that.'

Grandpa put two fingers in his mouth. He whistled sharply.

The dog jumped up, alarmed.

Isobel slammed her hands to her ears. 'Shh!' Isobel looked at the house across the street. 'We're meant to be hiding!'

The dog looked between the two of them and lay down again.

Grandpa lowered his fingers from his mouth. 'That's how I get Goldie back from the field.' Grandpa scratched his chin. 'Unless she's stumbled across a carcass, then there's no fetching her.'

'Can you show me how to whistle like that?'

'See, you put your fingers here,' Grandpa held her fingers next to her mouth, 'and blow.'

Isobel blew hard. There was a watery hiss.

The dog didn't even open her eyes.

'It takes practice,' Grandpa said.

Isobel tried again. She felt the front middle bits of her lips flap softly together. Another wet hiss.

'It doesn't come at the first go,' Grandpa said. 'Anything worth doing takes practice.'

Isobel kicked out in frustration. 'I can't do it.'

Her foot made contact with the display of crisps and the display shuddered.

Isobel turned to Grandpa. 'I didn't mean to do that.'

Grandpa smiled. 'Didn't you?' He drew his foot back. And *he* kicked the crisp display.

Isobel put her hands to her mouth. 'Grandpa!'

'I've always hated these crisps.'

'I prefer Wotsits.'

'So do I.' He glanced at her. 'Do you know much about Wotsits?'

'I know they taste good. And they make your fingers orange.'

'Do you know Wotsits are a maize-based snack? Not made of potato but corn? They're an entirely different product from potato crisps.'

Isobel put her head to one side. 'Which type would burn best?'

Grandpa relaxed back against the glass. 'Do you know what other crisps are maize-based?'

Isobel shook her head.

'Quavers,' Grandpa said. 'Monster Munch. French Fries.'

'OK,' Isobel said.

'Space Raiders. Ringos.'

'You know *a lot* about crisps,' Isobel said.

'We used to sell them all.' Grandpa stared straight ahead. 'The kiddies used to come in with their pocket money every day, between three fifteen and three forty-five. It was always buzzing. I only let two kids in at a time, and had signs up saying "beware of the camera". I wasn't born yesterday.' He shook his head. 'Your dad took those signs down when he put the tables and chairs in. But then, he stopped trying to attract the after-school crowd, so they all go to Cheryl's newsagents instead.'

Isobel kicked the crisp display again. 'They're good crisps, those maize ones. So much better than Dad's ones.'

Grandpa smiled at her. 'Exactly.'

Isobel smiled back.

Grandpa straightened his trousers out. 'Have you enjoyed the party?'

'This has been the best bit so far.'

Grandpa smiled. 'I agree. Completely.'

They sat in silence for a while.

'I'm pleased you weren't a burglar,' Grandpa said.

'I'm pleased you didn't shoot me.'

'I couldn't have shot you. My gun's in the shed.'

'But it would have been good if you did have a gun with you. As long as you didn't shoot me.'

'I'd never shoot *you*, little one.' Grandpa leaned over and squeezed her hand in his. He put his hand on the floor and pushed himself to standing.

'Where are you going?' Isobel asked.

'One sec.'

Isobel watched Grandpa walk away, the stupid dog trailing behind. She'd barely spoken to Grandpa today. Why had she bothered playing with those little kids, when she could have been playing with him?

He came back and sat down. 'Just checking the freezers were locked. The seals are perishing. They can spring open in the night and waste electricity.'

'That's good for the planet, Grandpa. Thank you,' Isobel said. 'Most grown-ups don't get how important it is.'

Grandpa looked at her for a moment. He looked away. 'I suppose I'd better get on.'

He sounded grumpy. Isobel wondered if he was cross, but he squeezed her hand so tightly it hurt.

He stood up again. 'I'm going to get something to show you. Wait here.'

Isobel listened to Grandpa's footsteps as he walked away
– *step, step-squeak, step, step-squeak.*

She put two fingers in her mouth again. She concentrated,
trying to arrange her fingers like Grandpa had. She blew again.
Again, she felt the air against her fingers. Hiss, no whistle.

Isobel took her hands from her mouth and fingered the
lighter in her pocket. It was an automatic thing, just checking it was still there really. Now she was on her own, she
didn't feel like setting fire to anything.

She tried to whistle again, but it just wasn't happening.
And now her mouth hurt.

Where was Grandpa?

She fingered her lighter again.

She supposed she was here now. And those crisps *were*
stupid.

Isobel looked at the display. Maybe she'd set fire to just
one little packet. Just while she was waiting.

Isobel straightened the paper corner of the nearest crisp
packet. She got out her lighter and flicked it close to the
corner. At the last second, she pulled her hand back.

She could do with Grandpa coming back in the room
before she did something bad. It was like biting that skin off
her cheek all over again. She knew it would hurt, she knew it
wasn't a good idea, but . . .

'Grandpa?'

Nothing. Isobel wondered whether he'd gone to the storeroom or left the shop.

Isobel flicked the lighter on again. She stared at the
beautiful flame, glowing orange and yellow as it waved. She
moved her hand around, making the flame dance.

She held the lighter closer to the edge of the highest crisp
packet. Then closer.

She'd get *so done* for this if anyone saw her.

She let the flame lick the edge of the packet. But she was only playing chicken.

The crisp packet took alight immediately.

Oops.

Isobel watched.

I should have got some of these crisp packets earlier, she thought. *They're better than paper.*

The flame was taller than she expected.

Good, Isobel thought. Then, *Wow, that's getting really tall.*

And now, somehow, the flame had travelled downwards to touch the packet beneath. Fire wasn't meant to go down, but here it was. Going down anyway.

That's a lot of fire, Isobel thought, *for just two packets of crisps.*

Isobel was still smiling, kind of, but she felt unsteady on her feet. She took a step backwards.

There was a *poof* sound. The fire got hold of the cardboard crisp display.

She took a deep breath. *It's OK.*

By the time Isobel finished that breath, the flames were nearly at the ceiling. And Isobel was jumping to her feet and running for the door.

52

George had had it with socialising with these people. He'd passed on all of the butler's messages, he'd done his bit.

He stood alone in Stella's old bedroom. He wanted to get ready for bed, but he didn't have any stuff with him. No T-shirt, no shorts, no toothbrush. And to get ready for bed, you needed props.

Bloody dying Margaret and her ambushed sleepover.

It was quite a sign of the woman's impressive character, George thought as he removed his jeans, that he could still be cross with her on the day that he found out she had months to live.

The music doubled in volume downstairs. The eighties guitar-bounce of 'Girls Just Wanna Have Fun' was audible through the closed bedroom door, as were the heavy footsteps. The dancing was starting.

George heard laughter, followed by smashing glass. The laughter stopped abruptly, replaced by hushed apologies.

George looked at the 'bed' Margaret had put together. He hoped Stella wouldn't remember he'd said he'd sleep on the chair and flopped backwards onto the lilo half. It rippled beneath him. His bum, heels and shoulder blades touched the hard floor beneath.

George got under the duvet. He leaned over and switched off the bedside light.

His eyes adjusted to the darkness. He looked round at the shapes: the piles of unwanted teenage books, the Blu-Tack marks on walls where posters had once been. He looked at the handful of gym medals, the fliers for nightclubs that Stella had used to make a dado rail round the room.

George let his eyes close. He lay there in a simulation of sleep, hoping eventually to be fooled by it.

The door cracked open. The opening strains of another song – The Who's 'Baba O'Riley' – grew louder.

George shuffled up the bed.

Stella stepped into the room and closed the door behind her. She held a blanket, folded over one arm. 'I can't talk to you.'

'I'm so sorry,' George said.

'I have no option but to go to bed. So I'm only talking to you to tell you not to speak to me. This is the start – and the end – of this conversation.'

She threw the blanket at George. It hit him in the face.

The fluff made George cough. He peeled the blanket from his face. 'Stella—'

'*Don't.* I've told you my wishes.'

'I need to tell you how sorry I am. Don't you think talking is good?'

'Nope.'

She stripped down to her underwear and George looked at the floor. He saw her clothes hit the carpet. He felt her lift the duvet and get into bed.

George got out of his side of the 'bed'. He sat on the chair and arranged the blanket effectively over him.

The chair was more upright than he imagined. Cold air circulated around his lower legs.

George thought about putting his jeans back on, but he couldn't sleep in jeans. There were people out there who could sleep in clothes, on buses, trains – *at work* even. A mixed blessing, George thought – but he wasn't one of those people.

George reached for his pillow. He wedged it at the back of the seat, to make the chair fit him better.

It didn't work.

He moulded the pillow round his neck, trying to twist it into a C-shape like those pillows organised people took on planes.

Whichever way he twisted his head, he felt the strain in his neck.

'You comfortable like that?'

George closed his eyes. 'Very.'

'Looks cosy.'

'I thought you didn't want to talk.'

'Fuck you.'

A new, unexpected pillow hit George full in the face.

'Ow!' George threw the pillow on the floor in frustration. 'Stop throwing things, Stella! That hurt my neck.'

'You're very delicate, apparently,' Stella said. 'And it was an accident.'

'Is this what I have to expect, airborne attacks in the night? What's going to be launched next? The bedside light?' George leaned over and switched the light on. 'We can talk or not, but it's going to be hard enough to sleep in this chair without having to anticipate acts of violence.'

Stella had her head turned away. 'It was just a pillow.'

'A *heavy* pillow. Your parents have meaty ones. As you know.'

'I was angry. I wanted to do something.'

'I'm going to have a crick in my neck tomorrow. I'll charge you for the osteopath.'

'Like *you'd* ever go to an osteopath.' Stella sat up in bed. 'Though you *have* been dating someone else, I suppose. So that's very go-getting of you. Maybe I don't know you as well as I thought.'

George sighed. 'You ended it, Stella. You said you didn't want me. I frustrate the hell out of you and I *don't understand you*. I heard you tell Grace that a thousand times.'

Stella turned her head to meet his gaze. 'But how could you let me find out you were seeing someone from my dad? That's *shitty*.'

George closed his eyes. 'I'm an idiot. I was ending it with her. I shouldn't have let you find out something that would hurt you.'

'Don't flatter yourself.'

'Oh, stop being a child. And I shouldn't have let your dad hear me.'

'I *lied* to Dad. I gaslighted the guy for you, said he'd misunderstood what he'd heard. When he's already feeling vulnerable, how fucked up is that? I'm going to hell for that one.'

There was silence.

George switched the light off. He closed his eyes and tried to sleep.

There was a click; the room filled with light again.

'So what was it like?' Stella stared at him. 'Being with someone else?'

George paused. 'Do you really want to know?'

'I'm going to have to be with someone else at some point, aren't I?'

George didn't say anything.

'But I hate the idea of having to sift through other men. Like, Scott's gone to his mum's house, trying to find me an old dance CD he put together in the nineties. Apparently it meant something to us in childhood and I'm supposed to find it meaningful.' She shook her head; it looked like despair. 'How the fuck am I meant to date other men again? There are too many knobends out there.' She glanced at him. 'But that's all it is. I'm furious with you. I'm scared of dating in the future. But I'm not sad.'

George still didn't say anything. This conversation, he reflected, was dangerous.

'So what was it like?'

George glanced at her.

'I want to know.'

'It was weird,' George said eventually.

'Weird-good?'

'Everything was different. You and me were together a long time.'

Stella's voice was small. 'Was it nice?'

George didn't have a clue what Stella wanted to hear.

He was too exhausted to tell her anything but the truth. 'It was nice at points. But it also felt awkward and fake. I've never felt less sure of myself than I did on those first dates. And, of course, I should have been able to dust off all the old anecdotes, but, when I tried, it was like they didn't fit the conversation.'

'Which classic anecdotes did you wheel out?'

'The swimming pool turd.'

'Not first-date material. Did you do the accent?'

'Of course. It's not as good without the accent.'

'That accent has really improved over the years. What else?'

'I talked about my thoughts on social media.'

Stella winced. 'You know people don't want to hear that smug stuff, right?'

'I toned it down. I was pretending to be all nice and reasonable, but it was like I'd forgotten how to play myself. I was really easy-going about her taking photos of her meals—'

'You didn't call her *vapid and shallow?*'

'—and I always shut the door when I went for a piss. I squeezed the toothpaste tube from the bottom. And I rinsed my toothbrush afterwards, remembering what you said about our sink always looking like a child had got loose in there with some white paint.'

'Lucky woman.'

'It was a stress, to be honest. Being a better George.'

'Poor you.'

'I know you're being sarcastic, but it was exhausting to have to pretend to be open-minded and *fresh*. I don't think I can be with anyone now who doesn't know I'm faintly inadequate and has made peace with that.'

Stella pushed some hair away from her face. 'I didn't think you were faintly inadequate.'

'You did in the end. Definitely.' He paused. 'Though I don't think you ever made peace with it.'

Stella didn't say anything.

'It was so awkward, trying to be a better person,' George continued. 'I started rinsing plates before I put them in the dishwasher and—'

Stella pulled back the duvet and leapt up.

George felt the air in the room change.

Stella stood completely still. 'You did *what?*'

'Stella?' George said uncertainly.

Stella rubbed her hands up and down her arms, stiff with anger. 'You rinsed your plate? Every *fucking* time?'

'Why are you going mental?'

'I can't believe this.' Stella paced across the room, narrowly avoiding the bed. 'The toothpaste thing was bad enough, but I asked you *a hundred times* to remember to rinse the plates, especially after you've had something that had crusted over, and you always said it was hard to remember. But you'd do it for her. *Her*, who meant nothing. Did you do it every time? Even if you'd had a drink, after late-night kebabs?'

George stared at her, helpless. Was that a real question?

'Tell me, did you rinse your plate specifically after a kebab? Did you throw away the salad on the night and *rinse it immediately*?'

George looked away. 'I'm not having this conversation. That's why we split up. So I didn't have to have these conversations anymore.'

'So you did hear what I wanted, after all. You just decided I had to suck it up and that you'd save your thoughtful behaviour for a new woman.'

'That's not how it was.'

'That's *exactly* how it was.'

George was about to say something – he didn't know what, but it was definitely going to be cutting and appropriate and argument-winning – when he heard a flurry of footsteps downstairs. A charge of activity, people moving from one side of the room to the other. He heard panic in the overlapping voices.

'It can't be!'

'Is that flames?'

'Someone call the fire brigade!'

Stella and George stared at each other.

'What the fuck?' George said.

Stella shushed him.

George strained to listen.

'Does Margaret know?'

'Someone needs to go in! Help us!'

'Margaret! Where are all the fucking phones?'

Stella ran to the window, George hurried behind. She pulled the curtains apart. The two stared outside, wordlessly.

It wasn't dark outside, not anymore. That was the first thing George registered. Now, there was a source of light. A large, flickering source of light.

And smoke. And heat. And flames.

It was unthinkable. But unmistakable, when you put it all together.

Because, somehow – and really, it must be an elaborate party hoax, surely? *Surely?* – somehow, inexplicably, the shop was on fire.

53

'It's a fire!'

Helen didn't recognise the voice, but she heard the panic in it.

Around her, people ran to the lounge window.

Instantly, Helen looked for the kids.

There was Charlie, standing with Mum. But where was Isobel?

Helen pushed people out of the way, out of the door and into the street. 'Isobel!'

She looked at the shop and faltered. It was so bright, like being at a bonfire. The closer she got, the more the heat became overwhelming.

'Who's got a phone to call nine nine nine?'

Jimmy's calling on the landline. She couldn't take the landline.'

Helen put her hand up to shield her eyes. She looked at the burning building. It still looked like the shop – just a surreal version of the shop. The same shop, in the same place, yet this version had flames dancing like figures behind the windows. She couldn't read the letters of the *Le Jardin* sign anymore. The paint had curled and blackened on the wooden awning.

In front of Helen's eyes, the *Under New Management*

banner caught fire, blistered and crisped. Flaming sections wafted to the ground.

Helen looked around in desperation. 'Isobel!'

She ran up to a group of children who were milling around, pointing at the fire, talking to their parents.

'Have you seen Isobel?'

They all shook their heads.

'I saw her let herself out of the side gate,' the girl with the French plait said. 'She looked sneaky.'

Helen ran towards the shop, dodging a piece of falling awning. She reached to grab the shop's door handle. She knew it would be hot, but she didn't have time to cover her hands, and she wouldn't need to. At times like this, mothers could lift cars and ward off brown bears, even repel *Avada Kedavra* spells, and—

Fuck!

Helen jerked her hand away from the hot metal.

'Where's Nathan?' Helen was screaming at nobody and everybody. 'Is Isobel with him?'

With Helen's remaining good hand, she fumbled her keys from her pocket. She shoved the key into the lock and – *wow, keys get hot quickly*, and—

Helen dropped the keys to the floor. 'No!'

Isobel was missing.

It was Helen's fault Isobel was missing, because Helen put herself first and hadn't thought things through enough and—

'Mum.'

Helen span round.

Isobel took up very little space on the street. *Meek* was not a word Helen had ever associated with her daughter, but here she was now. Decidedly meek.

'Isobel!' Helen scooped her up into a hug, wincing at the impact on her bad hand. She held Isobel there in silence, gently rubbing the protrusions of Isobel's bony shoulder blades. The pressure in her chest told her Isobel was hugging her back.

The two stayed locked together in silence, with no protests from Isobel.

Eventually, Helen pulled back. 'Where's your father?'

'He wasn't in the shop.'

'Oh.' Helen wanted to lean back in relief, but there was nothing to lean on. She righted herself. 'Thank God. But . . . But how do you know? Were you in the shop?'

'It was an accident,' Isobel said.

Helen shook her head ferociously. 'Of course it was. You don't need to say anymore.'

Isobel looked at her feet. 'Crisps burn, Mum. Like kindling. They weren't on fire, and then suddenly they were, and then they were *really* on fire, and then—'

'I *know* you didn't do this.' Helen hugged Isobel again. 'I love you. I'm just pleased there was no one inside.' She wanted to hold on to this moment.

Her daughter was *safe*.

'Grandpa was there,' Isobel said. 'At the shop with the dog. That's how I got inside. He was fixing the storeroom tap.'

That quickly snuffed out Helen's sense of warm, pulsing relief.

'Then he was sitting staring at the crisps in the window and told me to hang on while he got something to show me. I shouted to him, but didn't hear a reply. I'm pretty sure he'd left.'

No.

No, no, no, no. NO.

'Dad!' Helen let go of Isobel and pushed through the crowd. 'Dad!'

She whirled around.

'Has anyone – *anyone* – seen my dad?'

54

Once they'd processed it – and really, Stella thought, you could say it to yourself loads of times, *the shop is on fire*, without actually processing it – Stella and George ran outside.

'Come on!' Stella shouted.

'I'm trying to get my belt on,' George shouted back.

They reached the front door, then the front garden. They faltered and stared wordlessly at the burning shop.

This was a fire. A *real-life fire*.

Stella had never seen a real-life fire before. But it turned out a fire looked exactly – *exactly* – as she would have expected. Like the time she went to Paris and trekked to Notre Dame Cathedral in the rain. She blinked at it for as long as she needed and thought – *yes. Gargoyles, and big windows. On to the Arc de Triomphe.*

'It's hot!'

Stella looked down. Her nephew, Charlie, stared up at her.

'Hey, Charlie mate,' George crouched down. 'Stand with us. Let's link hands.' He reached out to Charlie.

Stella reached out too, and Charlie took her hand with his other one.

'Stay with us, OK?' Stella said. 'Right between us. And have you seen' – she thought – 'Grannie?'

'Grannie?'

'Gran? Grandma? Nana Margaret? The lady in the purple dress who keeps telling people what to do?'

'Grandma's in the kitchen, handing phones out of a bowl. People are shouting at her.'

'Too right they are,' Stella muttered.

Helen ran across the road towards the shop. '*Isobel!*'

Stella watched Helen try and fail to wrench open the shop door.

Stella's legs felt unsteady. 'Look after Charlie, George.'

She ran towards her sister.

Isobel emerged from behind the industrial bins and Stella slowed. She hadn't realised she'd been holding her breath; she let it out.

She watched Helen and Isobel embrace, Isobel's thin arms wrapped tightly round her mother. They had a few moments of conversation, then Helen looked panicked again and pushed through the crowd. 'Dad! Dad! Has anyone seen my Dad?'

Stella went cold.

Helen ran up to her. 'Dad might have been in the shop!'

'He left,' Isobel ran after Helen. 'Before. I think so.' She looked at Stella. 'Or I wouldn't have. . .'

'He could be inside?' Stella said.

Isobel turned to her with wide eyes. 'He left, I'm sure he left.' Isobel gestured to the shop, engulfed in flames. 'There was no one in there.'

Helen turned to Stella. 'I'll check the office. You check the shed.'

Stella ran through to the back garden and sped to the shed. Please. *Please*, no.

Not Dad.

55

The fire was shocking, obviously. But the shop was closed for the day, so there was no one in there. And Margaret couldn't believe how difficult people were being. Everyone was *just horrible* about the mobile phones, hovering over her bowl and pecking away with their fingers, not waiting their turns, making it hard to think straight. It wasn't her fault everyone's phone looked the same and some of the Post-it notes hadn't been stuck on firmly enough, was it?

'Shall I help, Margaret?' Cheryl took the bowl from her gently. 'You must be in shock.'

'Of course I'm not in shock,' Margaret barked.

Cheryl dipped into the bowl and pulled a phone out and unwound the bubble wrap. 'Samsung. Black case.' She pressed the button; the screen lit up. 'Baby in a blue hat, gurgling.'

'Mine,' a neighbour said.

Margaret stared at the neighbour. She knew his name, of course. He'd lived on the street for a decade. So why . . .?

Cheryl unwound more bubble wrap. 'iPhone with a crack across the screen. A cat on a rug, belly-up.'

'Is the cat a Siamese?' another neighbour said.

Cheryl looked at the screen dubiously. 'I don't know. It looks . . . smug?'

She showed the woman the phone.

The woman took it. 'He's not smug, he's just happy with his lot.'

'If you say so.'

'And hang on, I'm sure the crack across the screen wasn't that big before!'

Cheryl unwrapped more bubble wrap and pressed another screen. 'This one has a picture of a dog dressed like a sailor in a little hat.'

'I don't know why we have to hand out *all* the phones,' Margaret said. 'The police and fire engines are here.' She indicated Cheryl and the bowl. 'But I'm going outside. Help yourselves if you must.'

She stalked out to the street.

A crowd had gathered on the road outside the house. People milled around while yellow-helmeted firemen hosed the shop down.

One of the firemen turned round, and Margaret realised this fireman was actually a woman, but she didn't have time to think about this right now.

She stared at the shop. *Their* shop. So they didn't own it, Scott owned it, but it was just a money-maker to him. He had loads of properties. If truth be told, Margaret thought, too many. She'd found that kind of thing more impressive in the past, but now there were *so* many more homeless people on the streets than she ever remembered. And surely five bedrooms and two cars was impressive enough for anyone?

No, this wasn't Scott's tragedy. It was *their* shop.

Their business.

Their life.

Margaret shook her head. *Sentimental.*

She looked around at the people, milling around, losing their heads. At the people—

'Stop taking photos!' She marched over to them. 'Is this what you wanted your phones for? *Please.* Have some respect!'

Over the road, a taxi slowed. Margaret narrowed her gaze.

Rubberneckers were the lowest kind of people. People who actively sought drama, or created it from nothing – or even inserted themselves into other people's problems and made them worse.

The taxi slowed to a stop. Margaret marched over to the man getting out of the nearest back door of the taxi. He was pulling a bag onto his shoulder.

The man stared at the fire, wide-eyed. 'Wow.'

'*Wow* indeed. Now move along,' Margaret said. 'Let the fire engines do their work and don't you dare get your phone out to take pictures.'

'Mum?'

The voice came from the other side of the taxi.

Margaret took a step backwards. 'Pete?'

Pete grabbed his bag from the seat and slammed the car door. 'Mum, what's going on? Well, obviously the shop's on fire, but are you OK? Is everyone OK?'

'So many questions!' Margaret hurried over to hug him. 'Everything's fine!'

'But – can I do anything?'

She smiled. He was so calm, her boy. So selfless. All these people were losing their heads, and her Pete was still calm. 'Oh Pete, I'm so pleased you made it! Did you get stuck at work? Was there a problem with the trains? I know London's so hard to negotiate these days, what with all the roadworks and tube strikes and—'

'Mum, seriously. What's going on?'

'An accident of course.' She turned to Pete's companion and gave a mini-curtsey. It felt too coquettish; she hoped no one had noticed. 'And who is this?'

'This is Jin,' Pete said.

Margaret looked between Pete and Jin. From her generously sized son to this really good-looking, similar-aged (and obviously very charming) man who was *arriving at her party* with him.

Margaret smiled wider.

'Strange timing. Hi, Margaret.' The handsome man – Jin – put his hand out awkwardly. 'Can I call you "Margaret"?'

'Absolutely, you must!' Margaret said breathily. 'I wouldn't accept anything else!' She grabbed his hand in both of hers.

She turned to Pete and hugged him again.

'I can't breathe, Mum.' His voice was hoarse.

'Am I hugging you *that* tightly? It's just that it's so nice to see you.'

'Seriously, I can't breathe. A lungful of smoke has gone down the wrong way.'

Margaret released Pete from her arms. He bent forward and gave a guttural cough.

A piece of sooty paper wafted down and landed on the pavement in front of her. She kicked it to the side with the suede tip of her party shoe.

'I've heard so much about you, Margaret,' Jin said.

He really had the most charming smile. 'And I've heard so much about you!'

'No you haven't.' Pete tried to stop coughing. His voice was strained, his eyes wet from exertion. He turned to Jin. 'I haven't mentioned you.'

'Haven't mentioned me?' Jin grinned again. 'Then we'll have to get a drink and catch up, won't we?'

Margaret let out a peal of laughter. The *humour* of this delightful man.

She quietened. Dare she ask?

'But is Jin . . .?' Margaret trailed off. She indicated from one man to the other.

'He's my boyfriend,' Pete said. 'Yes.'

There was a sound of crashing from within the shop. Together, the three took extra steps back.

The fire raged behind her and Margaret let out a happy sigh.

56

Stella shoved open the gate and ran into the back garden.

Dad couldn't have been in the shop, could he? But Stella knew he could. Because that would be just how he *would* go. He would even have rushed back in after the fire started. Martyred for no cause; going down with a ship that was no longer his. Saluting, back straight, while the water engulfed him in the shadow of the iceberg.

Stella threw the shed door open. She blinked.

Dad stood in the centre of the shed, Goldie standing at his feet. He was holding his air rifle.

'I'm not going to shoot myself,' he said quickly. 'God, no. I never was. That's ridiculous.'

Through her relief, Stella registered what he'd said. 'Hang on. What?'

'I was making sure it wasn't loaded. I'm taking it to show Isobel.'

Stella was panting with exertion. She never would have thought she'd be so relieved to see her Dad carrying an air rifle with uncharacteristic purpose.

'Why were you' – *puff* – 'going to show Isobel a gun, Dad?'

'She wanted to see it. And besides, you really should knock before going into a man's shed.'

'Stay there. I need to tell Helen you're OK.'

'If you must.' Dad let his gun droop. 'Though I don't think I am OK, you know.'

'I didn't mean that sort of OK. I mean – more immediately OK. Alive.'

'You all right, Stella? You look a bit red of face.'

Stella paused. The shed had one tiny window, facing away from the shop.

How could she do this to him? Tell him *this*?

'I' – she panicked – 'I need to tell Helen you're here.'

She ran out of the shed.

Helen stumbled across the lawn towards her.

Stella jerked her thumb behind her. 'Dad's in the shed. With Goldie. That's everyone accounted for?'

Helen slowed her pace. She put her hands on her hips. 'Thank God.'

'But he doesn't know.'

They both stared at each other as the wail of the fire engine got louder.

Nathan stepped into the garden from the house, his face blank. He turned to Helen wordlessly.

Stella watched Helen rush over and pull Nathan towards her.

'The kids are safe,' Helen said. 'Everyone's safe.'

Nathan clung to Helen, his face in her hair. 'I don't—' he said. 'I just don't—'

'I know,' Helen said into his neck. 'I know.'

Nathan lifted his head. 'But the shop . . .'

He lowered his head and put his face back into her hair. Helen rubbed his back.

'Helen?' Dad came out of the shed, still holding his gun. 'Helen, what's that smell?'

Helen and Nathan unwound from their hug.

Dad turned towards the shop.

Stella looked where he was looking. At the smoke, billowing in the sky.

'Isobel's in there!' Dad cried.

'Isobel's fine,' Helen said quickly. 'She got out.'

There was a crash as flaming wood hit the pavement. They all watched the burning building.

Stella turned to look through the open gate, at Scott running down a side street, arms pumping, a CD case in one hand.

He slowed as he reached the shop. He put his hands up to his face, covering his mouth and nose in shock.

Stella looked at Dad. He still hadn't reacted.

The siren grew louder and a fire engine pulled up outside. There were shouts and ladders and hoses, and barked instructions.

'Move away!'

'Get back!'

'Everyone back!'

'Dad?' Stella said tentatively again.

Dad stared ahead. 'The shop's on fire.'

'Yep,' Stella said.

'*My* shop.'

'I know.'

'My shop. *Mine.*'

'I know.'

'I fixed the tap,' Dad said. 'It just needed a new washer.'

Stella put her hand on his shoulder. 'And I bet you did it well.'

'I fixed the tap,' Dad said again. 'Just now, Stella. I *fixed* it.'

57

George handed Charlie over to Helen in an awkward exchange. He lifted Charlie's hand and placed it in Helen's.

There was something about the way Charlie was looking at George, like he was some kind of hero. When George was around, exciting things happened. Like *fires*.

George smiled back. Charlie should know that days with George were usually more about toast and scrolling mindlessly on his phone, and – in an unwelcome, recent development – occasional *oof* noises when straightening up from putting on his shoes. But if Charlie wanted to think he was all about flames and sirens and heroic firefighters scaling ladders, George wasn't going to ruin his impression.

George gave Charlie's hot little hand a final pat.

'Thanks for looking out for him,' Helen said.

'No problem.'

'Look!' Charlie turned to Helen with wide eyes. 'It's a real-life fire engine!'

'I know,' Helen said. 'So let's leave them to save the shop without bothering them.'

George gave her an encouraging smile. If Helen hadn't realised the shop was unsalvageable, she wasn't going to hear it from him. George was going to make an effort not to *rain on parades* anymore, as Stella put it.

'I want to watch the fire people,' Charlie said. 'My favourite is the lady up that ladder. She's the shoutiest.'

'We need to go soon,' Helen said. 'They're nearly finished now.' She pulled Charlie away.

George heard raised voices. He looked over to where Margaret appeared to be in an altercation with some strangers who were getting out of a taxi. Except now it wasn't an altercation. And Margaret was hugging one stranger who, George now realised, wasn't actually a stranger.

Pete had arrived.

Even with the fire going on, and everything else he had to think about right then, George automatically reached for his phone pocket. But his pocket was empty, the phone left by the bed.

Still. He didn't need a phone to tell him that Pete had turned up several hours late. How Stella had put up with being seen as the slack one in this family without exploding with frustration, George didn't know.

George felt a softening in his chest that he *needed* to ignore.

George wandered over to see Pete. 'Hi.' He nodded at him and the two shared a loose hug. George released Pete and looked him up and down, at the battered trainers and the old sweatshirt. He sometimes forgot this guy actually existed. That he wasn't just a notorious celebrity, or Margaret's imaginary friend. 'Better late than never.' George patted Pete on the back. 'Though you missed a fun murder mystery. Apparently that solicitor part was made for someone with your acting skills.'

'The mystery's not over yet. And he had trouble with the trains, unfortunately. George, this is Jin.' Margaret stared at George meaningfully. 'Jin, this is George, Stella's husband. You'll have heard of him, I'm sure. Pete talks about the family all the time.'

George and Jin made eye contact.

'We'll fill you in on any tiny gaps,' George said.

'Jin's an actor,' Margaret said.

'And a call centre worker,' Jin said. 'I sell insurance.'

'How interesting.' George smiled politely. 'Will I have seen you in anything?'

'No,' Jin said. 'But I might have sold you critical illness cover.'

Margaret scowled. Over George's shoulder, she shouted, 'Martin!'

George turned to look. 'Martin' froze in the street.

'Where are you going?' Margaret said sharply.

Martin looked tentatively from the house to the shop, and back at Margaret.

'The party's not over!' Margaret said.

A piece of rotten wood shifted and fell to the ground.

Martin looked at the shop and back again. 'It *looks* over.'

'Rubbish! We haven't even had the fireworks yet, or the bacon sandwiches. We haven't found out who the murderer is!'

Martin moved from foot to foot. 'I'll just call a taxi anyway. Just in case.'

Margaret shook her head. Something else caught her attention. 'Adele! Don't tell me you're leaving!'

Adele tried to kiss Margaret on the cheek; Margaret dodged to the left. Adele tried again, Margaret dodged right.

'I won't have this,' Margaret said.

Adele gestured towards Scott. He was in wide-eyed conversation with a woman in a fire outfit. 'Scott's shop's burned down, Margaret. We've had a bit of a shock.'

'But it's our family business, and I'm not letting it ruin the night, am I? Scott'll have to stay here anyway to talk to the fire people. We might as well make a night of it. Get on with some dancing.'

'Margaret. Please.'

'The night's still young! Pete's just got here! And you need to meet Jin!'

'Wait up!' Cheryl hurried towards them, vicar's gown hitched up with one hand. She waved Margaret's Act Three card with the other. 'While you've all been out here, I was making myself useful. I've put everything together, going over the clues, and I've solved it! When you think about it, with everyone dead—'

'Cheryl!' Margaret clucked her mouth. 'Can't you see we've got bigger fish to fry right now? And Pete's here, look! We need to take a break for Pete to get his outfit on before we get to the solution.' Margaret turned to Adele. 'See? The party's definitely still going!'

Adele gave an embarrassed wave and stepped back.

'Please, no one leave. What am I going to do with all the bacon?' Margaret brushed hair out of her eyes and looked from one to another – to Cheryl, Pete, George and Jin. She looked at the other party guests beyond and raised her voice. 'Please, everyone! You can't leave *now! Pete's* here! And someone get Tommy. Tell him we can get that photo now we're all together!'

People made awkward smiles and took tiny steps away. Even Cheryl was doing it now, Margaret saw.

'Hang on, come back, Cheryl! I still want you to give the solution, I just meant not right now!'

Cheryl hung back. But everyone else kept leaving.

Margaret threw her hands up in frustration. 'And it's Pete! Pete's here! Surely, *surely,* you all want to see Pete?'

58

Isobel didn't like seeing a big fire as much as she thought she would.

Once Mum had told Isobel Grandpa was fine, she wasn't scared anymore. Or maybe she was, but a different kind of scared. A kind of scared that made her want to circle her arms round her body and cuddle herself close.

It wasn't her fault.

She shuffled back to sit on the damp leaves in the ginnel behind the house. Everyone else was in the street, watching the firefighters. Even the three teenagers looked impressed, pointing and taking pictures with their phones.

But Isobel didn't want to watch the fire anymore.

And she *definitely* didn't want to think about how the fire started.

Isobel looked at the bucket she'd used earlier to burn all the paper. She picked it up and walked to Grandma's black wheelie bin. She threw the bucket away and sat down on the lawn. She pulled her feet up to her bum, wrapped her arms around her legs and let her face rest on her knees.

She was feeling more like a little girl by the moment. Smaller and smaller.

No, she *was* a little girl. And that meant this whole thing wasn't her fault.

She'd only been playing.

She'd only held the lighter next to the crisp packet, she never meant to *light* the packet. There must have been a gust of wind or something.

And she hadn't known those crisps would go up like that.

How could she have known that? No one had told her.

From where she was sitting on the lawn, she could see the whooshing water on the other side of the fence. She could hear the shouting.

It must be a very big fire.

She stood up and peeked through the hole in the gate.

She watched as the firefighters spread around the building, moving fast in their chunky uniforms, moving like they already knew the next steps in a dance. They all surrounded the building, except the one person in a fire uniform who stood still in the street. She stood watching the others, not even trying to help.

Isobel took a breath. She let herself out of the back gate and stood next to the watching woman.

The woman said nothing.

Isobel inched closer.

The woman nodded at Isobel and continued watching the fire.

'Why aren't you going in?' Isobel said eventually.

'I'm the crew manager,' the woman glanced at Isobel and back at the shop, 'it's my job to watch.'

'Do you get to go up the ladder too?'

'Not today.'

'I'd want to go up the ladder.'

The crew manager shrugged.

'Are you scared?'

She stared at the building. 'No.'

'Are *they* scared?'

'They feel safe.' The woman didn't look at Isobel. 'They're trained for this and they have all the equipment.'

'Is it good equipment?'

'These uniforms are tested up to a thousand degrees.' The woman gestured over the road. 'But they've done their job, look. The fire's under control. It's nearly out now.'

Isobel turned to look properly at the shop. The fire looked more like steam and smoke than flames now.

'Fascinating, isn't it?' The woman glanced at her. 'Fire is beautiful but deadly. That's why we have to train people to control it.'

Isobel gave a long breath. She tried to imagine being able to control fire.

She realised the woman was watching her.

'We'll be here for a while till the investigations are finished. If you like' – the woman peered at Isobel – 'you can come on my engine?'

Isobel went still.

Mum hurried up to them, holding Charlie by the hand. 'I'm so sorry if she's bothering you.'

'She's not bothering me. This your daughter?'

Mum nodded.

'She has a calm demeanour.'

'Yes,' Mum said.

'She could be a firefighter when she grows up.'

Mum turned to Isobel. 'We've got to go.'

'This lady says I can go on her engine.'

Mum gave her a long look.

The crew manager looked at Isobel. 'If you want to learn more about being a firefighter, we could come in to your school.'

Isobel held her breath.

'Get your teacher to call the station,' the woman said. 'And we'll see what we can do.'

'Thanks very much.' Mum pulled at Isobel's arm. 'Let's go.'

They hurried past the group of teenagers and Isobel shook Mum's hand off her arm. She stopped.

The boy with the eyeliner looked from the fire to Isobel. 'That's your dad's shop!'

'Yes,' Isobel said.

'It's on fire!'

Isobel nodded to accept his approval. She let Mum grab her arm again and pull her along.

'Isobel! Helen! Charlie!' Grandma shouted at them from a few metres away. 'Before you go, we have to take that photo.' She pulled on Grandpa's shirt. 'Tommy, go get your camera, quick smart.'

Grandpa looked towards the house and back. 'But the lighting! I haven't got the right film loaded.'

'I'm sure any old film would be fine.'

Grandpa shook his head. 'It doesn't work like that. I'd need the HP5+. And I'd have to set up the tripod.'

'Tommy, we haven't got time.'

'I'll take the photo on my phone.' Cheryl stepped forward. 'Come on all of you. Bunch together. And smile.'

They all stood together in the street. Stella and George and Grandpa and Grandma. Mum, Dad, Isobel and Charlie.

'And Pete. And you, Jin,' Grandma said. 'Of course.'

Two strangers moved to stand with them. Isobel took a step away, though one of them now looked familiar.

'That's your uncle Pete,' Stella whispered, 'and his boy-friend, Jin.'

'I've heard a lot about Pete,' Isobel whispered back.

'Yes,' Stella said. 'Yes, you will have done.'

Cheryl lifted her phone to take the photo.

'George,' Grandma said, 'where are you going?'

'Isn't it better if it's just immediate family?'

'George!' Grandma frowned at him. 'We don't have time for your messing around now. People are *leaving*.'

George paused, then stepped forward again.

Isobel felt her nose wrinkling up because of the smoky air. She tried to unwrinkle it for the photo.

Cheryl lifted her phone. Isobel smiled widely as Cheryl took their family picture.

It was only once Cheryl lowered her phone again, once Grandma had run back over the road to tell people the party was still going, Isobel realised Cheryl had taken the photo a bit from the side. Which was a real shame, Isobel thought, because it meant she wouldn't have got any – not even a tiny little bit – of the fire engine in the picture.

59

Back in the bedroom, George and Stella looked at each other.

'So, here we are,' George said. 'Again.'

George glanced at the chair and back at Stella.

'It's your choice,' Stella said. 'But it feels quite unnecessary.'

George looked at the chair again. At the hard seat. At the unforgiving slope of the back.

'But what do I know? I'm not the one who has to sleep in it.' Stella pulled her shirt over her head and threw it across the room. 'You just don't have to make a point *all the time.*'

George looked away. He pulled his socks off and unbuckled his jeans. He put his clothes in a pile on the floor and slipped under the duvet, onto the sagging lilo.

Stella got into bed. 'At least Pete turned up in the end.'

George felt his bum and shoulders touch the carpet beneath. 'Your mum looked so happy. She was glowing with pride. Though it could have been the reflection from the flaming building.'

'She looked happy?'

'Definitely.'

He felt a warmth coming from Stella's side of the bed. He inched away, in case he started to like it.

'Since when do you care about my mum being happy?'

'That's what I'm here for, isn't it?' George closed his eyes.

He wasn't ready to process the events of the day. He just wanted to go to sleep without thinking.

With my eyes closed, I can't see anything. I could be anywhere. I'm not here, Stella's not here, I'm at home alone. If I opened my eyes, I'd see my bedroom table with the broken lamp and the empty cups. I'm not here, not in bed with my soon-to-be-ex-wife, not in Margaret and Tommy's house. No way.

He stopped himself belching. In the absence of many other guests, Margaret had fed him *a lot* of bacon sandwiches.

'Poor Dad,' Stella said. 'This is going to kill him. And poor Nathan.'

'Poor Scott as well.'

'You feel sorry for Scott? Are you two *mates* now?'

'No, I actually think he's a bit of a tool. But even if you've got loads of properties, I'm sure it's a shitter to have one of them burn down. Is that reaction OK? A tiny bit of human empathy?'

'I suppose so.'

When Stella spoke again, her voice was quieter. 'Did we do OK today?'

George kept his eyes shut. 'Kind of. Your family don't know we split up. Your dad does think I'm having an affair, but hopefully he's been distracted by the massive roaring fire.'

He felt something on his naked shoulder. The touch of a hand.

He tensed.

But then his shoulder felt cold again. The hand had gone.

Eyes still closed, he tried to work out if he was imagining it.

Maybe I've imagined all of today. Maybe I'm still in my room at the house. If I open my eyes, I'll see a broken lamp and manky coffee cups. If I look to the left, I'll see the sofa part-blocking the door.

'I touched your shoulder as mates.' Stella's voice was a whisper. 'Just to be clear. To say you're a good guy. To say thank you for coming today.'

George stayed completely still. He heard a car whoosh past the window and, in the distance, the beeps of a van reversing. A faint shout.

He waited.

Stella said nothing else. Did nothing else.

George lay there, unmoving, trying to work out exactly what had just happened. Wondering about the effect smoke inhalation had on the brain – and whether it had affected the decision-making part of Stella's brain, or the perception part of his. Or both.

He lay still. Wondering whether, either way, there was any chance whatever was going on would last until morning.

60

The cars and taxis had gone now, and the fire in the shop was officially out. The only people left on the street were the firefighters and Scott, and the odd drunk, shuffling home from somewhere.

And Tommy.

Tommy couldn't bring himself to leave the site of the fire, despite Margaret's coaxing to come into the house and have a drink with Pete and Jin.

Margaret had brought him out a bacon sandwich on a napkin, and set it down next to him. Tommy didn't react, and still didn't react when, initially tentatively, then with increasing openness, Goldie ate the sandwich.

Tommy sat on his front step and stared at the shop.

At what was left of the shop.

Somehow it looked less like Nathan or Scott's shop, but more like Tommy's, now it was destroyed.

A fixer-upper, Tommy thought. *Not the finished article; something with potential. Like something you'd find in a skip.*

Tommy was good with things you found in a skip.

Someone opened the front door behind him. Tommy righted himself so he didn't fall backwards.

Nathan walked out. He looked at Tommy for a moment, then gestured to his step. 'Do you mind?'

Tommy didn't move.

Nathan hovered for a moment. There wasn't room on the step next to Tommy, so Nathan lowered himself until he sat cross-legged on the cold drive, next to Tommy and a sphinx-posed Goldie.

In a row, the three of them stared at the ex-shop in silence. 'Excuse me.'

Tommy looked up at a man in overalls and a hard hat, who was walking up to him with Scott in tow. 'I'm the watch manager here. You are Tommy Foy and Nathan Wheatley?'

Nathan got up and dusted himself off. 'Yes.'

Tommy looked down. 'I suppose so.'

'The proprietor' – the man indicated Scott – 'said you might be able to help with some questions about the fire? I can't leave the site until we've fully investigated the scene.'

Tommy stared at his shoes. 'It's not my shop anymore. It's nothing to do with me.'

The watch manager indicated Scott again. 'Mr Prentice said you're the one who'd know the ins and outs of the building in most detail.'

Tommy acknowledged this truth with a nod.

'So can you both follow us across the road? I'd like to ask you some questions.'

Nathan nodded. 'Of course.'

Eventually, Tommy stood up too. He brushed down the seat of his trousers.

The watch manager looked down. 'I'm afraid the dog can't come.'

Tommy looked at the now-standing Goldie. He opened the front door and gave Goldie's rear a shove. She finally got the message and loped through the doorway.

Tommy shut the door behind her and followed the man and Scott and Nathan over the road. The burning smell still hung tartly in the air.

He could barely bring himself to look. 'What happened?'

'We're just working that out.' The man peered at him. 'What do *you* think happened here?'

Tommy looked around now. He surveyed the ash on the ground, the remnants of broken awning. 'What happened is my world went up in flames.'

There was an awkward silence. The three looked away, and Tommy looked down at his feet.

A little melodramatic. But it couldn't be helped.

'Was there anything particular' – the watch manager indicated an area just behind the shop front – 'just here?'

'There was a display.' Tommy narrowed his eyes. 'A display of crisps.'

'Anything specific you can tell me about it?'

Tommy turned to look at Nathan. At the accusation in Tommy's eyes, Nathan looked down, now fascinated by the ash on the ground.

Tommy stood straighter. 'There were exposed electrics here. Fancy lighting, woven into cardboard. An all-singing, all-dancing display.'

Nathan shoved his hands in his pockets.

The man in overalls nodded. He wrote something on his clipboard.

'Could it have been an electrical fire?' Tommy asked.

'I'm just making notes for now.'

'Did whatever it was here catch fire?'

The man smiled. 'I'm afraid I need to keep asking the questions for now.'

'Of course.' Tommy sucked in his breath. 'But those *crisps!*'

He glared at Nathan and looked back. 'Did they spontaneously combust?'

'That would be unlikely.' The watch manager glanced at Tommy's face; he let his clipboard drop to his side. 'If they were packaged in paper and high in fat, they might have acted like kindling. But it's too early for me to make that assessment.'

Tommy widened his stance. He glared at Nathan again. 'They were *unnecessarily* high in fat.'

Nathan rocked awkwardly on the balls of his feet.

'And I *still* don't understand,' Tommy continued, 'why the smoke alarm didn't go off. I'd made it clear in the detailed shop handover document that the batteries needed checking each month.'

Nathan fixed on something over Tommy's shoulder. 'I'm just . . . going to check something with Margaret.' He strode off, hands in his pockets.

Tommy kicked a piece of wood on the floor. He looked from Scott to the watch manager. 'They said those crisps came from a *farm,* can you believe that?'

Scott's face was blank, but the watch manager studied his clipboard.

Tommy shook his head. He adjusted his position till he stood taller still, his feet now even wider apart.

'Cowboys.' He shook his head again, feeling the sparks of life reigniting in his chest. 'Unlucky, son.' He patted Scott on the shoulder. 'You've learnt a life lesson and learnt it the hard way. There are some unscrupulous people out there. And, unfortunately, some manufacturers are bloody *irresponsible* cowboys.'

THE DÉNOUEMENT

A Detective Speaks

To be read out by the solicitor, Mr Shaker (a.k.a. Pete Foy) when someone has correctly identified the murderer.

Congratulations for solving the case!

You have, of course, identified that Lady Brockenhurst was the murderer, and it was she who sent the note of adoration to the love of her life, Lord Brockenhurst. She killed her love rival, Agnes, and then killed Lord Brockenhurst when she realised Agnes was just one of many lovers. Lady Brockenhurst decided she couldn't live without his fidelity, and that he wouldn't live without her. The gassing of the couple in the second Bentley was a murder–suicide.

You are also aware Lady Brockenhurst killed Miss Evangeline before the vicar could reveal that she had discovered the love letters were clearly produced on the typewriter in Lady Brockenhurst's study (which was obvious because of an imperfection on the 'N' key).

She forged and stole the will to throw early
suspicion on Mr Owlish – knowing, of course, that
after Lord B died intestate, his estate would pass
to his brother and heir, Ashley. Remember: Lady B
was the only one who knew that Ashley had secretly
married Ellie, so she knew her ward, Ellie, would be
financially taken care of.

You have identified that the theft of Ellie's late
mother's necklace was a red herring: that it had
been accidently taken to the attic and placed in the
dressing-up box by an absent-minded servant.
Congratulations again for solving the mystery!

Please accept this Star Detective Badge and the
one-of-a kind, specially printed, I Solved the Murder
at Brockenhurst Manor mug, that are both currently
being presented to you by my glamourous maternal
assistant.

For the others who didn't solve the mystery,
commiserations and better luck next time.

Happy future sleuthing!

61

They say that, after something dramatic happens, you don't remember it for the first few seconds on waking. You lie there reliving the remnants of your old life, and then think – *oh. That happened.*

But that wasn't true. Not for Stella, not the morning after the party.

A noise from downstairs made her stir. Before she'd even opened her eyes, the facts dropped into in her consciousness, in an ordered yet simultaneous list.

Wrong bed.

Kidnapped by Mum at their house.

George next to me.

Shop fire.

Stella decided to focus on the least complicated of these points. She pulled back the duvet and strode over to the window.

The fire itself was long out, leaving a blackened shell, the building significantly smaller and emptier than before. Stella could see right through it, from the shopfront to the charred back yard. There was red-and-white traffic tape fencing off the shop. The glass in the windows had gone, blown out or melted, or just – disappeared. The *Le Jardin* awning was gone too, so you couldn't tell the building was even a shop anymore.

Several passers-by stood chatting, peeking into the build-ing unashamedly, like it was a stop on a walking tour.

'Is the shop still gone?' George's voice came from the bed. 'It hasn't regenerated overnight?'

Stella let the curtain fall back into place. 'Still gone.'

George hooked his naked arm over the duvet. Stella felt a thud of déjà vu and a rush of heat to her face. She looked at the carpet.

George shuffled up the bed. 'Is that Pete's voice?'

Stella strained to listen. Sure enough, that was Pete's voice downstairs, his words followed by her mother's laugh. A laugh that sounded too joyous for the circumstances.

'Your mum sounds like she's having a great old time.'

'I'm guessing Pete and Jin stayed last night.'

George looked down at the lilo/mattress combo. 'They must have had an even worse sleeping arrangement than us.'

Stella hopped back under the duvet. 'I wouldn't count on it.'

She lay facing the ceiling, ensuring no part of her touched any part of George.

It was a moment of weakness, touching his shoulder last night. When she'd briefly forgotten that hard-learned lesson. That they were terrible together, and happier apart.

At least George hadn't acted on her touch. One of them was being sensible. And she hadn't totally humiliated herself. She'd kept things vague. She could deny her intentions, if necessary.

'Your parents know how to throw a party,' George said. 'They'll be an Instagram sensation.'

There was another peal of Mum's laughter from down-stairs. A shriek of excitement.

'Like she doesn't have a care in the world,' George said.

They both stared ahead.

'Stella—'

'Don't.'

The duvet rustled next to her. In her peripheral vision, Stella saw George try to face her.

'Should we talk?'

'No.'

'I'm so sorry about Nancy. We have to discuss it.'

'We don't *have* to discuss it, we don't *have* to do anything. We're divorcing.'

Stella folded her arms in a clear sign.

George didn't say anything. He retreated out of her peripheral vision.

Stella heard furniture being moved across the room downstairs. 'I need to go and check on Mum and Dad.'

'Before you do.'

'*No*, George.' Hadn't he listened?

'It's something else. Something I found out yesterday.'

Stella turned her head to face him. 'You look serious.'

George indicated the space between them with a hand. 'Whatever's going on here—'

'Which is nothing.'

'Which is nothing. There's something else going on, and I don't know whether to tell you yet.'

She sat up. 'You have to tell me now, obviously.'

He glanced at her. 'Really?'

'You can't stop now. *Whatever it is, tell me later*, who in the world has ever said that?'

'I didn't think it through.'

'Is it another secret girlfriend?' Stella made herself sit up straighter. 'Have you been gallivanting all over town?' She sharpened her voice. 'Rinsing off plates for all the girls?'

'It's not that.' His voice was . . . not normal.

Stella looked into George's eyes. She'd seen this look before. When he'd come into the bedroom to wake her first thing in the morning, and said, 'There's something I need to tell you.' When she knew someone must have died, and she'd sat up to receive the news, her brain ratcheting through a list of who it might be and how. She had just settled on *Dad, adjusting the aerial and falling off the roof like Rod Hull*, when George had finally broken it to her, in his saddest voice, that the Wi-Fi was down.

'Has the Wi-Fi gone again?'

George gave a small smile. 'No.'

'It's not even our house, so what do I care if—'

George stopped smiling. 'I'm afraid you've got to listen to something. And it's going to be tough.'

Stella's stomach dropped. 'Have I got to be brave? Have I got to be a brave little soldier?'

George reached for her hand. He looked away then back.

And that's when Stella knew it wasn't the Wi-Fi.

George took a deep breath.

'Spit it out.' Stella spoke harshly. 'Come on, I haven't got all day.'

George held her gaze softly. 'I'm afraid there's something I've got to tell you. And I'm afraid it's about your mum.'

62

The morning after the fire, Helen decided it was important – *really* important – to organise something. Yes, the fire had sent her family into chaos, but every action needed an equal and opposite reaction. Regaining an element of control was what was required here.

And you know what Helen could control? The *freezer*.

Helen tied her hair back and stormed into the kitchen in her pyjamas. She flicked the freezer power switch off and arranged a towel on the floor.

She started pulling out drawers. She deposited cold, hard, often mysterious items onto the floor.

Her internal monologue was fast and jumpy.

I mean, freezers aren't even meant to need defrosting these days, so where has all the ice come from?

Don't think about the fire.

How many pitta breads? *That's just a waste of valuable freezer space.*

No one in your family started the fire. Definitely not Isobel. Definitely not Nathan, trying to cover his tracks and hide his fraud.

Wow, my hands are cold.

Helen put her oven gloves on and returned to her task.

She studied a Tupperware container, turning it over in her hand.

Soup or stew?

She rummaged some more.

Oh, I did have one of those pies left after all.

She sat back on her heels.

Did Nathan start the fire?

She hadn't seen him all morning. He was out somewhere, probably dealing with the emergency services. He'd left when she was in the shower. Almost as if he didn't want to tell her where he was going.

If it wasn't for the money, I would never have considered that the fire could have been set by Nathan.

The thought had blossomed in the threat-happy part of her consciousness at about 2 a.m. Usually, the 2 a.m. worries lessened in the warm light of morning.

Usually.

Helen continued depositing freezer food on the table. She found some raspberries she'd frozen in case she ever needed instant cocktail ingredients – in case she'd suddenly turned into a Real Housewife of Cheshire.

She dumped them straight in the sink. Helen was not the kind of woman who had people round for impromptu cocktails. She needed to admit that to herself, and be fine with it. And save herself some freezer space.

She fetched the hairdryer from the bedroom and blow-dried the inside of the freezer, watching as ice turned to water and ran onto the towel.

'Do you want some help?'

At Isobel's voice, Helen frowned. 'Thanks, darling, but you don't need to help.'

'Why are we doing this today?'

Helen gave a too-high laugh. '*We* aren't, *I* am. Go and watch telly or something. Or eat one of those ice pops

335

on the table, but I don't know how old they are.'

'Can I talk to you?' Isobel's voice was small.

'I need to do this now, I'm afraid.' Helen stood up purposefully. 'It's important we take stock and reflect after an incident like yesterday. And I'm taking stock and reflecting that the freezer needs clearing out.' Helen strode towards the table. 'While you're here, how old does this lasagne look to you?'

'I think I might have started the fire, Mum.'

Helen placed the lasagne down firmly on the table. 'No you didn't.'

'I think I did, though.'

Helen shook her head, hard. 'You can't make things happen just by thinking them. Are you sure you don't want to go back upstairs?'

Isobel just stared up at her.

Helen felt her shoulders slump and looked down at her oven-gloved hands. She fussed over the freezer food for a minute more. She risked glancing round.

Isobel was still staring at her.

Wearily, Helen sat down at the table. She gestured for Isobel to come closer. She peeled off her oven gloves.

'But if you *had* set the fire,' Helen said, 'it would have been an accident, right?'

Isobel looked at her shoes.

'I'm sure that's the only way it could have happened,' Helen said.

'I don't think it can have been a *complete* accident.' Isobel's voice was so quiet. 'Because I definitely held the lighter near those crisps on purpose.'

Helen closed her eyes for a second. 'But you never meant to set them aflame.'

336

'I don't know. I don't *think* so. And I was only pretending to set one packet on fire. I didn't realise the whole display would go up so quick. I thought fire only went up, not down. I didn't mean to ruin anything.'

Isobel started to cry.

Helen pulled her daughter towards her. 'Of course you didn't.'

Helen patted Isobel's back softly as Isobel sobbed into her. Helen patted and rubbed. Her chest filled with warmth where her daughter's head lay.

Helen tried to work out why this didn't feel like the most awful thing ever. That her daughter was a fire-starter. (A twisted fire-starter.)

She stroked Isobel's hair.

Maybe it was because Isobel was *telling her*. She'd confessed. Integrity and honesty and remorse – all the right emotions were here in her daughter, present and correct.

There were no classmate-shooting *Kevin* behaviours here.

Helen pulled back from the hug and looked into Isobel's eyes. 'But why would you even *pretend* to set a packet of crisps on fire?'

'Because those crisps were rubbish. Grandpa hated them. And it was fun, for a few seconds. But then it went bad, really quickly. And it was too hot and smoky for me to do anything then.'

'That's fire for you,' Helen said. 'Hot.'

'I'm never setting anything on fire again.'

'Good girl,' Helen said.

'Do we have to tell the police? And the fire people?'

Helen stroked Isobel's back. 'I'm afraid so. But if we tell them it was an accident, they will understand. Kids don't always understand the impact of their actions.'

337

'I'll go to prison.' Isobel sniffed.

'You're not going to go to prison. You're a child, you didn't understand what you were doing.'

'I'll get a criminal record.'

'They don't give kids criminal records,' Helen said firmly. She hoped it was true.

'I'm so sorry, Mum.'

'Course you are, darling,' Helen said. 'That's all that matters.'

'Do you think Dad's going to mind?' Isobel looked up through wet lashes. 'About the shop?'

'I think ... I think he'll be disappointed.' Helen stroked Isobel's hair and, amazingly, Isobel let her. 'But he won't blame you.'

'Maybe he can go back to being an estate agent,' Isobel said into Helen's T-shirt. 'They can give him back that car to drive with the writing on the side.'

'Yes,' Helen said. 'Maybe.'

'I liked the car with the writing. Except that it didn't have back doors.'

'That *was* annoying,' Helen said.

'But I always knew which was our car in the car park.'

Charlie shouted something from upstairs. Something about dinosaurs. Helen couldn't hear him clearly, but, from the tone of his voice, it couldn't wait.

'I think Charlie's found a T-Rex under the bed again.' Helen got to her feet wearily. 'I need to take you both to Katrina's pizza party in a little while. Do you want to help me put things back in the freezer?'

Isobel shrugged. 'No. Not really.'

'OK.'

'I'm not bothered about helping with the freezer, really.'

'Right,' Helen said. 'That makes sense.'

'I just wanted to talk to you. I'll have an ice pop though. If there isn't anything better.'

'There isn't,' Helen said.

Isobel picked up an ice pop. She studied it at arm's length.

Helen watched Isobel amble with it into the lounge. She packed a bag for the pizza party and wondered how it was she was still standing here, functioning. How she wasn't collapsed on the floor in a motionless, foetal ball.

63

George told Stella everything. How he'd worked out her Mum wasn't having treatment. The conversations of the day before.

Stella tried to process what he was saying, point by point.

Mum was pretending to have treatment lined up for the cancer, but she had no intention of going through with it.

This party had been a funeral. A funeral, that Mum could plan, supervise and *attend*.

The situation was surreal. Devastating, brutal, and impossible to influence.

This situation was so . . . *Mum*.

'Are you OK?' George said.

'I think so.'

'You seem . . . dazed.'

'I think I knew.' Stella felt a complete, notable absence of emotion. 'Or I'm in shock. I knew or I'm in shock, it's one or the other.'

'Your mum has planned her exit,' George said. 'Controlled everything. How can she be so matter-of-fact about *this*? I can't stop thinking about your poor dad, and how he's going to cope.'

'Oh, God,' Stella said. 'Dad.'

And at that – the image of her dad's lost, sad, face, the thought of him negotiating this empty house – Stella put her head on George's neck. The tears finally came.

An hour later, Stella left George in her old bedroom and walked down the stairs alone. She paused, looking at the lounge, delaying going into the kitchen to see Mum.

The lounge was back to pre-party normal. Emergency chairs and disco lights removed, rug back down. Furniture moved back into the centre of the room, blankets removed from the sofas. Glassware stacked up and in the cupboards, figurines back on the mantelpiece.

If it wasn't for the side table missing a (now smashed) lamp and the rust-coloured stain on the carpet, you wouldn't know there had been a party at all.

Stella heard Mum singing in the kitchen. She took a breath and went in.

Mum smiled at her from the fully cleared kitchen table. 'Sleep well?'

Mum made no mention of the fire. Stella wondered if she'd moved it into her past already. *A shop? Oh, yes, we did have a shop once.*

'Where's Dad?'

Mum looked away.

'Mum?'

'He's writing letters. Upstairs.'

'Right.'

'I can hear muttering and swooshing of papers from the study. He's keeping himself out of trouble.'

Stella wasn't sure that was true. She'd seen her dad's TripAdvisor reviews, and his letters to the council about the rubbish collections could only be described as *provocative*.

Stella sat down. 'That's good.' She reached for Mum's hand. 'Mum. George told me.'

Mum shook Stella's hand off. She stood up quickly. 'I need to work out where to put all these.' She turned her back and reached for the anniversary cards on the side. 'So much fuss over nothing, isn't it? And how long am I meant to leave them up collecting dust?'

'Mum . . .'

She kept sorting through the cards. 'I don't want to talk about it.'

'I do.'

'But I don't. And you can't ruin today! Today is a momentous day! The angels are out in force for the Foy family today.'

'What?'

'Let's wait for George, so I can tell you both the news together.' Mum headed to the bottom of the stairs and shouted up. 'George! Can you hurry down please?'

George ambled downstairs, his unbrushed hair sticking up at one side.

He looked from Mum to Stella in a question.

Stella shrugged.

Mum ushered George into the room. 'Pete's just told me some news!' Mum looked from one to the other. She clapped her hands together. 'He and lovely Jin are getting married!'

Stella smiled. 'Congratulations, Mum.'

'You mean *Congratulations, Pete*! They've had to head into town because Pete has some urgent business with a contact, but they'll be back later, so you can congratulate them.'

George leaned forward and kissed Mum on the cheek. 'Congratulations, Margaret. I'm so happy for you.'

'I need to start planning!' Mum said.

'You do?' Stella said.

George opened a kitchen cupboard. 'Gonna grab some cereal now, if that's all right?'

'Don't eat it all, George. Pete and Jin might want some later. Pete always did like cereal in the afternoon.'

Stella and George glanced at each other.

'And Pete's promised to have the wedding by the end of this year. For obvious reasons that we aren't going to discuss.' Mum beamed at them. 'Do you think it'll be a big wedding?'

'I'd manage your expectations a bit,' George said.

'Do you think there'll be a chocolate fountain?'

George glanced at Mum. He poured himself some Honey Nut Loops.

'I'd love it if there was a chocolate fountain.'

Stella made herself smile. 'You never know, I suppose. Maybe – maybe this one time – Pete will surprise us.'

64

Helen dropped Isobel and Charlie off at the pizza party. She had just finished restocking the freezer when she heard the front door slam.

Nathan threw his keys onto the kitchen counter. He slumped into the chair next to hers.

Helen waited. She didn't trust herself to speak first.

'*Le Jardin's* destroyed.' Nathan pinched the space between his eyes. His left eyelid stress-flickered. 'That's it. Over.'

Helen wiped her hands carefully on the tea towel.

'They could rebuild it, of course.' Nathan didn't seem to notice Helen hadn't spoken. 'But why would Scott bother rebuilding a shop when he could build flats there instead and charge twice as much?'

Helen stared at him. She placed the tea towel back on the hook. 'Where've you been?'

'With the fire people.' Nathan's eyelid twitched for a third time. 'Then I borrowed your parents' dog and took it for a walk.'

'You don't ever walk the dog.'

'I wanted to *do* something purposeful. If you go for a walk without a dog or a destination, you're just drifting.'

Despite all the real emotions about Isobel and the fraud playing out in her tight chest, Helen couldn't help being momentarily distracted by this bad logic. That Nathan also didn't understand about *being in the moment* and to *take the time to study the surroundings and simply be,* and other stuff she'd picked up from Sunday supplements that told her she'd been going for a walk wrong for forty years.

'But it was wary of me the whole time,' Nathan continued. 'Kept looking back at the car. It hates me, that dog.'

Nathan was clearly expecting to hear soothing *no he doesn't* sounds. Noises Helen would normally have made, even though he was right, and Goldie definitely had no time for him.

Nathan slumped further back in the chair. 'Where are the kids?'

'At Katrina's pizza party.' She picked up her car keys. 'Let's go for another walk. You and me but no dog, this time.'

'Helen—'

'On the walk.' She reached for her coat. 'We talk outside.'

She headed out of the front door and waited for him to follow.

Helen drove to the brown-signed quarry car park in the next town. She and Nathan set off round the man-made lake.

Helen tried to focus on the air, the leaves, the smell, the grass. She took deep breaths, like she was meant to. Her hands were still shaking. It was a challenging day to go for an in-the-moment walk.

Focus, Helen.

The problem was, she really didn't want to be in the moment right now. Not *this* moment, anyway.

She tried again to be mindful.

Look at that leaf, the way it changes colour partway down. Nature's magical.

My daughter's an arsonist.

Helen stopped walking. 'Isobel started the fire.'

And there it was.

Nathan stopped. 'She can't have.'

'She said it was an accident. She was playing with a lighter near the crisp display.'

Helen studied Nathan's face.

His eye might be stress-flickering, but he didn't look surprised enough, she decided. Even though he'd always dismissed her concerns about Isobel. *She's just a child* or *kids are kids, they experiment*, his reassurances making her feel like she was fussing.

Right, Helen thought. *So it wasn't just me. Not deep down.*

'Aren't you going to at least act surprised?'

She should be angrier with him, she thought. But he looked so hunched over. And that bloody twitching eye. It earned him pity he didn't deserve.

'I can't take it in, Helen. Where did she get the lighter?'

'School? The pavement?' Helen shrugged. 'Anywhere.' Helen deliberately wouldn't look at that eye. 'We're going to have to tell the police.' She made herself continue walking. 'Surely she won't get in trouble? A *child*. She didn't mean to do it.'

Helen caught Nathan's gaze; she looked away.

The two said nothing for several minutes.

'Say something,' she said.

Nathan raised his palms. 'I'm just – give me a minute. I can't take it in.'

'I want us to find a way of making this OK. Can you think of one?'

Nathan looked down at his boots.

When he didn't reply, Helen continued. 'I think she only

meant to start a little contained fire, just one packet of crisps. She didn't mean to burn the shop down.' With her out-stretched hand, Helen caught a low branch. She moved it to the side so she could pass. 'Does that make it OK?'

Nathan kept looking at his boots.

'And she's sorry. She's really sorry.'

That part was definitely accurate. *Of course* it was. She'd seen her daughter's face that morning.

When Nathan didn't respond, Helen couldn't hold back anymore. 'I'm actually relieved it was Isobel. Because I know now the fire was an accident.'

Nathan shoved his hands in his pockets. 'What?'

'I thought *you* might have set the fire. Deliberately.'

Nathan turned to her. 'What – the *actual* – hell?'

'Because of the fraud.' Helen kept her voice level. No anger, no tears, just facts. 'Because of all the extra money going through the shop. The mythical two hundred cappuccinos drunk every day by one elderly lady and a low-slung dog.'

Helen waited.

She waited some more.

This was Nathan's silence, and he was *bloody well* going to have to fill it himself.

'I *knew* you'd notice.' Nathan shook his head. 'I *told* Margaret you'd notice. I said "Helen knows the business. And she's not stupid."'

At Mum's name, Helen pulled her scarf round her neck more tightly.

She looked at her hands. 'The two of you have been keep-ing secrets from me.'

'No!' Nathan spoke hurriedly. '*She* was the one keeping se-crets. I knew nothing. It was already happening by the time I found out and, well, you can imagine, I was furious.'

Helen thought. *Could* she imagine that? Did it make things better or worse? 'Tell me. Everything.'

'I didn't notice at first, I was just pleased that we were making such a good turnover after all my new ideas.' His eye flickered; Helen focused on the other one. 'It felt great, after the redundancy, to be successful at something again. And I didn't mind that the profits weren't going up with the turnover because it felt like I was developing a healthy business. But then – I couldn't ignore it anymore. I knew it wasn't right. And it turned out Margaret had been laundering money the whole time.'

This was unbelievable. 'And what did she say when you confronted her?'

'She said to keep you away from the accounts, and it had already happened, so there was nothing I could do about it, but I could restock the place however I wanted. I got all that new signage without a peep from her. Not a single complaint.'

Helen reflected on this.

'She said she'd take the fall about the money and nothing would have my fingerprints on. Though she'd already done it by the time she told me – I couldn't have stopped it if I tried. Not without turning back time, or grassing up your mother. Which didn't feel like an option.'

Helen looked up at the sky, wondering if this conversation was actually happening, and whether she was *inside* it. In previous weeks, she might have been able to have floated away and watched herself holding this conversation at a distance.

She couldn't watch herself at a distance now. Unfortunately this was the real Helen, the real grounded Helen, who was having this real and extremely unwelcome conversation.

'I don't want her doing dodgy stuff in my new business, do

I?' Nathan pressed the heels of hands to his eyelids. 'I would never have chosen this to happen. But she just did it without asking.'

He brought his hands away and made twitching eye contact with Helen.

'Mum did this,' Helen said dully. *Of course she did.*

She hadn't wanted it to be Nathan, she realised. But this . . .

'I hoped I'd made a mistake. That you were going to point out how I'd misunderstood.'

'She kept saying it was only for a few months,' Nathan said. 'She said it was a victimless crime.'

'Mum oversimplifies things to suit herself.'

'What was I meant to do – *shop your mother?*' Nathan shook his head. 'Isobel and Charlie adore her. And Margaret said by the time it got discovered – *if* it ever got discovered – she'd be . . . gone. That's the word she used, *gone*. And she'd made sure all the evidence pointed to her. Her logic was twisted but surprisingly hard to argue with. I've never heard anyone talk about their death as a problem-solver the way your mother does.'

Helen said nothing.

'I was furious, obviously – can you imagine?' Nathan hunched his brow. 'You put your name on a new business and think it's a new start, and then you find out there are illegal shenanigans and your mother-in-law is using you as a massive stupid *pawn*, but what could I do?'

'There were a few things you could have done.'

'Tell me then. What should I have done?'

'Told *me*.'

'I was trying to protect you.'

'You should have told me anyway.'

Nathan said nothing.

Helen made her voice level. 'Why did she do it?'

'She said it was "family reasons". Once I realised I wasn't going to do anything about it, I didn't want to know anything. I just wanted her to stop and she promised it would be over in a couple of months.'

Helen closed her eyes. 'Pete's in debt again.'

'I assumed so.'

'But why didn't you tell me?'

'Oh, God.' Nathan pushed his hands roughly through his hair. 'I wanted to. Don't you remember me asking you, time and again, not to do the accounts? Saying you're too busy with the kids and your day job, and isn't it a critical time for Isobel, with all her . . . special challenges?'

'I thought you were saying I was a bad accountant.'

'I'd never think that.'

'And a bad mum. I thought your comment was a shortcut to cover both bases.'

'I was trying to make sure you didn't get involved.'

Helen pushed a branch out of her way, using more force than necessary.

'I've been avoiding you.' Nathan looked down at his hands. 'Spending so much time in the shop and with suppliers. I can't tell you evasions.'

'Lies of omission, Nathan. And you should have told me.'

Nathan shoved his hands in his pockets. 'You're right.'

'But this still doesn't explain why you ended up getting me that patronising book about being calm for Christmas.'

'OK.' He held up his hands. 'OK, that was nothing to do with the shop. That was a mistake.'

Helen watched a duck skid across the lake, wings held wide as it landed on the surface. She thought of all the years that shop had been in her family. Could Mum really have risked all this?

'Are we going to be OK?'

Helen glanced up. She saw the vulnerability in the round of Nathan's shoulders.

When she didn't answer, he added, 'Should I give you time? I can give you time.'

Helen made herself focus on Nathan. 'You should have stopped her.'

'OK.' Nathan kicked an empty drink can along the path. 'I don't know how anyone stops her from doing anything, but OK. Have you ever been able to stop her doing what she wants? How do you manage that?'

Helen looked away. She was the victim here. Her role was to be the outraged party, not to problem-solve, and Nathan had had loads more time to think about this than she had. It wasn't fair to put this question on the victim.

'Please, Helen. Look at me.'

She looked at Nathan blankly.

'I know there's loads to talk about. But just reassure me. That we're going to get through this? That I haven't ruined everything?'

Helen folded her arms in a self-hug.

'Please. Just tell me we'll be OK.'

'Don't push me today. If you make me answer today, you won't like the answer.'

Nathan took this in. 'Do you want me to leave you alone?'

Helen kept walking. Nathan hurried to catch her up.

Finally, she turned to him. 'You didn't have anything to do with it? You were really a pawn? If I ask Mum,' Helen pulled her coat lapels closer round her, 'will she say the same? Or will she say *she* was *your* pawn?'

Nathan snorted. 'Your mother is no one's pawn.'

Helen shoved her hands in her pockets. 'No.' She still couldn't think about how long Nathan had kept this from her. What it said about them that they'd ended up here, only discussing this now.

But there were layers of betrayal here. Helen needed time to process the layers. Some were more complicated than others.

All she knew, right now, was that she was never going to be able to forgive her mother this time.

65

By lunchtime, George was all Foyed-out. They just needed to get Stella's car out from behind the one on the drive, then he could forget this whole weekend.

He was *so nearly* out of there. Nearly out of that family, in fact. If this hideous experience was a trip to IKEA, he'd trudged painfully to the end of the arrows and was in the queue for the tills, able to see the windows and the tempting glint of outside beyond.

But he hadn't reached the exit yet. So here they were, still at the kitchen table, still listening to Margaret muse about the elements that might make up Pete's wedding day. She was hoping for a lot, George decided. A string quartet. A four-course meal. A swooping, ring-delivering owl. Margaret speculated on Pete's intentions and Pete, George thought, sounded increasingly like a man she'd never met.

There was a scraping sound from upstairs – Tommy moving a chair in the study – followed by the sound of Eeyore-paced footsteps on the stairs.

Tommy's shape loomed in the kitchen doorway and George looked away quickly. He'd avoided Tommy since the row about the call with Nancy.

'We're out of printer paper,' Tommy said.

'There are some emergency sheets in the cupboard. And,

love,' Margaret looked up, 'you need to drive to Jane's. So we can pick up her car keys and move her car.'

'I need to see Helen before we go.' Stella looked from George to Tommy. 'Do you want to go with Dad to pick up the keys?'

George gripped the seat of his chair.

There was a long pause.

Tommy turned to George. He looked deliberately over George's shoulder. 'Have you got your shoes on?'

'I'll get a taxi. It's fine.'

Tommy made eye contact, finally. 'A *taxi*? To *Bolton*?'

'It's not a problem.'

'You *can't* get a taxi to *Bolton*. It's unheard of.'

George looked at Stella for help.

Stella stood up. 'What's Helen's address, Mum? I can walk from here, right?'

Tommy got his car keys from the hook under the kitchen cabinet. 'Look lively, George.' He walked out of the room.

George got up slowly. He flicked one last desperate glance at Stella and followed Tommy out.

Tommy set out his intentions for the car journey by putting on Radio 4 before they were even out of Cole Street. He turned the volume way up.

Tommy drove, staring straight ahead, his hands in the ten-to-two position.

George closed his eyes.

'—*even claims that the moon landings were a hoax, and that terrorist shootings were staged by crisis actors. The dismissal of expert views on unregulated online forums*—'

George heard the *tick tick* of the indicator. He felt Tommy brake, then speed up.

That *tick tick* again.

George set his jaw. This was *fucking unbearable.*

'Stella and I went through a difficult patch.' He couldn't take it anymore. 'We separated, briefly. I dated someone else, briefly. It's long over.'

Tommy flicked the indicator on again. *Tick tick.*

He adjusted the volume of the radio, up a little.

He adjusted it again. Down a little.

George pressed his fingers into his thighs.

'*—underestimating the human cost and the real-world impact, that this leads to vulnerable people with already-shattered lives receiving death threats—*'

George had just accepted that Tommy was pretending not to hear him, when Tommy put his hand back on the wheel. 'Are you through the bad patch?'

George glanced at Tommy, who stared firmly at the road ahead.

'I don't know,' George lied. 'We're trying to make it better.'

'You haven't treated her badly?'

'Not in the way you think.' He thought of Stella, sitting at that kitchen table in her gloves on *Jurassic Park* day. 'Maybe I did treat her badly, in some ways. Maybe I didn't support her enough. Or talk enough, or listen enough.'

Tommy fiddled with the radio volume again.

'*—increasing rapidly as trust in the mainstream media breaks down. A recent study that sixty per cent of the British public believe in at least one false narrative—*'

'Talking's overrated,' Tommy indicated to take the exit off the M60 onto the M61. 'I don't know why everyone goes on about talking. Look at me and Margaret.'

He seemed to be waiting for a response.

George adjusted his seat belt.

'Yes?' he said eventually.

'We never talk. Or only about shopping lists, or the overnight frost, or the state of the grouting. We understand each other perfectly.'

'Right.' George thought about this. 'Do . . . do you want to know more about me and Stella?'

'None of my business.' Tommy took the exit. 'You both say you haven't betrayed her. So that's that. And, George' – Tommy glanced up and back at the road – 'no more talking today.'

Tommy turned the radio volume way up.

'—*with the long-discredited belief in a link between autism and the vaccination of children still widespread*—'

Tommy shifted to face George. 'Do you understand all this? All this stuff about crisis actors and people thinking the moon landing was faked?'

'I wasn't listening.'

'Then listen.'

'—*and the debate rages on over balancing the right to free expression with the risk to society of the erosion of trust in facts*—'

'Do you get it?'

George realised Tommy was staring at him with an interest that bordered on the aggressive.

'There's a lot to think about,' George said.

Tommy sniffed. He reached over to the central console and changed the station to Radio 1.

An EDM song played, the singer's voice auto-tuned and reedy.

'I suppose this is really what the kids listen to these days?' Tommy said.

'I'm nearly forty, remember,' George said.

Tommy sniffed again. 'I'll ask Isobel.'

'Oh.' George spun to face Tommy. 'You'll like this. Speaking of being forty, you know Scott?'

Tommy glanced at George.

'He hides the fact he smokes from his mother. Has done for twenty-five years.'

Tommy nodded.

'Why the nod?'

'He's being respectful. His mother wouldn't want to know.'

George looked down at his lap. 'Really?'

'Absolutely.'

They pulled up at Jane's building.

'It's that maisonette there, on the bottom. I'll wait in the car while you get the keys. You can *hold* car keys, I assume?' Tommy switched the engine off. 'I don't need to go in. I spent far too much time with Margaret's friends yesterday.'

66

Helen kneeled on her driveway in her gardening gloves, pulling out the weeds by hand.

Today was a gloved-task day.

The freezer was done. But the drive had been going wild for a long time. She'd been meaning to get to it, but life got in the way. Every time she left the house, she saw the drive and thought, *I need to deal with that. Another thing for the list.*

And here she was. Dealing with it. In her gloves.

She pulled on a stringy weed and added it to her pile.

Amazing what she could get done in one day when trying not to think about Isobel. Or Mum and Pete. Or Nathan. Or pretty much the whole family, actually. And the state of the world, of course. She couldn't even let herself *begin* to think about the state of the world. That really wouldn't help right now.

Helen pulled on a particularly stubborn thistle.

She probably should have got some kind of product to kill the weeds. She'd seen other people in their driveways with sprays on sticks. But that wasn't what she needed today. Today, she needed to *yank*.

'Hi.'

Helen looked up, confused.

Stella stood over her, wearing the (still slightly flour-speckled) silk shirt and velvet trousers of the day before. 'You look pretty cross with that thistle.'

Helen looked down at it. She released it and pushed herself up to her feet, one knee at a time. 'I didn't think you knew where I lived.'

'I got a taxi. Don't tell Mum.' Stella looked around. 'This is a nice area. Trees on the street and everything. New house?'

Helen brushed the debris off her gloves. 'We've lived here since I was pregnant with Isobel.'

Stella put her hands in her trouser pockets.

'Tell you what.' Helen pulled off her gardening gloves by the fingers. 'Since you're here, why don't you actually come inside?'

Helen did the tour and Stella made all the right noises.

Now they sat with cups of tea, side by side on the bench, looking out at Helen's decked back yard.

'So why *are* you here?' Helen asked finally.

'Can't I just come and visit my sister on a whim?' Stella glanced at Helen. 'OK, I don't usually, but I *could*. And you were the person I wanted to tell.' Stella took a deep breath. 'Mum is over the moon this morning. Pete's getting married.'

Helen had been lifting her mug to her mouth. She stopped lifting mid-air. 'Really?'

'*Really*. Unless Mum's got the wrong end of the stick, and I don't think even she could dream up something that unlikely. *Can you imagine* how happy she is?'

Helen thought. 'I don't even think I can. She'll be exploding, I'm guessing.'

'She's got big dreams for the day. Soundtracks. Chocolate

359

fountains. Buttoned-up page boys and flower girls sprinkling petals. She's even hoping for a wedding website.'

Helen and Stella looked at each other. They both started to laugh.

Then Helen remembered: *the fraud.*

She stopped laughing.

'What?'

'I've just remembered, I'm furious with both of them. *Furious.* Mum's done it this time.'

'Interesting. Why?'

'You've got enough on your plate with George.' Helen felt an unfamiliar emotion. The need to protect her sister. 'And I'm overreacting. You know, just Mum stuff. And Pete stuff. The usual.'

'Call me if you want to rant. Always happy to join in a rant about Mum and Pete.'

Helen eyed her up and down.

'What?'

'I'm not sure you've ever told me to call you before.'

Stella shrugged. She took a long sip of her tea.

When Stella spoke again, her voice was soft. 'Did you know Mum's not having the treatment?'

Helen put her mug on the decking. Slowly, she straightened up.

Stella waited.

'She told me,' Helen said finally. 'Said she had to share it with someone so they could plan to look after Dad. Should I have told you?'

'I just wondered if you knew.'

'There's no convincing her, you know. I think we have to let it happen.'

Stella nodded.

'She told me not to tell anyone.'

'I don't think I mind that she told you not me. I'm the irresponsible one, and you're the one who gets the worry. That's OK by me.'

Helen smiled. 'Great.' Her smile faded. 'Mum's terrified though. She'd never show it and she won't even admit.' Helen shook her head firmly. 'But I don't want to feel sorry for her today. It should be *scientifically impossible* for me to feel sorry for her today.'

'What's she done?'

Helen bit her lip. 'Nothing major. You really don't want to know.'

'I *really do* want to know.'

'Just – party stuff. Little things. Selfish Mum stuff.'

Helen picked up her mug again. The two drank their tea in silence.

Helen glanced at Stella. 'And I've got another big addition to the *my life's going to shit* list.'

'Surely not?' Stella frowned. 'Not in the last twelve hours?'

'This one's massive.' Helen took a deep breath. 'Isobel started the fire in the shop.'

Stella didn't react.

'How about that? My daughter's an arsonist, and she did it because she was bored. We're going to have to tell someone. It's all going to come out, isn't it?' Helen paused. 'They don't send kids to prison, do they?'

'Shit, Helen.'

'Do they? Do they send kids to prison?'

'I don't think so.'

'I mean, they can't – can they? A child?'

Stella shook her head. 'They won't have room for kids in prisons anymore. Haven't you been reading the papers?

They'll just do one of those "scare them straight" things, like when they send cons into schools. George says it doesn't work that well these days, the kids barely raise an eyebrow.'

Helen peered at her. 'How *is* George?'

Stella shrugged. 'He's in a car with Dad. He'll be having a hellish time. The tension in that car will be choking.'

'You know what I meant.'

Stella looked straight ahead. 'He'll be fine. I'll be fine. We've both moved on. So everyone's fine.'

'That was three *fines*.'

'You can never have too many *fines*.' Stella set her mug down onto the decking. 'I should go. It's only fair to leave George with Dad for so long. He has done me a favour this weekend, after all.'

'Do you want a lift back to Mum's?'

Stella stood up. 'If you don't mind?'

'Of course not.' Helen stood up. 'But don't let me see Mum right now. I'm so angry with her, I don't know what I'd do.'

67

Margaret headed back inside after seeing Pete and Jin off in a taxi.

It was such a shame they had to head back to London so soon, but, of course, Margaret understood. Entrepreneurs could never truly switch off – she, of all people, knew that. After all, she'd been married to one for forty years.

The doorbell went, and Margaret went back to the front door.

Cheryl stood in the doorway. She held up a faded supermarket bag for life. 'I've got some things for you.'

Margaret stood back to let her in. 'Really?'

Margaret waved Cheryl inside.

Cheryl reached in her bag and pulled out Margaret's old turquoise cardigan. 'Thank you for lending this to me.' She handed Margaret a CD. 'And this was outside my shop. We haven't sold CDs in years. I wondered if it was from the fire?'

Margaret looked at the writing on the CD. *Floorfillers: Hands in the Air.*

'I think it's Stella's. Scott brought it for her.' Margaret put it on the hallway table. 'Thank you.'

'And this is for you.' Cheryl handed Margaret a piece of paper. 'It's not a good copy. I did it myself at home, you'd need to get a proper one at the print shop. But I thought you'd want to see it straight away.'

Margaret got her reading glasses from the side.

She looked at the paper. She smiled.

The photo wasn't great quality. It was on flimsy paper and Cheryl had clearly been running out of printer ink. In the picture itself, all their eyes were all too shiny from the flash. But, still, there they were. Her whole family, in one place. Margaret and Tommy. Pete and Jin. Stella and George. And Helen and Nathan and – most importantly – Isobel and Charlie. Looking perfect, of course.

Was that smoke in the background?

No, it definitely wasn't smoke. It was just a trick of the light.

'I was going to get one printed properly,' Cheryl said, 'but the photo shop is shut on Sundays.'

Margaret looked up. 'Thank you.' She grabbed Cheryl's hand with her free one, still looking at the picture. 'And thank you for solving the murder mystery when everyone else was losing their heads.'

'It was an honour.'

Margaret took her reading glasses off. 'Do you want to tell me your solution now?'

'I certainly do, Margaret. *You* did it, you sly old fox, even though you were dead!' Cheryl beamed. 'That naughty Lady Brockenhurst. It was like in ... well, I'm sure you've read the book, but I gather from the Internet that people don't like spoilers.'

Margaret nodded. She put the photo on the side table. 'Wait here.'

She went to the kitchen and found the game's final envelope from the side. She handed it to Cheryl.

Cheryl opened the envelope and pulled out the folded paper. She held up the sticker that said *Star Detective*. 'Oh, how wonderful!'

'Give it to me.'

Margaret peeled the sticker off and stuck it to the breast pocket of Cheryl's cardigan.

Cheryl looked down at it in wordless awe.

Margaret tapped the piece of paper in Cheryl's hand. 'Here's the solution, if you want to check.'

Cheryl opened the paper and started to read.

Margaret waited. What was that feeling in her stomach? It couldn't be *nerves*.

She moved her weight slightly from one foot to the other.

'The imperfections on the "N" key – yes!' Cheryl spoke without looking up. She read some more, and nodded. 'Help me with something I'm not clear about though.' She folded the paper and placed it back in the envelope. 'I still don't understand why the will had to be stolen when—'

Margaret interrupted Cheryl before her own logic could be questioned. 'There's also . . . Wait here.'

Margaret went into the odds and ends cupboard and pulled out the *I Solved the Murder at Brockenhurst Manor* mug.

She handed it to Cheryl. 'And very – *very* – well deserved.'

Cheryl looked down at the mug. She looked back up at Margaret with shining eyes. 'I'll use it every day.'

Margaret smiled.

Cheryl turned the mug so she could see it from a different angle. 'It seems such a shame the mystery's all over, after all that work you put in.' She looked up. 'Maybe you could write the story up as a screenplay?'

'Maybe,' Margaret said.

The two stood in a content silence.

'Shall we do another mystery at mine soon, do you think?' Cheryl put her hand to her chest, pressing her sticker to make sure it was firmly adhered. 'I'd like to write one. I'm sure it won't be as good as yours, but I can try. I've got an idea about a smashed watch that points to the wrong time of the murder, but please forget I said that.'

There was something about the way Cheryl was standing there, pressing her badge to her chest with pride, having solved the mystery and brought Margaret the photo.

Margaret didn't know what was coming over her. 'Can we make sure we do it *quite soon*, please? I'm not well. I've got a year.' Margaret felt a prickle in her stomach. The prickle multiplied and travelled to her arms and legs. 'Maybe.'

Cheryl didn't speak.

Margaret picked up the family photo as casually as she could. She tried to study it. 'I've got cancer and I'm not having the treatment. I don't want to say any more than that. But I've said it now, so that's that.'

Carefully, hoping Cheryl wouldn't notice, Margaret put her free hand against the wall for support.

When Cheryl still hadn't said anything, she looked up.

The two held eye contact.

'I'm sorry,' Cheryl said softly.

Margaret held up a hand, palm out in a stop sign.

The grandmother clock chimed the quarter of the hour.

Cheryl looked at her mug. 'Let's do it, then.' She set the mug down on the hallway table with a purposeful bang and looked back up at Margaret. 'Next month. I'll write something set at the Pyramids. You can be a Golden Age film star and wear a feathered headdress. I'll be an exotic Egyptian heiress, all in gold, like Cleopatra. A month should be long enough to get our outfits together. Just *please* forget what I said about the smashed watch.'

Margaret gave a faint smile. 'Cheryl, have you been lonely since Malcolm died? What's it been, five years?'

'Seven.'

'And you're good with a slow cooker.'

'I am.'

'Maybe when I'm gone, you can marry Tommy? Not straight away, of course.'

Cheryl smiled. 'You know I think very highly of you, Margaret. *And* Tommy.'

Margaret nodded.

'But I'm not going to marry him.'

'That's fair,' Margaret said. 'I did just spring this on you. I'll let you think about it.'

'No, I'm not going to marry Tommy *at all*. But if it gives you some peace, I'll do him a plate of roast lamb every Sunday. Anyway, I thought you said that if you couldn't have him, no one could?'

'That's Lady Brockenhurst. You're mixing me up with Lady Brockenhurst again. I want Tommy to be happy.'

Margaret put her hand on Cheryl's arm. She felt slow. Jet-lagged. She stumbled backwards.

'I'm fine.'

Cheryl put her hand under Margaret's arm. She steered her into the lounge, into Tommy's armchair.

'Ignore me,' Margaret said. 'It's been a big weekend. I just felt dizzy. I'm all right.'

'Of course you're all right.' Cheryl peered at her for a second, then turned away to look out of the window. 'You have a goldfinch! How wonderful. Look at those mark-ings!' She glanced at Margaret and back into the garden. 'I suppose you put out something special to get a goldfinch?'

Margaret closed her eyes and tried to control her light-headedness. But she didn't know which internal switch to press, which button to push.

It was the heat of the day. She hadn't eaten since breakfast, and there'd been all the excitement of the wedding. That's all it was.

Margaret swallowed. Hard.

She forced her eyes open. 'I put out a niger seed feeder. You wouldn't believe how bitter my war with the squirrels is getting, I'm thinking of asking to borrow Tommy's air rifle. And, Cheryl?'

Cheryl turned.

Margaret said, 'Don't tell anyone. About my . . . thing.'

Cheryl frowned. 'Of course not. It's your business. Why on earth would anyone need to know *that*?'

An hour later, *Death at the Pyramids* had been written in two diaries and Cheryl had left. George and Tommy had returned and Tommy had moved Jane's car, freeing Stella's.

Now Margaret stood with Tommy on the driveway, with Goldie sitting slightly behind.

They faced Stella and George.

Margaret held *Floorfillers: Hands in the Air* in one hand. 'Such a shame you couldn't see Pete and Jin again. But Pete had an important meeting back in London.'

'Sadly, it was not to be.' Stella shrugged. 'I'll see them at the wedding, maybe? If I'm invited?'

'Of course you'll be invited, what a silly thing to say.' Margaret tried to hand *Floorfillers: Hands in the Air* to Stella. 'This is yours.'

Stella glanced at the CD. 'It's not mine.'

Margaret waggled it at her. 'Scott wanted you to have it.'

Stella shook her head – ungraciously, Margaret thought. 'I haven't got anything to play it on, even if I wanted to. Which I don't.'

'Don't be difficult.' She nudged it against Stella's unopen hand. 'Scott brought it especially for you. You *have* to accept a gift.'

Stella looked again at the CD. She took it. She leaned in and kissed Margaret. Stella held her arm tightly, for longer than needed.

Gently, Margaret shook Stella off. Tommy was looking at the shop so she manoeuvred him by the elbow so he was facing the opposite direction. She watched Stella give him a hug and felt a wave of affection.

'Great party.' George kissed Margaret goodbye. 'You're quite the host.'

'I am,' she said.

'I read that piece of paper in the hall, by the way.' Stella gestured back at the house with her CD hand. 'The one with the solution to the murders. And Ashley Brockenhurst was definitely Ellie's *actual* uncle. Ellie married her blood uncle and we're all meant to be fine with that?'

'Yesterday's news,' Margaret said. 'We've all finished the game now, darling. If you were going to get irate about that, you should have done it yesterday.'

George reached out to shake Tommy's hand. Tommy took it formally.

Stella and George got in the car.

Margaret linked her arm in Tommy's and waved them off. She watched the two chat as Stella turned and reversed out of the drive.

'Were they arguing yesterday?' Margaret said.

'The usual nonsense, probably,' Tommy said gruffly.

Margaret watched the car pull away. She thought she saw a small item fly from the car into the shop on the way past, but she must have imagined it.

She realised Tommy was staring at the shop again. 'Stop looking. It won't change anything.'

Tommy put his hands in his pockets. 'I was thinking about trying to buy the land from Scott. Rebuilding from scratch.'

Margaret took her reading glasses out of her pocket in a slow, deliberate movement.

'But I don't suppose we've got the money,' Tommy added. 'Or the time.'

Margaret checked the lenses were clean. She put the glasses back in her pocket again.

'Or I could get a little job in a garden centre? A couple of days a week?'

Margaret beamed. 'That's a great idea!'

Tommy nodded.

'But make sure you can get time off. We're going to do quite a lot of holidays this year.'

'Are we?'

'I want to go on the Orient Express. And the pyramids. Maybe an archaeological dig. If they're actually still a thing, I haven't researched it.'

They both watched the car indicate and turn the corner, out of sight.

Tommy coughed. 'We'd need to do a bit of planning. Make sure it's off-season.'

'Of course.'

'And the insurance will be expensive.'

'We'll cross that bridge.'

He nodded.

'Tommy. About tomorrow. The appointment at the hospital.'

Tommy put his hand on her arm. 'You don't have to tell me. I know.'

She furrowed her brow.

'I've always known,' he said softly.

'Did Helen tell you?'

'Margaret. We've been married forty years. How could I *not* know?'

They stared at each other.

'I didn't want to upset you,' she said.

He nodded

A family walking with a pushchair over the road stopped in front of the shop. Margaret and Tommy watched them look at the burnt shop with obvious excitement.

'Then' – Margaret looked back at Tommy – 'let's change the subject. Happy Anniversary, love. They've been forty very happy years.'

Tommy felt himself choking up. 'Yes.' He reached for her arm and clung onto it. 'Happy Anniversary.'

He dropped her arm.

Margaret widened her eyes. 'The cheek!'

Tommy watched as the family over the road started taking photos of the shop.

They looked at each other. Tommy and Margaret turned slowly towards the house and started walking, with Goldie padding a step behind.

Tommy reached down to ruffle her ears.

'So.' Margaret's tone was breezy. She linked her arm with his. 'Any news with George from the car?'

Tommy sniffed. 'Only that Scott hides the fact he smokes from his mother. Has done for twenty-five years.'

Margaret nodded. 'Very respectful. He's a good boy to Adele, in lots of ways. And it was very thoughtful of him to get that CD for Stella.'

They reached the front door.

'But speaking of George,' Tommy opened the door with a purposeful jerk, 'whatever those two are arguing about, it doesn't change anything.' Tommy let Margaret go through the door first; he shook his head. 'I don't care what Stella thinks on the topic and how modern she is. She'll never convince me. That man really *should* learn to drive.'

68

George clicked his seat belt tight with satisfaction. *Finally.*

'He brought me a fucking CD!' Stella threw her handbag and the CD into the passenger footwell. 'Ugh. Can you believe it?'

George looked down at the CD. *Floorfillers: Hands in the Air.* He picked up the cracked case. 'Where did he even find this?'

Stella turned to face behind and reversed the car out of the drive. 'He went to his mother's to get it. Just before the fire.'

'Why's he so weird with you? Are you *that* hard to get over?' George felt a throb of something and looked away.

'Oh, it's nothing like that, don't flatter me. I think because it makes him feel young. But *honestly.* And Mum wasn't going to let me bin it here.' Stella paused; she gave a last wave at her parents. 'I'll bin it back at the flat. No, in fact—'

Stella reached for the CD. She slid down the driver's window and threw the CD into the burnt shop.

'Nice.' George waved at Margaret and Tommy. 'Let's hope Margaret doesn't find it.'

Stella drove away.

George watched his in-laws grow smaller and disappear. 'Do you think I should make more effort with Pete?'

That was out of nowhere, George thought. 'Why?'

'You know.' Stella indicated left. 'Family. And he did come in the end and he's nice when he's there. And I liked Jin.'

George watched Cole Street fade into the distance.

'Maybe it was hard for him,' Stella continued. 'Growing up in our house, with Mum with all her expectations. Then all her *other* expectations when she realised he was gay.'

'Wow. Even *you're* making excuses for him now. How he behaves is nothing to do with who he does or doesn't choose to have sex with.'

'Are you sure? We don't know that. I think I've been too harsh.'

'You're letting him off the hook? You sound like Margaret!'

'George!' She couldn't have sounded more wounded if he'd slapped her in the face. 'I definitely *do not* sound like my mother.'

'The thing is,' George adjusted his position in his seat as they tuned onto the dual carriageway, 'I've been reflecting, and I'm starting to think he's actually doing your mum a kindness. It might be a good thing she hardly ever gets to see him. He's letting himself be to her what she wants him to be. This way she gets to enjoy him as he isn't – to enjoy all those mythical chocolate fountains – without being hit by brutal reality.'

'I'm not sure Mum's a fan of brutal reality.'

'She thinks it's a massive buzzkill.'

Stella turned to glance at him. 'But she's so happy today, isn't she?'

George stretched his legs out in the footwell. 'I can't believe you let her get away with that so lightly. Lying to you, and everyone.'

Stella reached for her sunglasses in the driver's door. 'What can't you believe?'

'Don't you think she should have been pulled up for that behaviour?'

'But you can't have a go at her now.' Stella put her sunglasses on. 'Not in her condition.'

'Even if she really deserves it?'

Stella focused on the road. 'I don't think so.'

George relaxed into his seat. 'Oh dear.' He closed his eyes. 'Then I think we can expect, when she works that out, she's going to properly milk this situation.'

George and Stella spent most of the two-hour journey to Birmingham in silence.

Ten minutes from home, Stella's phone beeped. She kept her gaze on the road ahead. 'Can you get that for me?'

George looked at the phone doubtfully. 'Are you sure?'

'What do you mean, "am I sure"? You want me to get it when I'm going at ninety? I know you expect me to do everything round here, but—'

'I meant, *you stupid arse,* in case it's private?' George swallowed. 'Something you don't want me to see?'

Stella flicked a glance at him and looked back at the road. 'And what kind of message would that be?'

Instant, unwanted images flooded into George's head. A younger guy, pecs as hard and shiny as chestnuts, going down on Stella expertly in a candlelit hotel room.

Thanks for a special night, the message would say. It would be signed something like *H x*

George wondered what *H* might stand for.

Stella was still talking. 'And if it's any of my mates slagging you off, there would be no surprises there. They say exactly what I say about you. And I say it to your face.'

'Could be a dick pic?'

'Who do you think I hang out with now? Besides, if it's someone sending a dick pic, you can open it with my blessing.'

No, George thought. Of course, it wouldn't be a dick pic. H would be way too smooth for that.

George banged his hand against the armrest.

Stella turned to him. 'What?'

'Nothing.'

George put Stella's old password into the phone before he could develop H's backstory and proficient sexual technique any further.

The screen unlocked. 'You should really change your passwords now we're divorcing. I know them all. I could get into your bank account any time.'

'You gonna spy on me? Steal from me now?' Stella kept her gaze on the road. 'I'm pretty sure you're not.'

'Thank you.'

'I didn't mean it as a compliment.'

'You say that, but how could it *not* be a compliment?' George looked at the screen. 'It's Helen.'

He read the message out.

I've decided that I really do appreciate having you in my life.

Stella snorted. 'She needs to have a long hard word with herself.' She banged the steering wheel. 'OH MY GOD!'

George started. 'What?'

'I've just realised, not only did Mum actually have me murdered, *she was the one* who'd actually murdered me!'

'Hang on. What?'

'She killed me!' Stella pulled her sunglasses down her nose so she could look at him over the top, George suspected so he could fully appreciate the outrage in her eyes. 'My *own mother* killed me!'

George thought about this. 'But she killed your dad as well.'

Stella deflated a little. 'Ye-es.'

'And herself.' George pointed out.

Stella deflated a little more. 'I suppose.'

'Maybe . . .' George traced a finger along his jeans casually. He side-eyed her. 'Maybe if you'd been a little more *humble and grateful*?'

Stella frowned at him and looked back at the road. 'So, let me get this straight. I had sex with my father and got killed by my mother.' Stella shuddered. 'How very *Oedipal*.'

'Could have been worse,' George said. 'At least no one had to fuck Goldie.'

They pulled up outside George's house.

Instantly, the atmosphere in the car lost its warmth.

Stella looked at the house. 'This it?'

George watched the man heading out of the front door; he raised a hand in greeting. 'Home sweet home.'

'That a friend of yours?'

'Ground floor at the back.'

'What's his name?'

'*Ground floor at the back.* Or *Kill Bill waffle guy*.'

Stella looked at George.

'He likes Tarantino films *a lot*. And he really likes potato waffles.'

They sat watching the man walk to the bus stop.

'When's your lease for the room up?' Stella asked.

'Three months. Do you . . .' George leaned forward, feeling the need to concentrate on wiping a mark off the dashboard. 'Do you want to see it? I could make you a cup of tea. I might even be able to swing you a waffle.'

Stella didn't answer.

George rubbed the dashboard harder. 'But you'll have to climb over the sofa if you want to see my bedroom.'

'Why would I climb over the sofa?'

'It doesn't fit in the room.'

'Then why did you take it?'

George shrugged. 'It was a principle thing. It didn't seem fair that you got the flat *and* both sofas.'

Stella closed her eyes.

Neither spoke for a minute.

Stella still didn't open her eyes as she said, 'How did we let this happen?'

George leaned towards the mark on the dashboard again. He rubbed more softly this time. 'Two in five marriages end in divorce.'

'Do you think,' Stella said, 'if we'd tried a bit harder, we'd have been able to do anything different?'

George's chest was full. He struggled to speak. 'I don't know. I really don't know.'

They sat in silence.

'Though – I've decided I'm going to have driving lessons.'

'Really?' Stella opened her eyes. 'I thought you said there was no point because self-driving cars would be coming in.'

'I've decided it's time. Even if it's just for a few years.'

'You mean you're stuffed because you don't have me to ferry you around anymore.'

George looked at his knees. 'I'd learn to drive whatever. Because I want to.'

When he looked up, Stella was staring at the house. George looked through her eyes, at the bin bag by the door that had been ripped open by some animal. A carton of milkshake mix pushed visibly through the plastic; a lump of congealing meat spilt over onto the concrete step.

'So, do you want to come in?' George concentrated even harder on the dashboard. 'It's not as bad as it looks. And there's not normally a pile of rubbish there.'

They both watched a bus pull up ahead, and an elderly man get off.

'No,' Stella said finally. 'No, I don't want to come in.'

'Right.' George felt a pang. 'Fair play.'

'I need to get back today.' Stella took off her sunglasses. She shifted position so she could look at him face-on. 'But one night this week maybe? Tuesday? Maybe we could go for a drink?'

George held her gaze. 'Could we get a kebab after?'

'If you like.'

'You want to come here?'

Stella frowned. 'Not *here*, obviously. God, no.'

George gave a carefully casual shrug. 'OK.'

'A pub or something,' Stella said carefully. 'Like the old days. The White Swan? Seven p.m.?'

'Right.'

They looked at each other for a moment.

George forced himself to open the car door. 'See you Tuesday, then.'

'OK.' Stella put her sunglasses back on. 'See you Tuesday. Don't forget.'

'I promise you.' George got out of the car. 'This time, I definitely – *definitely* – won't.'

69

Helen tried and tried, but she couldn't leave it any longer. She found herself knocking on Mum's door.

'Well, come in then!' As always, Mum had the air of someone who'd been expecting her. 'It's like Piccadilly station round here today.'

Mum turned and walked into the lounge. Helen followed her and sat down in Dad's armchair.

'Mum. You've let me down.'

Mum gave an irritated fly-swat with her hand. 'I've had a difficult weekend, Helen.'

'You made my husband commit fraud.'

'I haven't.' Mum sat in her own armchair with an indignant thump. 'His hands are clean. I kept up a Chinese wall at all times. There's nothing anyone could pin on him.'

'Let me be clearer on this, Mum. *You* committed fraud. In a business you asked *the father of your grandchildren* to run.'

'It was an ends-justify-the-means thing.'

'That's Machiavelli, you know. Can you hear yourself?'

'You think I don't care about family? I did it *for* family.'

'For Pete, you mean.'

'Pete has been having some cash-flow problems. He's been under pressure with his latest investments.'

Helen tapped her hand against the side table. 'But why would putting extra money through the business help with Pete's gambling debts?'

'His got himself in trouble with some investors.'

'The word is "bookies", Mum.'

'They were nasty people and he was in physical danger.' Mum shook her head. 'They needed him to process some stock for them in exchange for writing off his debt.'

'Laundering.'

'Not *laundering*.'

'It sounds like laundering.'

Mum gave a wave of the hand. 'Anyway, it's over. All the money has gone through now and Pete's paid his investors off. He's done what he needed to do to get back on the straight and narrow.'

Helen raised an eyebrow. 'You're not selling two hundred cappuccinos a day anymore?'

'Pete's marrying Jin now. He won't need to stay in with that bad crowd anymore. Because that was the problem, he was in with the wrong crowd.'

'Did you just say he was "in with the wrong crowd"?'

'He's easily led.'

Helen sat back in her chair. Why did she ever think this would go any other way?

Mum glanced at Helen. 'How is Isobel? In herself? Today?'

'This isn't over,' Helen said. 'The conversation about the fraud.'

'Of course not.'

'But why do you mention Isobel right now? In the context of bad crowds?'

'She started the fire, didn't she? Tommy told me she was in the shop, though I don't think he's made a connection.'

Margaret shook her head sadly. 'That little one's always liked fire.

Helen said nothing.

'Even as a toddler, she stared at the flames in our hearth like it was television.'

Helen still said nothing.

'Tommy put in those safety hooks round the fireguard, remember? Just in case. But I'm sure it was a crowd of them that did it? Egging her on, at least? Not just little Isobel?'

Helen looked out of the window.

'We can't let her suffer for this.' Mum shook her head. 'Do you need me to say I caused the fire? I'll take the fall. I'll say I was carrying a special anniversary candle and I slipped. I've got just the right candle for it somewhere among these presents.'

'What?' Helen blinked at her. 'No. Mum. You *have* to stop lying. Please. I'm going to take Isobel to the police and they won't press charges. She's *ten*. They don't do anything with ten-year-olds. I think.'

'I don't want this hanging over her life. She's a good girl. I'll take the fall, it's not a problem.' Mum gave Helen a reassuring smile. 'I won't be around long enough. I won't *actually* go to prison.'

'Mum. I know this is hard for you to take in, but you don't solve everyone's problems by taking falls. Isobel has to tell the truth, and it will be fine.'

'I know you're worried,' Mum said, 'but that girl's perfect. I will not let her life be ruined by something as silly as this.'

The trill of the landline made Helen start.

Mum stood up. 'You're jumpy today.'

Helen watched Mum move to the sideboard. 'You're *still* using that chicken phone Stella bought you?'

'It's perfectly functional.' Mum picked up the phone and put the beak to her ear. 'Six oh five five?' Mum listened to the caller. 'OK. I'll tell her. Her phone's on silent, you think?'

Shit. Helen scrabbled for her phone in her pocket. She looked at the screen.

Nathan. Three missed calls and a text.

Call me now.

'I'll pass the message on.' Mum hung up the beak.

'What did Nathan want, Mum? Is it something bad?'

Mum turned to look at her. 'It's Isobel. She's fine, but she's left the pizza party without Katrina's parents noticing.' Mum shook her head. 'And guess where she's turned up?'

70

Tommy sat at the desk in the study. He listened to the rise and fall of Margaret and Helen's conversation below.

This weekend had been all about arguing. But he wasn't going to intervene. He didn't want to know anything else. About anything.

The phone rang. A minute later, the front door slammed.

Tommy looked out of the window; Helen rushed towards her car and – a few seconds later – roared away from the curb.

Tommy looked back at Margaret's computer.

He supposed it was *his* computer too. But there was still an unspoken rule about it – that if Margaret wanted to use it, he got off it.

Tommy wondered if he wrote down all the systems and unspoken rules that were in place in the last forty years of this household, whether the resulting manual would be bigger than the Bible.

He got some satisfaction from this. All these rules, accumulated over the years, so reliable and unchanging. His kids might laugh at the mechanics of his marriage, but at least he knew if he lifted the bonnet up on it and poked around, he'd be able to tell how it worked. How many of them could say that?

On the computer, Tommy created a new document. *Council Complaint July 15. Crescent Road.*

He started typing.

242 Cole Street
Manchester
M16 7XX

Dear Sirs/Madams,
I wish to make you aware of the incidents of unauthorised
parking in loading-only areas on Crescent Road and the impact
this has on the flow of traffic on Cole Street. It is essential that
traffic wardens patrol the area with more frequency to avoid a
potentially catastrophic outcome. I shall list times and details of
twelve near-miss incidents below to illustrate my point.

Tommy flicked through his notebook to the right page and
held it open with his elbow as he typed.

Incident 1. 7 June 15.46 p.m.
Cooksons Delivery van servicing The Corner bar parks for
two hours in loading bay and driver returns, bold as brass, with
several bags from supermarket. Impact –

Tommy was interrupted when Margaret appeared in the
doorway.

'What are you doing, love?'

'Writing a letter to the council.'

Margaret was still looking at him.

'What?'

Margaret put one hand on his shoulder. 'Isobel was the
one who started the fire.'

Tommy put his hand behind him and grasped for his
chair. '*Isobel?*'

'She's a good girl though.'

'Of course,' Tommy said in haste.

'Do you need a minute? I know you find things like this hard.'

Tommy just stared at her. He wondered what kind of things had happened previously in his and Margaret's lives that she could possibly categorise as 'things like this'.

'And she didn't mean to do it,' Margaret added.

Tommy sat back, weary. 'Of course not.'

'She was playing with a cigarette lighter near the crisps. She was bored, and that's on us. We should have made sure there was more going on to entertain the kiddies, got a clown or a face painter in. The devil makes work for idle hands.'

Isobel.

Tommy tried to take this in. He tried to ignore the implications of this 'devil makes work for idle hands' statement. He hoped Margaret wasn't going to find God at this stage of life. It wasn't unheard of, but he felt the last thing Margaret needed was an all-powerful spiritual ally.

'Isobel will be fine,' she said. 'We need to protect her now. Make sure she doesn't feel the pain of this.'

'It can't be her fault. She will never have meant *this* to happen. Besides . . .'

'What?'

Tommy cleared his throat. 'I found out last night that Nathan never checked the batteries in the shop's smoke alarm. *Never.* Even though it was clearly documented as a monthly task in my handover document.'

'It *was* a long document though, Tommy. Even *I* stopped reading at page twenty.'

Tommy shook his head in disappointment.

Margaret sat down on the emergency beanbag, a relic from

Stella's teens. 'There's something I have to tell you about the shop. You'll be angry at first, but please hold it in until you've had a chance to process it. I don't want you to say anything you'll regret.'

Tommy turned to face her.

He listened, as Margaret told him about Pete and his financial challenges.

About Pete's professional investors, and how he had asked Margaret to help with their demands.

About how this resulted in inflated cash flow in the business.

About how they weren't *actually* selling two hundred cappuccinos a day.

Tommy was aware his mouth had dropped slightly open. He closed it and wiped at the trickle of spit at the side of his mouth.

'How could you?' he said finally. 'In my business? My father's business?'

'It was for family, Tommy. Was I meant to just let Pete sink?'

'But ... my business. My *legacy*.'

'If you're going to make me say it, then I'm sorry. There. Are you happy now?'

Tommy shook his head. He let it hang down.

He tried to take in what he'd heard. It was devastating, obviously. And yet, he felt a spark of something within. There was a really, *really* important point in there somewhere, and it felt like he was missing it.

He thought some more, until—

Tommy snapped his head back up. 'Nathan wasn't making profit with his stupid stock?'

'Not even close.'

'In fact, he was making less money even than when I was heading up the shop?'

'We don't know that for definite, Tommy.'

Tommy sat up as straight as he could.

Margaret reached out awkwardly from the beanbag. She strained to put her hand on his leg. 'It'll take some time to get used to.'

'I'm just trying to put this all together,' Tommy said. '*Isobel* set the fire—'

'Accidentally,' Margaret interjected.

'*Pete*'s in debt again.'

'It's not his fault.'

'*Nathan* didn't check the smoke alarms and wasn't making any profit.' Tommy jiggled in his seat. '*You* were money laundering—'

'Not "laundering". You weren't listening properly.'

'—and somehow, those crisp villains are off the hook, because it wasn't the electrics. So everyone was at fault here.' He sat up straighter. '*Everyone*.' He paused. 'Except me.'

He turned to Margaret to see if he'd understood it right.

She gave a firm nod.

Tommy sat back in his seat again. *Incredible.*

'But *are* the crisp people off the hook? I'm not so sure.'

Tommy stopped jiggling his leg. 'What do you mean?'

'It might not have been the electrics, but you wouldn't expect normal crisps to go up like that, just because of a harmless child with an old lighter.'

'That's true.' Tommy sat up straight again. 'That's *very* true. He scratched his chin. 'Margaret' – he turned to her with the most joyous of sorrowful looks – 'I can only think there must be something very, very wrong with those crisps.'

71

After Isobel finished her food at the pizza party, she looked at Katrina's mum, who was sitting at a table in the restaurant a few away from the party table. She had papers spread out in front of her, a phone against her ear.

Perfect timing.

Isobel went up to her. 'You working?'

Katrina's mum looked up, eyes blurry with thought. 'Hang on.' She kept her phone to her ear. 'Hi, Isobel. Do you need something?'

'Mum just rang me. She said I should meet her at the park now. Something's come up.'

Katrina's mum looked at the clock. 'That was quick.'

'But she's going to come later to get Charlie anyway. Nice to see you and thanks for the pizza.'

Katrina's mum smiled.

Isobel headed out of the restaurant door. She stopped for a second, trying to work out which way to go to get to the underpass that went under the dual carriageway. Then she set off again, shaking her head.

Katrina's mum hadn't even asked where Isobel had got a phone.

*

An hour, a few attempts to find the underpass and two dual carriageway crossings later, Isobel walked right up to the fire station reception desk. 'Can I see the crew manager from last night please? The one who went to the fire at the shop on Cole Street.'

The man on reception blinked at her. 'She might not be working today. We're not all on shift, all the time.'

Isobel pulled on the sleeve of her jumper and twisted it. 'But is she here?'

The man got up slowly and shouted through to the back. 'Lois! You have a visitor.'

The crew manager walked through to the reception area. She saw Isobel and stopped. 'Hello again.'

'Will you really come into my school?'

The crew manager glanced at the man on the desk. 'Your teachers would have to want us to. We couldn't arrange it just with you.'

'But what if I told you I set the fire? Then you'd need to come into school.'

'*You* set the fire?'

'By accident,' Isobel said.

'You spilt something flammable?'

'I went too close to the crisps with a lighter.'

The crew manager rested her hand on a plastic reception chair. She sat down slowly.

Isobel sat in the chair next to her. 'But I didn't really mean to make a proper fire. I thought fire only went upwards. Listen.'

And the crew manager listened, blinking, while Isobel told her everything.

*

Half an hour later, the saloon doors of the fire station flew open; Mum rushed in, all red-faced.

'Isobel!' Mum hugged her from above, then crouched into the hug without letting Isobel go, until she was way too close. 'Never, ever do that to me again. You crossed two dual carriageways on your own! And now you've—'

She looked at Lois. She hitched her bag further onto her shoulder and smoothed her hair down.

'Thanks for keeping an eye on her. Again.'

Lois nodded. 'It's been enlightening.'

'Has she said . . . much?'

'It's fine, Mum.' Isobel waved a hand. 'I've told Lois everything and she's coming into school to teach us about fire safety. It's all sorted.'

So Lois and the fire people were coming into school with their engine in two weeks to do a whole-school assembly. Which would have been exciting in itself – even *before* you knew they were coming in because of Isobel. And Isobel got to correct the teachers about the words they used. 'You don't say *firemen*. You say *firefighters*.'

Isobel was a playground celebrity. Everyone wanted to hear the story about the fire, and Isobel told them – a little bit, at least. Mum had said it was fine to talk about the flames and the smoke, but best not to mention how the fire started.

And Mum was being different. Something had happened since the fire. Isobel first noticed it when she heard her on the phone to Katrina's mum after the pizza party.

'You *should* be fucking sorry. You let my daughter walk off on her own? Like I'd tell her it was OK to go and yet tell Charlie to stay there? That's a parenting basic, come on,

Angie. Always check the alibi. How naïve are you? I'd even told you she *doesn't have* a phone!'

And there was other odd stuff going on. Isobel was eating a yoghurt in the kitchen one day after school, when she heard Mum snort while looking at her phone.

Isobel looked up from her yoghurt. 'What is it?'

'It's Stella.' Mum looked up from her phone. 'You know Uncle Pete's getting married?'

'Pete?'

'The one who turned up late to the party. The one in the picture. You remember.'

'Sort of.'

'Well, he's invited us all to his wedding on an email. Not even an email *e-invite*. Just an email with the date and time. And it's at a registry office. Your poor grandma.'

'I don't understand,' Isobel said.

'No,' Mum said. 'No, I suppose you wouldn't.'

Isobel looked again at the card Mum had put up on the fridge – the card with '*Happy New Home*' on the front.

Isobel put down her yoghurt. She pulled the card out from behind the magnet and looked at the message inside.

Just wanted to let you know that we <u>both</u> appreciate having you in our lives. Stella and George x

It made no sense. Not even when she'd heard Mum talking to Dad about it the other evening, on what was becoming their joint sofa. '*This is how she tells me they're back together. Typical Stella.*'

Isobel looked from the card to Mum. 'I still don't understand why it says '*Happy New Home*' on the front. We've lived in this house as long as I've been alive.'

'It's a private joke, darling,' Mum said. 'It's all a private joke. Stella can't say anything directly, it's her thing.'

Isobel stared at the card. She slid it back behind the magnet and carried on eating her yoghurt.

That night, Mum took Isobel along to her book group.

'It isn't an extra punishment, in itself,' Mum explained as they stood outside the front door of the house. 'You're just here because you're grounded.'

Mum muttered something that sounded like 'bring it on'.

'What?' Isobel said.

A woman in a long dress opened the door.

'Yes, I've brought my daughter,' Mum said. 'And, yes, I know the rules, but I can't get a babysitter. I'm sure it's not the end of the world if a child sits quietly in the corner for one week, is it?'

The woman blinked and reversed, letting Mum and Isobel in to her house.

The people all sat round a table in the kitchen and Isobel sat on the floor next to Mum's chair. She touched the cold metal of the table. It reminded her of the school trip to the abattoir that had caused all that fuss.

The woman in the long dress looked round the group. 'Last week, we discussed *We Need to Talk About Kevin*. Does anyone else have anything they reflected on about it since then?'

'No,' Mum said.

The woman gave Mum a too-kind smile. 'No?'

'Do we really have to talk about *Kevin* again? Aren't we done with him and all those eyeballs by now?'

The woman frowned. 'Don't you mean eye-*ball*?'

'Eye-*ball*,' Mum repeated. 'Singular, of course. Yes.'

The woman folded her arms. 'Sometimes people like the chance to reflect over the week—'

'But I don't want to reflect on Kevin anymore.' Mum's

voice went high. 'Anyone else?'

Mum looked round the faces in the room. Everyone seemed to be looking at something else.

Mum turned back to the woman. 'I spent all weekend reading *Wolf Hall* for today.' She brushed something off her jeans. 'So, unless anyone's feeling really strongly, let's all move on, and – for once – let's cut Kevin's mother some slack.'

After the book group, Isobel let Mum lead her down the street to the car.

Mum beeped the car open. She turned to Isobel before opening the door. 'I didn't handle that conversation very well. I got cross.'

'I know.'

'You shouldn't get cross with people. It's not how you win an argument.'

'But you did win the argument, didn't you?'

'That's not the point.'

Isobel shook her head. She got in the car without being asked, and clipped her seat belt on.

Mum glanced at Isobel as she switched the engine on, and Isobel gave Mum her best, encouraging smile. 'What was that about an eyeball?'

'Nothing. I love you,' Mum said.

'I love you too.'

Mum didn't smile, but she stared at Isobel with soft eyes. For ages.

Isobel shifted so Mum couldn't see her face. 'Aren't we going home?'

Now, Mum did smile. She turned back to the road.

Still, the two sat there in silence for what felt like a long time before, eventually, Mum drove away.

EPILOGUE

When George first became a teacher, all those years ago, he learnt he could never go about his daily business in anonymity again. He'd be ambling along the road, thinking about what he was going to eat that night. He'd be picking up a coffee, or doing up his shoelace in the street, and those heart-freezing words – *sir, sir!* – would strip any sunny casualness from his day.

In becoming a teacher, George had achieved the status of (incredibly minor) local celebrity, getting accosted by kids whose smiles implied they'd caught him out, just by him *existing outside of school* – even if all he was doing was something as benign as dumping a broken chair at the tip.

Often, the first he knew of those sightings was when he got asked strangely specific questions in front of the class.

Knowing smile. '*Like Toblerones, Sir?*'

Deadpan innocence. '*Are you thinking of getting new glasses, Sir?*'

Each time, the class collapsed into giggles. And George knew something had gone round the school, and was forced to guess what it was.

I saw Mandani in the ticket queue for Galaxy Destroyers *on his own, the sad fucker. He was carrying a big Toblerone. And he brought his own drink from home.*

I saw Mr Mandani trying on frames in the optician's in town. All the frames he tried on were shit.

And there was no right way of answering the kids' questions. If George answered the question straight – 'yes, I do like Toblerones, do you?' – some of the class crowed, like they'd won a prize.

Others just stared at him. *What a twat,* their expressions said. *Going round eating Toblerones.*

Before one particular day, a few weeks after the party, George always thought that the most humiliating thing that could happen in a supermarket was running into one of the kids from school.

But it turned out that wasn't the most humiliating thing that could happen in a supermarket.

The shopping trip started in the usual way.

Stella looked him up and down with disgust. 'We don't need those.'

George looked down at the punnet of raspberries in his hand. The two of them hadn't even got past the fruit and veg aisle before Stella started with her 'advice'.

He looked back at Stella. 'Why don't I want these, please?'

'Because you never get round to eating fruit, and raspberries go off in a day. Better just to fill the bowl with apples, they take longer to go brown. You won't be shamed by your fruit so much that way.'

'I'm planning to start being healthier this week.'

'I'm sure you are, but don't bother congratulating yourself in advance.'

George clicked his tongue in irritation.

'I just think,' Stella said, 'you should recognise what kind of person you are.'

George clutched his raspberries closer to his heart, both literally and metaphorically. 'And *I just think* you should recognise what a massive controlling *witch* you are, and stop ruining my attempt to be a better person.'

'Well, I think you should take your raspberries and—'

Stella stopped smiling instantly.

'What's up?'

Stella stood up straighter. '*Grace!* Hide!'

Immediately, George ran round the side of a display stand of toilet roll, still clutching his raspberries.

He stood as still as he could, despite the thudding in his pounding heart.

Surely everyone could hear his heart? His stupid tell-tale heart? He felt as tense as that time he did Laser Quest at a stag do.

Eventually, he peeked out from behind the stack.

Stella had remained where she was with the trolley in the fruit aisle. She was now studying a grapefruit with an intense level of scrutiny.

She looked up from the (fascinating) grapefruit and jerked her head back in feigned recognition. 'Grace, hi!'

Grace was pushing a trolley beside a much younger man and a toddler. In her trolley were bread and apples, along with a twenty-four pack of Guinness and several bottles of Pinot Grigio.

Interesting.

'Hello,' Grace said pleasantly without stopping.

Stella turned to the younger man. 'Where are my manners?' She beamed. 'I'm Stella. I'm one of Grace's sad sacks.'

Grace slowed the trolley. 'I use the word "clients".'

'I'm joking.' Stella stopped smiling. 'Look, I know it's been weeks, Grace, and you've been trying to get hold of me. I've been meaning to get in touch but—'

'That's wonderful.' Grace gave a non-committal smile back. 'Please call my office to arrange something.'

George accidentally touched the toilet roll display with his ear, pushing one package off the top of the stack. The package bounced once towards Grace's feet.

Grace leaned down to pick up the package. She stepped towards the stack, then paused.

Without changing her expression, she placed the package on the stack, next to George's head.

George cleared his throat. 'Grace,' he said casually.

Grace made brief eye contact. 'George.'

George stepped out from behind the stack and indicated Grace's trolley. 'You like the wine, I see. That's good to know in a counsellor. Humanising.'

Grace said nothing.

Stella stepped towards Grace. 'I think we owe you an explanation.'

Grace flapped an arm at the surroundings. 'Not here.'

Stella held up a hand to Grace's shopping companions. 'Two secs. You see' – Stella looked to George and back to Grace – 'the party was an absolute nightmare, but it brought George and I closer. Because my family are weird and it made us realise we fit together, you know?'

'This isn't the place.' Grace started pushing her trolley past them. 'I hope you both have a wonderful day.'

George and Stella watched the back of Grace's duffle coat. She hurried round the next aisle, the toddler and younger man slightly behind.

'Huh.' George turned to Stella. 'Grace wears trainers. I wouldn't have seen her as a trainers person.'

'Do you think she's angry with us?'

George thought about this. 'I don't think she's allowed to be angry, is she? That wouldn't be professional. Besides, do we even care? We aren't going back.'

'I reckon she was angry,' Stella said.

'She would say you're projecting.'

'She fucking would as well, with that superior look on her face.' Stella shook her head. 'Like *she's* never projected in her life.'

'See, we know the language now, we're experts.'

'This is why we don't have to go back and see her anymore. We know it all already.'

'Agreed.' George placed his raspberries in the trolley. 'And I prefer to argue with you unsupervised and for free. By the way, I'm definitely having these raspberries.'

Stella looked where Grace had been standing. 'I feel a bit shitty. She did try to help us. Should we thank her?'

'I reckon she'd probably rather we didn't.'

Stella leaned with her arms onto the trolley's handle-bar. 'Do you reckon she thinks we shouldn't have got back together?'

George weighed this thought up. 'It's not up to her, is it?'

'No,' Stella said thoughtfully. 'I suppose not. But what if she's right? What if we haven't learnt anything? What if it isn't any different this time round?'

George thought. 'The thing is, it doesn't matter. I want to be with you anyway.'

Stella stood there, completely still.

Then she shook her head. 'You absolute sap.'

'You started it!'

'I mean, honestly.' Stella shook her head in disgust and walked away, pushing the trolley. 'We're in a *supermarket.*'

George followed her down the fruit aisle. He was going to reach for a pineapple, then thought – *no. Baby steps.*

Stella stopped and turned. 'Did you see how much booze Grace had picked up?'

'She might be having a party.'

'It was just Guinness and Pinot Grigio. If you have a party, you get a variety of drinks.'

'You're right. That was a proper boozer's trolley.'

'*And* her boyfriend looked young,' Stella said. '*If* that was her boyfriend. If he's an elderly son, she must either have had him as a pre-teen, or she's had loads of work done.'

They carried on shopping for a while.

They turned into the canned goods aisle.

'There she is!' Stella said.

They watched Grace put a tinned meat pie in her trolley.

Stella made eye contact with George. He knew they were both thinking the same.

Tinned meat pie. Well well, Grace.

George smiled at Stella and she smiled back.

George finally understood the pleasure his kids got when seeing him those afternoons, before they came into school with their deadpan questions.

'Do you like Toblerones, sir?'

⌁THE GOURMET SNACK COMPANY⌁
Feeding quality conversations since 1993

Tommy Foy
242 Cole Street
Manchester
M16 7XX

Dear Mr Foy,

Thank you for your letter regarding our hand-cooked 'farmer's market' snack range, specifically your concerns about the flammability of the Manchego Burst flavour.

We were sorry to hear about the fire at *Le Jardin*.

We take any concerns very seriously and our R&D department are currently reviewing this issue. We will not be recalling this product, or repackaging it as firelighters as you suggested. However, while investigations into the snack are ongoing, we have changed the exterior packaging from paper to cellophane. This is purely a precaution.

Whilst we do not take responsibility for the fire, please be assured any ongoing conversations will take place with the authorities and the proprietor, as necessary. We cannot enter into correspondence with other parties.

We do, however, appreciate your interest in our products. As a gesture of goodwill, please find enclosed a complimentary box of a new product. Crave is our new boutique range of organic chickpea snacks, retailing at a recommended price of £5.49 per 90g item.

We hope you like them, and would love to receive your feedback at www.gourmetsnackco/cravethefuture/ advocates.

This is an opportunity to become one of our first Crave Snackvangelists – and we'd be delighted if you'd share your thoughts on social media!

Please accept our best wishes,

Jez and Ethan

Directors

The Gourmet Snack Company

CREDITS

Caroline Hulse and Orion Fiction would like to thank everyone at Orion who worked on the publication of *Like A House On Fire* in the UK.

Editorial
Emad Akhtar
Lucy Frederick
Bethan Jones

Copy editor
Jade Craddock

Proof reader
Mariian Dreid

Audio
Paul Stark
Amber Bates

Contracts
Anne Goddard
Paul Bulos
Jake Alderson

Design
Debbie Holmes
Joanna Ridley
Nick May

Editorial Management
Charlie Panayiotou
Jane Hughes
Alice Davis

Finance
Jasdip Nandra
Afeera Ahmed
Elizabeth Beaumont
Sue Baker

Marketing
Anna Bowen
Helena Fouracre

Production
Ruth Sharvell

Publicity
Alex Layt

Sales
Jen Wilson
Esther Waters
Victoria Laws

Rachael Hum
Ellie Kyrke-Smith
Frances Doyle
Georgina Cutler

Operations
Jo Jacobs
Sharon Willis
Lisa Pryde
Lucy Brem

If you loved *Like A House On Fire*, don't miss Caroline Hulse's hilarious and heartwarming debut novel . . .

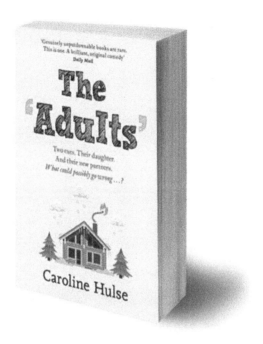

Two exes. Their daughter.

And their new partners.

What could possibly go wrong ...?

'Funny, dry and beautifully observed. Highly recommended for anyone whose perfect Christmases never quite go according to plan!'

Gill Sims, author of *Why Mummy Drinks*